This book

RISE of a FALLEN MAN

belongs to

____

____

____

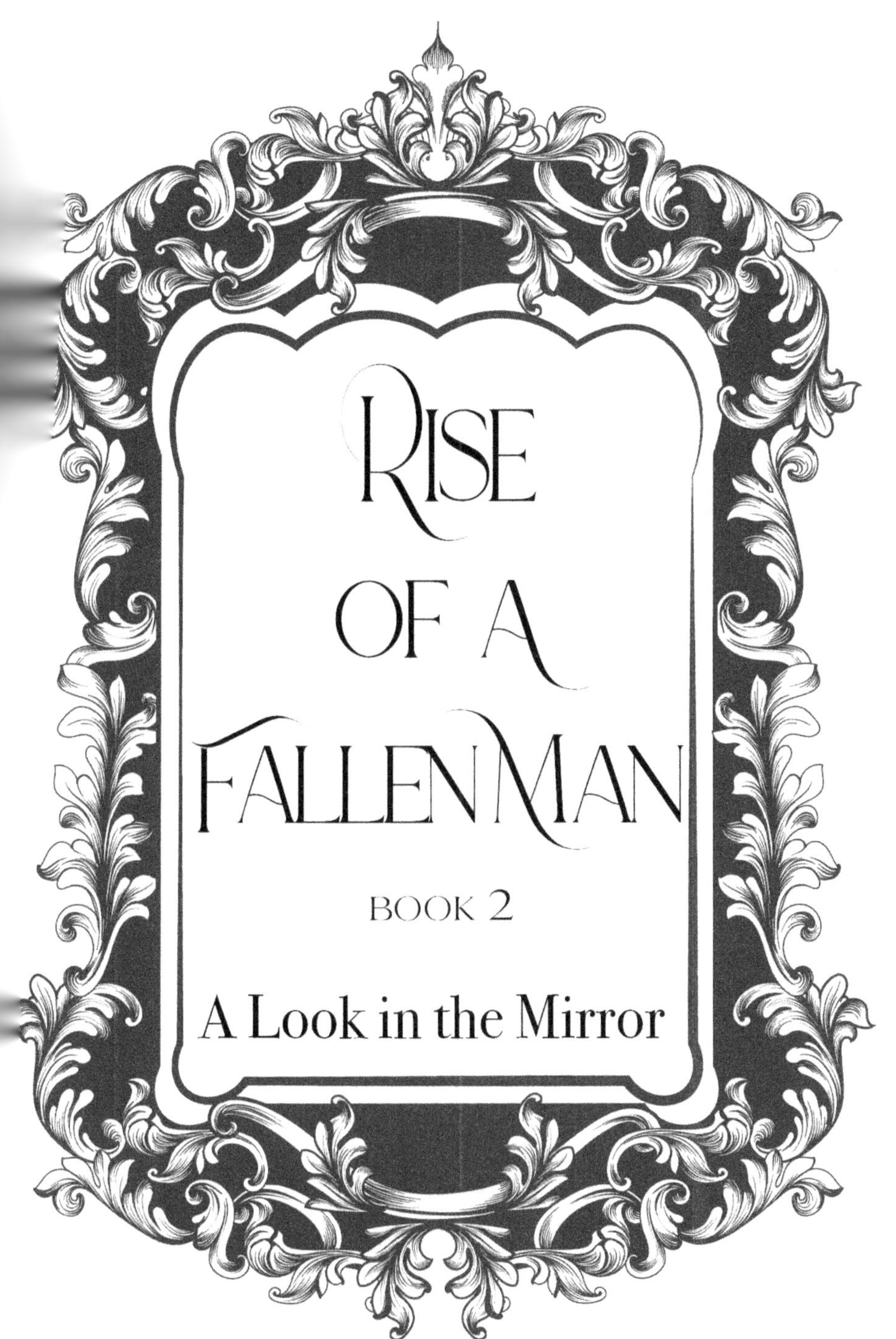

Marina Simcoe

Rise of a Fallen Man
A Look in the Mirror

This book is a work of fiction. Names, characters, places, and incidents are a product of the author's imagination. Locales and public names are used for atmospheric purposes. Any resemblance to actual people, living or dead, or to businesses, companies, events, institutions, or locales is completely coincidental.
Spelling: English (American)
Cover design by Hannah Sternjakob, from www.hannah-sternjakob-design.com
Illustrations by Marina Simcoe
Image source depositphotos.com

No generative artificial intelligence (AI) was used in the writing or illustrating of this book. The author expressly prohibits any entity from using this publication to train AI technologies to generate text or pictures, including, without limitation, technologies capable of generating literary and artistic works.

Rise of a Fallen Man contains graphic descriptions of intimacy, discussions on adult themes, and possible triggers.
Intended for mature readers.

Rise of a Fallen Man

A LOOK IN THE MIRROR
BOOK TWO

MARINA SIMCOE

One

SALAS

"**T**his way, son. In the bucket it goes." Father directed the heavy sword blade that required two pairs of tongs to hold toward the barrel of water.

Gripping the handles of my tongs with both hands, I strained my muscles and bared my teeth from the effort. The water bubbled and hissed as we plunged the hot metal in it.

"Well done, Salas," Father said after we had finished for today.

He wiped his sweaty brow with his thick forearm. And I mimicked his gesture, wiping my forehead with my sleeve. The pounding of horse's hooves against the packed dirt road came from behind the workshop.

"Mother is back." Father took my leather apron from me. "Go check on the pie and see if she needs help to unload. I'll close up the shop for the night."

"Yes, Father." I took off my work gloves and placed them on the shelf by the door before leaving.

"And fetch some wine from the cellar, boy," Father shouted after me. "She likes a glass of wine after a long day at the market."

I dashed into the main room of our log house. With a large hearth in the center, this space served as a kitchen, a dining room, and a living room all at once. A square wooden table took most of the space in front of the river-rock hearth. I'd already set it up with the earthenware bowls and carved wood spoons for our dinner.

There were just three people in our family. I was an only child. Mother said there had been a time when she wished to have more children, but the gods decided otherwise. Sometimes, I wished to have a brother who'd share the chores with me. But when I worked with Father at the forge, I loved having his undivided attention.

After taking the rabbit pie out, I set it on the table. The thudding of hooves and clanking of metal grew louder in the yard.

"Stand still, you demon!" Mother yelled at the horse.

She sounded frustrated, clearly needing help out there. Leaving the wine in the cellar, I ran into the yard to help before her frustration would blow into anger. She wasn't a cruel woman, but got angry and snappy at times, especially when she was tired.

"Greetings, Mother."

I grabbed the reins of our horse. He shook his head, impatient to get the harness and the collar off.

"Oh, there you are, Salas." Mother looked exhausted but relieved to have help.

Children's laughter came from the road on the other side of the house. My ears almost twitched with excitement resonating through my chest. A year ago, I'd be running out there, too, to play tug or hide-and-seek with the neighbors' kids.

But once I'd turned twelve, Mother decided I was too old to go outside unchaperoned, especially since some families on our street had girls my age.

"Girls are nothing but temptation and trouble," she'd said. "You better stay home, my boy, keep your father company, and learn the trade. People like to wag their tongues and make stories out of nothing. If you're home, no one can say a single bad word about you. This way, it'd be easier for you to find a good woman to marry when the time comes."

There were a few boys my age on our street who were still allowed to play outside. None of them were as tall as me, though.

The last time I had gone to the market with Mother, a customer ran her gaze up and down my body and smacked her lips.

"Are you looking for a wife for that one already?" she asked.

"No. He's way too young," Mother snapped before sending me to sit in the wagon, out of sight.

"Couldn't be that young." The woman laughed. "He's as tall as me."

"He's barely twelve. Hey, how about this sword for your husband?" Mother grabbed a weapon, turning the blade to reflect the sunshine.

The woman ignored her, staring at me as I tried to hide in the wagon by folding my legs under me. All my limbs seemed to have grown way too long lately. Mother often complained about how fast I was growing out of my clothes.

"Twelve, you say? What are you feeding him to grow that big? My husband is twenty-seven. But I bet your boy would wrestle him to the ground before we could even blink. Look at those arms of his!"

Mother huffed, losing her patience.

"Here." She grabbed another sword. "This one is nice and light. Perfect for your puny husband, who can be so easily over-powered by a twelve-year-old boy."

Ever since that day, she'd stopped bringing me to the market or letting me play outside. As much as I loved spending time with Father, sitting at home got boring sometimes. It didn't help that I didn't even understand the reasons for Mother's worries. How could girls mean trouble for me? Boys were more likely to start a fight.

A peal of girly laughter trickled from the road into the yard. It tugged at something inside me. I wished I could be playing with the others out there, but the pull was deeper than that, like a twist of longing for something I couldn't name.

"How was the market?" I tied the horse to a hitching post.

"Good, good." Mother ran a hand over her face. "I sold a lot. There isn't much left to unload. Leave it for your father to deal with." She waved a dismissive hand at the horse and the wagon. "Make me some tea instead, will you?"

"Sure." I ran back into the house ahead of her.

As she entered with slow, heavy steps, I filled a metal pot with water and set it on the fire to boil, then grabbed a porcelain tea set from the glass cabinet. The set was a part of Father's dowry and had Mother's favorite teacup that we didn't take out very often. I hoped it'd cheer her up to drink from it tonight.

"Father told me to fetch some wine too." I made a move toward the trapdoor to the cellar dug under the floor, but she stopped me.

"Leave the wine for now, my boy. Tea is great." She folded her tall frame into the armchair at the head of the table.

Mother was a large woman—tall, strong, and solid. She lifted the crates with heavy swords as easily as any man I knew. I once saw her stop a running horse in its tracks.

The last time she'd slapped me, it was for dropping a pot on her foot. My hands were covered in flour after kneading the dough. The pot slipped from my fingers and hit her foot. She swore and swatted me aside as if I were a fly. Propelled by the impact of her blow, I'd hit our kitchen table and shoved it all the way to the wall.

"Watch it, boy," she'd growled, limping out into the yard.

That limp was gone the next day. Mother was strong as a bear and healthy as an ox. Until just a few weeks ago, she'd unload the wagon and tend to the horse all by herself after spending the entire day at the market. Today, she slumped in her chair, waiting for me to get her tea ready. She breathed heavily, as if lifting an anvil, even as she just sat there, not moving a limb.

Father came in, wiping his hands on a clean cloth.

He hugged Mother's shoulders and kissed her cheek. "How did it go?"

"Good." She patted his hand before reaching into the pocket of her skirt. "Here." She dropped a leather purse on the table. It landed heavily, thick with coins clinking inside. "They really liked those hunting knives you made. The arrow heads sold well, too, like always. There isn't much to unload, but the horse needs to be tended to."

"I'll do it," he said, heading out into the yard.

"Your tea, Mother." I filled her cup. "The meat pie is ready if you're hungry. Or do you want some sweets and cookies with your tea instead?"

Her asking for tea at dinnertime confused me. She usually had it after work in the afternoon, often when other women from the village came to visit or her friends from the Blacksmith Guild dropped by. Then I served them tea with cookies, jams, and meat sandwiches. For dinner, we usually had a stew, a roast, or a meat pie. Now, I wasn't sure what to serve her.

"No. Just tea for now, Salas. Tea is good." She leaned back in the chair and stretched her legs in front of her. "Help me take these boots off, will you? My head spins when I bend down."

I kneeled by her feet and pulled her short, worn boots off one by one.

"Ahh," she exhaled, as I gave her feet a quick rub to relax her a little. "You're a good boy, Salas. Strong. Hardworking. Kind. All you need is a good woman who would appreciate everything you have to offer." She sighed heavily. "If only—" A rough, coarse cough cut off her words.

She bent over, coughing so hard, as if trying to hack a passage in her throat for her next breath. Her shaking hand rummaged in the pocket of her skirt before pulling out a handkerchief and pressing it to her lips.

"Mother..." My voice came out small. I wasn't used to seeing her weak like this.

Fear wormed its way into my chest. Mother had always been the epitome of strength to me. Father might be slightly taller and considerably wider in shoulders than her, but he was softer at heart. He would often keep quiet, while Mother was never afraid to speak up.

"Mother?" I placed a hand on her shoulder, wishing I could stop her body from shaking from her chest-ripping cough. "What can I do to help? More tea?"

I moved the cup a little closer to her.

She waved a hand at me between the bouts of convulsions.

"Go—" she squeezed out in an altered, strangled voice. "Go, boy... Help your father outside."

I took a step toward the door, torn between the need to obey her and the fear of leaving her alone like that.

"I..."

"Go, I said," she snarled, wiping her lips with her handkerchief.

Bright red stains bloomed on the beige linen of the handkerchief. My fear turned into a lead-heavy ball of dread in my chest.

"Go, Salas." She waved a hand at me, looking deadly tired. "Just go, will you? I don't want you to see me like this."

Her voice turned soft. Pleading. I'd never heard her speak like this before, and it terrified me even more.

I turned on my heel and ran.

DURING THE LONG months of Mother's sickness, her body lost most of its bulk. The strong, solid woman I knew most of my life had melted down to just a wick of her former self. She'd turned thin and frail. With her skin paled, she'd look like a ghost if it weren't for the feverishly bright red spots on her cheeks.

As the village's healing witch shook her head, talking to my father in a subdued voice, I gathered the bloodied pieces of cloth from around Mother's bed, then gave her a clean one.

"Salas," she said, her voice sounding like a rustle of a breeze in fallen leaves. I had to lean closer and strain my hearing to catch her words. "Bring me a piece of paper and a quill. I need to write a letter," she explained, answering my questioning stare. "I'll be gone soon—"

"No, Mother," I interrupted her. She was weak. She might look like a corpse already, but my childish optimism still made me believe my parents were invincible. They had to be. She and Father were my world. What was life supposed to be without one of them? "You'll get better."

She lifted a hand, stopping me while fighting another bout of a body-shaking cough.

"I will be gone soon," she repeated after the coughing fit had finally subsided. Every word was a struggle for her, and I didn't interrupt her this time, not wishing to force her to repeat. "I've been trying to make sure that you're taken care of. You and your father will be alright. I promise."

My wishes and prayers for Mother's life proved useless. She died, no matter how well father and I took care of her.

It was a sunny but frigid day when she passed. The weather remained freezing the day of her funeral too. The villagers had to burn bonfires for the entire night prior to thaw the ground enough to dig a shallow grave.

The priestess of the Great Goddess Nus said a few words over the casket. She spoke about Mother being a well-respected woman, an honorable business owner, a long-standing member of the Blacksmith Guild, a wife, and a mother, survived by her loyal husband and son.

Father stood by the gaping hole of the grave, silent and grim. His eyes remained dry. He didn't cry. But a ripple of *reflection* ran over his large body with a shudder now and then.

I'd cried so much in the past few days, I had no tears left

either. They just burned now in my chest like a ball of inextinguishable fire.

I held Father's hand in mine, watching the *reflection* momentarily discolor them both into the grays and browns of the surrounding landscape.

Father was scared, and so was I. What would happen to us with Mother gone?

Her younger sister came down from the mountains for Mother's funeral. She glared at Father and me from across the open grave.

My aunt was a tall, broad woman, just like my mother. The similarity between them was so strong, it made my heart ache.

While the priestess spoke, the aunt sobbed, dabbing at her eyes with a lacy handkerchief. After the priestess had finished and the first shovelfuls of dirt hit the pinewood lid of Mother's casket, the aunt left, not sparing me or Father another glance.

People came by to offer us their condolences and to shake Father's hand. Eventually, everyone left. Only Father and I still stood over the freshly filled grave. Frost in the air bit my face. Cold wind seeped through my coat and woolen pants.

"Let's go home, Father." I tugged at his hand.

He squeezed my fingers in his. "That house is no longer ours, Salas."

With a shiver running through his body, his skin and clothes changed their color, *reflecting* the frozen hill and the black stones of the cemetery. He turned nearly invisible, blending into our surroundings to hide from the world. Now that it was just me and him, he no longer had to keep his fear at bay, and the fear urged him to hide.

I'd rarely seen Father *reflect* before. Granted, when Mother was alive, he had fewer reasons to feel fear or shame that caused *reflection*. But I also *reflected* far less than other children did. Mother had wondered if I was less sensitive than most. But Father had told her that the men in his family generally *reflected* less than normal, even when they were genuinely scared.

Now Father must be terrified, turning practically invisible against the bright winter day.

"Why can't we keep the house, Father?" I asked, squeezing his hand tighter.

His broad chest expanded with a deep breath as he took control of his emotions once again. The *reflection* passed, allowing his image to solidify again.

"Your aunt owns both the shop and the house now. Like the law says, 'the next living female relative...'" He rubbed the back of his neck. "She's always hated me. Their whole family does. Your mother came from a well-to-do family up in the mountains, Salas. And I was a nobody when she met me, the fifth son of a goat shepherd with nothing to my name. My parents couldn't even scrape enough for a dowry. But your mother married me, anyway."

"That's not true. You had a dowry," I objected. "Our tea set is a part of it."

He huffed a laugh. It was a sad, miserable laugh, but it was still better than tears.

"That tea set was all my parents had of value. A family heirloom, you see?" Father pulled his hat lower over his head and hiked up his collar to hide from the bitter wind. "The set is your aunt's now, like everything else. But she didn't want to keep you. She has three boys of her own. All will need a dowry at some point, and you'd be just another mouth to feed. Her husband also said he'd hate to have more men in the house, so..." He waved a hand in the direction of the village as if rejecting that entire place after they had rejected us.

A heavy feeling pressed on my chest. The house where I'd spent all my life was no longer my home. We had no shelter to get out of this cold.

"What are we going to do?"

Father patted my shoulder reassuringly.

"We'll go to Lady Lana's manor, son. She owns everything around here." He swept with his arm toward the frozen fields that surrounded the cemetery and the dark strip of the forest in the distance. "Surely, she'll find a place for you and me." He took my hand again, tugging me along the path toward the road. "Your mother wrote to Lady Lana, asking for her kindness. The lady agreed to take you in as a companion for her son. He's about the same age as you."

I'd never been to a lady's manor. Living in one seemed exciting.

"What does it mean to be his companion? What will I have to do?"

"It's kind of like being his friend," Father explained. "You'll play with the little lord, sit in the lessons with him, learn everything they teach him."

"Like what?"

He shrugged. "To read the right books, to dance, and to fence with a sword like a gentleman."

"I know my way with a sword already. You taught me."

"It's not the same." Father shook his head, huddling into his coat against the wind as we left the cemetery behind. "Noble folks have their own ways of doing things. When they teach you, you'll learn how to act just like them."

"What for?"

"For your future, boy. You'll have a chance of a better marriage if you speak and act like a highborn. If you gain Lady Lana's favor, she'll find you a good wife and may even offer a dowry for you. You'll have a chance at a much better life than any man in our family ever had, son."

I hadn't met a noble lady before. I had no way of knowing whether marrying one would be a good thing, but Father seemed to think it was. His face lit up with hope, and I didn't question it.

"And you, Father? What will you do when I get married? Will you stay with me and my new family?"

He grunted uncertainly, then tugged his coat closer around him.

"I'll be around," he replied evasively. "But you're getting way ahead of yourself, boy. Let's just get there first."

The road ran down the hill. My boots slid on the hard, frozen dirt mixed with ice and snow. Freezing wind pelted my cheeks and nose, no matter how hard I tried to hide my face in my coat. But Father's hope proved contagious. Huddling into the coat I'd already outgrown since the last winter, I hurried along, lured by the promise of a better life.

Two

Otto, Lord Emil's fencing teacher, launched forward in an attack. I deflected it, lunging forward in turn. He leaped aside, the cork on the tip of my blade brushing past his ribs on the left.

"Very good, Salas." Otto panted, catching his breath.

I grinned, and he moved again, the corked tip of his sword poking in my chest with enough force to leave a bruise.

"And that's how you win." Otto smirked. "Don't let flattery distract you, boy. Pretty words aren't worth dying for."

I stepped back, rubbing my chest.

"My turn!" Lord Emil rushed me, wielding his sword.

I stepped aside. Following the momentum, Emil lost his balance, tripped over his feet, and fell.

"Use it, Salas!" Otto shouted. "Use his mistake to win."

I raised my sword, standing over Emil who sprawled in the grass of the riverbank behind the manor of his mother, Lady Lana.

The victory was right in front of me. One thrust, one touch of the cork on my sword to the chest of the young lord, and I'd be declared the winner of this training session. But Emil was a year younger than me and of a much slender build. My instinct was to protect him, not to hurt him.

With his reddish-blond curls spread on the grass, his large blue eyes filled with genuine fear, he *reflected* the green grass he lay on. Helpless and afraid, the sight of him disarmed me. This wasn't the same as fighting Otto, the grown man of my own size.

My hand with the sword wavered.

Emil's eyes glinted with excitement, spotting the opportunity.

"Got you!" He shoved his sword up and into my belly.

I hauled in pain, doubling over. He'd thrust so hard, it felt like a punch to my stomach, even as the cork prevented the blade from piercing my skin.

"I won!" Emil cheered, jumping to his feet. "I won! I won!"

"That's your problem, Salas." Otto took the sword from my hand. "You're too kind. It's not enough to be fast, strong, and skilled. A warrior must be ready to kill. You have to be ruthless if you want to succeed."

A loud, slow clapping punctuated his words from a distance. We all turned at the sound. Lady Lana approached on horseback from down the stream. She'd draped the reins of her horse over the bow of her saddle, and was now clapping with her gloved hands.

"Mother! I won!" Emil hopped with glee. "Did you see it?"

"Well done, my son."

Lady Lana threw her leg over the saddle, then hopped off the horse.

"Otto, take the horse back to the stables for me." She tossed the reins to the teacher, then pulled her riding gloves off on her way to her son and me. "The boys and I will stay here for a bit. Right, boys?" She brushed by me, her shoulder touching my bicep. "I swear, Salas, every time I see you, you appear to have grown even taller." She tilted her head back, looking up at me.

She was a short woman, plump, with soft curves to her face and body. Standing toe to toe with me, with her face turned up, her forehead was just below my collarbone. I'd be glad to stop growing. But at fourteen, they said I had quite a few more years to go.

"Not only taller but wider too." She stroked with her finger across my chest, then down my arm. "Look at these muscles," she murmured. "You're practically bursting out of your shirts. I can't buy new sizes fast enough for you."

I wasn't sure what to say to that. It wasn't my fault I was bigger than most boys my age. Both my parents were tall and what they called "big-boned." I felt bad for the lady spending money on the shirts that I kept outgrowing. But she didn't seem angry or offended. Her voice was a thick, low murmur I hadn't heard from a woman yet and didn't know how to respond.

Her touch was light and pleasant. Too pleasant, I realized, as shivers rippled down my belly to my crotch. I couldn't define the feeling, but I instinctively sensed it wasn't proper, especially toward Lady Lana.

The last time I touched a woman—the only time, really, except when tending to my mother during her illness—was at Emil's birthday ball three months ago. His dance teacher had spent weeks teaching Emil and me to dance. Emil took to it much faster than I did. After weeks of daily practice, I'd only mastered the waltz well enough to do it at the ball in front of everyone.

Several unmarried young women had been invited to the ball. All were a little older than me. I got to dance with three of them. The memories of touching their waists and hands as we danced still haunted me at night, bringing all kinds of shameful thoughts and feelings.

I remembered Father's words about Lady Lana possibly finding me a wife. Back then, the idea of marriage was nothing but words. After the birthday ball, however, I wondered if my future wife could be one of the girls I'd danced with.

I didn't even remember their faces and had barely exchanged a handful of words with any of them, trying so hard not to mess up the steps or accidentally step with my giant shoes on their delicate satin slippers. Ultimately, I decided it wouldn't be the worst thing in life to have a girl like that to take me as her husband.

It'd be nice to find a friend in my wife, someone to care for and who'd care about me. I hoped her family would like me and that my father could come live with us, too. He'd been gone from the estate, working on some far-away farm on Lady Lana's orders.

I had no idea how my marriage was supposed to be arranged. But I didn't believe it involved Lady Lana touching me the way she was right now while practically purring into my ear.

"We should go," I croaked, backing away from her hands.

"What's your hurry?" She smiled, unbuttoning her dress. "Let's swim a little. You're covered in sweat." She wrinkled her nose.

"But..."

I darted a glance around in search of an escape. I couldn't tell exactly what was wrong about her taking her dress off in front of me or asking me to go swimming with her. It was a hot day. I had worked up a sweat while practicing swordsmanship with Otto and Emil. A swim would be great. But it still felt wrong.

"What's the matter?" she teased. "It's not like you're scared or ashamed. You're not *reflecting*."

I wasn't scared. Confused mostly. I also didn't want to offend the woman who'd let me live in her house for the past two years.

Emil jogged back from Otto, who led the horse away and took our weapons with him.

"Yes, let's go swimming!" Emil pulled off his boots.

With him being here, the tension paralyzing my limbs eased a little.

"Come on, Salas." Lady Lana gestured for me to follow her into the river. "You can keep your clothes on. I'm not taking off my undershirt either. See? It's all as proper as could be."

Wearing only his shirt and underpants, Emil ran past us and into the water. His mother followed him, gingerly holding up the hem of her long undershirt. I took off my waistcoat, boots, and pants, then joined them in the stream.

The water felt chilly but refreshing against my flushed skin. I splashed around with Emil, playing tag in the water with him. Then, we competed to see who could hold his breath the longest.

Lady Lana slowly swam around in circles, floating on her back, with her face up to the sun. She whelped suddenly and splashed, looking like she was about to go under.

"Mother?" Emil made a move to go after her. But she was closer to the middle of the river, too far for him to swim safely.

"Wait here." I stopped him. "I'll get her."

I was a much stronger swimmer than Emil and reached the lady in a few long strokes.

"Lady Lana?"

She wasn't fighting the stream anymore, treading it confidently with a smile on her lips.

"What happened?" I blew the water out of my face, tossing my wet hair back.

"I think I got bit by a leech," she cooed, as if talking about something sweet and pleasant.

"Ew, a leech!" Emil screamed and rushed out of the water, wildly splashing around.

I wished I could join him. There was nothing pleasant about leeches. But I couldn't leave the lady all alone here, even if she didn't look like she was in trouble.

"Where?" I looked over her arms and shoulders. "I don't see any leeches on you."

"On my leg? Maybe?" she said playfully.

I believed she was lying, but of course I couldn't tell her that to her face. Turning around and swimming away would be rude too.

"Let's get out of the water," I suggested. "We can see it better then."

"Great idea, Salas. Only I don't think I can swim that far." She batted her eyelashes at me.

"I'll help you."

I took her arm and put it around my neck, helping her swim.

The moment my feet reached the bottom, however, Lady Lana flexed her arm around my neck, then floated forward and into my arms.

"You're so strong." She bent her legs, pressing herself to my chest, as if I were carrying her in front of me.

I kept walking, pushing her ahead of me and toward the riverbank.

The water sluiced around us. Lady Lana giggled, raising her shoulder. Her leaving her shirt on accomplished nothing, I realized. The thin fabric had turned nearly transparent in the water. The stream pushed it off her shoulder. The lacy edge got caught on the bud of her nipple, otherwise it would have slid off completely, exposing her breast.

She noticed me looking and sighed with a half-moan, not bothering to adjust the shirt or cover up.

I stared straight ahead, painfully aware of blood rushing to my crotch and my cock swelling embarrassingly hard. It'd been happening often enough for me not to freak out now. But never before had it been as a reaction to Lady Lana, especially while she was right there, giving me a knowing smile.

"I think I can touch the ground here." She dropped her legs down.

Her thigh bumped into my straining cock, sending a fresh shot of heat through it.

"Ooh." She slid her hand under the water to stroke me briefly. "Impressive. Even the chill doesn't affect you."

I just stood there, rooted in place, as she sauntered past me and toward the riverbank. Her hips swayed, water sluicing down her curves. Her wet shirt clung to her skin, leaving nothing to the imagination. And I stared, hating myself for it.

She winked at me over her shoulder before picking up her dress and strolling after Emil, who had run back to the manor.

I was not supposed to feel this way toward Lady Lana. She took me in as my benefactor. Until now, I'd felt nothing but respect and gratitude toward her.

All my life, I'd been striving to do the right thing, the way my parents, my teachers, and the priestess of Yarnus, the God of Purity, had taught me. And it all was undone now by one stroke of Lady Lana's hand.

This was sinful. Wrong. Leaving me feeling filthy and filled with guilt. Clearly, something must be wrong with me if I had this kind of reaction to the woman who had practically replaced a mother for me.

I stayed in the water until my teeth chattered from the cold and my cock shriveled and drooped. Then I climbed out of the river, put my clothes on, and headed back to the manor, knowing that nothing would ever be the same. The pure, innocent part of me, the part that was the most treasured in a man in this world, stayed in the river, forever lost in its stream.

"Where is he?" Lady Lana shrieked in the hallway.

Emil dropped the book he was reading while sitting in the window seat in my room. I put down my pencil and looked up from the picture of a sword I drew while laying on my belly on the floor rug.

The lady's footsteps came closer, her heels clicking against the wood floors of the hallway.

Emil held his breath. The question *"You or me?"* floated in his wide-open eyes. The timid wave of *reflection* momentarily made him disappear. And for a second, I foolishly wished it was me whom his mother was looking for. I could take her wrath and punishment better than Emil. He was such a sickly, fragile kid.

The door to my room slammed open, and the lady marched in.

"There you are!" She glared at her son, a white sheet clutched in her hands, a riding crop gripped under her arm. "Care to explain, Lord Emil? What is this?" She tossed the sheet to his feet.

Trying to make as little noise as possible, I rose from the floor and shoved my drawing out of the way.

Emil turned almost as white as the sheet she was pointing at accusingly. The fabric of it was slightly discolored in the middle. It looked like the spot had been starched, then scrambled, crusting over in the creases as it dried.

"You spilled your seed!" the lady shrieked, her face turning red to the roots of her reddish-blonde hair. "How dare you?" She moved on to him, holding the riding crop in front of her like a weapon.

"No, Mother..." Emil shrank back into the window seat. "I didn't. I..."

"Then what is it?" she demanded.

"It wasn't me." His eyes roamed in panic before stopping on me. "It was Salas."

"What?" I blinked, momentarily lost for words.

"Salas?" Lady Lana turned to me slowly, like a snake searching for the best moment to strike.

Emil's eyes shifted from wall to wall across the room. "Yes. He...um, took a nap in my bed while I was in my music lesson. He did it."

"I didn't come to your room today," I protested.

By now, I'd spilled plenty of my seed, but only in my own bed and only at night in my sleep when I couldn't help it. Unfortunately, some dreams ended with a sharp shot of pleasure followed by a release. They left me sweaty in the morning and my thighs slicked and sticky. There was no way of stopping these dreams. Gods knew I'd tried.

The difference between Emil and me was that I wasn't a lord and had no valet. I changed my own sheets and cleaned them myself as needed, with no one knowing.

"He did it!" Emil's conviction increased as his lie grew more elaborate. "I found him there after the lesson."

Lord Ciric, the lady's husband, appeared at the threshold of the room, probably alerted by the screams of his wife and son.

"What's going on? Why is this noise?"

"Leave, Ciric," his wife hissed at him through her teeth. "This does not concern you."

"Why not? It's about my son, isn't it? What did he do?" His gaze dropped to the sheet with the crusty stain on the floor. An understanding spread on his face. "Lana, leave the boys alone. Please."

"Leave them alone?" She walked menacingly slow to the cord of the bell by the door. "Of course that'd be your advice. Useless, like always. Do you even care about the reputation of my name or the marriage prospects of your son?"

She yanked on the cord with so much anger that I wondered how she didn't rip it off.

I'd been told not to use the bell. The servants brought me food when instructed to do so by the mistress of the house. The rest I did on my own. But when Lady Lana rang it, a footman appeared almost immediately.

"Take Lord Ciric to his rooms," she ordered. "He needs some rest."

"I'm not tired," the lord protested.

"Are you raising your voice on me?"

"No I'm not," he spoke so quickly, he almost stuttered, tripping over the words.

She propped a hand on her hip, tapping her boot with her riding crop.

"It sounds very much like you are, husband. A rest would do your temper good. I'll order to bring you some tea with the sleeping potion for you."

Lord Ciric ran his hands through his light brown hair, his fingers trembling slightly.

"No. Not the sleeping potion, please. I'm not angry," he said slowly, measuring every word. "I'm speaking reasonably."

"And now you're agitated. See?" she shrieked, poking with her riding crop at him like with a sword. "Do you need another trip to the water caves, Ciric? The witches there are so good at dealing with the male temper. They'll calm your volatile nature in no time."

His face paled, then turned mahogany brown, blending in with the wooden panels of the room in the *reflection* of fear.

"No, Lana, please don't do that again," he begged. "Don't send me to the caves."

"It's for your own good, darling. The treatments proved beneficial for your frazzled nerves the last time. You were so quiet and docile when you returned from the caves. And now, look at you again. You can't even follow a simple instruction." She folded her arms across her chest, the riding crop dangling in her fingers. "Let the man take you to your rooms, Ciric. It's too stressful for you to stay here. I'll handle all problems with our son, including this one."

Lord Ciric was bigger than his wife. She wouldn't be able to physically overpower him. But she didn't need to do it herself. She paid men to handle him for her. A second footman showed up. The two servants then led the lord away as he gritted his teeth. Defiance burned in his eyes, but he didn't dare let it out.

"You." She turned to her son again after her husband's departure. "Take this sheet down to the kitchen and wash it yourself. I want you to do it in front of all the servants. Let the shame stop you from ever doing something like that again. Then you spend the rest of the day praying to Yarnus to grant you the virtue that you so clearly lack."

With a sniffle, Emil grabbed the sheet and ran—angry, scared, but relieved to get away, no doubt.

I sidestepped Lady Lana on my way to the exit, but she shot her arm out, stopping me with her riding crop.

"So, is that true, Salas? Did you climb into my son's bed to take a nap? Did you touch yourself while you day-dreamed? What was that dream? Tell me. Who did you dream about while you stroked your cock?"

"I didn't, my lady. I never went to Emil's room today. Ask the servants. We've been here since lunch."

Only I had a feeling she didn't care about the truth. She lived in her own fantasy, the one where I was in bed with my cock in my hand.

Pressing the end of the riding crop to my chest, she circled me on her way to the door, then closed and locked it. Her hand went to the buttons in front of her dress.

Alarm shot through my body with both chills and heat.

I swallowed hard. "My lady. I need to go. Please."

The riding crop swished through the air, searing my cheek with a burning slap. I gasped, cupping my cheek, heat flaming under my palm.

"You do what I say," she snapped. "And I say that you stay."

"No." I whipped toward the door.

She grabbed my hair, yanking back my head. Pain jolted my instinct of self-defense. Swinging a fist, I spun to punch her and... froze.

She was a woman. So much smaller than me. Soft and vulnerable. She belonged to the house where I lived. She was a part of the family that my guts demanded I protect. My fist was almost as big as her head. If I hit, I'd injure her, badly.

Everything inside me rebelled against hurting anyone, especially someone who looked like her, even if she had hurt me first.

She pulled me down by my hair until her hot breath hit my temple.

"You do as I say, Salas, like everyone else does around here. Your life is mine. As is the life of your father. It's up to me to make it hard or easy for him. And it all depends on how well you'll please me."

Her mentioning of my father further paralyzed me. She saw the effect of her words on me and smiled, letting go of my hair.

"Now, be a good boy, and we'll be friends. You want to be my friend, Salas, don't you?"

She slid her dress off her shoulders. There was no undershirt this time. Her breasts spilled from her bodice. The tips tightened into buds in front of my eyes. I didn't know a woman's body did that. I had no idea what that meant, but I just couldn't stop staring as my mind raced.

Even if I brought myself to hurt her, there'd be consequences. An assault on a woman was a crime punishable by death. I'd be executed. I didn't know exactly what she'd do to my father after that, but I knew it wouldn't be good.

But there was more to my feelings than fear of death. As she shoved her dress down her hips, then took her underwear with it, I couldn't take my eyes off her naked body. Some dark, sinful part of me wanted to stay and see what would happen next.

"It's wrong," I muttered, licking my dry lips.

She came flash to me, naked, save for the milky-white stockings held up by the pink ribbons over her knees. The stockings were so thin, they looked like mist sprayed over her legs.

"How can it be wrong when it feels so right?" She gripped my cock through my pants. To my mortification, it grew harder in her hand.

"I must save myself for my wife, my lady." My words came out hollow, as if from someone else's mouth. My body no longer felt like my own either.

"Oh, but a wife needs to be pleasured," she murmured. "Let me show you how." Stroking me with one hand, she took my hand with the other and pressed my palm to her breast. Her body felt soft and inviting. My fingers curled around the pillowy sphere as if on their own. "You're such a handsome boy, Salas. If you make me feel good, I'll let you have some pleasure too."

Maybe I should've pushed her away after all. Maybe I should've chosen the execution over degradation and shame. I would've given half of my life to be able to flee that room. But I also wanted her to keep touching me. And I wished to touch her back.

"Good boy." She slid her hand into my pants. Her cool fingers wrapped around my heat.

Instead of fighting her grip, I leaned into it. The throbbing ache in my cock grew stronger, and everything else fell into the background.

Without fully realizing it then, I fell that night. And I kept plummeting further down ever since.

THE MIRROR STOOD on the floor, propped against my bed. I sat on my knees in front of it, naked. Red welts from Lady Lana's nails and her riding crop decorated my chest and shoulders.

She rarely hit hard enough to break the skin, but always strived to inflict enough pain and shame to make me *reflect*. She loved watching the ripples of *reflection* quiver through my body. For her, it was as much a goal of all our encounters as her climax.

Over the past few months, she'd visited my room much more frequently than her own husband's. To make me comply, she used both the proverbial stick and carrot. The "stick" was quite literally her riding crop, as well as the threats to hurt my father. The "carrot" was the possibility of my orgasm that she dangled in front of me as the ultimate reward, occasionally granting it to me.

I couldn't fight her. But I never stopped searching for ways to deny her, if not the access to my body, then at least the pleasure of seeing my shame and my fear.

I lifted the riding crop I'd stolen from the stables. Keeping my eyes on the face of my reflection in the mirror, I swung the crop and hit myself on the back. Hard.

My skin flared with searing pain. The boy in the mirror winced, baring his teeth like a cornered dog. I raised the crop again and paused, allowing him to take a good look at it, then brought it back again, ready for another strike.

A barely perceptible wave moved across my face in the mirror as I brought the crop closer to strike. I braced for the blow. As the sting burned my back, however, the wave faded and disappeared.

It wasn't the blow or the pain that scared me the most, I realized, but the anticipation of it. If I learned to wait for it without trepidation, there'd be no *reflection*. If I resigned to the inevitable, I could combat fear.

Acceptance became my weapon against shame.

There was no point in striving to be good anymore. What Lady Lana did with me at night was wicked. Rotten. Bad. It made me wicked too. I had let the sin tempt me, and I'd succumbed to it. There was no coming back now. No saving me. Bad boys didn't deserve good things. Those who had forsaken decency had no right to feel ashamed.

Without fear or shame, there was no *reflection*.

Lady Lana had taken my innocence, but there was one thing I could and would deny her—the pleasure of seeing my weakness displayed to her.

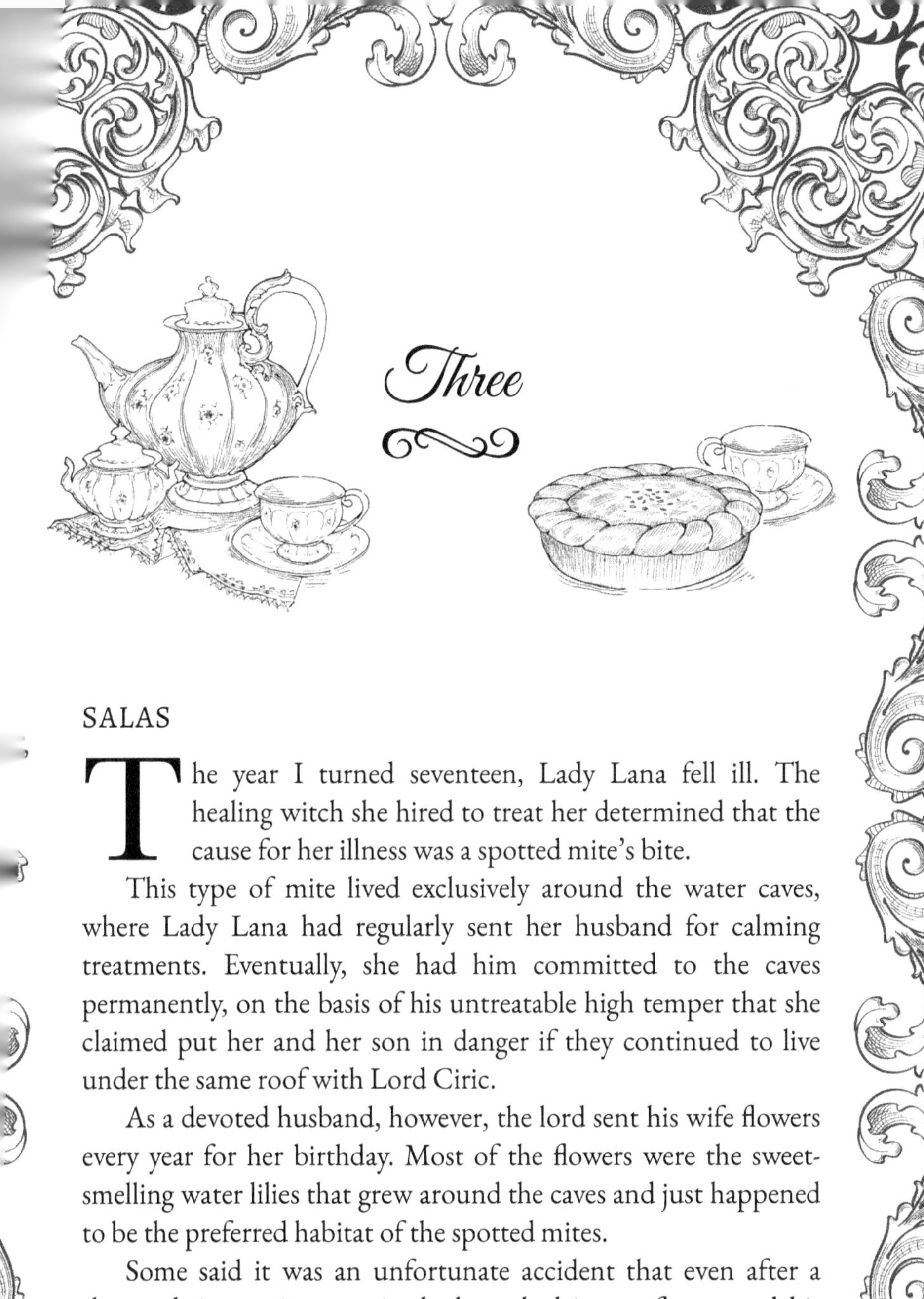

Three

SALAS

The year I turned seventeen, Lady Lana fell ill. The healing witch she hired to treat her determined that the cause for her illness was a spotted mite's bite.

This type of mite lived exclusively around the water caves, where Lady Lana had regularly sent her husband for calming treatments. Eventually, she had him committed to the caves permanently, on the basis of his untreatable high temper that she claimed put her and her son in danger if they continued to live under the same roof with Lord Ciric.

As a devoted husband, however, the lord sent his wife flowers every year for her birthday. Most of the flowers were the sweet-smelling water lilies that grew around the caves and just happened to be the preferred habitat of the spotted mites.

Some said it was an unfortunate accident that even after a thorough inspection, a mite had sneaked into a flower and bit Lady Lana when she received the bouquet. I chose to believe that Lord Ciric got his revenge in the end. It made me feel better to think that there still was some justice left in this world.

The lord died shortly after Lady Lana fell ill, and she didn't have it in her to shed even a single tear for her husband.

Just as calmly, she had informed me about the death of my father a year prior. She said he'd worked himself to death, then gave me a night off from her visits to mourn him. Just one night was supposed to be enough, in her opinion, before she snuck into my room the following night again.

As she slept in my bed that night, I thought about how easy it'd be to place a pillow over her face and end it all, both for her and me. No one would even miss her. Not her son, whom she terrorized more and more the older he got. Not her older daughter, who'd moved out of her mother's house the first chance she got.

Yet I let Lady Lana live that night and every night thereafter. It wasn't the fear of prosecution that stopped me, not even my innate disgust for cruelty and murder, but the dread of complete and utter loneliness. My father was gone. And now, by some perverted, disturbed twist of fate, my tormentor was the only person in the world who cared whether I lived or died. Without her, I'd have no one.

Only after she got sick and her condition deteriorated did she stop visiting my room. Instead, she ordered me to visit hers daily. The nature of our encounters had also changed. Instead of her lover, I became her caregiver. I brought her food, read books to her, and helped with her baths.

"You're a good boy, Salas," she said one afternoon, lying in her bed, as I was reading her a fun, lighthearted novel. "But you're a wicked boy too. No woman will ever want you but me. You have to take good care of me because without me, you have no future."

Until the day she died, Lady Lana believed she would recover. I shed no tears when she died, but on the day of her funeral, I felt irritable and upset. Against my every intention, Lady Lana had become a part of my life. A dark, rotten part that I should be glad to get rid of. Yet her death left a gaping hole in my existence with nothing to fill it in.

She was the only woman I knew intimately, and I missed the intimacy. Not just the sex, but also the touch, the company, the falling asleep next to someone. Ours had been a twisted relationship, but it was the only relationship I'd had.

The moment the dirt covered her casket, her daughter informed me I was no longer welcomed at the manor. Apparently, the word about "my wicked ways" had spread, and the heiress worried that my tarnished reputation would cast a stain on her brother, Lord Emil, and ruin his marriage prospects.

I was shown the door.

By now, I'd gained several skills, some more useful than others. I could read and write, fence, dance the waltz, and take care of the sick from feeding to bathing them. My math skills were far superior to those of a common man. And I still remembered how to fire up the forge and assist a blacksmith.

At seventeen, my strength rivaled that of a grown man. I'd heard there was plenty of physical work available for a pay. I didn't shun from hard labor. What I didn't take into account was how far the word of my reputation would spread.

The daughter of Lady Lana refused to give me a character recommendation, and without her good word, every door I'd knocked on in search of work closed in my face.

In the middle of the bitter winter that year, I realized quickly that if I didn't get out of the cold soon, I'd simply freeze to death on the side of the road somewhere.

"Get off my property. You're a loose man," the woman behind the last door I knocked on growled at me like a dog, protecting her house from me as if I were the sin reincarnate. "The place for the likes of you is in the fun house."

At that point, "fun house" sounded better than "dying from cold and hunger," so I found out where it was, then walked for an hour to get to that town.

By the time I reached the high fence of the fun house, I couldn't feel my feet inside my boots or my fingers inside my gloves.

A man of about forty opened the gate. He huddled into a thick scarf, the wind blowing a few long hairs over his otherwise bald skull.

"What do you want?" He gave me a measuring look, taking in my well-made clothes.

"Work," I croaked.

His water-blue eyes focused on my face.

"Do you know what we do here?" he asked. "Have you done this kind of work before?"

A gust of wind and snow forced me to hide my face in the raised collar of my coat before I could answer.

The man cursed the weather under his breath, then opened the gate wider.

"Come in, boy. Let's talk inside."

We crossed the narrow courtyard, then entered the front room of the house. It was spacious but cozy, with flower-print curtains on the windows, plush armchairs with starched doilies laid out on their high backs, and thick rugs on the floor.

A middle-aged woman sat by the fire, smoking a pipe. Her graying hair was braided into a long plait that circled her head like a crown.

"Another one?" She squinted at me, cuddling into a fuzzy gray shawl. "This weather tends to bring them here in droves."

"It's fucking cold out there." The man rubbed his arms, disappearing through a door into the adjacent room. "I'm Erif," he shouted out of sight. "And this is Traeh, my wife. She owns this place."

The woman put her pipe down and smoothed her brown woolen skirt over her knees.

"Come closer. Warm up a bit." She gestured at the second armchair by the fire.

I didn't wait for her to repeat the invitation. Frozen to the bone, I plopped my butt into the chair and shoved my hands and feet as close to the fireplace as I dared without burning my skin or setting my boots on fire.

"What's your name?" Traeh asked.

"Salas."

"How old are you?"

"Seventeen."

"So young." She clicked her tongue in disbelief, sliding an assessing glance down my body. "You don't look it."

"I know. I've been told so before." I nodded, trying and failing to stop my teeth from chattering.

Now that the warmth from the fire had worked its way under my clothes, ice seemed to thaw in my muscles. The parts of me that felt frozen solid before started to move, shaking me with a violent shiver.

Erif returned, bringing a plate with a few wedges of turnip and a thick slice of bread.

"Here. I thought you might be hungry." He put the plate on the small table next to my chair. "Sorry, we've already had dinner, and there are no leftovers. All I have is this. But I put the water for tea on the stove. Should be ready soon."

Someone's footsteps sounded on the floor above us, then the furniture creaked. Treah and Erif ignored the noises, so I did too, giving my full attention to the food instead.

"Thanks." I was too hungry to say much more before stuffing my face with bread while grabbing a piece of turnip with my other hand.

"Do you know what this house is, Salas?" Traeh asked after the tea was ready and I'd taken a few scorching hot sips from the mug Erif had brought for me.

The hot tea slid down my throat like a molten lava. But I welcomed the heat spreading through my body and bringing it back to life.

"Do you know what the men who work here do for a living?" She kept questioning me.

When my parents were alive, I didn't have the slightest idea what happened in places like this one. They were called "fun houses," which sounded playful and innocent to a child's ear. As I grew older, I also learned other words they were known by, such as "brothels" and "bawdy houses"—crude words that many used when cursing.

I'd heard things about the men working in these places too. None of what I'd heard was good. But I also didn't believe there was much good left in me, either. Lady Lana had taken from me everything that the world deemed of value. And now, the world turned its back on me, leaving me to die in the cold.

In this house, I got shelter and food. And at the moment, that was all that mattered. I was too tired to think far past today.

"I do," I said. "I know what the men here do for a living."

"Is that something you want to do?"

I shrugged, quickly polishing away the remaining food. "I don't have a choice."

Erif brought a mug of tea for Traeh.

"There is always a choice," she said. "Even if you don't like the alternative."

I took another sip of my tea, washing down the food. Sadly, the tea didn't get rid of the bitter taste in my mouth caused by her words.

"My alternative is to die in the snow out there. And no, I don't like it very much. Despite everything, I'm not ready to die yet," I admitted. "But I have nowhere else to go."

She nodded, as if expecting it. "No family, I take it?"

"None who'd want me."

"There are still options out there for you, boy," she argued. "Go do something else."

"I tried. No one would hire me."

"Why not? There is nothing wrong with you." She tipped her chin at me. "You're strong and healthy. There is enough work out there. Hard, back-breaking work maybe, but people will respect you for it. There will be no respect if you stay here."

I shifted in my seat uneasily. "No one will hire me. I've tried."

Erif squinted at me, leaning with his shoulder against the mantle of the fireplace. Recognition spread across his face.

"You're Lady Lana's kept boy, aren't you?" He pointed at me. "I heard on the market that her daughter yapped in church to anyone who cared to listen about how you deceived and seduced her poor mother to gain the lady's favor."

I managed to control the *reflection*. But my cheeks flared with heat that didn't come from the tea or the fire.

"That's not how it happened," I said, staring into the flames.

"Maybe it isn't." Traeh reached for her pipe again. "But truth doesn't matter as long as people believe the lie. No one will let you in their house now, boy. In their eyes, you're tainted, ruined, and soiled. Wicked. The town folks think that wickedness is like a disease that can spread on their pure, innocent sons." Her voice gained intensity as she leaned closer. "But working here will make it worse. You'll never wash off the stain of being a whore for hire. Never. If there is anywhere else you can go, any place at all, go there and stay away from houses like ours."

Fear clawed at my chest that they would send me away. Now that they had warmed me up and fed me, going out into the dark, freezing night felt worse than death. The chances of me surviving another night in the open were slim as the storm moved in.

"That's the problem, madam. I have nowhere else to go," I said.

"Right." She leaned back in her chair, puffing on her pipe again. "You're too young to even sign a slave contract."

Erif cleared his throat. "Who is to say that slavery would be a better choice for him than this? Slave work has killed many strong men."

Traeh gazed at me with undisguised pity. "Your freedom or your body, Salas. Either way, you'll have to give up one. It's not an easy choice to make, is it?"

"It wouldn't be an easy choice," I agreed, "if I had it. But I don't even have that one. You said it yourself, I'm too young for the slave contract." Now I knew exactly what Lady Lana meant when she said I'd have no future. She truly left me with nothing.

No woman would marry me. The only path I ever knew in life was now closed to me. "All I have is this. If you have me."

"Well..." Traeh grunted, getting up. "It's getting late. Erif will take you upstairs. You'll bunk with the boys in the attic. The second-floor bedrooms are used for work only. It's slow today. The weather keeps people at home. Tomorrow doesn't look like it'll be much better, either. Rest, take a bath. Tomorrow night, you'll show me what you know about pleasuring a woman. Then I'll teach you the things you might not know yet."

THE FOLLOWING NIGHT, Traeh took me to one of the neatly furnished bedrooms on the second floor of the house. After closing the door, she turned to me and heaved a sigh, looking me over.

I avoided meeting her eyes. I wasn't worried about failing her test, or whatever this was supposed to be. But ever since Lady Lana had first laid her hands on me, I'd had to brace myself for the touch of another being. I was not looking forward to taking my clothes off for yet another stranger, another woman more than twice my age.

I swallowed the knot of nerves and apprehension in my throat before bringing a hand to the buttons of my shirt.

Traeh stopped me by covering my hand with hers.

"Keep your clothes on for now, boy. Let me just tell you something first."

I looked up, finally meeting her dark-eyed gaze.

"You have three things that make you what you are, Salas. Your body." She pressed a hand to my lower belly, just below my belt. "Your heart." She touched my chest next. "And your mind." She tapped with her finger against my forehead. "Don't give all of yourself to this work, and you'll survive. You'll have to use your body to give the clients what they pay for. But keep in mind the things you need to get out of it—things like food, shelter, money, and whatever pleasure you may get from being with a client. Most importantly, however, leave your heart out of it completely. Your heart is yours and only yours. Keep it that way."

I nodded, not entirely understanding the full meaning behind her words yet, but grateful for them anyway. There was more to me than Lady Lana had taken. She ruined me but didn't destroy me. I survived her. I would survive this too.

Watching my face, Traeh nodded with satisfaction.

"And don't let the judgment of others get to you," she said. "This is a job, like any other. It just occasionally requires you to wear less clothes than most." She pulled her blouse off over her head. "Keep your pants on for now. Your work will be mostly about the women you're with. Not all of them will ask you to undress. They'll pay you to touch them, not the other way around. Now, kick your boots off and hop in the bed. You may end up having fun still."

Four

SALAS

8 YEARS LATER

"**A**nd that's how it's done!" I smirked triumphantly, wiping my mouth with the back of my hand. "You're on fire tonight, my lady."

Madam Edirp, the banker from Main Street, moaned one last time, then closed her legs, and rolled to her side.

"Did I beat my last record, Salas?"

"Close, madam. If we count from before the dinner tonight, this was your orgasm number seven."

"Really?" she murmured, raking her fingers through the hair on my chest. "You're simply magnificent tonight, sweetie."

"You flatter me, my lady." I caught her hand and removed it from my chest.

At times, I felt worn out to the point when physical contact irritated me. I placed a kiss on her hand to make it look like a caress rather than what it really was—a rejection.

She giggled like a girl half her age. "It certainly felt like you sent me all the way to the afterlife a time or two. Come here, handsome." She hooked her arm around my neck to pull me closer. "You deserve a kiss."

Kisses were not necessary. I worked for money, not kisses. My job was to give Madam Edirp as many orgasms as she could handle. In exchange, she paid Traeh handsomely, and Traeh provided me with room and board, as well as put some money aside for when I'd be too old or too sick to work.

But of course, I couldn't pull away from Madam Edirp, not without risking to offend her. So, I let her guide me down to her puckered mouth and parted my lips when her tongue prodded against them.

"Hmm," she hummed in pleasure, breaking the kiss after a moment or two. "I love tasting me on you. It's so deliciously wicked."

Wicked boys grew into wicked men.

I'd been working at Traeh's fun house for eight years now and had grown rather comfortable here. Most clients treated us kindly. There were a few who preferred to dominate. Some were even aroused by cruelty, just like Lady Lana. But unlike before, I was never left to deal with them on my own. Traeh and Erif had rules to protect the men working for them and tried not to let any situation get out of control.

By the age of twenty-five, I had a solid base of regular customers. Most, like Madam Edirp, paid for an evening and the entire night after. For many, sex wasn't the most important or even the most requested activity. Madam Edirp, for example, went through this type of multi-orgasmic indulgence only about once a month. If she visited me on any other night in between, she usually just ordered me to make her tea and spoon her as she slept. She claimed that my tea improved her digestion and the spooning was good for her backache.

I had one client who only requested a massage of her legs and feet. While I delivered it, she liked to complain out loud about her neighbors, her store's customers, and her in-laws. Our conversation rarely required any input on my part.

Another one liked to recount to me all the dreams and night terrors she'd had since the last time she saw me. I'd serve her tea and listen patiently as she talked. Some nights, she'd allow me to make her come on my fingers. Other nights, she wouldn't let me touch her at all.

I tried to make sure my clients enjoyed the time spent with me, but there was one thing I couldn't give them, no matter how much they offered to pay me. It was love.

Most women understood that their money bought them only my time and access to my body. But some had the love fantasy in mind. They demanded an emotional involvement, too, and that was impossible to feel for me and very hard to fake. Despite my extensive experience with sex and pleasure, I still knew nothing about love.

Regardless of whether it was sex or love they searched for in a fun house, loneliness was the main reason that brought many of my clients into my arms. And in that, we were similar. Despite falling asleep while hugging a woman almost every night, I often felt alone.

Madam Edirp stretched in bed, her eyelids drooping.

"Oh, I'll sleep so well tonight," she murmured, relaxing into the bedding.

I pulled the covers over her bare shoulders. The old house sometimes got drafty at night.

"I'll be right back," I said and padded into the adjacent bathroom to brush my teeth.

I changed from my pants into a pair of long underwear that I liked to sleep in. During the entire night so far, my pants had never come off. For a man of my occupation, I didn't have nearly as much sex as the general population might think.

Like Traeh had warned me back when I'd first crossed the threshold of this establishment, our work here was all about the clients' pleasure. Women paid me for their orgasms, not mine.

Some enjoyed the actual fucking, but not everyone requested it and not for every visit. Even when a penetration was requested, my climax was never the goal. If I came, it often happened as a side effect.

The visits when I was required to be inside a woman were when the clients brought their daughters to me to help them get rid of their virginity.

These visits were often shorter. The daughters acted uneasily around me, looking like they couldn't wait for it to be over with. Some focused too much on the process, as if I were giving them a lesson in class. They clearly were educating themselves on what to do with their virginal husbands afterwards.

Once we finished, they would shove a silver coin or a cheap cigar into my hand as a personal thank-you for the experience, then leave promptly to marry their innocent grooms with unsoiled reputations.

It hadn't been hard to follow Traeh's advice and keep my heart to myself. At first, I had occasionally longed for a connection. But as the time passed, my heart grew numb and my mind tired.

I no longer missed the physical intimacy. On the contrary, I often loathed it. So many women had come and gone. I'd grown tired of so many faces and so many different bodies in my bed, treasuring the rare nights when I got to sleep alone in my bunk in the attic.

Worn out by all her orgasms, Madam Edirp snored softly by the time I returned to the bedroom. I took a spare blanket and lay on the other side of the bed. There would still be enough time to spoon her before morning as she'd requested and paid for. Until then, maybe I could get some sleep too.

Erif shook me awake, frantic with terror.

"Salas, fire!" He coughed in the smoke that was filling the room through the open door. "The house is on fire. You need to get out."

Alarm speared through me, sending me into action. I tried to wake Madam Edirp, but she only rolled her head on the pillow, keeping her eyes closed.

"Smoke. She must've breathed it too much." Erif ran out the door. "Get her out. I'll wake the others."

Taking shallow, careful breaths, I carried Madam Edirp out of the room. The fire had nearly completely taken over the main floor. The flames licked under the stairs, their bright tongues flicking through the gaps in the boards.

Pressing the unconscious woman to my chest, I ran down the stairs as fast as I could, leaping over two steps at a time.

The cold winter air met me outside. The flames brightened the night, flooding the fence and the frozen ground with a sinister red glow.

Wearing only her nightgown, her long hair unbraided, Traeh ran to me with a blanket in her hands. "How is she? Alive?" She tucked the blanket around my client.

"I think so." I gently laid Madam Edirp down a safe distance from the fire. She groaned, then coughed, gripping her throat.

Traeh clawed at my arm. "Where is Erif? Did you see him?"

"He was inside, waking everyone."

Someone else ran out of the burning house, and Traeh rushed to them with another blanket.

The freezing cold bit my skin and seeped through my thin linen pants. Frost covered the ground, numbing my bare feet. I ignored it, looking around wildly.

What happened?

Why was the world ablaze?

A window frame collapsed, shuttering the glass panes. Flames burst out, illuminating more of the yard.

"Burn the evil in the cleansing fire!" a female voice shouted over the roaring flames and the crashing of burning wood. "Burn the wicked!"

Wind tore at the pristine white robes of the priestess who stood in the gap in the fence around the yard, surrounded by townspeople. She wore white—the color of Yarnus, the God of Purity. The priestess held a long pole with a ring mounted on top. It represented the circle of life, the symbol of marriage and procreation.

"Burn the wicked!" a man parroted, kicking another section of the fence in.

He tossed his torch through the kitchen window, as if it would make any difference at that point. The house I'd called home for the past eight years was burning to the ground, and nothing would either save it or make it burn faster now.

"There are people inside!" Traeh screamed at the priestess and those who came with her. "You're burning people alive, you monsters!"

Except that for them, we weren't "people." They held us below the animals. We were whores, with less right to exist than scum under their shoe.

Traeh frantically dashed between the men and women in the yard, checking on them and counting the survivors.

Madam Edirp coughed again, then sat up, staring at the fire in horror.

"What's going on?"

"Are you alright?" I kneeled at her side and pulled the blanket higher over her shoulders.

She spotted the townsfolk by the broken fence and shoved me away.

"Don't touch me," she hissed in a half-whisper. A ripple of *reflection* pulsed through her body. "Where is my wagon? I've got to get out of here before anyone sees me with you."

She paid me to fuck, kiss, and cuddle her in private, but wouldn't accept a friendly touch from me in public, ashamed to be seen with me. Her rejection burned, but I tamped it down promptly before even a hairline of *reflection* could mar my skin.

No one could ever see me *reflect*. No one could know how much their insults hurt me or how scary the world's disdain could feel.

Since *reflection* was a public display of fear and shame, a part of dealing with it was to control those emotions. The other part was to physically hold back the ripple, which I'd learned most people couldn't do. I started training this ability of mine back in Lady Lana's manor. By flogging myself with the riding crop, I'd learned how to hide my fear of physical pain. During my years at the fun house, I'd trained to conceal my shame too.

"Salas!" Traeh rushed to me. "Erif... He didn't come out. Everyone is here now, but he's still inside."

A beam crashed in the kitchen, sending fireworks of sparks out of the broken windows all around the house.

"Oh no. No, no, no... Erif." Traeh wailed, falling to her knees beside me.

"I saw him on the stairs," one of the men said. His leg was bleeding, either burned or cut.

"Erif!" Traeh lurched toward the house, but I managed to grab her just in time.

"You need to take care of the men." I pointed at the one with blood dripping down his arm and all the others huddling in the yard, half-naked and shivering.

The villagers poured through the broken fence. They threw torches and curses at the house. I feared they might turn their wrath from the inanimate objects like the fence and the house to the people who were taking shelter in the yard.

"Stay here and keep the townsfolk at bay," I told Traeh, then tipped my head to the closest of our men. "Keep her here. I'll be right back."

I picked up the blanket that Madam Edirp had dropped in her escape to her wagon. Throwing it over my head, I ran back into the burning building.

A wave of heat slammed into me inside. The smoke proved disorienting. I dropped to the floor, where the smoke wasn't as thick, and crawled toward the stairs.

The staircase had burned through and prolapsed. Erif lay at the bottom, his foot stuck between the boards of the lower step. He didn't move when I grabbed him under his arms. I hoped with all my heart he was just unconscious, not dead.

I freed his leg and dragged him to the exit where Traeh was waiting for us.

"Oh, thank gods...thank gods..." She grabbed Erif's arm.

Two other men from our house rushed to help.

With a loud cracking, the door frame collapsed. The top beam just missed my shoulder, but the side post caved in, crashing down and scorching my side on the way. My right pant leg caught on fire. The searing pain sent me out into the yard. I fell and rolled on the frozen ground, trying to kill the flames that burned my skin and flesh.

Terror and agony ravaged me. Shame pulsed through it all, fanned by the screams from the crowd higher than the flames. But I didn't let a single line of *reflection* show anywhere on my body.

The world did not deserve a visual display of the torture it'd been putting me through.

"Burn. Burn. Burn," the villagers chanted. "Burn, filthy whores!"

Five

SALAS

7 YEARS LATER

The crowd screamed as the royal gladiators and I entered the arena. These were the screams of cheers and support, but they echoed with the chants "Burn, filthy whore!" ringing through my memories.

I was the same man, with the same body and soul, and the same shameful past. Only the place had changed. And here, they admired me instead of despised. I wondered how long it would take for the cheers to turn to sneers if they found out who I really was and how I came to be here now.

After Traeh's fun house had burned to the ground, I spent weeks recuperating from my burns in a rented room. As my injuries healed painfully slow, I had plenty of time to contemplate my future.

The decision was simple because my choices were fewer than ever before. I was a fallen man who'd worked in a fun house for eight years. There was only one place for me to go now—another whore house. Even a slave contract was out of reach with the past like mine. There was no such thing as a "former whore." Traeh had been right all along. A stain like this remained forever. It became a life sentence.

A working boy was required to be registered to a brothel and confined to a fun district. Legally, I wasn't allowed to leave the district without permission or accompanied by a woman.

Traeh gave me a letter of reference for another establishment like hers. As soon as my burns healed enough for me to walk, I headed to the town where it was located.

Once again, I walked along a frozen dirt road to a place I'd never been to before. This time, however, I had the money to stop at a tavern and buy a meal.

By pure luck, I found a letter of reference in the tavern, dropped by someone, probably after a night of heavy drinking. The letter had no name. I couldn't return it. So, I used it to sign my first slave contract.

As a whore, I could only keep my heart to myself. But as a slave, I kept more. I no longer had to share a bed with anyone. I was not required to fake emotions I didn't feel or to have strangers' hands on me when I didn't want to be touched. As long as I did my work during the day, my body remained my own.

Later, I learned, of course, that slaves were still despised and looked down at by free folks. Yet the status of a slave was higher than that of a whore because every slave had a chance at redemption, even if many of them never got free again.

After that first contact, getting the next one proved easy. As long as I worked hard and asked for little, slave owners didn't dig deep into my past.

Nothing in my life had predicted my being in the gladiators' arena now. A position like that was highly coveted by many and was granted to very few. Still, when Lady Gem had offered this opportunity to me, my first instinct was to decline.

The gladiators' games rivaled the queen's parades in popularity. They attracted enormous crowds, and in my case, too much attention could be deadly. I'd broken the law by concealing my past to become a slave. If discovered, I risked the death penalty.

But in the end, I had accepted the offer. A part of me wished to experience at least a moment of the respect and admiration that society showered the royal gladiators with. I wanted to know what it felt like to step in front of a crowd with my head held high.

The other reason was her—Princess Aniri. As a royal gladiator, I got to stay in Egami, where she lived.

My mind demanded I get away, but my heart decided otherwise. And that was the problem. That girl with her freckles, and her glasses, and her tragic secrets had made her way under my skin, getting dangerously close to my heart.

SHE WAS the only woman I'd ever met who made me feel like her equal, despite our positions being so impossibly far apart. The feeling came as a true shock, and I still wasn't sure whether it was her who was so down-to-earth or me who felt elevated in her presence, but with her, the slave felt worthy of the princess. She never treated me as a lesser being, not even after she'd found out the whole truth about my past.

The gladiators formed a circle around the arena, framing it in a single line. Queen Anna and her royal consort King Trebor walked down the long rug laid over the sand. Regal and dignified, the royal couple crossed the arena toward the lavishly decorated sitting platform on the opposite side.

I thought I was prepared to see her again. I'd waited for this moment all morning. But my breath hitched when Princess Aniri stepped out into the arena after her parents.

She held her chin up, not letting her tall crown weigh her head down. The long train of her formal gown sparkled like a starry sky, stitched with diamond stars. The starched lace collar rose from around her shoulders like a wide flower petal, not letting me see her face until she stopped in the middle of the arena and raised her hand in greeting.

Ari turned around slowly, waving to the crowd. Hiding behind the visor of my helmet, I greedily soaked in every detail about her.

The sun reflected in her glasses, hiding her eyes from me. Did she see me? I was standing too far away, and she was looking up at the cascading rows of seating from where the people who'd come from all over the queendom waved and cheered.

A different kind of images entered my mind as memories rushed me. I remembered how her glasses fogged with my breath while I kissed her freckles. I never forgot the sensation of her hair gripped in my fingers while she held my cock in her mouth. And how she sobbed in my arms, recalling things that no girl should have to live through.

The princess was a survivor. Like me. I sensed our connection from the first words she said to me. That was the only reason I'd agreed to come to her bedroom that first night.

The generous sum the crown offered for teaching the princess the ways of sex would've enticed many. But for me, it was useless. I didn't plan to buy my freedom because there was no future for me beyond slavery.

I had no desire to work as a hired man of pleasure ever again, not even for one night, not even for the crown princess. But I had to make sure that Princess Aniri was simply the spoiled little girl like most nobles were. Born in miracle and raised in luxury, she couldn't possibly have anything in common with me.

How badly I'd been mistaken, and how wrong she'd proven me. Since that first night, I couldn't get her out of my thoughts.

Throughout my life, women had been many things to me. My mother was a source of strength and safety. Lady Lana became my source of pain and humiliation. Later, being with women delivered some pleasure and even comfort. My clients had been my job that I did well but didn't think about once it was done. I hadn't pleasured a woman since the night of the fire and hadn't missed it.

But with Ari... With her, I let it all spiral out of control, and I wasn't sure when or how it had happened.

It wasn't Ari's fault. I knew who she was from the very first moment I laid my eyes on her. I had no business falling for the crown princess. But there I was, falling, plummeting so hard, my head was spinning, and I had to stop it before I crashed.

She crossed the arena and climbed the stairs up to the royal balcony under the awning of gold brocade. The train of her priceless gown stretched over the stairs like a waterfall of diamonds and sunshine. I watched her climb higher and higher to the heights where I could never follow her.

As she took her seat next to the queen, I forced my thoughts out of the past and into the present.

Instead of remembering how Ari's arms twined around my neck with her naked body pressed against mine, I recalled the purpose of all of us being in this arena today. The purpose of this event was for Princess Aniri to welcome to Rorrim Queendom the three high-born princes. Before their visit was over, she'd choose one of them to be her lawfully wedded husband.

By the end of this year, another man would share her bed, touch her body, and kiss her freckles. And it wouldn't be me.

A fallen man could never claim the crown princess for his own.

Ari wasn't mine and could never be.

THE HELMET DID A GREAT JOB, concealing my face from the audience in the arena. But on a hot day like today, it turned impossibly stuffy inside. I grunted with relief when taking it off upon our return to the gladiators' quarters.

The three wings of the two-story building framed a large courtyard in the middle. In the summer, the men preferred to take lunch outside. A wide awning hung from the tall fence poles to the left, shading several long tables with benches on both sides. The cook and her helpers brought out huge platters with food from the kitchen and put them onto the wooden tables for our midday meal.

The aroma that drifted from the platters made my mouth water. I got up late that morning and only had a few gulps of hot tea and a slice of bread for breakfast before Lerrel, the games master, dragged me into the practice rink to get ready for the ceremony in the arena.

Marching in the arena required far less strain and energy than hauling bricks or rocks as a slave, but I was used to eating my fill, even as a slave. A single slice of bread was not nearly enough to sustain me for the entire morning. By now, I felt famished, looking forward to finally getting some food.

I hung up my helmet on the hook on the fence, next to the props and costume pieces of the other men.

Raob, a stout man with copper-red hair braided in long pleats and a beard that reached down to his chest, carefully placed his elaborate headdress on the shelf nearby. His helmet was decorated with a wide strip of thick brown fur, a pair of tusks, and a snout pierced with a thick bronze ring in the middle.

"This fucking thing gets boiling hot like a teakettle in the sun," he muttered, running his hand over his sweat-slicked braids. "You must be cooking under that hide, too, boy?" He tipped his chin at the bear fur over my shoulders.

I nodded, unbuckling the belts that connected the hide to my shoulders.

"I've been waiting to get rid of it all morning," I admitted.

The fresh breeze blew over my sweaty back the moment I removed the hide. I stretched my shoulders, reveling in the relief it brought.

The rules of modesty and propriety didn't seem to apply to gladiators. Many of us remained topless, both in the arena and here now. A few men threw on their light shirts or robes after removing their armor, and I wished I'd brought my shirt down here too. I wasn't used to being half-naked like this, even less so when taking my meals. But I was way too hungry to run inside for a shirt now.

I took a seat at the end of the bench, grabbed a plate, and piled it high with food from the platters. I'd never felt this hungry, not even as a slave. It wasn't in the owner's interest to starve us. But the watery potato stew and the undercooked barley normally served to the slaves had been barely eatable compared to the gladiator's fare of roasted ribs, steamed vegetables doused in buttery sauce, and freshly baked bread. I tried not to drool, breathing in the appetizing smells.

Regit, the young gladiator, originally from Tresed Queendom, slid onto the bench across from me.

"So, what did you think about the arena, Reab?" he asked before biting into a piece of bread.

Reab.

That was the name I gave to the games master when she asked how I wished to be known to the public. The less people knew about me, the safer I was.

"It's a big arena," I replied, tearing a piece of warm bread from a thick slice.

Somehow, Regit managed to stuff his face with food and chat simultaneously without choking.

"I bet it feels different when standing in it than when looking at it from the audience during the games," he said between the bites of the meat and forkfuls of the vegetable dish.

Before that morning, I'd never been to the Royal Gladiators' Arena either as a performer or a spectator. I grew up in a small village, quite a distance from Egami. Lady Lana's estate was deep in the country, too, far away from the capital. I'd first arrived in the city when I was already a slave, and of course, the owner never took her slaves to see the games. Why would she?

Obviously, I wasn't going to explain any of it to Regit.

"It's different," I agreed, bringing the bread to my mouth.

Falo, another gladiator, dropped his plate on the table next to mine and stepped over the bench on my right.

"Make space, big boy," he growled, squeezing between me and Raob. "This place was just right for the forty-eight gladiators. And now, it feels way too *tight.*"

He slid along the bench, slamming his side into me. Not expecting it, I lost my balance and nearly fell off the bench. Dropping the bread, I grabbed on to the table, shifting the whole thing toward me.

"Hey!" the other gladiators yelled, catching their plates to stop them from sliding off the table.

I jumped to my feet. Falo rose from the bench, too, jerking his chin up in challenge. The midday air sizzled with tension around us. Even the clanking of the dishes stopped abruptly.

A single clap came from behind us, sharp like a crack of a whip. Lerrel, the games master, propped her hands on her hips, glaring at us as she approached the eating area.

Of an average height and size for a woman, she looked tiny compared to the gladiators. Yet she didn't need a size advantage over the men for them to do as she said. Her words lashed harder than a whip.

"You two. On the rink. Now." She snapped her fingers and flicked her wrist at the oval rink roped off in the middle of the courtyard.

Packed with dirt and sawdust, the rink was smaller than the Royal Gladiator's Arena, but it had the same shape and proportions. We'd used it to practice our formations that morning. And now, Lerrel wagged her finger between Falo and me.

"Whatever is going on between you two, get on the rink and work it out. Now."

Cursing under his breath, Falo stomped over to the rope stretched between the low poles that marked the rink.

I tossed a wistful glance at the succulent ribs on my plate and my uneaten slice of bread before following him. My empty stomach spasmed in protest, but no one seemed to dare disobey the games master, and I wasn't going to be the one to set that example.

Judging by Lerrel's clothes, she was a Roamer from the traveling tribes. Roamers were notorious for their street fighting skills, but Lerrel had made a career out of it, rising all the way to the Games Master of the Royal Gladiators.

She was dressed in a frilly, colorful skirt and a sleeveless blouse with flowery embroidery in the front. Her black, thick curls were cut to just above her shoulders and held away from her face with a red scarf tied around her head. With her hands propped on her hips and her dark eyes narrowed at us, she watched closely as Falo and I stepped over the rope and got into the rink.

Falo spat on the ground. "Lady Gem doesn't give a fuck about you, Raeb. Don't you imagine even for a moment that you're her boy now just because she put a word in for you on a whim."

I shrugged. Lady Gem spoke to me for the first time ever just a day ago. She'd talked through her teeth, avoiding eye contact and clearly hating every minute spent in the same room with me. She might've given me the official reference, but I had a strong feeling she wasn't really the one behind my sudden rise from a slave to a gladiator.

As Lady Gem had reluctantly explained, there might be a murder accusation looming over my head. She also had made it clear that becoming a gladiator might shield me from my past catching up with me if I remained a slave. It seemed I had a high-standing benefactor who was concerned about my safety, but it couldn't be Lady Gem. Princess Aniri was the only one who'd shown me any kindness lately, and I believed it had been her idea all along. There simply wasn't anyone else who would care about me or my future.

With his fists raised, Falo circled me, and I rotated to keep facing him.

"Stay away from the lady chamberlain," he snarled.

"Gladly."

But he was too wound up to listen to reason. Launching forward, fast like lightning, Falo executed a maneuver I'd never seen before, slamming his fist into my ribs.

"Slow like molasses," he gloated. "You're a waste as a gladiator. You may've gotten here by giving Lady Gem a satisfying fuck or two, but that's as far as you'll go."

He kept jumping around me, searching for another chance to strike. His leaping around proved disorienting, giving me a headache.

"What are the rules?" I asked.

"There are no rules, you oaf," he spat out.

Lerrel grabbed a roasted rib from Falo's plate and ate it with her foot propped on the bench.

"The rules are no killing your opponent and no broken bones on the training rink," she said between the bites. "Save the real stuff for the arena."

That was good to know, since I'd broken a man's arm in my last fight. It hadn't been intentional. I'd grabbed his wrist, and when he'd jerked one way, I'd pulled in the other. The bone had snapped.

That day, we worked on fixing a giant pothole in the road leading to the palace. A few wagons passed by, and I recognized one as Traeh's. I should've just let her pass. But I hadn't seen Traeh for years and didn't give it a second thought, running up to her to say hi.

"Traeh, it's me, Salas. How have you been?"

She squinted at me, her hand pressed to her chest. "Salas? Is that really you?"

She didn't recognize me, unsurprisingly so. I hardly recognized myself when I had a chance to look in a mirror. I'd grown wider and rougher since my days at the fun house. I'd also stopped shaving, letting my beard grow.

Seven years had passed since I saw her last. Her face, however, held the mark of sorrows worth far more than just seven years.

We chatted briefly. Erif had survived the fire but died five years later, succumbing to the aftermath of the injuries he'd gotten that night. All the other men who'd worked for Traeh had found positions in other fun houses.

"You're the only one who never went back," Traeh said.

"Pure luck and a lie helped me get away."

She shook her head, her lips pressed together in concern.

"You know what the law is. If your past is discovered, you won't live long."

"I know. But for as long or as short as I have, I'll live the way I want, not the way the law forces me to."

"Are you content with your life then?" She didn't ask if I was happy. True happiness wasn't for the men like me.

"It is what it is." I shrugged.

I went back to hauling the gravel to fill the pothole, and Traeh was on her way to the farm of a distant relative. She'd never opened another fun house while taking care of Erif. After he died, she decided to move to the farm and help around for as long as she could.

When I returned to the slaves working on the road, one of them recognized Traeh's wagon.

"Hey, I saw that wagon years ago. People on the market said that woman was getting groceries for a whorehouse."

"Do you want to become a whore, Salas?" the other one snorted.

"That bitch would take you for all you've got, make money off you, then fuck you herself for free," the first one added.

The third slave made a sign of a circle over his forehead—the ring of purity in honor of God Yarnus, "Cursed is she and all those who are with her. May they all burn in a purifying fire."

The others laughed and cursed, saying things about Traeh she didn't deserve. The brunt of our stigma scorched her too.

"Shut up," I snapped.

Traeh wasn't perfect by any means. But who was? She had taken me in when every door had closed on me. She showed me kindness when no one else did.

They taunted me and insulted her, delighted in having someone below them to look down at and spit on. One of them shoved me, and I threw a punch in response. Five more men jumped at me, and I hit left and right without looking, until a bone snapped and a man yelled in agony.

"No breaking bones." I nodded, repeating Lerrel's words.

Falo hit again. The blow to my chest left me winded. He was too fast, jumping around me like a rabbit. I figured out the pattern of his jumps and leaped aside to evade his next strike. Then I moved behind him and hugged his arms to his torso.

"Hey!" he yelled and sputtered, squirming in my tight embrace. "That's not how it's done. Fight me, you coward!"

"You said no rules." I wrapped one arm around his middle, holding his arms to his body, then lifted him off his feet.

He kicked, so I shifted him under my arm, holding him horizontally to the ground. He kicked and screamed but couldn't free his hands or reach me with his feet.

"Set me down, you fucking clumsy bear!" Falo yelled, dangling in my hold like a toddler throwing a tantrum.

Lerrel's mouth dropped open, the half-eaten rib dangling in her fingers.

The rest of the gladiators erupted in thunderous laughter. Raob all but fell off the bench, holding his sides. Regit laughed so hard, tears were rolling down his cheeks.

"Don't you squirm like that." I adjusted Falo under my arm. "Or you'll break your ribs, which is against the rules." I turned to Lerrel. "Where do you want him, master?"

Lerrel blinked, then swallowed, hiding a giggle behind her hand.

"Well." She stepped over the rope and onto the rink with us. "Set him down. The fight is over, Falo." She shoved the rib bone with little meat left on it into his hand. "Go eat your lunch."

"The fucking ogre has no clue how to fight!" Falo glared at me, storming off the rink.

A reflection wave of embarrassment ran over his skin and clothes, momentarily blending his shape with the fence and the ground. He tossed the half-eaten rib into the bucket on the ground, then grabbed his plate from the table and stomped toward the building, chased by the teasing shouts of the gladiators.

"I never said I knew how to fight," I explained to Lerrel. "I'm much better with a sword than with my fists. Especially if you don't want any bones broken."

"But you sure made it entertaining." She smirked. "Which is actually the most important part of what we do around here. Above all, the public must be entertained. Let me think. What can we do with you?"

She stepped around me, assessing me with her stare.

I was wearing long linen pants and knee-high boots made from a soft, thin leather held up by a rope zigzagging up my calves. Instead of a shirt, a pair of wide leather belts crisscrossed my chest, with two metal buckles on my shoulders that were used to hold the bearskin.

Lerrel splayed her fingers on my right bicep.

"Flex," she ordered.

I raised my forearm, straining the muscles. She added the

second hand but barely made it half-way around my upper arm with both hands.

"Well, shit." She gaped at me. "Huge like a mountain and hard like a rock."

Taking a step back, she stared at my chest for a few seconds, then slid her gaze down to my abdomen. Without a warning, she poked her finger in my belly. I jerked, my muscles flexing instinctively.

She traced a square of an abdominal muscle, muttering, "A bit too lean, but that's to be expected, considering what you did before. No worries, we'll put some bulk on you yet." She walked around me. "What exactly did you do as a slave?" I turned to face her again, but she twirled a finger in the air, signaling me to spin around. "I need to see your back."

As requested, I presented her with the view of my back again.

"Is that from the flogging you got for that fight Lady Gem mentioned?" She traced a scar on my back.

"Yes."

"It's healed well," she commented matter-of-factly. "So, what else did you do, other than fight?"

"I helped fix the castle walls with the others," I said over my shoulder. "And before that, I helped lay the garden paths. And before that—"

"How exactly did you help, Raeb?"

"I carried rocks and bricks, brought gravel in a wheelbarrow. That kind of things."

"I see."

I felt the press of her fingers on either side of my spine.

"What did they feed you to keep you working?" she asked.

"Mostly, a potato stew or boiled barley, with other grains sometimes."

"Really? How long were you a slave?"

"Long enough," I replied evasively, afraid to give her the exact number, lest she dig deeper into my past.

"How long?" she insisted. "Months? Years?"
  "Years. Many years. Almost three contracts' worth."

"Hmm. And all those years, you ate mostly barley and potato stew?"

"Pretty much."

She poked and prodded down my spine then around my lower back, sliding the tips of her fingers under the waistband of my pants.

I tensed my shoulders but didn't stop her. Lerrel's attention, though uncomfortable, didn't feel sexual or suggestive. She inspected me the way a farmer would inspect a horse that she considered buying. Some men might still find it offensive, but I'd been through similar assessments a few times already, when signing the slave contracts.

"Have you ever had any back pain?" she asked.

"No. Not yet."

"You're lucky." She completed her walk-around and stopped in front of me again, tapping her chin with her finger. "Maybe I should cut down on meat for my boys here too? Switch to barley and potatoes instead?"

The gladiators grumbled, shifting uneasily at her words.

I flinched, casting a longing glance at my plate of ribs on the table.

Lerrel laughed.

"Don't worry. For one, our chef can prepare any grain much better than those in the slaves' kitchen, I'm sure. And two, I know I can't take meat from them completely or I'll have a mutiny on my hands." She tilted her head. "Well, you look like the gods have hewed you out of a mountain rock. A bear indeed."

A loud clapping came from the direction of the building, accompanied by a female voice, "Big like a mountain and strong like a bear. Why do you think I gave him that bear hide to wear this morning?"

A couple walked to us from the open door of the gladiators' building. The woman had introduced herself to me as Naeco that morning. She'd said she was the choreographer for the gladiators. Because apparently, the great fighting skills weren't enough to put up a satisfying show for the audience. Each fight had to be carefully choreographed for the arena, even as the risk of injury or death remained very real too.

Naeco's snow-white hair, eyebrows, and eyelashes, as well as her light-blue eyes, subtly tinted with violet, told me she was one of the Frosted people who looked like Eci, the Goddess of Winter. Every now and then, gods sent someone looking like Naeco into the world to remind us that beauty had many forms and the mortals' appearance was as varied as that of the gods.

The man who accompanied Naeco was Noil, Lerrel's husband and the gladiators' mentor. He trained the men to fight while Naeco made sure they looked good when fighting.

Naeco squinted in the sunshine before putting a pair of dark-tinted glasses on to peer at me through them.

"Fur suits you," she said.

"It goes well with the hide he has growing on his chest." Noil chuckled, then beelined for the table with food.

"Mountain Bear," Naeco murmured, raking with a finger through my chest hair that had fully grown out after the last grooming. "That's what you should be called in the arena. Mountain Bear. What do you think, Lerrel?"

I glanced at the games master.

"Works for me." She tipped her head at the table. "Go eat. I know you're hungry. It wouldn't do for us to starve you, especially if we're going with that bear-like persona for you."

"Thanks." I headed to the table, not waiting to be asked twice.

Noil took the place on my right, the one vacated by Falo.

"So, here is what's going to happen." Noil grabbed a rib from his plate, using it to articulate his words by waving it in the air. "You'll figure out all that costume shit with Naeco today. We'll get you the gladiator's ring tomorrow." He tapped against the table with the heavy silver ring on his right middle finger. The ring was engraved with the golden crown of Rorrim in the oval frame of the gladiator's arena. "I allowed you to sleep in this morning, but you're getting up early with the rest of the boys tomorrow. We train before and after breakfast. The first two weeks you'll help with the games and practice your own act. A week after, we'll try your act in the arena, see how it goes, and go from there." He bit into the rib, tearing a huge strip of meat from the bone. "And no women during the first month," he said around a mouthful. "I need you fully focused on the games, at least at the beginning."

"Fine with me." I reached for my plate. "I'm not interested in women."

"That's too bad, because if you prefer men, they can't pay much. Women are the rich and powerful ones. They make the best benefactors."

"No. Not interested in men, either." I picked up a rib and finally sank my teeth into the succulent meat. The flavor gave justice to the aroma that had been teasing me all this time.

Noil raised his bushy eyebrows, then shrugged his shoulders, and dug into the vegetables on his plate. "Suit yourself. You can certainly survive without a benefactor. But with a rich woman taking care of you, your life would be much easier."

The one and only woman who'd ever caught my interest I couldn't have. I'd shot way too high. Even a royal gladiator was way below a princess.

Her true match could only be a prince.

Six

ARI

The Royal Gladiators' Arena was filled to the brim with spectators, like always. What was happening in it, however, was not typical.

Instead of its usual elaborate settings filled with obstacles and traps for gladiators to overcome, hurdles had been placed at even intervals for horses to jump over. A long rail marked the jousting area. And instead of the beefy gladiators in their fantastic outfits, three fashionably dressed princes trotted gracefully on horseback.

"Ari, dearest, just look at them." Mother waved with her silk fan at the three riders circling the arena. The three princes paraded for the audience, their long decorative spears raised in the air. "So much class and elegance in their postures. Don't you think?"

"Absolutely, Mother. All three have class and elegance in spades."

The weather was cloudy today, finally providing some relief from the summer heat of late. However, Mother's dark satin gown still seemed too hot for the occasion, prompting her to work her fan relentlessly.

"Do you feel any preference for any of the three?" Mother

asked. "I'm not trying to push you into deciding on the spot, of course. You do have time. But I haven't noticed you leaning toward any of the princes yet. Do you feel any pull at all, however slight it may be?"

It'd been three weeks since the princes' arrival to Rorrim. In that time, Mother had held plenty of balls and parades in their honor. Every day had been packed with events and festivities. The usual council sessions had been put on hold, replaced by quick briefings with the queen for the most necessary discussions and decisions.

The influx of people to Egami had been disrupting the routine of the city dwellers. But there was also excitement in the air, both in the city and in the arena right now. The crowd shouted and clapped as the princes made their horses jump over the various hurdles erected for that reason.

So far, there hadn't been any "pull" on my part, however. Not at the slightest.

"Do you not have any preference at all?" Mother insisted.

"I already told you my preference, Your Majesty."

She sighed. "Yes, I know. You decided on Prince Leafar. But that was before you even met any of them. You made that decision based solely on the dowry agreements. I've been hoping that after you've spent some time with the princes and gotten to know them, you will form a connection with one of them."

So far, there had been no connections formed. I'd met all three princes together and individually. I'd danced at the balls with them and had a few conversations with each. They all acted appropriately and said all the right things, with nothing particularly standing out for me to like or dislike.

"I see no reason to change my decision, Mother. Prince Leafar will make a fine king consort for Rorrim."

"And for you?" She tilted her head to get a better look at my face. "Don't forget, you're not doing it only for Rorrim. The man you'll choose will also be your husband and eventually the father of your children."

I inhaled deeply, curling my fingers around the carved armrests of my brocade upholstered chair on the royal platform.

Accepting my upcoming marriage as my duty was one thing, but sharing my bed with one of the princes, touching him, kissing him, having sex with him, and ultimately starting a family with him... That was a whole other undertaking that felt like an unwelcome chore at best.

I intended to postpone the intimacy between us for as long as possible. Hopefully, I could drag out the period of getting to know each other until I'd grown used to having a husband and he'd also grown a little older too. Maybe after having been married for a while, we'd grow closer, find many things in common, and the intimacy between us would come naturally at some point. At least, that was my hope.

The crowd clapped enthusiastically as Prince Leafar's horse cleared a piece of a fence painted green to look like a hedge. I clapped too, keeping the mandatory smile on my face.

This was the second tournament where the princes had gotten a chance to display their horse-riding prowess. Prince Elbon had very narrowly won the last one. And this time, Prince Leafar seemed to have a lead, though I couldn't say for sure since I hadn't been paying attention or keeping the score.

The gloomy weather and, frankly, not that much action on the arena invited sleepiness, forcing me to fight to keep my eyes open. The princes pranced on their horses politely, neatly jumping over the pretty obstacles in the exact same way they had done it the last time.

Thankfully, the crowd cheered, having a great time, its enthusiasm likely fueled by the free meat pies and fruit wine served to the spectators at the crown's expense.

Finally, the tournament ended, with Prince Leafar being declared the winner this time. He received a white sash over his shoulder and a diamond-studded ribbon. As a part of his prize, he also got to sit on my right for today's gladiator games.

As he climbed up the stairs to the royal platform, his cheeks rosy and his blue eyes shining with excitement, my smile turned genuine. It proved impossible not to share his joy.

Mother folded her fan, put it on her lap, and clapped her hands. "Congratulations, Prince Leafar. Well done."

He gave her a deep bow, then took a knee in front of my chair.

"Congratulations," I said sincerely.

He looked elated and so proud of himself, it was hard not to feel his excitement.

"Your Highness," he said, placing his winner's ribbon at my feet. "From now on, all my victories belong to you. Everything I achieve, I do for you and in your name only."

"I'm flattered and eternally grateful, my prince." I accepted the ribbon because doing otherwise would be rude and even cruel. "Please, sit with me." I gestured at the armchair on my right.

He took the seat, beaming with pride.

"You are an excellent rider," I said.

The blush deepened on his clean-shaven cheeks.

"Thank you. I've been riding since I was two."

"Two? That young?"

"I started with a pony, of course. It's a mount of an appropriate size for that age."

"Still, it's impressive."

Prince Leafar was undoubtedly lovable. It should be entirely possible to fall in love with him. Maybe I just hadn't tried hard enough?

I smiled at him again, making an effort for the smile to look warm and gentle.

The crowd exploded with a sudden burst of excitement, bringing my attention back to the arena. It had been cleared from the hurdles. And now, a procession of gladiators entered it.

All my best intentions in regard to Prince Leafar momentarily evaporated. Instead, I found myself searching the arena for the man I'd promised to stay away from.

Among the guards carrying the queen's standard, the marching band of musicians, and even among the colorful group of the tall and well-muscled gladiators, Salas would be easy to spot. He usually towered over both men and beasts.

During the past two games, I'd caught glimpses of him here and there. He'd been a part of several group battles. Though, he'd seemed to hold back and stay out of the spotlight to keep the crowd's attention on the well-known stars of the games.

Today, he was nowhere to be seen at all, not even in the opening parade that all gladiators usually took part in.

A tendril of worry slipped into my chest. Why was he left out of the games this week? Had he been hurt? Or did he displease the games master in some way? As the conductor of the queendom's most popular and beloved games, the games master held a power that rivaled that of an army general. If crossed, she could make a formidable enemy with plenty of means at her disposal to ruin a man's life.

I racked my brain about how to find out what happened to Salas. I had no direct contact with the gladiators' quarters. Gem had not been forthcoming with any information about him. Understandably so, she was still upset with me about the way I'd forced her to become his official benefactor.

I watched the first battle restlessly, as if sitting on pins and needles. Falo, one of the newer gladiators, took the spotlight on the arena. From the day he joined the games a couple of months ago, he'd quickly become the crowd's favorite.

Dressed in a spectacular outfit of golden armor and white feathers, he channeled the God Yarnus, the only son of the Great Goddess Nus. His performance was based on one of the legends about the goddess's children freeing our land from bloodthirsty beasts and monsters for the people of Rorrim to live in peace and prosperity ever since.

The music intensified as Falo reached the center of the arena. The drum beat grew faster. The crowd stilled in anticipation.

Wide golden pillars rose from the ground. Falo jumped onto one of them just in time as scorching hot lava spread through the arena. It melted the sand. White smoke rose into the air with a sinister hiss.

I gripped the armrests of my chair, my attention now fully focused on what was happening in the arena. Rumor had it that the games master employed dark warlocks to create the magical effects for the games. She had never denied or confirmed that, vigorously guarding all her secrets.

The skill and magic of healing witches was honored and celebrated. The wizardry of warlocks, however, was feared and forbidden, forcing them to practice their dark craft in secret. Collaborating with warlocks had consequences. Only someone as powerful as the games master could get away with it. All for the entertainment of the masses.

The golden pillars kept moving, sliding in and out from the floor of the arena and constantly changing their height. The one that Falo stood on slid down. The glowing red lava licked over its top, nearly scorching the gladiator's boots. He leaped up into the air, then landed on another pillar. The moment his feet connected with it, however, this one started moving down too.

Taking the coil of golden rope from his belt, Falo tossed it toward the next pillar. The rope uncoiled in the air. Its end caught the top of the pillar in a noose. Falo jumped, nearly losing his footing as the pillar he'd stood on completely submerged into the liquid fire. Swinging on his golden rope, he reached the next pillar, then climbed on its top.

I released a breath, allowing myself to be deceived into believing he was safe now when I should've known better.

Battle cries ripped through the air, coming from all around the arena. Dressed as savage cannibals, men rushed to Falo from all sides. They jumped from pillar to pillar, closing in.

He evaded the first attacker by leaping away. The second man rushed Falo. The gladiator punched him in the chest, almost losing his balance, before jumping to the next pillar.

Hopping from pillar to pillar, Falo tried to escape. But there were just too many of his attackers closing in on him from all sides.

I watched with bated breath, fearful of what might happen next. I'd never spoken to Falo, never even came close enough to shake his hand, but I rooted for him fiercely at that moment.

He drew his sword and stabbed through the chest of the man who'd blocked his escape. The man howled in pain, losing his footing as Falo shoved him off the pillar and into the fiery hell below.

He killed three more of his attackers before the cannibals finally retreated. Flames flared in long, sparking licks as the river of lava swallowed the fallen men. The crowd gasped. Smoke rose from the lava like a thick black cloud, shrouding the arena.

The music blasted anew. As the smoke slowly settled down, Falo emerged. Standing on the tallest pillar in the center of the arena, he raised his sword high and released a triumphant cry of victory.

The lava receded with a defeated hiss, leaving the scorched black ground in its wake. The golden pillars slipped back into the floor and out of sight, save for the one that our hero stood on. Chains rattled, pulling long wagons filled with sand across the entire arena. The back walls of the wagons opened, spreading fresh white sand to cover the devastation caused by the lava.

The crowd erupted into applause and cheers so loud, it sounded like a wave of explosion rolling through the arena. Women tossed bouquets of flowers with jewels and other gifts tied to their stems. They landed on the freshly spread sand to be picked up by the arena helpers and laid at Falo's feet.

I unclenched my fingers from around the armrests and leaned back in my chair.

"That was intense," I exhaled.

"Rather barbaric." Mother flinched, vigorously working her fan again.

I wished to believe with all my heart that the men whom Falo had sent into the river of fire were alive and well. It was all a show after all. The danger looked so real, but that was what made the games so exciting.

"Why do it then?" I asked the queen. "Why have the games at all? The crown is the owner and the biggest supporter of them."

"Well, look at the crowd, my dear." Mother waved her fan at the rows that were filled to the brim, with not a single vacant seat left among them. "People are drawn to violence. Sadly, it is a part of our nature. Isn't it best to satisfy their craving here, in the environment we can control, than let it spill into the streets where innocents may suffer?"

The real question was why were people drawn to violence in the first place? What excited us about watching men put their lives in danger? Why did we so easily accept that they might get hurt or even die for our entertainment? The crowd in the arena didn't just accept it, they demanded that thrill.

I had no answer to that. No explanation.

"I suppose it is, Mother," was all I said.

If Prince Leafar overheard our conversation, he didn't show it. The prince remained silent, as a well-raised man would when women talked in his presence.

Once all the flowers had been picked up and Falo finally left, followed by screams from the adoring crowd, the games master entered the arena.

She walked toward its center, her hips swaying in her wide skirt of multi-colored ruffles. The hem of the skirt reached the top of her short beige boots with kitten heels and floral embroidery on the side. A wide frill of her blouse draped around her bare shoulders, and a bright scarf was tied around her head with its long, fringed ends hanging down her back. A black coiled whip was clipped to her belt, and she carried a hollowed, varnished rhino horn in her hand.

Two gladiators followed the games master. Neither of them was Salas, I noted with a pinch of disappointment. When she stopped, the gladiators crouched down on each side of her. Hugging her legs, they lifted her to sit on their shoulders.

The games master raised the rhino horn to her mouth.

"And that was our very own Yarnus, son of the Great Goddess Nus! Against all odds, he lives on!" Amplified by the horn, her voice reached far and wide.

The crowd caught her words and sent them high into the sky. The whole of Egami must have heard the thunder of support for Falo. The games master smiled triumphantly, soaking up their delight.

"But that's not all, people of Egami. We have a mind-blowing surprise for you today!" she continued.

At that promise, the crowd's enthusiasm leaped into a near hysterical. They clapped their hands and stomped their feet, bursting with frantic anticipation.

As the games master spoke, the two gladiators rotated slowly, making sure her words spread around the arena.

"My boys trapped a different kind of beast for you," the games master announced.

A trap door opened in the floor of the arena, and a cage with bars as thick as my arms slowly rose to the surface.

"He comes from the high mountains where he wrestled bears before breakfast and hunted cliff goats for dinner. He drinks nothing but freezing glacial water and wears the fur of the animals he devoured. Ladies and gentlemen!" The games master threw her free arm up in the air dramatically. "I present to you the Mountain Bear!"

The cage was fully up now. It rotated on its platform, displaying the creature inside that truly looked like a beast.

It took a moment for the recognition to slam into me.

Salas!

A long, thick cape of ragged bear skins concealed his back. His helmet had been fitted with a row of chipped and broken animal tusks. Instead of pants, several layers of torn fabric were wound around his hips. On the left, the rags reached below his knee. On the right, they were shorter, leaving the scar from the burn on his thigh exposed.

The scar was a mark of the tragic night he told me about in private. Now, it had become a part of his costume, displayed for all to see.

"Behold the feral beast!" the games master shouted.

The gladiators set her down again. Then all three of them ran off the arena as more trap doors opened and more props rose to the surface.

Piles of rocks, tall trees, and sharp cliffs appeared from under the arena, quickly making the space look like a wild mountainside. There was even a real waterfall of "glacial water" that Salas supposedly drank.

From around the arena, cages clanked open, releasing brown mountain bears and white snow lions. They prowled the arena, sniffing the ground and climbing the trees.

Gripping the bars of his cage, Salas tossed his head back and roared. His deep voice needed no amplifier. It rolled out into the audience, met with their delighted shouts and applause.

Worry pulsed inside me. Was it all an act? Or did the games master do something to Salas? How did she turn the gentle, caring man I'd gotten to know into the wild beast I could hardly recognize now? Or was that wild, unhinged part in him all along? Had he just never let me see it before?

The bars of his roofless cage slid down into the floor, leaving him exposed to the predators prowling in the arena. Men, dressed like hunters, appeared from the fringes of the arena. They held weapons and carried nets and metal traps, closing in on the area where the cage used to stand.

Salas dropped into a crouch, carefully scanning his surroundings.

I gripped my armrests so tightly, my fingers cramped.

"He looks old for a new gladiator," Prince Leafar suddenly remarked.

"It may be the beard and all that rugged look they're going for that ages him," Mother replied casually. "The games master loves the details. Look at that gnarly scar they painted on him. Though you're right, he must be well past his teens to amass all that bulk."

I forced the air in and out of my lungs in even, measured breaths. Yes, Salas was well past his teens. His age was not a disguise or a part of his costume. His scar was also real.

How did he feel about being dressed like that and put on display? A man who'd been hiding from attention for years was suddenly thrust into the spotlight in front of thousands. And he had no one to blame for that change in his life but me.

Salas snarled and ran in a crouch toward the closest pile of rocks.

Two hunters leaped at him from behind the cliff. Spreading the net between them, they tossed it over Salas and trapped him.

He roared and clawed at the net, but its ropes held, digging into the bearskin on his shoulders. The hunters pulled on the ends, wrapping him tighter into the trap.

The crowd booed and cheered at once, either delighted for the hunters or disappointed by how easily they had trapped "the beast."

With a gargantuan effort, Salas rose to his feet. The muscles in his neck and arms bulged. Gripping the net, he spun around. The net twirled, knocking the hunters off their feet. They wouldn't let go of the net, however. As Salas turned faster and faster, the hunters spun around, holding on to the net and screaming for their lives.

The audience burst with laughter, thrilled by the spectacle. The hunters finally let go of the net. Blown away by the force of Salas's spinning, they rolled along the ground, stopping only by the rocks and the shrubs.

Salas tossed the net aside, then grabbed a giant boulder. He raised it over his head, stomping toward the closest hunter.

I held my breath. Would he attack the man? Would he kill him? The boulder was big enough to crush a skull.

As he passed a rocky cliff, a snow-white lion leaped onto his shoulders from above. Salas dropped to the ground under the weight of the beast, the boulder rolling away from him.

Judging by the shock on the hunters' faces, I feared that the animal attack was unscripted. Worry speared through me. I glanced around the arena, searching for someone to help. But no help was coming to Salas from anywhere. The hunters climbed to their feet, but they wouldn't come any closer.

The lion tore at the bearskin cape, lumps of fur flying in every direction. Its massive paws dug for the flesh beneath.

"Where is the games master? Can anyone help?" I whispered, afraid to breathe and unable to tear my gaze away from the man and the lion.

Salas struggled to get up with the beast on his shoulders. He swung the bearskin cape off, tossing it aside. The lion rolled in the sand, trapping itself in the hide. Salas staggered behind the rocks where another predator lurked.

A giant mountain bear rose on its hind legs, sniffing the air. At the sight of Salas, it roared and lurched forward.

Salas sprang backwards to where the lion had freed itself from the hide. The bear dropped to all four and charged the man. In two long leaps, it caught up with Salas and landed on his chest, crushing the man under its massive bulk.

My heart leaped to my throat.

This was no longer a game.

"Stop this!" I yelled.

But my voice was lost as the crowd screamed and roared, going wild like beasts themselves.

The bear and the man rolled on the ground in a giant ball of fur and limbs. The hunters finally ran closer but could do nothing but watch. The bodies of the beast and the man had intertwined so tightly, it was hard to tell them apart.

A bright streak of blood painted the white sand of the arena, and my insides froze. All sounds suddenly seemed suspended in the air as my heart leaped high with terror.

Was Salas hurt?

I jumped to my feet.

"Your Highness?" Prince Leafar blinked at me from his chair before remembering the etiquette and getting up too.

Mother placed a soothing hand on my wrist. "Ari, darling, I'm sure the games master has it all under control."

Shaking with panic, I was ready to run down to the arena.

And do what?

Fight that bear off Salas?

The most incredible thing was that I would. I would fight the bear to save that man's life.

"The princess rarely comes to the games," Mother tried to explain to Prince Leafar my frazzled state. "She's unused to such a graphic display of brutality."

"Understandable," Prince Leafar replied uncertainly.

Salas slid to the back of the bear and circled the predator with his arms while pinning it down with his legs. His arm muscles bulged out. He growled, baring his teeth, his whole body shaking. The bear roared, but the sound trailed off to growl before dying out completely. The bear's body slackened. Salas dropped his arms away from the animal, then rolled aside and heavily climbed to his feet.

Alive!

He was alive.

Air rushed out of me. My bones seemed to turn to mash with relief, sending me back into my chair.

With a triumphant roar, Salas raised his arms high, and the crowd went wild. They jumped off their seats, clapped their hands, and stomped their feet, cheering and yelling so loud no other sound could penetrate that noise.

Salas's left arm was painted red with blood. It dripped into the sand in thick steady drops, but no one seemed to notice it, not even Salas himself.

The bear's paws jerked as the arena helpers loaded the unconscious animal onto a wheelbarrow and rolled it away promptly.

The courtiers in the rows below the royal platform clapped

excitedly. Gem lowered her head toward another woman. Both nodded and gestured at Salas.

I knew the court ladies usually went to the gladiators' quarters after the games. Gem still refused to talk to me outside of the requirements of her job, but I could send someone to enquire about the health of the new gladiator. No one would question my concern after I'd witnessed him getting hurt. But it wouldn't be enough. I had to see him.

As the crowd finally calmed a little, the games continued. Only I barely watched any of it, waiting for it to be over.

When the show finally ended, and it was our turn to leave, I approached Gem on my way out.

"I'm coming with you," I said to her quietly but firmly, not leaving her a single chance to protest. "I'll wait in your carriage."

Seven

ARI

The gate in the high fence surrounding the grounds of the gladiators' quarters wasn't guarded from the outside, but it was closed and locked from the inside. The gladiators weren't slaves and could come and go as they pleased. But the games master strived to keep their training routine a secret from the public.

A servant opened the gate for us as Gem and I exited the carriage.

"The boys are receiving the ladies inside tonight," he said. "It looks like it may be raining soon."

He led us to the building that surrounded the courtyard from three sides with the main entrance in the middle. From the spacious front hall, tall double doors opened into a wide room with a vaulted ceiling.

Many gladiators and several court ladies already gathered here. Some filled their plates with food from the round tables on the left. Others sat around the game tables that were covered with green and had cards or game pieces laid out. Some of the men and women had already broken into pairs and occupied the cushy chairs and couches arranged around the large fireplace in the middle.

Four servants carried trays with finger food, offering it to the ladies. Two more servants weaved between the guests, refilling their wine glasses.

The games master rushed to us.

"Princess Aniri! Lady Chamberlain! It's an honor to see you at our small soiree." She gave me a deep bow. "It's such a rare treat to welcome you into our humble quarters, Your Highness."

"It's a pleasure to be here," I replied mechanically, searching through the people in the room with my gaze.

Salas wasn't here. The tight string of worry inside me vibrated more urgently. I had to know how he was. I needed to see him.

Falo rose from one of the couches and sauntered to us. After a polite but brief greeting to me, he grinned at Gem.

"I've been waiting for you, Lady Chamberlain." He took her hand in both of his. "I have your favorite tea served already." He gestured at the low table set with tea by the couch.

"Aww, aren't you the sweetest?" she cooed, letting him whisk her over to the couch and leaving me with the games master.

"The show was great today," I said, clearing my throat.

The games master's smile grew wider.

"Thank you, Your Highness. We do our best every week. But today was special. The crowd simply went wild with delight. It's so rewarding when that happens."

I could no longer put off the one and only thing I'd come here for.

"Master, how are the gladiators doing after today's games?"

"Oh, everyone is fine," she assured me confidently. "My boys are highly trained. They're used to pulling off miracles in the arena and escaping the most dangerous situations unscathed."

The image of blood dripping down Salas's arm was too vivid in my mind to believe her reassurances.

I couldn't keep beating around the bush anymore and asked directly, "The new gladiator got hurt today. How is he?"

"You mean our wild Mountain Bear? Oh, it was just a scratch," she dismissed with a sly smile. "Nothing that small could bring that beast down. Trust me."

The only thing I'd trust right now would be seeing Salas alive and well.

"Why is he not here tonight, then?"

"Right." She twirled between her fingers the fringed end of the scarf tied around her head. "He's with our healing witch. We treat even minor injuries with the utmost care."

That felt reassuring. At least Salas was getting the care he needed.

"Did you plan for the bear to attack him today?" I asked. "Was it in the script?"

The games master huffed in offense.

"We don't have a script, Your Highness. Everything that happens in the arena is genuine and spontaneous." She winked at me. "That's how I always answer these kinds of questions. Why strip magic from the show that so many people enjoy?"

"All right, but that gladiator—"

She glanced behind me. "And there he is. The man of the hour!"

I spun around to find Salas standing in the doorway. He was still wearing his costume, only his helmet was gone, and instead of the bear hide, a hunter-green dressing robe was draped over his wide shoulders. His arms weren't in the robe's sleeves. A thick white bandage on his left arm peeked from under the jacquard fabric of the robe.

His eyes found mine.

And time froze.

Here, outside of the arena, he no longer appeared like a feral beast or a stranger. He looked like the Salas I knew. Directed at me, his brown eyes filled with the familiar warmth—the expression I'd grown to like so much. A gentle smile played on his lips, partially hidden in the deliberately disheveled beard.

Relief flooded me in a tingling wave. They hadn't changed him. He was still him.

But he was hurt. And all because of me. I'd forced this on him. Once again, I'd stuck my nose into his life uninvited.

The games master spoke, popping the hazy bubble I'd found myself trapped in with Salas. "Her Highness kindly expressed concern for your well-being, Raeb."

Raeb? He'd changed his name? It made sense. A gladiator was in the public eye far more often than a humble slave. A new name reduced the risk of someone from his past recognizing him.

"Her Highness is very kind." He bowed his head.

His deep, rich voice descended into my chest with resonance throughout my entire being.

With all eyes on us now, I did my best to school my expression into something expected from a princess when meeting a stranger. Because in the eyes of everyone here, other than Gem, Salas was a complete stranger to me.

"I trust you're feeling well?" My voice came out a little rough, despite my best efforts.

"Yes," he matched my politely detached tone. "Thank you, Your Highness."

"And the bear?"

"The bear?" His eyebrows rose in question.

"The bear is fine," the games master chimed in. She then lowered her voice, speaking in an exaggerated whisper while hiding her mouth from the rest of the room behind her hand. "But please, let's let the public believe that our Mountain Bear is capable of killing wild beasts with his bare hands. It adds thrill and enjoyment to people's experience. After all, they're paying the admission price, fully expecting to be deceived by the magic of the show."

I nodded. "I believe your Mountain Bear is capable of squeezing the life out of any wild beast if he wanted to."

"That he is." The games master slid an appreciative glance down her newest gladiator's powerful body. "He sure knows how to give bear hugs!" She laughed, slapping him on his healthy arm.

And now I was staring at his arms, too, remembering how good it felt to be inside his "bear hugs." A swell of warmth washed over me with the memories, heating my face with blush.

The games master tipped her chin at the bandage on Salas's arm. "The healing witch has sewn you back up, I see."

"Yes. She did a great job." He moved his left shoulder. "It almost feels fully healed already."

I doubted it felt "fully healed." No witch was that good. But the royal gladiators had access to the services of the most skilled healing professionals in the country. At least Salas was in good hands.

"Our witches are beyond comparison," the games master boasted. "Her Majesty, Queen Anna, even allows us the use of her personal healing witch whenever needed." She slid her arm under mine, gently but persistently leading me to the nearest couch. "It's so kind of you to show concern for one of my boys, Your Highness. I know you don't come here very often, and I highly appreciate your visit, but I assure you there is no need to worry. All my men and all our animals are absolutely fine."

I allowed her to sit me on the couch, the skin on my back prickling with the awareness of Salas's gaze on me.

The games master grabbed a glass of wine from the tray of a passing servant.

"Have a seat and enjoy the evening, Your Highness," she murmured.

It was hard not to admire this woman's dedication to the games. I believed she genuinely cared about her men, too, since they were what made the games possible in the first place. Salas was taken care of. He looked well and smiled. There was no reason for me to linger around any longer.

Yet there I was, sitting on the couch, sipping the expensive wine that was undoubtedly a gift from one of the lady patrons. The crown provided the gladiators with everything they needed.

But the court ladies supplied them with the luxury items beyond that, such as expensive cigars, fine wine, jewelry, and imported silks.

"May I suggest a handsome boy to keep you company, Your Highness?" the games master offered. "Sadly, our Mountain Bear is unavailable for another week. Rules are rules. But anyone else of my boys will be honored to spend the evening with you."

The sensation of Salas's gaze zapped through me like lightning. Sitting with my back to him, I couldn't see him, but I felt his presence with my skin. It was a special kind of torture to have him so close to me, yet being unable to say a single unguarded word to each other.

"Well, I..." I drained the rest of my wine in one not lady-like gulp, then set the glass down on the side table. I had to get out of here. I needed to leave. "Where is the ladies' room, please?"

If the games master hadn't thought of me as flaky and irrational after my last visit here that ended in a panicked escape, she surely did now. But I couldn't bring myself to care.

I had to get away from the man I shouldn't want. I felt him in every particle of the air I breathed. I tasted him in the wine I drank. I wanted him here on the couch with me, or better yet, back in my bed where I could be myself again.

Only with Salas I felt safe to be myself.

"I'll be right back," I promised, knowing damn well I would not keep this promise.

Once again, I was fleeing the gladiators' party, feeling weak and defeated, but I had to put an end to this insanity.

The games master got up with me. "Allow me to escort you, Your Highness."

I kept my head straight as she led me out of the room. From the corner of my eye, I glimpsed Salas conversing with Naeco, the games choreographer, and another gladiator. Absorbed in their conversation, he didn't appear to notice my leaving, which was for the best. I didn't think I could manage to say goodbye without making it obvious how hard parting from him always was for me.

With the games master escorting me, I had to at least pretend I needed to visit the bathroom before leaving the gladiators' quarters. I followed her down the main hallway to where it turned into the left wing. The bathroom was a spacious room decorated with flowery wallpaper, upholstered furniture in gilded frames, and a marble sink next to a long vanity with a large mirror.

"Let me know if you need anything at all." With these words, the games master departed, finally leaving me alone.

I turned on the polished brass faucet, took my glasses off, and splashed the cool water on my face.

He shouldn't have this effect on me. Not anymore. Not now. I had my future laid out for me, and Salas couldn't be a part of it. His life was safer without me too.

Except that everything inside me ached for him.

When coming to the gladiators' quarters, I just hoped to make sure he was okay. But seeing him this close again was like all those weeks without him hadn't happened. Like I had every right to touch him again. To kiss him. To be with him.

My face in the mirror looked flushed. My eyes glistened as if ready to cry. How could I go back to that room now? How could I face them? Or him? I couldn't even say goodbye.

I had to leave.

I'd arrange for generous gifts to be sent to the games master later, as an excuse for yet another lame escape.

I turned the faucet off, wiped my face and hands dry, put my glasses back on, and left the bathroom. As a civilized adult, I should at least let Gem know that I was leaving and taking her carriage, that I'd send it back for her later, but the sound of the door opening and closing came from the central wing, and I realized I wasn't ready to face anyone right now, not even a servant to send the message to Gem.

The world inside me felt like a ravaged land after a hurricane. I needed a moment to compose myself, at least enough for my hands to stop shaking and my heart to slow down a bit.

The left-wing hall ended with a large stained-glass window

with partially opened curtains and a window seat. I hurried to the window, climbed with my knees onto the seat, and pressed my feverish forehead to the cool glass, hiding in the shadows of the curtains.

Heavy droplets of rain hit the glass, then rolled down, leaving behind trails like streams of tears. I desperately searched for peace inside me, and couldn't find it.

Eight

SALAS

I'd taken my eyes off Ari for a mere second, just to reply to Regit's question about the healing witch who had treated me. But when I glanced again at the couch where she'd been sitting with the games master, Ari was no longer there.

I hadn't expected her to come here today. They said the princess had only come to the gladiators' quarters once, years ago, and she hadn't stayed for long.

The urge to believe she was here because of me was too strong to resist, but it was a dangerous path to take. Three high-born princes vied for Ari's attention. Soon enough, one of them would become her husband. The best I could do for my sanity was to stay away from the crown princess.

Yet I'd lasted only for a minute in the room without her. The pull to go after Ari was so strong, I feared it would wrench my heart out of my chest if I didn't follow.

As soon as Regit and Naeco got distracted by a new group of fine ladies arriving at the party, I headed for the door.

A servant passed by with four empty wine bottles on his tray.

"I'll take them out," I volunteered, grabbing the bottles off the tray and leaving the room before anyone could stop me.

The central hallway was deserted.

Did she leave already?

It'd be for the best for both of us if she did. But sadness gripped my heart so hard, I was ready to run all the way to the palace after her.

I walked along the corridor to the corner with the bathroom, then turned, unsure what to do next.

At the end of the east-wing hallway, I spotted a flash of her royal-blue dress between the burgundy drapes of the stained-glass window. The rain clouds darkened the afternoon from silver gray to charcoal. With the scone lights off, the hallway descended into a soft semi-darkness. I wouldn't have noticed Ari kneeling in the window seat had I not been looking for her.

Everything inside me reached out to her. My arms ached to hold her. Setting the empty bottles down by the wall, I walked toward her. But she wasn't mine to hold. The only right thing to do would be to turn around and leave.

Turned with her back to me, she stood on her knees on the window seat cushion, her forehead pressed to the glass. Dressed in a formal gown with a voluminous skirt and a high collar, the tall crown gracing her swept up hair, Ari looked every bit the princess. Only I'd long learned to look beyond wealth and status.

I saw her shoulders rising and falling with her rapid, shallow breathing. I noticed her hands splayed on the window. Her fingers shifted subtly on the glass, as if searching for purchase to anchor her while she was being swept into her sorrow.

I knew her well enough to see that she was hurting, and I couldn't stand watching her in pain, especially since I knew exactly how to comfort her.

I walked closer until there was almost no distance left between us, until I could smell her perfume and feel the warmth of her body. The unconquerable need to touch her blinded all my senses, including common sense. I splayed a hand on the side of her waist.

"Ari..." Her name left my lips like a sigh of longing.

Sparks of thrill rushed up my arm from the place where my hand lay on her body. I might've given Ari her first time, but she had given me so many firsts too.

Before her, women had been my work, my torment, or my survival. None of them had ever been the source of the elation I felt with her. She made my heart soar.

She could pull away, tell me off, or even slap me. With our arrangement now complete, I lost every right to touch her. But with a shuddering breath, she leaned into my chest, and I let go of common sense completely. With both arms wrapped around her waist, I hugged her to me from behind.

She relaxed against me with a deep sigh of relief, as if she'd just been waiting for my hug to release her from whatever had been bothering her.

Leaning to her neck, I breathed her in, searching for the scent of her skin beneath her expensive perfume. She moaned softly, gripping my hands. It felt so right to hold her, as if she belonged right here, in my arms.

All thoughts deserted me as I let my feelings guide me. I kissed her skin, tasting it on my tongue, but the more she let me have of her, the more I needed.

Trailing my kisses along her shoulder, I tugged down the starched lace of her collar to free more of her skin for me to kiss. She tilted her head, granting me better access. It thrilled me how pliable she was in my hands, how her body seemed to melt into my touch. Blood rushed both to my head and my groin.

I yanked at the lacing on the back of her gown, loosening it in a desperate need to feel her body.

"Salas..." She turned around to face me, and my heart all but broke.

Unshed tears glistened in her hazel-green eyes.

I took her face between my hands. "Ari, sweetheart, what's wrong?"

"Are you happy here?" she asked, touching the gladiator's ring on my finger. "Did you ever want to be a gladiator?" She exhaled a bitter laugh. "I'm sorry. I know I should've asked this question much earlier."

I kept my hands on her. There wasn't a power in the world that would pry me away from her now. But I forced my mind to think about her question.

Happiness was a fairy tale, a myth that people chased just to have some purpose in life. But I didn't hate the arena. Most of my life, I'd seen hatred and scorn from people. Hearing cheers instead of taunts proved uplifting and invigorating, almost intoxicating at times.

"I'm glad to be here," I admitted.

"But, you got hurt..." With a shuddered breath, she touched my left arm just below the bandage. "I messed up. Again. I meddled in your life, and now—"

"Shh. Hush, Princess." I stroked her cheeks with my thumbs, stopping her self-loathing. "You simply gave me more options than I'd ever had before. Ultimately, the choice was mine."

Unlike with many others, with Ari, I always had a choice. She might've opened the door to the arena for me, but I'd entered through it on my own.

I smiled. "I always knew it was you, my true benefactor."

"And look where it got you." She shook her head, inconsolable. "Are you in pain? How bad is it?" She hovered her fingers over the bandage on my arm.

I shrugged. "It's just a scratch."

Three scratches, to be exact. The one in the middle was so deep, the bear's claw scraped against the bone in my arm. There was also another bandage on my back where the lion had clawed through the bearskin and tore my flesh. The third bandage covered my hip under the rugs of the loincloth that Naeco had put on me.

Of course, Ari didn't need to know about them all. The gladiators' healing witch proved to be a true master of her craft. The numbing potions and the healing ointments she'd used made the wounds feel like mere scratches now.

The concern on Ari's face didn't ease, however.

"I'll send my mother's witch to check on you," she promised. "You'll get the best care there is in Rorrim. And if anything is needed from overseas, I'll figure out a way to get it too." She drew in a heavy sigh, unshed tears glistening in her eyes, brighter than the diamonds around her neck. "This should not have happened. Did something go wrong with that bear? Please tell me this wasn't planned. You don't have to go through it again, do you?"

This was what proved the most irresistible about Ari—her compassion. She cared about me while I had long forgotten what it felt like to be cared about.

Turning down sex was easy. I'd gone for years without it, hardly missing it at all. The tenderness of an intimacy was harder to go without, but I'd managed that too. However, the feeling of worth that Ari woke in me was something I'd never experienced with any other woman before.

Ari saw a man in me before she saw a male. With her, I felt like not only my life, but everything else about me mattered. She cared about my health, about my well-being, about my happiness... She simply cared. And that was impossible to resist.

"I'm fine, sweetheart, I—" A warm glow in my chest grew, stopping my words.

She touched the side of my face, her fingers curling into my beard. Her eyes held mine, saying more than words ever could. She saw through to my very soul. She always saw me, all of me, from the first moment her gaze ever connected with mine.

I drew her to me, propping my knee on the window seat for balance. Her legs ended up on each side of my thigh. I slid my hands up her back. Her heart beat so hard, I felt it under my palm splayed on her back below her shoulder blade.

She ran her fingers along the leather belts across my chest, then buried her nose in my neck and inhaled deeply, hungry for my touch and my scent as much as I was for hers.

Princess Aniri might not be mine, but in some cruel twist of fate, our hearts beat in unison and our bodies belonged together. All her pieces fit perfectly with mine. We resonated like two fine-tuned strings struck in accord—a song with no words needed.

I didn't know who moved first, but our lips connected. It felt like coming home, even as I barely remembered what having a home felt like. I kissed her like a starving man. Because I had been starving for things that only she could make me feel.

Reaching inside her neckline, I cupped her breast. Her nipple pebbled under my fingers. I pinched it gently, eliciting a breathless moan from her lips. She pressed closer, trapping my thigh between her legs.

The need for her pulsed through my veins. Heat rushed me from head to toe. I hardly realized what I was doing, hiking her skirts up, hand over fist, in search of her hips. With a soft groan, she tore at the tangled strings of my loincloth, then gave up and lifted it instead. Her chilled fingers found my hard, aching cock, and I thrust into her hand with a groan.

It was like a dance that we'd learned to do so well together. When I pushed, she pulled. When I took, she gave. And when I gave, she took it all, then begged for more.

She helped me slide her silk undergarments down, then let me guide her left leg around my middle while leaving her other knee propped on the window seat.

"I need you, Salas. Goddess knows I do." She pressed herself to me.

It was a heady feeling to be needed this desperately.

I reached between us and slipped a finger inside her slick heat. She moaned, arching into my touch. She was ready for me, but I savored this moment, stoking her need. I stroked her slowly, massaging and stretching her from the inside. With my other hand, I gripped the back of her head as my mouth ravaged her in a frantic kiss.

When I couldn't stand our separation for another second, I finally brought my cock to her opening, and she moved forward as I thrust in. Warm pleasure coursed through me as our bodies connected. I could stay like this forever, devouring her with all my senses.

She wound her arms around my neck and buried her face in my shoulder, surrendering to me completely. For one precious moment, she was wholly mine. I held her body in my arms and her soul in my heart. I felt her with every part of my being.

I thrust harder, lost to the pleasure of owning her like this. I wanted her to feel it too. Gripping her hips, I angled them to deepen our connection. With tiny whimpers that I grew to adore, she rubbed against my ridge, chasing her pleasure.

Climax shuddered through her, and I let it go too. She clung to me, riding our joint orgasm together. With her forehead pressed to my chest, she gripped the belts on my shoulders so hard, like she would never let me go. And right then, I truly hoped she never would.

She inhaled deeply, pressing a kiss to my chest, then lifted her face to mine.

"Salas, I..."

The unfinished sentence levitated between us. I held my breath, hoping against all odds for it to bloom into something magical.

What was she about to say?

"I..." what?

"I missed you."

"I want to see you again."

"I need you in my life."

The sound of a door opening shattered the charged silence between us to pieces. And with it, my hope popped like a soap bubble.

"Ari?" Lady Gem called in a subdued voice.

Her footfalls moved closer, and Ari jerked away from me.

"I'm sorry," she finished her sentence in the most heart-breaking way.

As she hurriedly straightened her clothes, reality rushed in, and it was cold and brutal.

She wasn't mine.

"Princess." I reached for her as if grasping for the remnants of a disappearing dream.

She caught my hand before it touched her face and kissed my palm gently.

"I have to go," she whispered. "Please, please stay safe."

Then she was gone.

Nine

ARI

I yanked the curtains closed behind me, hiding Salas from view. Gem turned around the corner, searching for me. Her probing eyes found me in the dim light of the hallway.

"I needed a minute away from the noise," I explained, briskly walking toward her.

But the lady chamberlain wasn't so easily fooled. It took her less than a second to assess the disheveled state of my hair and the loose fit of my bodice. Next, her gaze flicked to the empty wine bottles standing by the wall.

"Is that so?" she asked flatly, her brow pinched in a frown. "Did you want a minute alone or a minute in the company of someone you know you shouldn't be with?"

If I felt guilty about what had just happened between Salas and me, it was not because of Gem. My relationship with my cousin had deteriorated. Part of me missed what we used to have, but another part of me always knew that the relationship between us was never balanced. It'd only worked because I'd allowed Gem's dominance, and it was destined to fail the moment I pushed back.

"I outgrew the need for a nanny long ago," I snapped, brushing past her.

She caught up with me by the front door. "Where are you going?"

"Back to the palace. I'm not returning to the party."

"Thank Goddess, you're not," she scoffed. "Not in that freshly fucked state."

My cheeks flared with blush. I brought a hand up to my hair, trying to smooth it down. Shame crept into my chest, settling in next to guilt. I hated it, hated to feel ashamed of Salas or of anything that we'd shared.

I shoved the front door open.

"I'll send the carriage back for you."

"No need." Gem followed me out into the courtyard. "I'm coming with you."

The worst of today's summer shower seemed to have passed, leaving behind the dark puddles on the ground. The air smelled like wet dirt now. The rain clouds had thinned but didn't disappear completely, saturating the courtyard with a fine mist of drizzle. I welcomed the tiny droplets on my flushed face. The gloomy day was turning into a calm, pleasant evening.

I wasn't looking forward to sharing the carriage ride with Gem on the way home. As short as the ride would be, her pursed mouth and determined stride didn't promise an amicable company.

"Wouldn't your golden-haired gladiator be upset if you left so early?" I asked, crossing the courtyard.

"He'll survive," she dismissed, gesturing to the servant by the gate to get our carriage. "And Falo isn't golden-haired, by the way. His actual hair is brown. The gold comes from the lemon-camomile brew the healing witch makes for him to wash his hair with."

I blinked at her, unsure about what to do with that piece of information. "I didn't know that."

"Few people do." She smirked, climbing into the carriage

when it had arrived. "Falo guards this secret rigorously. He only admitted it after I'd seen him with his pants off. Apparently, as wonderful as the witch's brew is for the hair on his head, he's afraid to use it around his cock." She laughed. "And so, his crotch remains very naturally dark."

I really didn't need to know any of that. But I supposed I should be grateful it was her gladiator we were talking about, not mine.

Mine.

I sighed at the tug of wistfulness from that word.

My irritation wasn't entirely Gem's fault. I came to the gladiators' quarters to check on Salas, to make sure he was okay after the animal attack in the arena. But it proved not enough. Seeing him wasn't enough. Even him making love to me was not enough. The crumbs of time I got to spend with him were wonderful but wouldn't satisfy me. I simply couldn't get enough of that man.

I hated to leave. I felt jealous of every person in that room because, unlike me, they were free to stay in the same place where he was. I envied the witch who treated his injuries because I wished to be the one to take care of him. I wanted to change his bandages, to feed him dinner, and to kiss him goodnight when he went to sleep. I wanted it all.

My loss of control around Salas and the overwhelming need for him to be a part of my life scared me, and I had no idea how to deal with it.

"You fucked him," Gem stated from her seat across from me in the carriage.

It wasn't a question. She didn't wait for a confirmation but for an apology.

I met her eyes but said nothing.

"You promised, Ari." The bitterness in her voice sent another spasm of guilt through my chest. "You gave me your word that you would never see that man again. That was the deal, wasn't it? That was the condition of my helping him. And you broke your promise."

She was right.

Gods, she was so right.

But the taste of Salas's kisses lingered on my lips. The sensation of him moving inside me was still too fresh and too wonderful for me to regret any of it.

"You have your gladiator, why can't I have mine?" I challenged.

She scoffed. "You know why, Ari. But if you forgot, I'll gladly refresh your memory." She leaned forward, whisper-screaming at me, "Because he's a whore and a criminal. According to the laws of our country—the country that you will rule one day by the law of the Crown of Rorrim that will grace your head—he should've been long executed. Every breath that man has taken for the past seven years has been a crime."

I raised a hand between us, like a shield against her words.

"I'm not having this argument with you again."

"You don't have to." She huffed in frustration. "Because nothing has changed since the last time we've had it."

Her eyes shone with energy. Her cheeks flushed. Gem obviously felt strongly on the subject, and it wasn't just the fear of losing her standing in the royal court that made her feel this way. She truly believed in the laws she worked to uphold. As a crown princess, I should believe in upholding them too.

I turned to the window, watching the tiny drops of moisture from the recent rain gather on the glass outside to trickle down in thin rivulets.

Blowing out a breath, Gem slumped back in her seat.

"Ari, this is just an infatuation, believe me. He was your first. Some women hold a special feeling for their first one. But that's all there is. There will be more men in your life. You can have any other gladiator. Fuck, have them all after your marriage is done and settled. You wouldn't be the first or the last queen to have lovers."

In my mind, I agreed with Gem on one thing—I shouldn't want Salas. I should finally propose marriage to my future husband and make the official announcement about our engagement. The whole of Rorrim and the entire world beyond had been waiting for me to do that. It was my duty. I owed it to the queendom that had become my home.

"It won't happen again," I promised flatly.

But could I stand behind my word? Or would it be another promise I had no power to keep?

I didn't come to the gladiators' quarters to do what I did. Sex had been the last thing on my mind when I rushed from the arena to see Salas. Yet when I saw him, when I felt his touch, when I held him close, it proved impossible to resist. It all spiraled out of control quickly.

Salas had become both my torment and my salvation. And I had to have him, healing and hurting at once.

Gem shifted forward and placed a hand on my knee soothingly.

"He's so fucking lucky where he's right now," she said. "He has a safe place to live and great food to eat. He's taken care of in every way. But that all can change quickly." I glanced at her in alarm as she continued, "He needs to stay out of public attention, Ari. With the new stage name and with the costume that conceals his face, he can hide among the gladiators indefinitely. There are forty-nine of them now. Only those who stand out become famous." She lifted a finger for emphasis. "Now think about how much more attention would he get if he were to become the favorite of the crown princess? How much scrutiny would the royal court and the city people subject the gladiator who captured the attention of the future queen? How deep would they dig into his past, trying to find out who he is and where he came from?"

The answer was—all the way. The courtiers were relentless in their gossip. A love affair of the crown princess would be too juicy a morsel not to squeeze every drop of drama out of it. The potential for a scandal was especially high since I was about to get married. The newest gladiator had an unknown past. It'd give a great motivation to many determined people to dig for more, possibly to the very bottom of it.

Aware of the effect her words had on me, Gem squeezed my knee. "Everything I have done for him would be for nothing. If you don't care about me or your own promises, Ari, at least think about him. If you keep him in the spotlight of your attention, he'll be the one you'll hurt the most."

BECAUSE OF THE lingering mist in the air after the earlier shower, the dinner at the palace was served indoors that night. All glass patio doors of the formal dining room were closed, and the air inside quickly turned hot and sticky.

I'd long learned not to display my feelings in public. I ate my food, smiled, talked to people whom I had little in common with on topics I didn't care about. However, the turmoil inside me proved especially hard to contain today.

After Salas had barged back into my life—or more accurately, after I had barged into the gladiators' quarters, tormented by worries and longing for him—he was all I could think about.

I had no doubt he held some feelings for me too. I had little experience with men, but I knew enough to realize that an indifferent man wouldn't look at a woman the way Salas looked at me. He wouldn't kiss me or hold me the way Salas did, if he didn't feel at least a fraction of the affection I held for him.

A part of me wished to daydream about all the "what ifs."

What if we could give these budding feelings a chance somehow?

What if I could whisk him away to my summer house in the countryside? Or to Father's hunting lodge that he never visited? Or to Mother's lake house that she used as a retreat from the city once every few years?

What if we could run away for good, leaving everything behind—his past and my responsibilities?

The direction that my thoughts had taken proved I must be losing my mind, and with it, any control of the situation. Spontaneity often bordered irresponsibility. I couldn't afford that kind of behavior. Actions of the crown princess had far-reaching consequences with the potential to affect millions of people, not just Salas and me.

Gem was right, too. I was putting his life in danger by clinging on to him. The only sane thing was to let go. No matter how much it hurt.

As the dinner ended and everyone moved into the ballroom, I spotted Prince Leafar in the crowd. He was wearing a powder blue evening suit with his golden curls reaching the high embroidered collar.

Despite Prince Leafar's grand claims and pledges of devotion, I knew the prince didn't love me. He likely wouldn't fall in love with me for a long time still, if ever. But if I were to marry him, he had every right to my respect.

I wasn't born as the crown princess, but I had accepted that role with the best intentions to make the queen and the queendom proud of me and my choices. As such, I had to behave accordingly.

As the music played and the first couples entered onto the dance floor. I crossed the room toward Prince Leafar.

A hushed silence fell over the ballroom as I approached. The prince's cheeks flushed violently as all attention turned to us. His handlers—the high-standing ladies of his court and his gentlemen-in-waiting—stepped back, like a tide receding.

"May I have a minute of your time, my prince?" I extended a hand to him.

"Of course, Your Highness," he replied, somewhat breathlessly.

As soon as people realized this wasn't an invitation to dance, they inched closer, eager to find out the reason for me singling the prince out. I couldn't completely escape their attention, of course, but I could at least get us a few moments of relative privacy.

"Would you care to join me for a walk in the gardens?" I asked Prince Leafar.

"A walk?" He blinked, then glanced over his shoulder at his entourage for guidance.

My request clearly didn't fit into the script he'd been fed, and now he was confused about how to proceed.

"Right there." I gestured at the stone patio behind the doors that led into the palace gardens. "I promise we'll stay in the plain sight of everyone in this room. There is no need to bring a chaperone."

"Of course." He nodded politely, tossing a furtive glance at the grand duchess, his aunt, who stood just a half-step back to our right.

The grand duchess inclined her head in approval, and the prince finally took my hand.

I led him to the closest set of ornate crystal doors. Not waiting for the servants to get to us, I flicked the heavy bronze locks myself, then pushed the two doors wide open.

A warm, humid air rushed in from the outside, banishing the heavy fumes of wine and sweets served inside and the musky cocktail of the gentlemen's cologne.

"The rain has long gone," I said, stepping out onto the patio. "I thought you might enjoy getting some fresh air with me."

"Every minute spent with Your Highness is an honor and a pleasure." Leafar gallantly offered me his arm.

Resting my hand in the crook of his elbow, I led him off the patio.

The sun had set already, but strings of golden lights illuminated the paths between the flowerbeds.

I turned east at first. But as the heels of my dance shoes clicked against the bricks, I remembered that the path in this part of the gardens was damaged last winter. It'd been repaired that spring. The summer rains might've washed Salas's blood off the bricks by now. But I couldn't bring myself to have this conversation with Leafar while walking on the bricks that Salas had carried on his back.

"This way, please." I turned west instead.

The prince followed me without questions.

All the patio doors to the ballroom opened at once. As servants secured them in the open position, the courtiers spilled out from the crowded room. No one dared follow us into the gardens, but they didn't hide their curiosity, openly watching us from the patio.

I didn't mind the attention. Prince Leafar's reputation was safer this way. No one could accuse me of taking advantage of him or compromising his virtue when hundreds of witnesses were watching our every step.

"Do you miss home, my prince?" I asked him.

"As my homeland, Olakrez Queendom will always hold a special place in my heart, no matter where life may take me. But I grew up knowing I will have to leave it for good one day."

It was a good answer, but judging by how smoothly it left the prince's lips, he must've practiced answering this question.

"Do you not have something you'll miss when you leave? Special places? Friends? Pets, maybe?"

His brow furrowed for a second, but his voice came out just as evenly as before.

"Pets can possibly be brought along. New friends can be made. And special places can live forever in one's memories."

Another smooth, practiced answer. The conversation with him was easy. Easy and useless. We could spend an eternity tossing back and forth the canned questions and answers from our expansive collections of small talk tools and learn nothing about each other.

As we passed by a bush of fragrant jasmine, the prince tore a small bunch of partially opened ivory-white flowers.

"Do you like jasmine, Your Highness?" he asked.

"I do. I enjoy the smell."

He offered the flowers to me, and I accepted.

"Tell me about your childhood." I twirled the branch with the flowers in my free hand.

"There is not much to tell," he replied modestly. "But if Your Highness has questions, I'll do my best to answer them all."

What would drive him out of this polished shell that had been manufactured for him by his handlers? I knew what I had to do tonight, but I wished to get at least an idea of what kind of person Prince Leafar really was. It saddened me to think that there might be nothing real left behind his perfect behavior and well-rehearsed answers.

"What was it like to grow up as the youngest in your family?" I asked, not giving up. "Were you picked on by your sister? Did your parents spoil you?"

His facial features shifted again, but only for a fraction of a second. His eyebrows twitched, but he replied smoothly, just like before.

"My older sister is the Crown Princess of Olakrez. However, our Mother, the queen, has always treated us equally."

"I doubt that," I said, maybe a little more snappy than I should have. "Royal children are never treated the same. You didn't have the same opportunities as your sister. From the day you were born, your future was to leave your country, whereas hers was to lead it. Everything in your upbringing must've reflected that."

"Well, I..." He blinked, biting his lip. For once, the prince couldn't find any words in his pre-approved collection of answers.

A part of me felt sorry for him, but I had finally spotted a crack in his veneer and had to pry it open wider.

"I know what it's like to have a queen for a mother," I said. "She's never just your parent. The country often needs her more than her children do. But I was sixteen when my mother adopted me. I was old enough for her to teach and mentor me for my future role as her successor. We spent a lot of time together and grew close. Who was there for you when you were a child?"

"Um…" He twisted a silver button on his suit coat. "I have a stepfather. He is a strong, handsome man."

It was a well-known fact that Prince Leafar's biological father was executed for treason when the prince was only seven, but I didn't want to probe him about the tragedy. I hoped to open his heart with my questions, not to re-open any of his old wounds.

"I'm glad you're close with your stepfather."

"I didn't say we were close." The muscles in his jaw moved before he schooled his expression back into a polite semi-smile. "Though, the king consort certainly is a man worth the admiration of many."

"Many? But not yours?"

"Mine too, of course," he said quickly.

The prince lied. I could swear on everything I owned that Prince Leafar didn't have a great relationship with his stepfather, despite pretending otherwise, probably for as long as he knew him.

I slowed my steps, then stopped completely, because he seemed to be barely dragging his feet along as our conversation progressed.

"What is waiting for you back in Olakrez if you return?" I asked.

He ran his free hand up the front buttons of his suit coat, then tugged at its stiff collar.

"Disappointment, Your Highness," he blew out the words with a quick breath. "The queen's disappointment is the only thing that awaits me if I fail to secure your favor."

"It wouldn't be fair on her part. There are currently three candidates for my hand. No matter what, two will have to return to their homeland unwed."

"Her Majesty made it very clear, however, that I couldn't be one of the two returning. She made plans and put hopes in me, and she hates changing her plans or having her hopes crushed."

"But what are *your* hopes and plans? What future do *you* wish for yourself?"

"Me?" He looked at me as if I asked him if he could breathe fire. "A prince's duty is to serve the crown. That is the only fate I have."

I could argue with that. I could tell him he was a person before being a prince. A person should have feelings and aspirations of his own. But his words resonated with me in the way I didn't expect.

I too had a duty to my country. I'd been searching for something in common with Leafar when it was right there in front of me all along. The thing that could bind us was solid and real—our duty.

The prince stared at the path in front of him. His long pale fingers fidgeted with the same jacket button that he hadn't torn off yet only by a miracle.

"I was seven when my father was executed," he said in a hollow voice. "I saw his severed head roll down the scaffold. Mother made me watch so I would remember what fate awaited a traitor. She said I could never forget it, and I didn't."

Compassion squeezed my chest. All of us seemed to wear some kind of mask. Leafar hid behind the mask of a golden prince, the youngest, cherished son of a powerful queen. He wore it well. But I was grateful to him for letting me peek behind it.

"I'm so sorry, Leafar."

He spun to face me. I dropped my hand from the bent of his arm, but he caught it and squeezed my fingers in his.

"I would make the most loyal husband that Your Highness could ever have. I would follow the path of marriage dutifully because I know the price of a misstep."

"Fear is not a good reason to get married, my prince."

"But what reason could be better?" He shook his head. "Fear is one of the strongest emotions and one of the best motivations to do the right thing."

"To do right by whom?"

"By your spouse, your country, and the crown. For those born into royalty, the right thing to do is our duty." He squeezed my fingers lightly, emphasizing each word.

These might be the words taught to him since the day he was born, but the conviction behind them was his own. The prince genuinely seemed to believe in what he was saying. His eyes shone with passion, and his voice rang strong.

"Duty," I echoed.

Duty was the sort of prison with no honorable way of leaving it, no matter how much time had been served.

Well, I finally had to do my duty as well.

"Prince Leafar," I looked up, finding his eyes. "I will announce my choice at the ball tonight. But I wish to ask you in private first. Will you do me the honor to be my husband?"

He swayed with a soft gasp, making me fear he might pass out. But he was of royal blood, after all. He was taught to ignore his feelings in favor of acting in the way expected from him. And right now, he was expected to accept my proposal in the most dignified way, no matter how thrilled or relieved he might feel.

"It will be the highest honor to become your husband and your future king consort, Your Highness." He sank to one knee, holding my hands in his. "I'll strive to be the best spouse a queen can have. From now and always."

Cheers and clapping soared from the patio into the gardens. The court guests couldn't hear our conversation, but they obviously had been watching us closely and didn't miss the prince going down on one knee in acceptance of my proposal.

The two of us stood on the path between the flower beds of fragrant rose bushes framed by jasmine flowers. The strings of golden lights illuminated us.

The scene must look beautiful, only the hollow emptiness inside me felt ugly.

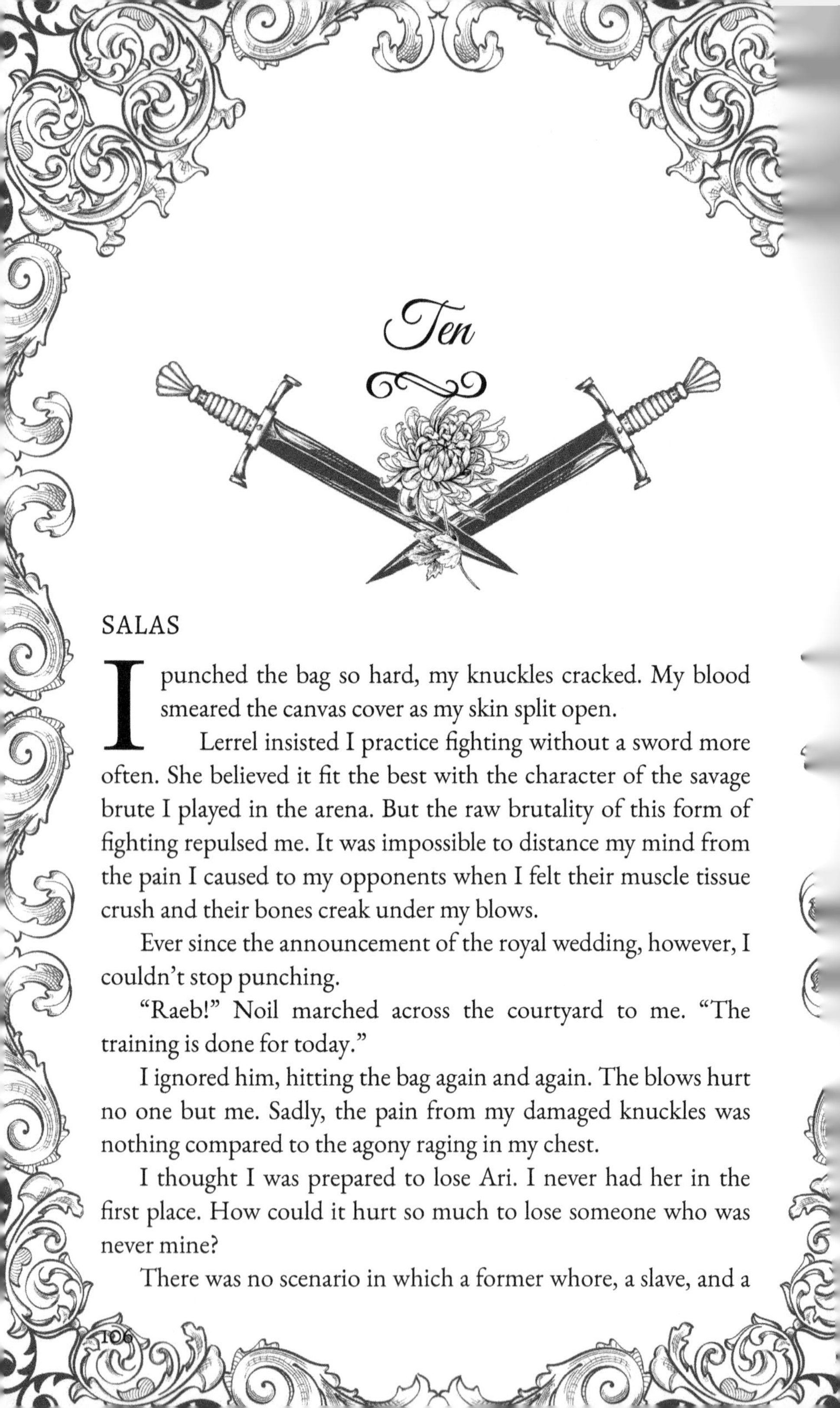

Ten

SALAS

I punched the bag so hard, my knuckles cracked. My blood smeared the canvas cover as my skin split open.

Lerrel insisted I practice fighting without a sword more often. She believed it fit the best with the character of the savage brute I played in the arena. But the raw brutality of this form of fighting repulsed me. It was impossible to distance my mind from the pain I caused to my opponents when I felt their muscle tissue crush and their bones creak under my blows.

Ever since the announcement of the royal wedding, however, I couldn't stop punching.

"Raeb!" Noil marched across the courtyard to me. "The training is done for today."

I ignored him, hitting the bag again and again. The blows hurt no one but me. Sadly, the pain from my damaged knuckles was nothing compared to the agony raging in my chest.

I thought I was prepared to lose Ari. I never had her in the first place. How could it hurt so much to lose someone who was never mine?

There was no scenario in which a former whore, a slave, and a criminal could publicly claim a crown princess as his own. I knew it all along. But it all felt exceptionally final now. Not only she wasn't mine, but she officially belonged with someone else.

Of course, I knew my only option was to accept it.

But acceptance proved hard to find.

"Raeb!" Noil shoved a hand in my ribs to get my attention.

I snarled, twisting toward him with my fist raised.

"What the fuck?" He caught my wrist, stopping the blow that would've smashed his face in. "I said it's done!" he yelled.

Lerrel appeared at his side, dressed in a pretty, white dress with bright red flowers. Noil had his best silk shirt on, too, his tawny hair and mustache trimmed and smoothed down in style. The palace invited all royal gladiators to attend the marriage ceremony of Princess Aniri and her chosen groom, Prince Leafar. Everyone was dressed and ready to go. Everyone except me.

The games master propped her hands on her hips, pinning me with her glare.

"Do we have a problem here?"

"Do we?" I jerked my arm out of Noil's grip.

"You've been doing this for almost two weeks now, Raeb," she stated. "So far, you've broken three training dummies and are about to decimate your fourth punching bag. More importantly..." she grabbed my hand, turning my bloodied knuckles to light, "you're damaging one of my most valuable assets—yourself."

"You're done here, boy." Noil unhooked the prolapsed, blood-smeared bag from the frame in the rink.

"Go back to your room," Lerrel ordered. "Clean the wounds. Get the healing witch to look at them when we all come back from the ceremony."

"And ask the witch for some mushroom powder to calm the fuck down," Noil muttered under his breath, taking the bag away.

"You're not coming with us," Lerrel said to me. "Not in this state."

"I wasn't going to, anyway," I snapped back at her. "I'm staying here."

She poked a finger into my sweaty chest.

"Whatever is eating at you, deal with it. Or I'll deal with it for you when I come back." She pointed at my hands. "Save this shit for the arena. Audience loves you. Don't fuck it up."

My room quickly proved too small to hide from my thoughts. I felt restless, unable to sit still or to focus on anything long enough before the images of Ari with her highborn groom assaulted me. He was everything I wasn't, which meant he was perfect, and she deserved the best. But that didn't make me feel any better.

Long before the lunch hour, I left the room with no clear destination in mind. I didn't feel thirsty, but maybe I should find a bottle of wine and drown the pain that burned through my insides like poison.

A moan sounded from behind the door of another gladiator. The sound wouldn't be unusual on a night after the games when the court ladies visited. But it wasn't even noon yet. Everybody had left the gladiators' quarters for the day. I thought I was the only one left.

I stepped back, staring at the door. This was Regit's room, the quick and always cheerful gladiator from the Tresed Queendom, who dressed as an elf in the arena. He had quite a few powerful women as his benefactors, but I didn't think any of them would be visiting him at this hour, especially on the day of the royal wedding.

Another moan came from behind the door. It didn't seem to be a moan of pleasure, I realized, as the sound descended into a sorrowful groan of pain.

"Regit? Are you alright?" I knocked on the door.

"Raeb?" His reply came in a subdued voice.

"Yes, it's me. Can I come in?"

"Sure." There was a note of resignation in his answer.

I pushed the door open.

Regit lay in his bed with the velvet curtains pulled back and tied around the carved mahogany bedposts. The thick embroidered drapes on the window of his spacious room remained closed. It looked like he hadn't been up yet. In the dim light of the glowing incense lamp on his night table, his eyes appeared sunken into their sockets. His normally warm-brown skin had turned ashen, with perspiration beading on his forehead.

"What happened, Regit?" I crossed the room toward him. "You look like shit."

"Thanks," he deadpanned. "You're not the most gorgeous man out there, either."

"I know." I shrugged. "Falo holds that title."

"Right. That handsome son of a—" Shifting under the quilted covers, he groaned again and winced in pain. "Fuck…"

"What's going on?" I touched his hand. It was feverishly hot. "Did you catch a trembling fever or something? It's common this time of year."

Regit's high cheekbones darkened with a subtle glow of blush. "No. Not a trembling fever. But it does feel hot and gives me shakes…" He peered at me intently, as if gauging how much he could divulge.

I didn't push him either way. We all had our secrets to keep. But if Regit felt I should know his, I was there for him.

After a moment of hesitation, he shoved away his silk cover.

"Does it look bad?"

"Fuck," I exhaled, staring at his bruised and swollen crotch.

Ink-black blotches covered his lower stomach and upper thighs. His cock bloated to several times of a normal size, its surface uneven and bumpy. His ball sack had completely disappeared behind his enormous cock. A black pearl of liquid beaded in the opening of his crown like a drop of seed. By the glossy silver sheen to it, I recognized the liquid onyx.

Now I knew exactly what Regit was going through. His pain resonated with a phantom ache through my own pelvis area.

I lowered myself into the chair by his bed.

"Why did you do it?"

"You know what it is?" he asked, arching an eyebrow.

I nodded. "I've seen it before."

I've lived through it too.

I didn't say that part out loud, afraid of questions I didn't want to answer.

"Where did you get it done?" I asked. "Where is the warlock who did the surgery? Did he give you anything to take after?"

I was certain the surgery had been performed by a warlock. Few witches had the skill to do this, intentionally so. The healing witches viewed operating on male "private parts" as something below their status.

"He gave me some powder for the pain." Regit reached for a silver tin on the side table. "But I've almost used it all."

Just a thin layer of pink powder covered the bottom of the tin. Even if the tin was full, however, a simple pain medication wasn't enough. Regis needed a healing ointment for the stitches and a special tea with a spell of magic to help his body absorb the liquid onyx.

The warlock who did this to Regit must be a hack, like so many of them were. The surgery was complex and required skills that warlocks often lacked.

Witches enjoyed the advantage of a far more thorough education, the apprenticeships with the best healers of the country, and the support of many affluent benefactors.

Warlocks studied the healing arts on their own. They often practiced in secret out of fear of being arrested and prosecuted for criminal ignorance in the profession they weren't allowed to study for in the first place.

"Why did you let a warlock touch you?" I scolded. "Why did you need to have it done? You're a gladiator, not a whore from a fun house."

Regit exhaled a humorless laugh through a grimace of pain.

"Do you think only whores earn their living with their cocks?"

"You're a gladiator, Regit. You earn your living in the arena.

Your occupation is far more honorable than that of a whore." I knew that for a fact because I'd done both.

"Honorable, all right," Regit scoffed. "For as long as I can leap like an elf to the delight of the audience, I'm fine. But what about when I can't do that anymore?" He peered at me. "How old do you think I am, Raeb?"

Regit was tall but lean and agile. His body was wired with ropy muscles. In the arena, he wore a pair of iridescent wings and was so light on his feet when leaping over the obstacles, it often looked like he indeed was flying over them.

"Umm, you're twenty-three? Twenty-four maybe?" I ventured a guess, scratching my beard.

He relaxed in the pillows with a sigh.

"Good. That's what you say when anyone asks. Deal?" He waited for my nod before continuing. "But I'm actually turning thirty this year. Thirty," he moaned as if that number hurt him even more than the pain from the surgery. "I found a gray hair last week. Already. Can you believe it?" He touched his hair that was neatly woven into the slim, long cords that reached his waist.

"I'm thirty-two," I admitted, trying to console him.

"And you look it. No offense."

"None taken." I shrugged.

Regit shook his head with a somber expression. "Your ragged charm and recent success may carry you through for a while. But at our age, we can't count on being a gladiator that much longer. The crowd feeds on our youth. The arena swallows us young, devours our health, and spits us out old and injured within just a few years. If you don't die, you'll get out of here with enough aches and pains to last for the rest of your life, however long or short that may be. And then what?"

"The crown pays a pension to the retired gladiators."

"That it does. But the money is only enough to rent a room in the city or a small house in the country." Distaste etched on his handsome face. "I'm not a country boy. I need the excitement of the city, Raeb. But I don't want just a plain boring room in a boarding house somewhere. Look at all I have now." He gestured at the lavish furnishings of his bedroom—the silk sheets on his enormous poster bed, the priceless rug on the floor, and the glistening pile of jewelry on a silver tray on his night table. "How can you give it all up after getting a taste? I want to keep sleeping in silk and eating the best food out there. I want to have servants to look after me when I'm old. I'll need more than the crown will pay, and more comes from women. I need benefactors to sponsor the lifestyle I'm accustomed to. But rich women prefer young boys with wrinkle-free skin and energy in spades. To stay in their favor when I'm past my prime, I must offer them something they'll be willing to keep paying me for."

I squinted, making a guess. "Your cock?"

He nodded.

"A better cock than most have. The best that money can buy."

"So, you let a hack warlock cut you up, stuff you with fish bladders, and pump you with liquid onyx, all for women's pleasure?"

"Exactly."

I didn't judge. I'd done the same years ago. My reason for that had been even simpler than Regit's. I didn't care for silk sheets or jewels, I'd just tried not to go hungry and hopefully save a coin or two for a rainy day. Men with those bodily modifications tended to earn more in the fun house. It seemed to apply to the gladiators too.

Regit put the covers back over his mangled member and growled, throwing his arm over his eyes.

"I'll need more of that pink shit," he squeezed through his clenched teeth.

"You'll need more than the pain powder if you want to recover fast enough to even walk before the next games. Without the proper aftercare, I'm afraid all the magic of the queendom won't make you well enough to do your usual act anytime soon."

"The games master will kill me," Regit moaned.

"The black puss building up in your cock will kill you before she does if we don't do something about it." I got up to my feet. "Tell me where to find the warlock who did this to you."

Regit peeked at me from under his arm. "What are you going to do?"

"I'll go to the city, find the bastard, and get from him what he should've brought to you already."

"I'm not sure he'd appreciate your visit. He doesn't want the public to know he offers this kind of service."

"I'm sure he doesn't, but I don't care how he feels about it. If he doesn't want any follow-up visits to his place, he should've done his job and come here himself."

"What if he refuses to give you anything?"

"Then, I'll make him. Don't let my sweet appearance fool you." I smirked, making him smile, too, despite his pain. "I don't like hurting people, but I can be very persuasive if I have to."

"Well…" he sighed. "It's not like I can ask the healing witch for help here."

"No witch will get involved in this now," I agreed. "The warlock started it, he needs to do it right."

Going to the gladiators' healing witch would get Regit in trouble. As much as the court ladies might end up enjoying the "improvements" to Regit's cock, surgeries like that weren't approved by the crown.

"When was the last time you took the powder?" I asked.

"Just now."

"Don't take more, then. Too much of this stuff can be bad for you. Take the rest with dinner, and I'll bring you more to take for the night."

"Raeb," Regit stopped me as I placed a hand on the door handle. "Take a horse from the stables. It's allowed. And… Thank you. A lot."

I nodded before leaving his bedroom.

After grabbing a cloak from my room, I left the building, but I didn't go to the stables. The less I saw of a riding crop, the better off I was. Ever since leaving Lady Lana's manor, I couldn't bring myself to hit another living being with a crop, be it myself or an animal.

Instead, I walked past the tall red barn where the games master supposedly held a three-winged dragon from the faraway Ekans Isles, then circled the wide dome of the underground terrarium with the fire-breathing mud worms, and made a brief stop at the animal enclosures.

The bear I'd nearly choked to death while fighting for my life in the arena had recovered by now. The lazy bum was napping on a flat rock over the pond in his special enclosure. A black-and-white beetle buzzed over the bear's ear before landing on his nose. The bear swatted at it with his paw and rolled over on his other side without even opening his eyes.

The games master strictly forbade the gladiators from approaching the animals. We weren't to form any kind of relationship with them for two reasons.

One, it wouldn't work for the show if the predators recognized us in the arena and acted friendly while being presented to the public as wild.

And two, if we had to kill one in the arena, it was easier to do so when the animal wasn't raised as a pet.

Watching the bear relax in the sun, I found it hard to believe that this was the same beast who'd nearly tore my arm off less than two weeks ago. The games master mentioned the attack wasn't the bear's normal behavior. She hadn't allowed for the bear or the lion that had mauled me to return to the arena since, worried that they had become unpredictable, unmanageable, and therefore too dangerous.

"Bye, buddy," I said quietly enough for the bear not to hear me.

Before leaving the grounds, I pulled the hood of my light linen cloak lower over my face. The chances of someone from my distant past recognizing me had been going down, the more time had separated me from those years and the more occupations I'd changed since, but it didn't hurt to be careful.

I hitched a ride with the family of a teacher who was returning to Egami after visiting relatives in the country. Her wagon moved slowly toward the city center, as the road was already congested with both carriages and pedestrians.

"We should've left earlier," the teacher lamented. "I knew the royal wedding ceremony was today, but I hoped we'd make it home before the crowds gathered."

The ceremony wasn't until the afternoon, with the special reception beforehand for the invited guests. It'd be followed by a celebratory dinner and a ball later tonight. But the crowds were already flowing toward the palace.

Their excitement was palpable. This wedding was a joyous occasion that the entire country had been waiting and praying for.

The city had been decorated with colorful banners and ribbons. Posters with the portrait of the couple hung in almost every window. It was hard to avoid looking at them, no matter how hard I tried not to look.

There hadn't been time to paint a proper official portrait of the bride and groom. Instead, the artist appeared to have joined the two existing individual pictures simply by linking their hands.

Dressed in her formal attire, the princess wore the same dignified expression she had in all her official portraits. The prince was staring straight ahead, with his arm bent and his bride's hand resting on it.

I tried to steer my feelings away from the matter. There was nothing I could do and nothing I could change. I just wished I could feel nothing too.

On the outer edge of the city center, I paid for the ride and said goodbye to the teacher and her family, then found the address that Regit had given me.

The door to the warlock's place was at the end of a deep stairwell of an old decrepit building that housed a storage facility for broken carriages and horse tack. It felt like I was descending into the depths of the afterlife when climbing down the narrow, crumbling stairs.

No answer came when I knocked. I slammed my fist into the door harder, refusing to leave without the tea and ointment that Regit needed.

"What do you want?" finally came in a rasping voice from behind the door.

"I heard you perform certain body modification surgeries," I said carefully.

Warlocks might not be well skilled in magic, but their ignorance often made them even more dangerous, like a child with a sword they didn't know how to use. It didn't hurt to be polite, at least until I had a good reason not to be.

The small window in the door opened, and a wrinkly face appeared in the rusty frame.

"Maybe I do," the old man said, squinting at me.

"I came from a client of yours. You haven't finished your job."

A quick wave of reflection momentarily obscured his features. He attempted to close the window, but I shoved my hand against the shutter.

"All I want is for you to honor the agreement you made with my friend."

He darted a frightened glance at my hand, pausing it on my ring. "You're from the arena."

"Yes. You operated on a gladiator—"

He brought a finger to his lips, cutting me off. After peeking over my shoulder at the staircase behind me, he stepped back from the window. Next, I heard the lock on the door clink open. It took several more clicks and clanks, as there must have been several locks and chains, before the door finally opened.

A stale, musty smell drifted from the dark space inside.

"Come in," the warlock ushered me through the door, then promptly closed it behind me. "No need to chat about my business out loud, where everyone can hear," he muttered grumpily.

"I wouldn't be here at all if you conducted your business properly," I said, taking a look around the dwelling.

Despite the warm summer day, it was cold inside with a hint

of moldy moisture in the air, but the metal stove in the only room remained unlit. The tiny, cramped place with a packed dirt floor and low ceiling was illuminated by a single candle on a rickety table next to an open book and a collection of glass vials.

The old man drew a tattered blanket tighter around his hunched shoulders. "I do my work well. The surgery was a success. Your friend will please all his women once he heals."

"How can you be so sure about his healing when you abandoned him with no means to manage the pain or to bring down the swelling after your spells?"

He shuffled over to a chipped wooden cabinet and opened one of its many drawers.

"I didn't abandon him. I made it all the way to the gladiators' quarters last night. They never let me in and refused to pass to my patient the ointments I brought for him." He took out a paper wrapped bundle from the drawer and glared at me from under his bushy gray eyebrows. "But you don't believe me, do you? Of course, what would a handsome gladiator like you know about the way warlocks are treated?"

I'd only had to deal with one other warlock before, and that was a quick and painful encounter I didn't care to remember. But I was no stranger to being treated like dirt.

"I know more than you think." I stretched my hand out for the parcel he was holding. With my other hand, I reached into the leather purse on my belt. Another significant difference between a slave and a gladiator was that I got paid regularly now. "Here." I offered a coin to the warlock. "For your trouble."

He shoved the parcel into my hand but shook his head, refusing the coin.

"It all has already been paid for. I just couldn't deliver it."

"It's not a payment, then." I placed the coin on the table, next to his short candle. "Get yourself some wood for that stove and a few more candles."

"I don't need charity. I have a practice." He hiked up his chin with pride.

"It's not a charity. Let's make it a compensation for the poor treatment you endured at the gladiators' quarters."

He chuckled. "If I were compensated for every ill treatment I've endured, I'd be living in the palace by now."

I knew for a fact there were no warlocks in the royal palace, and it wasn't the matter of riches or skills.

"Good day." Leaving the coin on the table, I hurried back into the fresh, warm air outside.

Eleven

SALAS

The streets, meanwhile, had gotten even more crowded. So many people moved on foot that wagons appeared to be frozen in place, with no room for the horses to stir in any direction. There was no point in looking for a ride in a wagon. I might as well walk.

As I made my way through the crowd, trying to ignore the pictures of the royal couple holding hands on the banners and the paper flyers everywhere, I found myself being carried off route by the stream of people. Instead of turning left and heading along the city wall to the gladiators' quarters, I ended up being shoved right, toward the open gates of the royal palace.

Apparently, I hadn't made enough effort to combat the crowd and now ended up in the place I had no intention of coming to today. The only sane, reasonable thing to do now would be to turn around and proceed on my way against the constant stream of people. But when it came to Ari, both sanity and reason deserted me long ago. The closer I got to the place where she was, the stronger the pull grew. I didn't fight the crowd, going with its flow instead.

The guards stopped me at the gate.

"Are you invited?"

"Yes." I presented them with my ring. "I'm with the gladiators."

"Gladiators?" The guard leader pivoted in my direction from the door to the gatehouse. "Really?" She squinted at me, then moved her gaze up and down from my head to my feet.

The shadows from my hood obscured my face, but my figure betrayed me.

"You're the Mountain Bear, aren't you?" She waved at the guards to let me through and for me to come closer. "By Goddess, you're even bigger up close."

The comments about my size were nothing new, and there wasn't much to say in reply.

"Yes, madam. I come from a family of tall people."

"Tall and massive." She nodded with delight, then grabbed a piece of paper and an ink pad from the gatehouse. "This is for my son. Could you please?" She thrust the paper to me.

Realizing what she wanted me to do. I dipped my ring in the ink then pressed it to the paper, leaving an imprint of the gladiators' crest—the Rorrim's crown inside the oval of the arena.

The woman cooed excitedly, smiling at the piece of paper as if it was a real treasure.

The public admiration still felt new and a little overwhelming. People who didn't know me as a person, who'd never met me outside of the arena, appreciated me and didn't hesitate to express their admiration whenever they got a chance to speak to me.

It was addictive. Every time I stood in the arena after yet another successful performance, showered with cheers and applause, I soaked up the public love, even as I knew the same people would rather see me decapitated if my past ever came to light.

I took the quill the guard leader handed to me and wrote my arena name under the gladiators' crest.

"Mountain Bear," she read with a bright smile. "Oh, this will make my little boy so happy. You're his favorite gladiator. He's been dragging me to the games every week since they trapped you." She gave me a once-over. "You're not really as wild as they claim, are you? Or have they tamed you?"

"Somewhat." I grinned. "Enough to let me go out in public unsupervised."

She laughed, matching my tone. "So, it's safe to allow you onto the palace grounds then?"

Except that getting onto the grounds wasn't easy. More guards gathered around me, along with the people from the crowd. After borrowing the ink pad from the guard leader, they asked me to stamp their royal wedding invitations, the flyers with the portrait of the couple, and everything else that would hold ink.

"Press it right here, handsome." A woman yanked down her dress, offering me her bare shoulder for the stamp. "I'll never wash it off." She winked.

Another woman pulled on my arm, bringing my ear to her mouth.

"You don't have to risk your life in the arena if you let a woman take care of you," she whispered while stuffing a piece of paper under my belt. "My name and address are here, sweetie. Drop by for a visit."

Only when the music blasted from the turrets of the palace, announcing the beginning of the ceremony, did the swell of attention on me ebbed. When everyone turned around toward the balcony over the main entrance to the palace, I used the moment to sneak out of the crowd and made my way to one of the pillars with lanterns that surrounded the front plaza.

The glass doors of the balcony opened. The Head Priestess of Great Goddess Nus stepped out, followed by a priestess of Rethaf, the God of Matrimony.

The priestess of Rethaf opened a scroll and read an excerpt from the scripture about the sanctity of marriage. A third priestess joined them. This one was wearing the white robes of Yarnus, the God of Purity.

Nus, Rethaf, and Yarnus. Power, Matrimony, and Purity. All were asked to shower their blessings on the royal couple.

As the priestesses stepped aside, Princess Aniri exited onto the balcony, and the ache in my chest leaped to new heights.

In the formal gown of red-and-gold brocade, with the heavy golden crown set over her swept up hair, Princess Aniri presented the image of royal power and grace.

People clapped, shouted greetings, and tossed flowers and colorful ribbons into the air.

"May the Goddess bless you!" the crowd cheered.

"May you give us an heiress soon!"

From the moment Ari first arrived in this world, the entire queendom rested its hopes on her shoulders. It was a heavy load to bear, but she carried it with dignity and quiet determination.

I knew she cared about me. We had an undeniable connection. She had shown her affection for me on more than one occasion. And I believed I could make that affection bloom into something far stronger if I had a chance.

If only...

A stab of regret hurt too much to continue that thought.

Shrinking into the shadows from the pillar, I searched her face for any clues about her true feelings.

It was her wedding day. Was she happy? Apprehensive? In love with her groom?

Love was hard to hide, they said. But Ari did a damn good job when hiding her emotions. Her face revealed nothing. Her expression was the same as in that picture on all the banners and flyers—dignified and neutral. A smile appeared briefly as she waved at the crowd. The smile blinked to life once more when her groom joined her on the balcony.

Prince Leafar wore a white suit, as was customary for men when getting married. Princess Aniri took his hands in hers, and the Priestess of the Great Goddess started the ceremony.

I wasn't supposed to be here. In fact, I'd made a considerable effort to stay away from the palace today.

Why did my feet carry me here anyway? For the dubious pleasure of catching a glimpse of Ari again?

I hadn't seen her for almost two weeks now. She hadn't been to the gladiators' quarters since the time we made love in the window seat. She hadn't even come to the arena for the games. And, well... I missed her.

It was a foolish, self-destructive feeling, but just for a moment, I allowed my imagination to take flight.

I imagined it was my hands she was holding, that she wasn't wearing a crown and the fancy gown with the train that draped from the balcony like a royal banner, billowing in the wind, but that she was just a girl I met in a city market or at a country fair.

I saw us facing each other, with bright genuine smiles on our faces. My fingers intertwined with hers as the priestess tied our hands with the ceremonial sash.

It'd be a far more modest ring in Ari's hands, but she'd be placing it on my finger. And I allowed myself to believe she'd be happier if she gave it to me instead of the prince.

After our ceremony, we'd come back to our true home, just the two of us. I'd make her the best meat pies in the world, and she'd cook potatoes for me in every way she knew how. We'd go on dates, swim under the stars, and make love whenever we wished, and no one could stop us. Because I'd be hers, fully and completely. And she would be mine.

I let the memory of her body held in my arms run through my veins once more. I held to the fantasy for one bright, sparkling moment longer. Then I let it fly away and disappear like the dream that it was.

The princess said her vows to her noble groom, "You'll have my trust and protection."

"I vow to cherish and obey you for as long as we shall live," the prince promised in return.

Nothing was said about love. But these vows weren't meant to be romantic. It was a political deal made between two queendoms.

As the priestess announced the royal couple as a wife and husband to the cheering crowd, I turned away and made my way back to the gate. I left before the bride kissed the groom because the only kisses I wished to remember were those she'd given to me.

Drawing the hood lower over my face, I made my way across the crowded road outside of the palace, then turned to go back to the gladiators' quarters.

I walked as fast as the crowd allowed. Even a good distance away from the palace, the roads remained packed. With no chance to glimpse the royal couple or even the palace gates, people still came out. The mood was cheerful. Clapping or shouting, and breaking into a song or even a dance, the city people celebrated along with the royals.

Tired of fighting to move against the stream, I left the road and headed closer to the city wall. Here, the crowd finally thinned. Keeping to the shadows from the wall, I made much better progress following the footpath here.

Eventually, the path turned completely deserted. The crowd remained closer to the palace, with not a soul in my way.

I took the hood off, letting the summer breeze cool my head. My chest remained heavy, with a gaping hole in my heart that I could only hope time would heal.

A strangled cry of terror came from a narrow street up ahead. It was cut off short, as if by a hand placed over the mouth or by a blade pierced through the heart. The voice was high, like that of a woman or a child, which made my hackles rise and my muscles tense instinctively. I had no weapons on me, but I rushed to the street ahead.

The high, windowless walls of the surrounding buildings came close to each other here, not allowing for sunlight to reach the ground. Groans and sounds of struggle from around the corner spurred me to run faster.

A woman lay on her back on the muddy cobblestones, her

clothes torn and smeared with dirt and blood. The man on top of her held a knife in his hand.

"Shut up, you monster," he gritted through his teeth.

He called *her* a monster? When *he* was the one acting like it?

Blood rushed to my head. Rage jolted me into action, numbing all other senses, including the sense of self-preservation.

"What the fuck are you doing?" I lunged at his back. "Get off her!"

I grabbed the wrist of his hand with the knife, stopping his next blow.

The woman's eyes met mine over the shoulder of her attacker. They were wide open and filled with horror as he clamped a hand over her mouth.

She was alive, thank Goddess, but terrified nearly to death. Blood smeared her blouse around her neck. Crimson droplets beaded from the scratch on her temple and cheekbone, glistening like rubies against her dark-brown skin.

The man growled like a feral beast when I wrestled his arm back, keeping the knife away from his victim. Letting go of her mouth, he swung a fist at me.

I grabbed his other wrist, blocking his blow. We both rolled off the poor woman. She sat up, gasping for air and pressing her torn clothing to her body.

"Run!" I shouted, needing her to be safe.

Thankfully, she didn't wait for me to repeat it. Scrambling to her feet, she ran as if demons were chasing her or a true monster was on her heels.

The man bucked under me, trying to throw me off him.

"Monsters..." he mumbled, saliva dripping from the corners of his mouth. "They're all vile. Kill them all before they kill you."

I shoved down on the hand with the knife. He unclamped his fingers, letting it fall onto the cobblestones. He kicked me, then twisted an arm out of my grip, and punched me in the ribs, knocking the air out of my lungs.

I bent over, gasping for breath.

He shoved me off and tried to gather his legs and feet under him, but I threw my bulk on top of him, pushing him back to the dirty cobblestones.

"Stay," I growled. "Stay and answer for what you've done."

I rolled him over to his back, seizing his both wrists and pinning his hips to the ground by straddling him. He snarled, trying to get away.

"What the fuck did you do to her?" I yelled, unable to comprehend this man and his actions. "How? Why?"

He eased his struggle, staring at me intently.

"Salas?"

The sound of my real name coming from the chapped lips of the stranger thundered through my mind.

"Do I know you?" I studied the scars on his face, searching for the features I might recognize. But his face was so disfigured, it looked like a grotesque, unfamiliar mask.

"You don't recognize me, do you?" He smirked. "Of course you don't. No one does anymore. It's me, Das. Remember? We both worked for Traeh, what feels like a lifetime ago."

"Das?"

I knew the name. It belonged to a dark-haired boy only a year older than me. He came to Traeh's establishment a month after me and stayed for less than a year. After several complaints from customers about him, Traeh asked him to leave. The women complained Das was too rough, even when they had paid him to be gentle.

"What happened to you?" I stared at the complex map of scars on his face.

The web of them covered his entire face and neck, descending into the neckline of his shirt too. Some were long and narrow, as if left by a blade. Others looked puckered and discolored, like burns. One scar slashed across his left eye. The eyelids healed in a way that kept that eye almost completely shut.

"Monsters, Salas," he croaked. "Monsters have been at it for as long as I remember."

"What monsters?"

"You call them women. I call them beasts. They love blood. Pay good money to see men writhe in pain. Even more money if they get to inflict it."

"Did they do this to you in a fun house?"

"A fun house?" He exhaled a coarse laugh. "They had fun, all right. But to someone like us, that's a place of horrors."

"Das, I'm sorry about what happened to you. But what you did—"

He jerked at the approaching sound of footfalls against the cobblestones. His one good eye opened wide. Horror replaced any sense of intelligence in his expression.

"Demons are here. Monsters are coming. They bring filth and darkness. Eternal night is near. Ghouls reign. Can't you see? They're too powerful. There is no salvation. No refuge from them. They... We need to fight them. You need to carve their hearts out... Slice their flesh..." His eyes bulged out, rotating wildly in their sockets. Saliva bubbled in the corners of his mouth. His voice descended into a barely comprehensible mumbling. "They thrive on pain. Give them pain. Until they are no more. That's the only way... The only way to save this world from evil."

The woman he'd attacked ran to us from around the corner, followed by the armed city guards.

"There he is!" She pointed an accusing finger at Das.

Her hands trembled as she clutched her ruined dress to her chest, but her eyes glared with determination and her voice was firm.

Das growled, then shrieked like a man possessed. With an unexpected burst of strength, he wrenched his arms from my grip, then punched me in the chest, knocking me off balance.

"Get him," the leader of the guards ordered.

"Monsters... monsters." Das fought his way from under me, chanting that one word under his breath.

Gripping my chest where the pain from his blow bloomed, I scrambled to my feet.

"Hold it!" A guard aimed her crossbow at me, drops of milky white sleep potion glistening on the end of the bolt.

"I mean no harm." I spread my arms in the gesture of surrender.

"This one helped me," the rescued woman said quickly.

The guard didn't shoot, but kept her crossbow trained on me.

"Perish, monstrous beasts!" Das took off in a mad dash.

Another guard released a bolt from her crossbow. It hit Das in the back, just above his right shoulder blade. He roared in pain.

The wound seemed to cost him whatever was left of his mind. He whipped around. His eyes bulged out of their sockets, foam dripping from his bared teeth.

"Evil!" he screamed. "All of you shall perish. Drown in your own blood!"

He lurched forward, clawing at the air, as if fighting something visible only to him.

A guard raised her crossbow, aiming it at his head this time.

"Don't." I grabbed her arm. "Please, he knows not what he's doing."

"Don't move!" The guard behind me shoved her crossbow in my back, the bolt's tip jabbing painfully against my spine. "Or I swear I'll shoot you."

Snarling and foaming at his mouth like a cornered rabid animal, Das made an unsteady step forward, then crashed to the ground face first. He rasped and hissed something incomprehensible, then stilled finally, succumbing to the effects of the sleeping potion. His eyes closed, and his mouth slacked.

The leader of the guards ordered one of her women, "Get two wagons, one for the lady and another one for the criminal." She then turned to me, sliding an assessing look down my body. "You'll have to come with us, too, boy. I'll need to ask you a few questions."

With the crossbow bolt still jammed between my shoulder blades, I slowly raised the hood over my head again.

"I have to get back to the gladiators' quarters before nightfall."

The fewer questions I answered, the better off I was. Also, Regit needed the pain powder and the magical tea before going to sleep. Otherwise, he'd get no rest.

She paused her gaze on the ring on my hand. "Are you a gladiator?"

"Yes, madam."

"You must be the Mountain Bear!" the guard behind me exclaimed, shifting her crossbow from my back to my arm in her excitement. "Sorry," she apologized as I winced. Then she put the crossbow away. "There is no one else quite this size."

I nodded, rubbing my arm.

"Well." The leader's voice softened considerably and her posture relaxed. She produced a pad of paper and a lead pencil from a satchel on her hip. "Let me just jolt down a few notes while the event is still fresh in your mind, sir. Then you can go. If I need anything else, I'll drop by the gladiators' quarters later."

The wagons arrived. The guards helped the woman into one of them, while several others loaded the unconscious Das into the second one.

"What is going to happen to him now?" I asked the leader.

"It's up to the judge to decide." She shrugged.

The guard, whom I'd stopped from shooting Das, shook her head.

"You should've just let me kill him," she said. "It would've been faster for him that way."

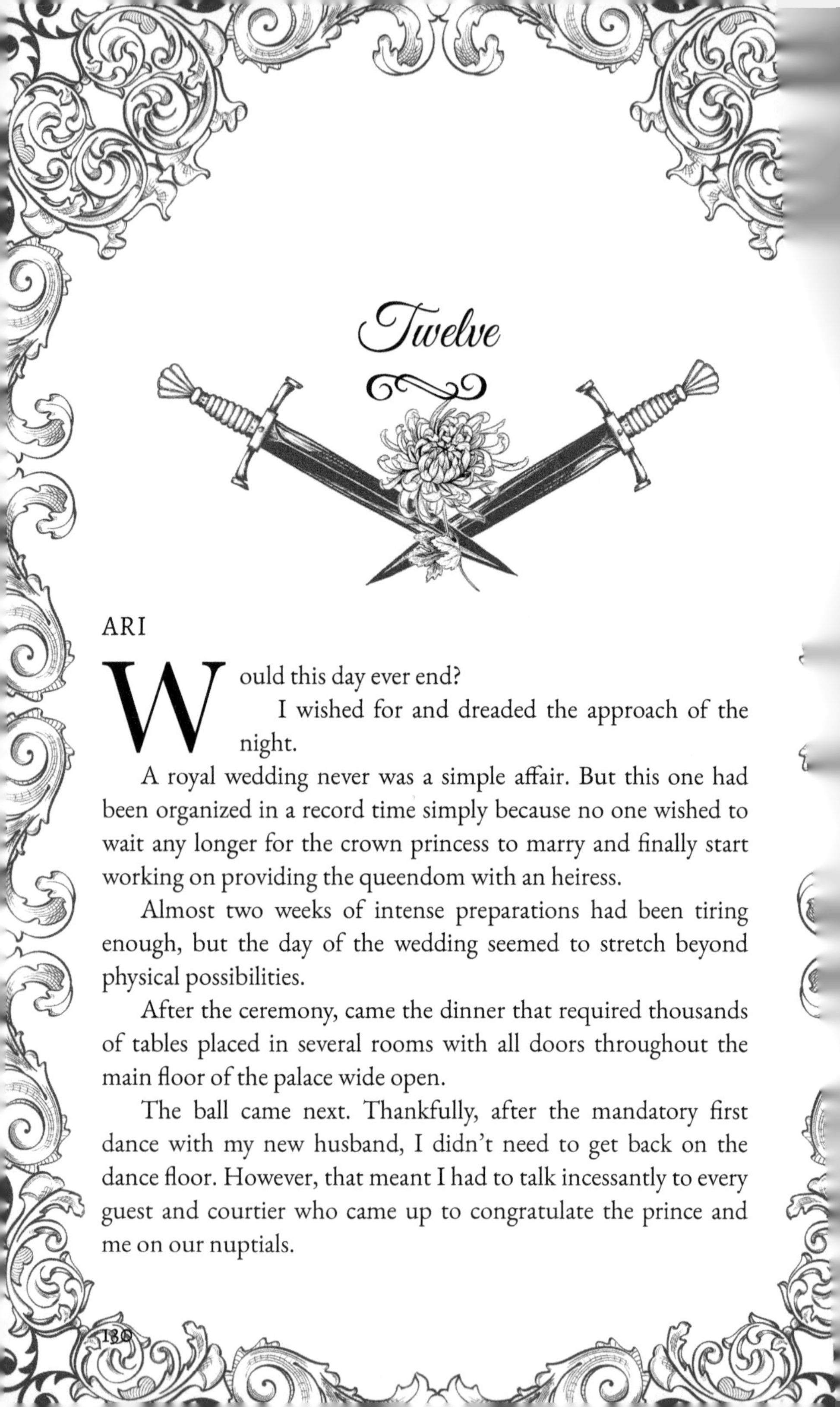

Twelve

ARI

Would this day ever end?

I wished for and dreaded the approach of the night.

A royal wedding never was a simple affair. But this one had been organized in a record time simply because no one wished to wait any longer for the crown princess to marry and finally start working on providing the queendom with an heiress.

Almost two weeks of intense preparations had been tiring enough, but the day of the wedding seemed to stretch beyond physical possibilities.

After the ceremony, came the dinner that required thousands of tables placed in several rooms with all doors throughout the main floor of the palace wide open.

The ball came next. Thankfully, after the mandatory first dance with my new husband, I didn't need to get back on the dance floor. However, that meant I had to talk incessantly to every guest and courtier who came up to congratulate the prince and me on our nuptials.

A couple of hours after midnight, I caught Leafar hiding a yawn behind his handkerchief.

"Tired?" I asked, feeling exhausted myself.

He gave me an apologetic smile. "I didn't sleep well last night."

I remembered what my father told me about the night before his marriage to Mother.

"Were you nervous?" I patted his hand sympathetically.

"Very," he admitted. "Still am."

I wished I could offer him some reassurance, but I had nothing reassuring to say. I was not looking forward to tonight, wishing I could just come back to my bedroom instead and try to fall asleep in hopes it'd work this time. A rest was way overdue for me. By now, I could barely think from exhaustion.

When it was finally acceptable for us to leave, I offered Leafar my hand. He gripped it with a long sigh escaping his lips.

The huge mirror stone glistened on his ring finger so brightly, I had to glance away. I'd put that ring on his finger that afternoon during our wedding ceremony. Leafar was now my lawfully wedded husband, and I had become his wife in the eyes of the gods and the law.

The notion still felt too foreign to settle in my mind with acceptance. I wished I'd asked Father or Mother how long it'd taken them to feel comfortable around each other. Because nothing about me leading Leafar down the corridor toward his bedroom under the scrutinizing stares of the wedding guests felt comfortable.

Reaching the doors to his suite, I wished him a good night, then pressed a peck on his cheek, as was required, and headed to my rooms.

I wished I could stay here, alone. But the delay was just to give the gentlemen-in-waiting enough time to get my virginal husband ready for our wedding night.

With the help of two maids, I had a bath, then put on a night-shirt and a dressing robe. While the maids dried and brushed my hair, I stared at the mirror reflection of the dark sky in the open patio doors behind me. My mind was blank, just the way I wanted it.

One of Leafar's gentlemen-in-waiting arrived a short while later to inform me that my husband was now ready to receive me.

A crowd gathered outside my door. The wedding guests formed a corridor along the hallways all the way from my rooms to Leafar's suite. Someone handed me a lantern decorated with flowers and golden ribbons. With the entire palace still wide awake, the role of the lantern was largely symbolic. It represented the means to light a wife's way to her husband.

Cheers, jokes, and encouragements accompanied me all the way to Leafar's rooms.

"May the loins of your husband be virile and fruitful, Princess Aniri."

"We're praying to the Goddess for a daughter for you, the heiress to the queendom."

"Make him moan, Your Highness!" someone shouted from down the corridor.

"We want to hear him scream all night!" another voice yelled, fueled by wine, no doubt.

"Make him scream your name."

"And 'Glory to Rorrim!'"

I smiled, waved in greeting, and even joked back once or twice, but released a breath of relief when I finally reached my destination.

As I raised a hand to knock on the door, Leafar's aunt appeared on my left.

"May the Goddess bless your coupling tonight, Your Highness." The grand duchess bowed her head, thrusting a white velvet cushion into my hands. A small golden key lay on the cushion.

"What is this?" I asked her.

"The key to your husband's virtue," she replied proudly. "We've preserved his purity for you."

By now, pretty much every person of the prince's escort had

praised his virtue to me. So, it wasn't too much of a stretch for me to accept the key as the symbol of his innocence.

"Well...thank you." I took the key from the cushion and shoved it in the pocket of my robe.

The door finally opened, and I hurried inside, glad to escape the crowd. But I got no reprieve in the prince's equally crowded bedroom. At least a dozen of his gentlemen-in-waiting were lounging about. The sound of their voices died out, cut off by my arriving into their midst.

Leafar's bedroom was round, with his bed placed opposite from the entrance. Glass doors on each side of the bed led out to balconies.

Several platters with tea, cheese, and sliced meat stood on the table and side stands in the sitting area to the right. Leafar sat in a high-backed armchair in front of a large mirror, surrounded by elegantly dressed gentlemen of all ages.

He jumped to his feet at the sight of me.

"Your Highness." He bowed his head.

His men got up too. They quickly gathered tea cups and plates from the furniture and put them on silver tea trays.

"Greetings, my prince." I gave him a nod, waiting for his men to leave the room.

They filed out through the door, taking the tea trays with them and bowing to me on their way out. When the door behind them closed, I leaned against it with a long breath out.

"What a day, right?" I said with a smile.

"It was quite intense," the prince agreed, not returning my smile.

His jaw tensed with a hard swallow. Lifting his hand, he started opening the small buttons in the front of his muslin night-shirt. He fumbled with a few, his trembling fingers disobeying him.

"Leafar, there is no need to hurry." I looked around the room, searching for the best place to set down my useless lantern. "In fact, I've been meaning to talk to you earlier, but it's been so fucking hard to find any privacy to have this conversation." He flinched at my cursing. "Sorry," I apologized mechanically. "What I mean is that we can wait, take our time to get to know each other." I walked to the side stand on my left and got rid of the lantern, then turned back to him. "Until we're ready—"

"I am ready." He opened his nightgown and shrugged it off his shoulders.

I blinked, met with the pale expanse of his smooth, completely hairless skin. Promptly diverting my gaze, I tried to look anywhere else but at him.

"Listen, um…"

"Is something wrong, Your Highness?" The worry in his voice brought my gaze back to him. He clenched his hands into fists at his sides, then splayed his fingers wide, looking more tense than ever.

I searched for something reassuring to say when a glimmer of metal in his pelvis area caught my eye.

"What is this?" I stared straight at it. It looked like an elaborate piece of jewelry obstructing his penis.

He glanced down at his body.

"A chastity cage," he explained proudly. "I've been saving myself for you."

"Oh, gods…" I pressed a hand to my chest, coming closer.

A set of golden rings enclosed his length. Thin chains connected the rings, making the contraption flexible for movement but preventing it from expanding in any direction. I imagined an erection would be impossible with this cage on. And that undoubtedly was its purpose.

Stunned, I ran a hand through my hair.

"It's quite literal then, isn't it? They actually caged you."

"You didn't know?" he asked, awkwardly shifting his weight from one foot to the other. "Is it not done to boys in Rorrim?"

"No. I don't think so…" I wavered in my answer, realizing I lacked the experience to speak for sure. "I've heard of those, but I thought they were the things of the distant past. I don't know of anyone still using them in Rorrim now, not as the means to force a boy's virginity, at least."

"All princes of Olakrez wear them," he said confidently. "Chastity cages are supposed to guard our thoughts onto a proper path. Prayers and magic spells further protect our bodies from the impure urges of temptation."

"Do they protect, really?" I asked sceptically. "Does it mean you've had no 'impure' thoughts whatsoever?"

He blinked rapidly before looking away. Deep blush colored his face. "I pray to Yarnus daily, and he answers my prayers by granting me peace...often."

My father came from Olakrez. I hated to think he'd been subjected to this treatment too. He never spoke about it to me, not even in that indirect way he employed when dealing with uncomfortable topics. Was he ashamed? Or did he simply take it for granted as something not worth mentioning?

"How long have you been wearing it?" I asked.

"For as long as I can remember. When I was little, I only had to wear it at night. Since I turned twelve, I haven't been allowed to take it off at all."

He must've expected me to be pleased. After all, he'd been put through it for my sake. All his life, he'd been told that abstinence in every form would make him the most valuable to his wife, the most desirable. But I simply couldn't muster any reaction other than horror, repulsion, and pity.

The key that his aunt had given to me turned out to be not merely symbolic. I yanked it out of my pocket.

"You can get rid of it now, please." I offered the key to him, but he wouldn't take it.

"I can't open it."

"I give you the permission to remove it," I insisted. "As your wife."

"No, I..." He ran a hand through his hair. "I can't even see the lock. It's designed so that I can't open it on my own."

"I see." I heaved a breath. "Well, where is the lock?"

"Under...um, underneath." He gestured stiffly.

"All right." I flipped the key in my fingers. "Would you mind lifting your... I mean *it* for me? Please."

Things that had been so easy to talk about with Salas proved impossible for me to even name in Leafar's presence.

We were married. The whole world expected us to be having sex right now. Yet even touching my husband felt wrong somehow. We've never gone past hand holding and an occasional peck on a cheek when necessary, and I didn't feel ready to move any further with him. At least not for the time being.

He lifted the cage with its contents up for me. Bending over, I looked under it and spotted the narrow lock fitted along the base ring of the cage just behind his ball sack. The lock was merely a slightly curved bar with a slim keyhole. It helped that the prince didn't have a single hair left in that area. Everything had been plucked, probably, for my viewing pleasure.

"It's so tiny." I pondered how to go about it. "Can you lie down, please? I'll bring the lantern over."

He did as I said, laying on his back on the bed, with his legs bent and his feet on the floor. I kneeled between his legs, bringing the lantern closer.

"Hold it up again, please," I instructed.

He lifted the cage for me. I slid the key into the lock and turned. It clicked open, making Leafar jerk.

"Did it hurt?"

"No," he replied quickly, biting his lip.

"I'm sorry if it did. I tried to be careful, but it's tricky..." I leaned back, letting go of the key. "Can you remove it yourself now?"

Rising on an outstretched arm, he slid the rings off with his other hand. Freed, his flaccid penis dropped on his thigh sideways.

"Here." I grabbed his shirt from the floor. "You can put this back on now. Unless you prefer to sleep naked?"

He gazed at me hesitantly.

"Shouldn't the clothes be off during the consummation?"

I sighed heavily, sitting down on the bed next to him.

"That's what I wanted to talk to you about. Can we wait with all this consummation thing for a little while?"

Worry crossed his handsome face. He pushed himself up, sitting next to me.

"Why? Do you not find me attractive? Am I not handsome enough?"

I waved a hand. "It's not about your looks or my attraction."

"I'll be a good father. If that's your concern," he added promptly.

"I'm sure you will be. One day. But... You see, I'd love for some emotional intimacy to form between us before we go ahead with the physical part. Does it make sense?"

I could tell by his expression that my request did not make much sense to him. A royal courtship and marriage customarily followed the same pre-established path. A wedding was always followed by the wedding night, which in turn was expected to result in a pregnancy and offspring. By asking him to deviate from that path with me, I confused him.

"It's not a rejection, Leafar," I tried to explain. "Please don't take it as such. We hardly know each other. Things have happened to us with little to no input on our part, and I'd like to change it as much as we can." I smiled, taking his nightshirt from his lap. "I'm looking forward to spending more time with you. But I also would like to give you some time to figure out what it is that *you* want. Not what your aunt, or your mother, or anyone else told you should want, but what it is that you desire for yourself." I held the shirt up for him. "Now, how do you prefer to sleep? Dressed or naked?"

He stared at the nightshirt, then moved his questioning gaze to me.

"How do you like me better?"

"No." I shook my head. "Make that decision on your own. Shirt on or off? What makes you feel more comfortable?"

He looked back at the nightshirt again, then nodded and

lifted his arms up for me to put it on him. I helped him to get it on, then got up from his bed.

"Well, since I'm expected to spend the night here, I shall stay. I'll take the couch."

His brows moved together, with a wrinkle of worry forming between them. His mouth flattened into a firm line of displeasure.

"You won't even share the bed with me?" he asked.

"Let us get to know each other a little better first, to get more comfortable with each other. Alright? It all just happened so quickly, don't you think?"

My hypocrisy didn't escape me. I'd shared my bed with Salas the very first night we got together. I'd known him then for a much shorter time than I'd spent with Leafar by now. But being with Salas always felt natural. My initial awkwardness around him was for different reasons because the physical attraction between us happened from almost the very first glance.

I missed that unconquerable pull toward a man, the need to have him as close as was humanly possible. With Salas, my chest seemed to burst open with emotions, with my heart ready to leap out into his hands.

Would that ever happen between Leafar and me? Was it just the matter of us spending enough time together? I feared it was not, but I'd made this step. Now there was nothing left to do but give my best effort to make this marriage work.

Still, I couldn't bring myself to climb into Leafar's pristine white bedding. At least not tonight.

"I'm a restless sleeper," I said. "I toss and turn a lot and wake up often. I'd keep you awake for no reason." He didn't look convinced, so I added, "I rest better when I sleep alone. We both need our rest after the long day we've had today."

With a sigh, he conceded, getting under the covers while I made myself comfortable on the couch with a pillow and a blanket.

Exhausted, I managed to fall asleep fairly quickly and woke up only at sunrise.

Leafar was still deep asleep, his covers tossed and tangled. I straightened them for him and covered him up. With his eyes closed, his mouth partially open, and his golden curls tussled, he looked even younger than his nineteen years. Whatever tender feelings I held for him at that point were those of an older sister, not a wife, and I feared that might never change.

Something clinked under my foot as I stepped away from his bed. The chastity cage lay discarded on the carpet. I picked it up, opened a balcony door, and tossed it out all the way into the gardens.

As part of my marriage vow, I'd promised the prince my protection, and that was a promise I fully intended to keep.

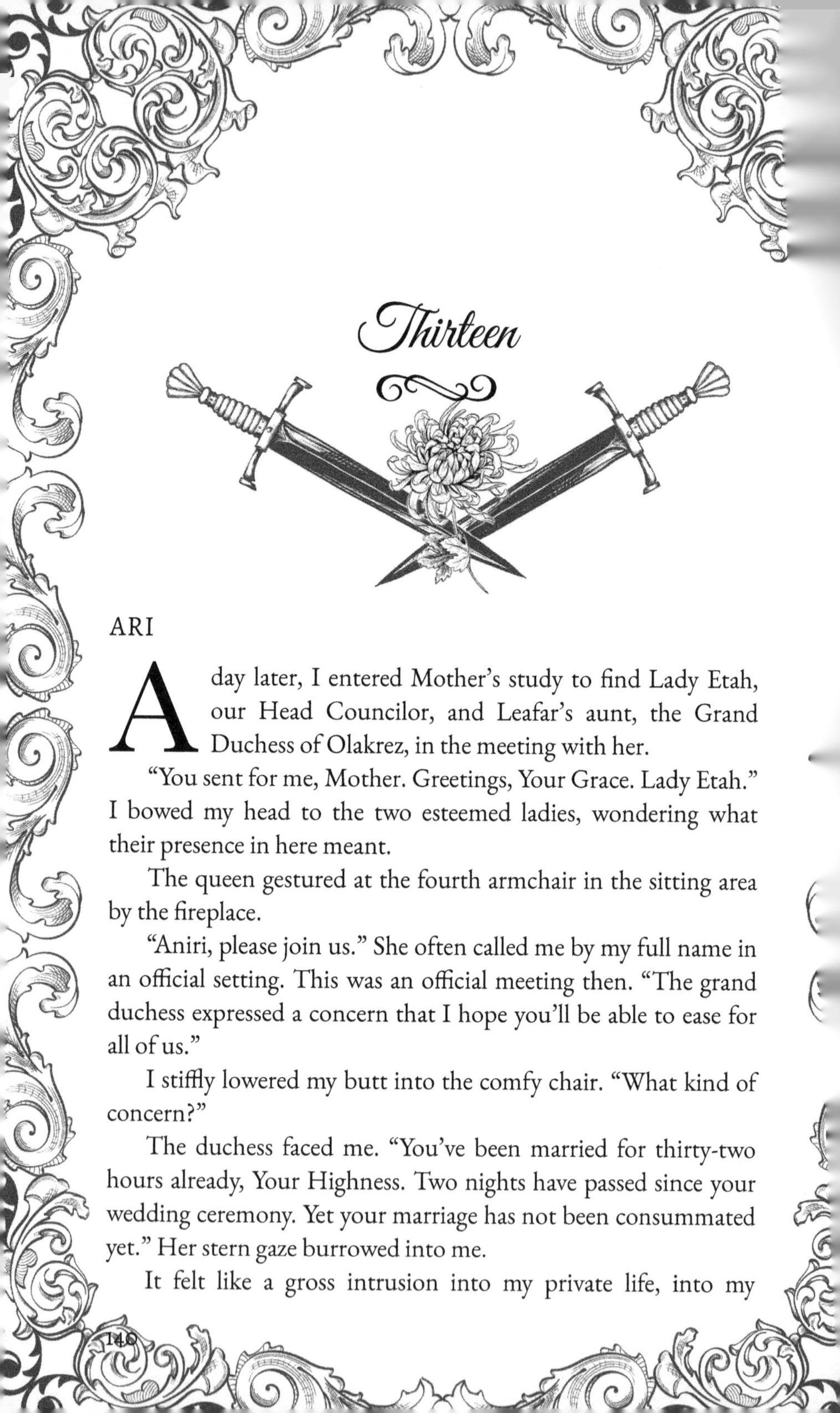

Thirteen

ARI

A day later, I entered Mother's study to find Lady Etah, our Head Councilor, and Leafar's aunt, the Grand Duchess of Olakrez, in the meeting with her.

"You sent for me, Mother. Greetings, Your Grace. Lady Etah." I bowed my head to the two esteemed ladies, wondering what their presence in here meant.

The queen gestured at the fourth armchair in the sitting area by the fireplace.

"Aniri, please join us." She often called me by my full name in an official setting. This was an official meeting then. "The grand duchess expressed a concern that I hope you'll be able to ease for all of us."

I stiffly lowered my butt into the comfy chair. "What kind of concern?"

The duchess faced me. "You've been married for thirty-two hours already, Your Highness. Two nights have passed since your wedding ceremony. Yet your marriage has not been consummated yet." Her stern gaze burrowed into me.

It felt like a gross intrusion into my private life, into my husband's privacy, and in the intimacy we were supposed to build with each other. But I could only afford a single breath to collect myself. Anything longer would've betrayed how much this conversation upset me, and I couldn't show the duchess such a weakness on my part.

I couldn't resist calling her out, however.

"How can you possibly know what happened between my husband and me behind the closed doors of his bedroom?"

If I expected her to be flustered or ashamed about her invasion in our privacy, I should not have held my breath. The duchess looked absolutely unaffected, clearly believing she had every right to know it all.

"It is my duty to be informed of the matter," she replied haughtily.

I should've known Leafar's entourage would question him about our first night together. Every part of his body belonged to his country, his every action did as well. He never had any privacy. All his life, his every move must've been watched and every step had to be accounted for. Of course, the Olakrez Court would want to know how his first night as a husband had played out.

I just wished he would've talked to me first. Together, we could've found a better way to deal with it.

"Is there a problem, Aniri?" Mother gazed at me with concern.

The duchess sighed heavily, steepling her fingers in front of her. "The prince is distraught that he might've disappointed Your Highness in some way."

Was that true? Was Leafar close with his aunt to confide in her about his true feelings? Did he not want to wait?

He seemed to have accepted my proposition for us to take time before having sex. But maybe I didn't give him enough choice on the matter? He didn't really argue with me about it, hardly objected at all, but he'd been taught not to speak in women's presence. He'd likely be reluctant to argue with me in earnest.

I should've taken more time to discuss this with him, but I was so deadly tired that night. I thought we'd reached an understanding. I believed he'd agreed.

"There is no disappointment on my part," I assured the duchess. "Prince Leafar is a delightful young man. For me, his worth extends far beyond his virtue."

Lady Etah shifted in her chair impatiently. "Then why a delay, Your Highness?"

"Well, that's none of your fucking business." I wished I could say to them both.

Oh, how I wished to storm out of this room right now and slam the door behind me.

"It's a private matter," I replied calmly instead. "One to be decided between the wife and her husband. I assure you, ladies, that my husband and I have no disagreements about it."

The duchess huffed indignantly.

Lady Etah squared her shoulders, as she often did when arguing with me in the council meeting.

"The marriage of the heiress to the queendom is hardly a private matter, Your Highness," she said. "As a state woman, you should know it."

Mother cleared her throat. "A lack of consummation gives grounds for an annulment, Aniri."

The duchess darted her a reproachful glance, then leveled her heavy stare at me.

"An annulment would not be a desirable outcome for Olakrez. Our queen gave to Princess Aniri the key to her son's virtue. He has spent two nights as a married man. There are plenty of witnesses that Your Highness visited his bed at least on one of those nights. His virtue has been gravely compromised already. As a woman of honor, you cannot discard the prince now. Doing so would upset our queen *greatly.*"

She put enough emphasis on the last word to leave no doubt an annulment would have dire consequences on the relationship between our countries.

I placed a hand over my heart in a demonstration of sincerity. "I assure you I am quite fond of Prince Leafar and have no intentions of 'discarding' him. As exciting as the wedding celebration was," I explained, "it left both the prince and me extremely tired on our wedding night." It was a lame excuse, but it was all I wished to disclose in this interrogation. "Instead of rushing through our wedding night, I believed that my new husband deserved a much better experience, even if at a later date."

The duchess pursed her lips. "It's been two nights, Your Highness. The prince is young and eager. He doesn't need that much time to recover his strength and deliver a consummation."

"Maybe," I replied diplomatically. "However, a woman's body needs some preparation in order to conceive. It's not the best time in my cycle yet. Isn't it in both our interests to ensure the optimal time for conception?"

The duchess looked like she saw right through my desperate attempt to postpone the inevitable.

"For the union between our queendoms to remain strong," she said, "the prince has to become your husband in every way. Your heiress shall have the blood of both Rorrim and Olakrez, especially since this is not so in your case, Your Highness."

My father was from Olakrez. He never made me feel like I was anything less than of his own flesh and blood. To him, I was his daughter with every right to his love. His home country, apparently, felt otherwise. Biologically, I wasn't his.

"My visit here is coming to an end," the duchess continued. "I'll be leaving your queendom in two weeks. Surely, that is enough time for the body of Your Highness to complete its preparations to receive the seed of your lawfully wedded husband in the most advantageous way."

"Some things just can't be rushed." My heart skipped a beat when I realized these were Salas' words I'd just repeated.

"Well, certain things must be performed in a timely manner, and a marriage consummation is one of them. I will not leave this palace until I'm certain that Prince Leafar's position is secure and his marriage is valid. My departure is scheduled for fourteen days from now. I will make the arrangements for a public consummation to take place on the day thirteen, unless I receive the news of it having happened before that."

I sucked in a breath and held it, keeping my wrath and indignity bottled tightly inside me, lest I explode with fury and destroy our fragile truce with Olakrez that Mother, Council, and I had worked so hard to achieve.

Neither the grand duchess nor the queen of Olakrez had any right to stick their noses under the covers of my marital bed. How dared they interrogate either me or my husband about the private things happening or not happening in our bedrooms?

Yet there I was, being interrogated, instructed, and even threatened about how to proceed. And all I could do was just smile and nod reassuringly.

Any power I thought I had was turning into an illusion. The crown princess could do as she wished, but only as long as it fell within the limits of the laws, the traditions, and everyone's expectations.

Ultimately, no one but Leafar and I knew what really happened between us at night. It was up to us to decide what to make public.

"Both Olakrez and Rorrim can have faith in me," I said. "Now, if you excuse me, Grand Duchess, Lady Etah, Your Majesty..." I gave a formal bow to each of the women, getting up. "I'll need to find my husband."

Mother got up with me. "The prince went on a ride with the king consort and their gentlemen-in-waiting this morning."

The duchess clicked her tongue disapprovingly, not missing the chance to shoot one last dart at me before my departure.

"It doesn't do for a wife not to know where her husband is at any given time," she pointed out curtly. "Too much freedom like that is a sure way to make a loose man out of even the most pious groom."

MOTHER FOUND me in my study a few minutes later. I paced the room, still reeling from the meeting with the duchess.

My study room with its tall bookshelves, the cozy sitting area in front of the river rock fireplace, and an oak desk with the most comfortable chair behind it always had a calming effect on me, similar to the palace's extensive library. Unlike the library, however, in my study I could be completely alone, and I often came here when I needed to mull things over in peace.

Except that peace was escaping me now. I felt too restless to sit, to talk, or even to think, unable to focus on any thought calmly.

Mother leaned with her back against the closed door.

"Ari, I thought that matter has been sorted out already." The accusatory note in her voice was unmistakable.

The heel of my shoe caught in the long pile of the rug, making me trip. I stopped in the middle of the room, running my hands over my hair. It was pulled up into a bun, but I found a loose strand to tug on nervously.

"What's going on?" Mother asked. "I thought you were fond of your husband. Was I wrong? What is happening between you two?"

"Nothing. Nothing is happening," I muttered.

"Nothing at all?" She heaved a sigh. "It's really concerning then. What is the reason for the delay? Have we not put in enough effort for you to become comfortable with men?"

It was so like Mother. She'd identified a problem. She'd put an effort into solving it. Now she expected it to be gone. And I was about to disappoint her.

"Achieving a certain level of comfort with one man," I said, "doesn't mean I'd be automatically comfortable with all of them, does it?"

Mother slid her fingers over the string of diamonds around

her neck. "I suppose you're right. But Prince Leafar is an agreeable boy, is he not? Is there something in him not to your liking?"

It had absolutely nothing to do with Leafar and everything to do with someone else.

I pulled at the strand of my hair again, as if the sting at the roots could sharpen my focus.

"Mother, you...you had other lovers before Father, didn't you?"

"Of course, I did. I had a few."

"Was it easy for you to give them up for Father's sake?"

"Well, it wasn't overly difficult. You see, dearest, sex is merely a physical act. It's the person you have it with who makes it either more or less important."

Her words had the opposite effect on me from what she must've intended. Now, my thoughts were with Salas again. Sex with him never felt like simply a physical act. He was important to me, even now.

"The moment I married your father," the queen continued, "I knew my duty was to give the queendom an heiress. That gave a purpose to the growing intimacy between us. Do you not feel the same about the prince? He is your husband, the only man who can give you legitimate children. That should mean something, at least for now. Stronger feelings may come between you with time."

I studied the pattern of the rug under my feet.

"What if I already have stronger feelings, Mother? But for someone else?"

She gasped softly in disappointment.

"Then I say that infatuation is unhealthy. Having lovers is one thing. Developing strong feelings for them is something entirely different, my dear."

"Is that why you don't have lovers now?"

"My decision on that is largely due to my personal preference. I treasure the stability of being with someone I know and trust over any temporary thrill a new lover may bring."

I appreciated being able to discuss it openly with her like that. But this conversation wasn't helping me in the ways I hoped it would.

The thrill of being with Salas wasn't temporary. It had lasted far longer than it should have. Thinking about him filled me with an ever-growing excitement, far more thrilling than the feelings I had for my husband. Could I hope it would change?

I hadn't gone to the games since the day he got injured. As promised, I'd sent the royal healing witch to assess his injuries, but after she told me he was healing well, I made no further inquiries about him. I had carefully avoided even a general conversation about the gladiators. Yet the longing in my heart never eased. If anything, I missed him even more now because the hectic activities of the past two weeks left me feeling more alone than ever.

It was a horrible situation all around.

"Of course, I also have to take your father's feelings into account," Mother said. "At this point, my replacing him with a lover would upset him. I care about his happiness too much to do it to him."

At her words, guilt pressed on my chest heavier than ever.

"I don't want to hurt Leafar in any way."

"The annulment would ruin him," Mother pointed out.

"It would," I agreed, rubbing my eyes. Harming Leafar seemed even more devastating than causing a war with Olakrez. He was an innocent boy trapped in the situation he had no control over, at the mercy of the forces that were far bigger than him.

Mother came closer and wrapped an arm around my shoulders.

"You have a good understanding of what's right for the queendom, Ari. I trust you'll do the right thing."

A dreadful feeling descended heavily into my stomach. There was so much I wanted to do for Rorrim to improve the lives of its people, but I could do it only if I followed the path leading me to the crown.

A future queen would always do what was right for the country. Peace was the most important thing for Rorrim, and the stability that came with a robust succession line of its monarchs. I could not risk that.

Someone knocked on the door before I could reply to Mother.

"Your Highness..." A maid poked her head into the room. The expression on her ashen face stopped the words in my throat. She saw my mother. "Your Majesty. It's the king. He was hurt. Trampled by his horse..."

Fourteen

ARI

Father lay in bed. His riding coat was off. His shirt had been cut open. A white sheet hid the lower part of his body from the waist down. Scuffs and bruises bloomed on his chest, but there were no open wounds visible and not much blood. Was it a good sign?

"Trebor." Mother rushed to him, no longer looking like a powerful queen but simply like a regular woman terrified of losing a loved one.

The royal witch was already here, organizing the small team of her helpers.

"Anna..." Mother's name drowned in a trickle of blood from the corner of Father's mouth.

A witch's apprentice wiped it off with a gauze, but another trickle came with Father's next labored breath. He closed his eyes, giving up on trying to speak.

Horror gripped my throat. His bleeding was internal. Father had some terrible wounds that we couldn't see.

I grabbed the royal witch by the sleeve of her ivory-white robe.

"How is he?" I asked.

She glanced at my parents uneasily.

Mother came to us, leaving Father in the healing team's care for a moment.

"Please be frank," she told the witch in a hushed voice for only the three of us to hear. "I need to know the truth."

The royal witch crumpled a clean piece of gauze in her fingers. "The king has excessive internal injuries, Your Majesty, to his chest and...um, his groin."

Mother swallowed hard, pressing her lips tightly together.

"Can you help him?"

To my relief, the witch nodded with a certain confidence. "As you know, I have diverse knowledge in healing arts. I have successfully dealt with similarly complex cases. In addition, I have already sent for lung and heart specialists. We will operate as soon as they arrive."

"What kind of operation does he need?" I asked. "What exactly are his injuries?"

"Several of his ribs are broken. One has punctured his lung." At Mother's strangled gasp, the witch leaned in, speaking firmly, "With our combined skills, knowledge, and magic, the king is in good hands, Your Majesty."

Mother inhaled a brief, shuddering breath.

"Will he live?" she rasped.

"We will do our best." The witch blinked, the confidence in her voice cracked a little.

"What concerns you?" I prodded.

"Your Highness..." the witch addressed me hesitantly. "This may be best discussed with Her Majesty alone."

Mother waved her off. "Princess Aniri has the right to hear the truth about her father's condition."

The witch inclined her head. "Very well. The king took a blow to his...um, male area. The damage is severe enough to require a... um, reconstruction of some sorts."

"Can you do it?" I asked.

"We will do our best. However, that is a very narrow field of knowledge that hasn't been thoroughly explored. Of course there are some options—"

"Do you not know a specialist who could successfully operate on a male's penis?" I cut her short.

The witch seemed flustered.

"We will do our best," she repeated the same thing again. "I do have to warn Her Majesty, however, that as a result of his injuries, the king may not...well... He may be unable to perform his marital duties in the future."

"I don't care about his *performance*," the queen exclaimed. "I just want him alive. Please do everything you can. If there is anything you need from the crown—"

The lung and heart specialists arrived—both middle-aged, self-assured women. Their teams joined them, immediately making Father's spacious bedroom feel cramped.

I could no longer come close enough to the bed to even see Father.

"We need some space here," the royal witch announced. "Anyone who is not assisting during the surgery, please leave."

"I'm not going anywhere," Mother declared resolutely, taking a seat at her husband's side.

No one dared argue with her.

"I'll wait outside." I gave the queen a warm smile in parting.

A crowd had already gathered in the king's front parlor outside his bedroom. Courtiers, servants, and Father's gentlemen-in-waiting spoke in subdued voices, speculating on the king's condition and waiting for updates.

Leafar was at my side the moment I closed the door behind me.

"Your Highness, I'm so sorry." He stopped short of taking my hand and twisted a polished bronze button on his riding coat instead.

I nodded, but said nothing, going over the words of the royal witch in my head.

"Such a most unfortunate accident." Leafar shook his head, his eyebrows raised in a tragic expression.

"You were with Father this morning," I remembered. "How did it happen?"

He cleared his throat, darting a glance aside.

"A few gentlemen-in-waiting decided to race along a trail with obstacles that included a farm fence. His Majesty joined them."

I scraped a hand down my face. "Oh, he should've known better."

Father wasn't the best on horseback. Riding wasn't something he enjoyed or did often. But I could see how he might've gotten excited and carried away in the company of the prince's younger entourage.

"Yes, yes. He most certainly should've known better," Leafar eagerly agreed. "The king is not in his best shape. He doesn't practice regularly, he admitted it himself. And in his age... Well, it's no wonder his horse didn't clear the fence. He shouldn't have even tried. It was stupid—"

I raised a hand, stopping him. What Leafar was saying might be true, but it was absolutely not what I needed to hear when my father was fighting for his life.

The door to the bedroom opened, and one of the healing witches exited.

"Any updates?" I accosted her before she even closed the door behind her.

She shook her head. "Not at the moment, Your Highness. The surgery is just about to begin. We are optimistic about its outcome. I need to fetch my trunk with potions. I don't trust anyone else to carry it. Some vials are so fragile."

"How long will the surgery last?"

"It depends on the full extent of the king's internal injuries that we will assess during the surgery, but I expect the initial procedure would take us about two to three hours with a possible follow-up later, including the amputation."

My breath hitched. "What amputation?"

"Oh, I thought the royal witch discussed this with you already." She glanced around, leaning closer to my ear. "Some of the king's injuries include those in a delicate area—"

"You mean the damage to his pelvis?"

"Yes, yes, that is exactly what I mean. His Majesty's..." She steepled her fingers in front of her, hesitating in her choice of words, "...male organ has been compromised. The best option we see right now—"

"Is to cut it off?" I finished for her, tired of her beating around the bush. "Without an attempt at reconstructive surgery?"

She cleared her throat. "It's a delicate area, Your Highness. Way too complex to operate effectively and impossible to preserve its functions."

"Impossible? Or you just don't know how to do it?"

It occurred to me that everyone in that bedroom right now was a woman, except for the patient. While men weren't explicitly forbidden to study healing arts, the medical college required an endorsement from a witches' coven for admission, and only women could be witches.

The healing witch hiked her chin, staring down her nose at me indignantly. "I have some of the highest qualifications in the healing arts—"

"I don't doubt your expertise, esteemed healer." I nodded. "It's just not exactly in the required area, is it?"

"It is unnecessary in this case. The king's ability to have children is no longer crucial. Her Majesty also agreed with us on the procedure."

Mother was too distraught and worried about Father's life. But Father deserved to have options.

"What does the king think about it?"

The witch looked at me, perplexed. "The king is in no position to give consent."

"Exactly. He can't consent to anything right now. And you're planning to cut off a part of his body without even an attempt to save it."

"With all due respect, Your Highness, that 'part' is no longer necessary—"

"With all due respect, I believe that if given a choice, my father would very much prefer to keep his penis attached."

She blushed when I used the actual name of "the part" in question. I recalled a conversation I once had during an official visit to the Egami College of the Healing Arts. A professor had explained to me that the male body is essentially the same as the female, with only some insignificant differences that don't warrant a development of a separate course of studies.

"You had no chance to learn much about that part, did you?" I sighed.

"I assure you I possess a vast academic knowledge and practical expertise that comes from the decades of tireless work healing my patients."

"Of course." There was no use in arguing since despite all that combined knowledge and expertise that was currently assembled in my father's bedroom, not a single person in there had the exact skill he needed.

That didn't mean the queendom had no experts of that kind. I saw the results of their work not so long ago.

"Thank you for the updates," I said to the witch. "I'll let you go get your potions to fix my father's lungs and ribs and save his life as you promised, but please..." I got hold of her arm, making sure she paid attention. "Please, don't let the royal witch amputate anything yet."

"What do you mean, Your Highness?" She looked confused.

I explained, "I need to make a few inquiries to possibly find an expert in the male area to aid your efforts." "Meanwhile, I don't want anyone to cut anything off. Do you understand me?"

She blinked at me rapidly, clearly lost for words.

"Do not amputate," I said loud and clear, then added a threat to ensure she understood, "Don't chop off anything until my return or I'll personally make sure that your head is chopped off for malpractice. Is that clear?"

She drew in a breath, her eyes opening wide in shock.

I left her and Leafar gawk at each other while I marched out of the room with a new mission at hand.

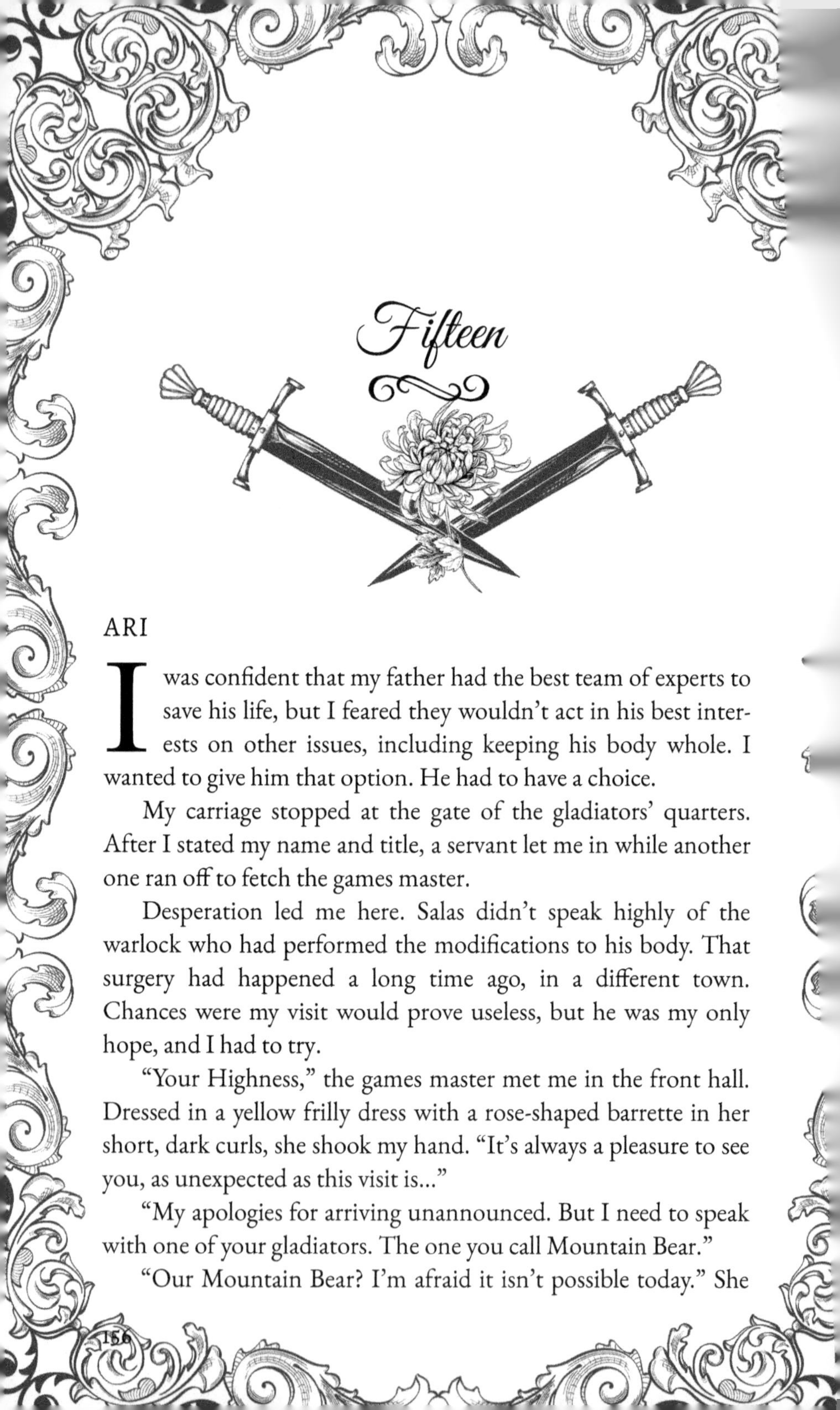

Fifteen

ARI

I was confident that my father had the best team of experts to save his life, but I feared they wouldn't act in his best interests on other issues, including keeping his body whole. I wanted to give him that option. He had to have a choice.

My carriage stopped at the gate of the gladiators' quarters. After I stated my name and title, a servant let me in while another one ran off to fetch the games master.

Desperation led me here. Salas didn't speak highly of the warlock who had performed the modifications to his body. That surgery had happened a long time ago, in a different town. Chances were my visit would prove useless, but he was my only hope, and I had to try.

"Your Highness," the games master met me in the front hall. Dressed in a yellow frilly dress with a rose-shaped barrette in her short, dark curls, she shook my hand. "It's always a pleasure to see you, as unexpected as this visit is..."

"My apologies for arriving unannounced. But I need to speak with one of your gladiators. The one you call Mountain Bear."

"Our Mountain Bear? I'm afraid it isn't possible today." She smacked her lips with regret. "He only opens a handful of appointments a month, and this month is all booked already."

"What do you mean?" I asked, and immediately regretted the question.

Did I need to know the activities filling Salas's schedule, especially if they probably involved the court ladies?

The games master spread her arms apologetically.

"His popularity in the arena is growing every week, Your Highness. And as such, he's become exceedingly popular with the ladies as well."

An unpleasant feeling that I couldn't immediately name scratched in my chest, sending a flush of heat to my face that I failed to control.

"Is he enjoying entertaining outside of the arena?" I asked. "Is that really what he wants to do?"

Catching the hard note in my tone, the games master raised an eyebrow indignantly.

"I do not run a brothel, Your Highness. Everything that happens under this roof happens with my boys' full consent and to their utter enjoyment."

"That's a relief to know," I replied, but the scratchy feeling in my chest didn't ease.

"Well..." The games master's expression relaxed. "You are such a rare visitor. It is a true honor to have you here, Your Highness. I may be able to shift the line in your favor and possibly arrange something for the end of this week. It's against the rules, of course, but since it's the first time you ever showed an interest in one of my boys—"

"Oh, I'm not interested in him," I protested promptly. "Not in that way, anyway. I need to talk to him about an important matter. My father got injured this morning..." Despite my best effort to keep it together, my voice broke off. The image of my father lying in bed, unable to even utter his wife's name and struggling to breathe, flashed through my mind with a stab of sharp pain through my heart.

The games master pressed her hands to her chest in alarm. "The king is hurt?"

"Yes..." I swallowed a painful lump lodged in my throat. "Some of his injuries are of the kind that the royal witch can't treat with the most desired outcome." Now, I was the one beating around the bush when there wasn't much time to lose. "Can I count on your confidentiality, Master?"

"Of course, Your Highness. In this place, we pride ourselves on our discretion. We know how to keep ladies' secrets."

"I need to find someone who is familiar with the biology and function of male reproductive organs. I hope your Mountain Bear might know a warlock who performs that kind of surgeries for a living."

She gave me a cautious look.

"A warlock? We don't employ them here, Your Highness." She shook her head adamantly, sending her curls into a bounce. "But I know the boys find ways to have certain surgeries done, anyway. They're so eager to please the ladies who show them affection and favor."

"Yes, so..." I rubbed my forehead between my eyebrows where the tightness of worry was steadily building up into a headache. "Can I speak with Mountain Bear or Raeb, please? I'm hoping he can direct me to someone for help."

"Why Raeb? Regit was the one who got the surgery done just a couple of days ago. Though Raeb met with the warlock who performed it, too, as I've learned. Regit is fully on the mend, by the way. I assure you his performance at the games will not be affected."

Her mentioning a recent successful surgery gave me hope.

"I'm glad Regit is well, but I prefer to speak to Raeb, please." I'd much rather discuss this with someone I knew and trusted than with a stranger. Also, I knew for sure that Salas would keep it a secret if I asked him. "My father needs help as soon as possible. I can't delay."

"Of course," the games master finally conceded, turning to

the main staircase that led up to the second floor. "We can certainly make an exception in this case. You can see Raeb right now. He has about thirty minutes before his appointment with Countess Ciryl."

Countess Ciryl.

The name brought to mind the image of the smiling, chatty woman I'd met many times. The countess served on several committees as a supporter of the arts and was the major benefactor of the Theater of Opera and Drama in Egami. She also had an exceptionally lovely voice and was often asked to sing at the events in the royal palace.

She'd be a pleasant companion to spend an afternoon with. I couldn't blame Salas for planning to do just that. Unlike me, the countess was also unmarried. There was absolutely no reason why a single woman and an unattached man shouldn't enjoy an evening together... possibly a night, too, if they so chose...

By the time I reached the top of the stairs, I felt as winded as if I climbed the highest peak of Drazil Mountains. My chest felt tight, like I was wearing one of Father's waistcoat corsets. And my hands turned cold and clammy like dead fish.

"Raeb." The games master knocked on one of the several doors along the second floor's hallway. "Princess Aniri is here to see you."

There was a pause in his response, and the games master didn't wait, pushing the door open.

"The crown needs your help, sweetie," she said. "I'll make sure the countess knows about a potential delay with your scheduled rendezvous." With a polite bow to me, she left, leaving me standing on the threshold to Salas's room.

Late summer air blew through the open balcony door, but I easily caught his scent in it, the scent I'd been hunting for in my dreams. I inhaled deeply and made a step in, closing the door behind me.

Holding a folded shirt, he stood by a tall chest of drawers

painted with swirls of stars. A laundry basket was at his feet with a stack of clean linen in it.

"It is really you, Princess," he said softly, as if afraid to scare away a dream.

Hearing his nickname for me knocked the air out of my lungs. The corset of longing tightened even more around my chest. Memories teased, both tantalizing and tormenting. Clutching handfuls of my skirts at my sides, I focused on every breath I took.

"Good day, Salas." I licked my dry lips and cleared my throat. "It's very nice to see you again."

"Nice" was such an inadequate word. The weather outside was nice—warm and pleasant. Seeing Salas again felt like a salvation I didn't search for and didn't know I needed.

With his eyes on me, he poked with the shirt at a closed drawer above the open one. Realizing his mistake, he sighed and dropped the shirt back into the basket.

"You do your own laundry?" I asked, wrinkling my skirts in my hands.

"No. The laundry is done for us. I just have to put it away."

"Sorry, I interrupted you. I just..." I felt suddenly so lost, like I'd been running tirelessly and resolutely along a predetermined path, only for it to disappear on me unexpectedly.

He frowned, taking a step toward me.

"What is it, Princess? What's wrong?"

The kindness in his voice undid me. All the emotions of the past few weeks—the uncertainty, the anger, the guilt, the fear, the helplessness, everything I'd pushed down and held in—rushed out at once.

My cheeks flared with heat. My fists unclenched, releasing my skirts. Tears burned my eyes.

"I... Salas, my father..." I couldn't bring myself to say the words, afraid the mentioning of my father's broken body would break me too.

"Come here, sweetheart." He opened his arms for me, and I ran into their shelter without a moment of doubt or hesitation.

"Father isn't well, Salas," I sobbed into his shirt.

It wasn't the shirt that I gave him, I noted, but a much nicer one, from an expensive silk in a glossy satin weave with buttons carved from iridescent mother-of-pearl in a golden setting.

He stroked my back, holding me in a hug that felt like no evil could penetrate.

"How can I help?" he asked simply, his cheek pressed to the side of my head.

He was helping already, and he didn't even know how much. Slowly, I could breathe again. I could talk.

"It happened this morning," I muttered against his chest. "He fell from his horse. Then got trampled by its hooves. Internal bleeding. Broken ribs. A punctured lung..." Through tears and only in short, fragmented sentences, but I talked while he kept all my pieces together in his big, strong arms, preventing me from falling apart completely. "They're fixing him. They know what they're doing. The witches are smart."

"They are." He glided a reassuring hand over my hair. "The royal witch must be at least as good as the one we have here. And our witch did wonders when healing my wounds."

"Are they healed?" I sniffled, looking up.

My glasses fogged up with my tears, and he moved them up to my head, allowing me to see his face.

"All healed." He smiled. "As good as new, just with a couple of scars left that Lerrel says look amazing in the arena." Reaching back, he took a freshly washed handkerchief from the pile of clean laundry in the basket, then wiped my tears off my cheeks. "The healing witches are women of high intelligence and stellar education. Your father is in good hands."

"They are. And he is." I nodded, clutching the shirt over his chest. I had no strength to leave the safety of his arms yet. "Only they don't know everything, Salas. The horse kicked him in his groin, too, and all the witches can do is just amputate..." My voice broke off again.

I closed my eyes and pressed the side of my face to his chest, finding his heartbeat. Strong, measured beat seemed to come way too fast for his size, but its rhythm and the warmth of his body soothed me, anyway.

"Is amputation the only option?" he asked carefully.

"No. I mean, I don't know... But they can't just cut it off like that. Not without at least trying a reconstruction. Except that they don't know how to do it. They wouldn't admit it, but I know they haven't been taught. Salas." I looked up at him again. "Do you know someone who can help?"

Once again, the irony didn't escape me. One of the most powerful women in the queendom was pleading for help with the man who had no right to even own a home in his name. But that was only what it looked like on the outside.

In reality, I felt helpless, not powerful. And Salas had always been the strongest person I knew. It wasn't just his physical strength, but the strength of his character too. He was solid, honest, and real in every way. And I used him as my source of strength, again and again.

I didn't even have it in me to feel guilty about taking his support, because the more I took, the more he seemed to have.

"You had a surgery done yourself," I said.

"I had. But I would advise everyone to stay away from the charlatan warlock who treated me."

"There must be someone better." I held on to every shred of hope. "The games master said that Regit had a successful surgery just a few days ago."

"Will you trust a warlock to treat the king?" he asked uncertainly.

"If you vouch for him."

He shook his head.

"I don't know this one well enough. He did perform a successful surgery that is healing well now. But I don't know how skilled he is in anything more complex than inserting fish bladders or injecting liquid onyx."

"The warlock wouldn't be alone. The royal witch and her

team are there. I'm not even sure if they actually would let him put a knife to the king. But I'd like to have someone with practical experience during the surgery, someone who could at least give a second opinion before they do something that can never be reversed."

"All right." He brushed a strand of my hair aside before returning my glasses to their usual position on my nose. His thumb stroked my cheek right below my glasses, and I wondered if he'd just connected my freckles into an arch on my skin. He blinked, his smile slipping away. "I know a warlock who might be able to help. He lives in the city. I'll have to go there. There is no other way. He wouldn't open his door to just anyone."

"I'll come with you."

"It's not the prettiest part of town, Princess. Noble folk avoid going that way."

"Well, then I should visit it for sure."

He gave me a penetrating look, but I held it steady.

"I'm not hiding from the sores of our society anymore, Salas. If I don't know what the issues are, how can I ever attempt to fix them?"

"Do you really want to fix things? Do you think life in Rorrim can be good for everyone?"

"That's the plan, to make it good for everyone. At least for when I get the crown." I winced, thinking back to my unsuccessful arguments in the council. "As the queen, with a new council, I'll have far fewer limitations to act than as the princess."

"Are there limitations now?"

"Quite a few." I sighed as he handed me a cloak. "Do I need to wear this?"

"Yes. There is no need to raise questions." He draped the cloak around my shoulders, then put another one on himself too. "Also, it's better for the peace and reputation of the man we're going to visit."

He opened the door for us to leave, and I took one last look at the place that he called home now.

It was a lovely room with a window, a balcony, and a large poster bed with green velvet curtains tied back with golden tussled cords. A writing desk stood by the window with a stack of sketch papers on it. The sharpened lead pencils lay in a small silver tray next to it. Pots of blooming rose bushes and colorful dahlias decorated the balcony, lending their sweet fragrance to the air.

It was a peaceful place, furnished with both function and joy in mind, filled with serenity and peace I only ever felt in his presence.

He waited for me, holding the door open.

"Is anything amiss, Princess?"

Everything in the world out there seemed to be "amiss" lately. I wished I could stay here, even if just to have some tea with Salas and take a nap in his four-poster bed with the green curtains.

"No." I forced a smile. "But...how about Countess Ciryl?"

"Who?" He lifted an eyebrow.

"Your appointment this afternoon," I reminded him.

"Oh. Don't worry about it. I'll tell Lerrel to cancel it on our way out." He closed the door behind us.

"Will the countess be upset?" I asked as we walked toward the stairs then down to the main floor.

"She'll reschedule." He found a servant in the main hall downstairs and sent him to let the games master know about our departure and the change to his schedule. "Is your carriage still here, Princess? It'd be faster than walking."

In the carriage, I expected Salas to take the seat across from mine, but he sat next to me instead. His arm pressed to mine. There simply wasn't enough space to accommodate his bulk and leave a gap between us, and I didn't mind it a bit.

As the carriage moved with a jolt, I struggled to resist the urge to lean into his warmth. I'd long lost the right to be this close to him. Every moment spent next to Salas now was stolen.

"I'm sorry I ruined your shirt," I said, pointing at the sliver of the tear-stained satin showing between the ends of his cloak.

"It'll dry." He shrugged, then added with a barely there smile, "It's not the first time you left me with a wet chest."

His words burst the door open for the memories I tried so hard to contain. It was not the first time I'd cried on his chest. He'd comforted me before. And shamelessly, I kept coming for more.

"But it was a cotton shirt before. This one is silk." I plastered a smile on my face to hide the persistent nagging of jealousy that I knew I had no right to feel. "Tears and satin aren't good together. I'm afraid this shirt is truly ruined now." I shifted in my seat, trying and miserably failing to hold back the next question. "Did the countess give this shirt to you?"

It made sense he'd wear her gift while waiting for her visit.

"Yes," he admitted simply.

I had no business to feel jealous, not when I was the one who'd put a wedding ring on another man's finger. But jealousy burned stronger in my chest, painful like a spill of acid.

"I'm sorry you had to cancel your date," I said, feeling not sorry at all.

He tilted his head, staring at me in that way that only Salas did, like he could read through all my carefully practiced neutral expressions and calmly delivered words.

"It wasn't a date, Ari. Just a lesson."

"A lesson on what?"

The memories of all the delightful "lessons" he'd given me fluttered through my mind like a kaleidoscope of sweet, cherished, colorful butterflies.

He shook his head, a corner of his mouth lifting in that half-grin that still haunted me at night while I tossed and turned, trying to fall asleep in the sheets that no longer smelled like him.

"A music lesson, Ari. The countess insisted on teaching me to play a lute."

"A lute?" I snorted a laugh in a very not-princess-like manner. "Why, by gods, would she teach you that?"

He leaned back in the cushioned seat. "She had a whim to

become a teacher, I guess. She said it'd give her a chance to talk about music in a new way. And let me tell you, the countess loves to talk." He chuckled. "We've had two lessons so far, but I'm yet to learn how to play a single chord. Though, I have learned a lot about the history of opera in Rorrim, the administrative challenges of the theater productions she's been overseeing, and the many ways that music connects to our bodies."

"How does it connect to our bodies?" I wondered.

Smile danced in his eyes, drawing me in like an undercurrent.

"According to the countess, every function of the body has a melody corresponding to it. Or resonating with it."

"Every function?"

"Yes, from speech, to digestion, to even, pardon me, the bowel movement."

"What? Really?" Laugh burst out of me, unconstrained. "What melody would that function have, I wonder?"

Salas watched me with a wide smile.

"Something involving drums, I gather. Or maybe a tuba?"

"Depending on what one ate!" I laughed harder, slapping his thigh. "What if it's beans?"

"There'd definitely be a bass involved." His deep, carefree laughter joined mine, momentarily banishing every shred of tension and worry that had been hanging over me lately.

From the pocket of the cloak, I grabbed the handkerchief he'd given me and dabbed at my eyes, wiping off the tears of laughter.

"This is so ridiculously good." I grinned. "I should give the countess a hug next time when I see her. But have you ever really aspired to play a lute? Or any musical instrument, for that matter?"

"I don't think I have the aptitude for it, to be honest. Even learning how to dance was a struggle. But I don't mind the lessons. Countess Ciryl has a pleasant voice and loves to talk without expecting my input. I've been catching up on my chores during our lessons, watering the plants on the balcony, putting away the laundry, or drawing."

I remembered the stack of sketch paper on his desk.

"What do you draw?"

"Weapons mostly. Swords. Noil, the games master's husband, allowed me to help in the workshop where they make and fix the weapons for gladiators. I've been designing a couple of swords for me to use in the arena."

I adored the enthusiasm that lit behind his eyes. He clearly loved going back to working at the forge. For once in his adult life, Salas did something for his own enjoyment, not just for survival or to please others.

"I'd love to see the swords you'll make," I said. "I should come to the games sometime soon if you promise me not to get hurt again." I managed to keep my tone of voice light, despite the grave reminder of his injuries he'd sustained the last time I'd visited the arena.

He patted my hand on his thigh reassuringly. I hadn't even realized I'd kept my hand in his lap all this time.

"I'm getting better at it, Princess. I don't make it easy anymore, either for a man or a beast to hurt me," he assured me.

I turned my hand with my palm up, and he curled his fingers around in, squeezing lightly. Despite all this time spent away from Salas, I realized that our connection hadn't grown weaker.

It should've alarmed me. But at that very moment, I smiled, feeling lighter at heart. It felt like after a stormy, turbulent journey, I opened my travel chest to discover with relief that my most treasured possession remained intact.

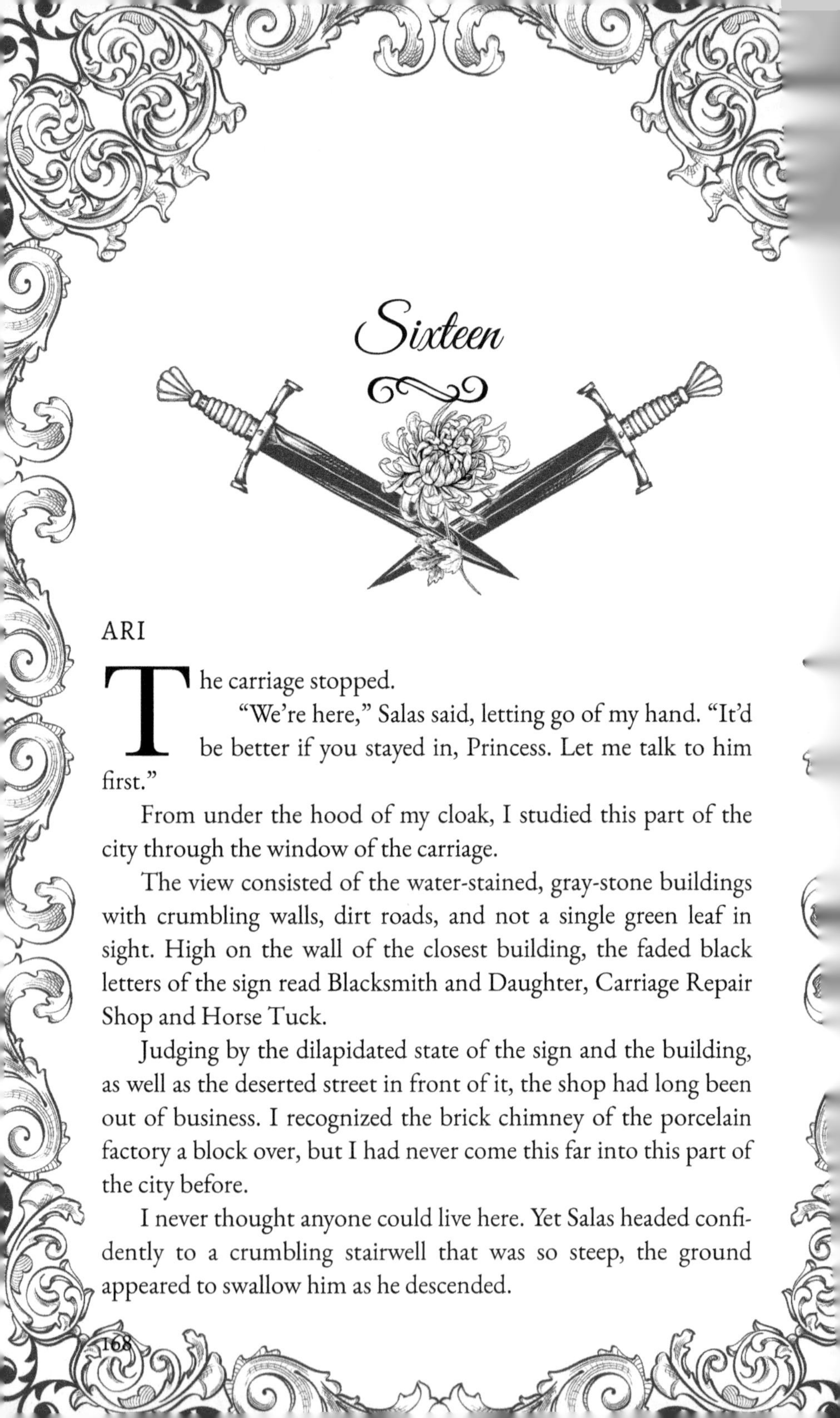

Sixteen

ARI

The carriage stopped.

"We're here," Salas said, letting go of my hand. "It'd be better if you stayed in, Princess. Let me talk to him first."

From under the hood of my cloak, I studied this part of the city through the window of the carriage.

The view consisted of the water-stained, gray-stone buildings with crumbling walls, dirt roads, and not a single green leaf in sight. High on the wall of the closest building, the faded black letters of the sign read Blacksmith and Daughter, Carriage Repair Shop and Horse Tuck.

Judging by the dilapidated state of the sign and the building, as well as the deserted street in front of it, the shop had long been out of business. I recognized the brick chimney of the porcelain factory a block over, but I had never come this far into this part of the city before.

I never thought anyone could live here. Yet Salas headed confidently to a crumbling stairwell that was so steep, the ground appeared to swallow him as he descended.

He returned a few minutes later, followed by a lanky, hunched over figure that huddled into a tattered cloak while carrying a large covered basket.

They both climbed into the carriage, with Salas taking his place next to me and his companion sitting down across from us.

I'd never seen a warlock from this close before. In the children's books that my father used to read to me when I'd just arrived in Rorrim, warlocks were always depicted either as despicable villains or as conniving charlatans. Either way, those stories taught children to stay away from them.

This time, however, a warlock might lend us some help.

"Good day," I greeted the man, shoving back my hood.

He paled, staring at my face for a moment, then without uttering a single word, scrambled for the door.

Salas stopped him by placing a hand on the door handle.

"Please. Just listen to what she has to say," he implored. "You can always leave after."

The warlock curled in the seat sideways, facing the door and cradling his basket to his chest.

"My life may seem pitiful to you," he mumbled, addressing no one in particular, "but I do not wish to end it just yet."

"What do you mean?" I asked softly, striving to sound non-threatening. "Your life is not in danger. My father's life is."

He sucked in a breath, glaring at Salas from under his hood. "When you said the gentleman was a highborn, you didn't specify he was the highest born in the queendom."

"Why does it matter?" I asked. "Would it stop you from helping him? If the surgery is a success, you will be generously rewarded."

"And if it isn't?"

"Do you have so little faith in your skills?"

I studied him closely. His once blue cloak had kept that color only in the seam under the hood, the rest had weathered to the pale gray. The wicker potion chest that he clutched to him looked like a beaten-up picnic basket with its corners cracked and its lead partially unraveled. His clothes emitted a faint smell of mold, but his chin appeared freshly shaven, and his hands were clean with neatly trimmed fingernails.

He looked old enough to have gathered the necessary knowledge and expertise, provided he had dedicated his life to learning and improving his skills. Of course, his age alone was not a guarantee of his expertise.

"Do you not think you have what it takes to perform a successful surgery?" I prodded.

He wouldn't look at me as he spoke. "The gods meddle in the affairs of mortals all the time. No matter how skilled a man is, there is always a chance of something going wrong during a surgery. With the king as my patient, if that happens, I hold no hope of keeping my head on my shoulders."

I clasped my hands together in my lap.

"The best outcome we're facing right now is an amputation. If that proves to be inevitable, I promise you'll keep your head. If you can deliver anything better than an amputation, I won't just pay you for your efforts, you'll receive a pension for life that will allow you to move to a much better place than this." I tipped my thumb at the crumbling building outside the carriage window.

"What good is in the promise 'for life' if there wouldn't be much of life left for me to live?" he wouldn't give up, mistrustful of anything I said.

"The princess gave you her promise," Salas snapped. "How dare you doubt her word?"

"You don't trust me," I spoke to the warlock. "Understandably so. You don't know me. But I'm taking a leap of faith with you too. A huge leap of faith. My father's health is vitally important to me, to the queen, and to the country. But here I am, begging a man with no academic credentials to operate on the king."

He sulked, tossing me a reproachful glance.

"Academic credentials are a privilege not available to men. However, my practical experience can rival that of the most accomplished of witches," he replied proudly. "I grew up on a farm and was lucky enough for the owner to take a liking to me. She indulged my interest in the healing arts from a very young age. She ordered text books for me, subscribed to publications, and even allowed me to use her outdoor kitchen to brew my potions. But everything else I've learned through practical work. As I grew older, I treated her workers, including the male farmhands. Among the various injuries I've healed, I also had to deal with the wounds from kicks of animal hooves to the groin area. There was also a particularly nasty incident with a farmhand falling onto a fence, straddling it, and severely crushing his manhood." He winced.

Salas grunted, shifting his legs closer together.

"After my treatment," the warlock continued, "that man went on getting married, and even blessing his wife with four healthy children."

The story could easily be a lie, an exaggeration, or simply wishful thinking. But I longed to believe in it with all my heart. I had to give both this man and my father a chance.

The warlock finished his speech with his head held high. "I do have the knowledge and the skills, at the very least, to assess the king's injuries and give you my opinion on the outcome."

"How can I convince you to do it?" I asked, afraid to hope.

Finally, he met my eyes straight on.

"My name is Rotcod," he said, clearly pronouncing each syllable of his name for me to remember. "If I assist during the surgery to His Majesty's satisfaction, I want my name to be added to every publication that goes out about this case."

"You want recognition above anything else?"

"At this point in my life," he nodded, "recognition is the only thing I'm still willing to risk my head for."

It surprised me at first that a man who had nothing would only ask for his name to be known. Then I realized it was his one and only chance to leave a mark on this world. For a man who had genuinely dedicated his life to his work, it'd be the best reward to be remembered and honored for it, even after his death.

"It's a deal, Rotcod." I offered him my hand to shake on our agreement. "If you contribute to my father's surgery in any meaningful way, your name will not only be in every publication known among the healing arts professionals, I'll personally see to it that it'll appear on the front page of the Rorrim Herald. Your name will be known to the entire queendom."

THE CARRIAGE TOOK us back to the palace. I ordered the coachwoman to bring it through the gate and as close to the front entrance as possible.

Salas opened the door, exiting first, then helped me and Rotcod to get out. As the warlock looked around uneasily, clutching his basket to his chest, I paused, leaving my hand in Salas's.

"Thank you. For everything," I said sincerely.

"Don't thank me yet, Princess. I hope it all goes well. Here..." With his other hand, he reached into the folds of his cloak and took out a small bundle wrapped into a piece of an old issue of the Rorrim Herald. "I got it from Rotcod for you."

"What is it?" I took the parcel.

"The tea to help you sleep."

"You remembered..." I exhaled.

"Well." He lifted a shoulder, looking a little awkward. "You aren't easy to forget, Princess."

I pressed the package to my chest with one hand, momentarily speechless.

"There is scarlet camomile," he explained quickly, pointing at the package, "wild lavender, and crushed fairy-dream berries gathered on the night of the new moon. No sleeping potion added, since you have a country to run and can't afford to be drowsy."

"Thank you," I repeated, reeling from it all.

He ran his thumb over the knuckles of my hand that he still held in his. "I hope it helps. Everyone deserves a good rest, at least once in a while."

I clung to his hand like to a lifeline, aware that if I let go of it, the hurricane of reality would sweep me away from him again.

"I... I just really, really hate saying goodbye to you right now," I confessed.

I needed him more than ever. But I couldn't come up with a single excuse to keep him with me any longer.

Today, Salas had been friendly, supportive, and understanding. But I sensed his tension as my own. He'd been holding back, maintaining the distance between us, as he probably felt he should.

For a moment, however, his polite composure slipped away. His thick eyebrows moved together, his eyes sparked with urgency as he stepped closer, placing his hands on my shoulders.

"Ari," he said. "If you ever need anything that you can't get in the palace, even if it's just a kind word and a hug. You come to me, do you hear me? Don't you ever hesitate to come to me for anything at all."

Kind words were sometimes harder to find in the palace than diamonds, and Salas's hugs were the best in the world. My chest hurt, squeezed with longing and gratitude.

"I don't deserve you, Salas. No one does."

He held my shoulders, and I gripped his forearms. Then I pressed my forehead to his chest and stilled, stealing one last moment of peace in the eye of the hurricane.

"Your Highness!" Leafar's voice shattered the silence. "Where have you been?"

His voice came like a slap on the face. My cheeks flared with heat. I whipped around to face my husband, who was crossing the plaza from the front entrance of the palace toward us. The priceless mirror rock of the ring on his finger cast a myriad of sparks onto the cobblestones—a splendid reminder of his status and mine.

"Who is this man?" He tossed a questioning look over my shoulder to where Salas stood by the carriage.

I placed a hand on Rotcod's shoulder instead, redirecting Leafar's attention.

"This man is here to help my father. Come with me, please," I said to Rotcod with a sweep of my arm toward the palace. "I'll introduce you to the rest of Father's healing team."

"Is that..." Leafar slid an assessing look down the warlock's lanky frame draped in the tattered cloak. "Are you bringing a warlock into the palace?"

"Yes. And I have little time to lose." I marched across the plaza, leading Rotcod with me and hoping that Leafar would follow.

It cost me an immense effort not to turn to Salas for one last glance goodbye. I had to pretend that he didn't matter, that he was a nobody, that he wasn't worth anyone's attention, even as he was worth a world to me.

Thankfully, it worked. Leafar hurried after Rotcod and me, leaving Salas alone. The small crowd, spilling out of the palace's doors, also focused on Rotcod as we approached, and I released a sigh of relief at the sound of the horses' hooves behind us as the carriage left the plaza, taking Salas back to his room filled with sunshine and flower scent.

Away from me.

Seventeen

ARI

I adjusted Father's blanket to cover his exposed foot. I did it carefully so as not to wake him, but his sleep remained deep, aided by the sleeping potion and a calming spell.

Rotcod snored softly in the chair nearby. The tattered book of spells lay open in his lap. Until two days ago, two witch apprentices also spent nights in Father's bedroom. But as his condition had been improving, they had moved into the front parlor to give him more privacy at night. Mother and I had been taking turns at Father's bedside to make sure he had someone from his family with him whenever he woke up.

It'd been a stressful week for all of us, a rollercoaster of emotions. But now, Father's health had been steadily improving. He'd had several surgeries that all went well. After an extensive consultation with the royal healing witch, Rotcod had successfully performed the reconstruction, and now the king was on the mend.

The door to the bedroom opened quietly, and Mother slipped inside.

"How is he?" she asked.

"Asleep." I stepped away from the bed and whispered, "Rotcod brewed him a healing tea with a drop of sleeping potion and gave him some powder to help manage the pain."

"Was he in a lot of pain?" She glanced at Father's bed over my shoulder.

"Not as much. He was in a very good mood tonight, actually." I smiled. "He even made me promise I'd take him to the games this weekend."

"The games?" Mother gasped. "Do you really think he'll feel well enough to leave the palace so soon?"

"If he's comfortable enough, I think a change of scenery will do him good. That's what Rotcod said too."

"It's so good to hear, Ari. There have been moments in this past week when I didn't think your father would ever leave the palace alive again..." Her lips trembled, her eyes shining with unshed tears.

Goddess knew I'd had many moments like that myself. Even as Father was recovering now, the fear for him hadn't released my heart yet.

"He's better, Mother." I gave her a firm hug, determined to stay strong for her sake.

"Well..." She sniffled, releasing me from the hug and quickly sweeping with her hand her cheeks under her eyes. "I have some good news too. Madam Trela reported she finished her investigation into the recent horrific murders. The case is now with the judge. The ruling will be quick. I requested a public execution of the murderer. People have to see with their own eyes that the threat to our peace and safety is finally eliminated."

"Is Madam Trela certain then that they got the right man?"

"All evidence is there, Ari. The owner of the fun house confirmed his identity. He was apprehended while trying to commit another murder. How can there be any doubts?"

"You're right." I nodded.

From the day the guards apprehended the suspect over a week

ago, there hadn't been any more attacks. Peace had returned to Egami.

"I shall let Rotcod go to bed." Mother made a move toward the warlock, but I stopped her.

"Let him sleep. He's been up a lot every night since he got to the palace. You can send him to bed if he wakes up on his own. Otherwise, I wouldn't disturb him."

She nodded, going to Father instead. "You haven't slept much either, Ari. Go to bed. I'll stay here with him."

I was tired. With Mother spending most of her time at Father's side, I had taken almost entirely over all her duties of running the queendom. I also tried to be with Father every spare second I got.

"You spent the last night here," Mother insisted. "But you didn't sleep at all. You were up and awake every time I opened my eyes."

"I don't sleep that much, anyway."

"Well, I think you should try to get some sleep tonight."

"But how about you?"

"I'm good." She smiled, sliding under the covers on the opposite side of Father. The bed was wide enough for her not to disturb him. "I sleep the best when he's near," she said and added almost apologetically, "I miss him."

Leaving the queen with Father, I went across the hall and past the grand marble staircase to my bedroom. Exhaustion weighed heavily on me, promising at least a few hours of sleep if I was lucky.

The guards at the doors to my suite bowed to me in greeting.

"His Highness Prince Leafar is waiting for you, Your Highness," one of them said.

"Leafar?" I paused in my tracks.

For a moment of weakness, I cowardly considered going to my study or spending the night in the library instead. But he was my husband. I'd asked him to marry me. I couldn't run from him now, no matter how tired I was.

Coming to my senses, I thanked the guards, crossed my sitting room, and pushed the door to my bedroom open.

The soft glow of the lit candles in the room momentarily conjured the vision of Salas making us tea while waiting for my return. The sudden memory came with a tug at my heart, both sweet and agonizingly painful.

"Your Highness?" Leafar rose from the couch, rubbing his eyes.

Without a suit jacket, a waistcoat, or even a cravat, he had the first few buttons of his shirt open, which I had never seen him do before. Such carelessness in appearance was not typical for the prince.

"Evening, Leafar." I spotted a silver tray with a liquor bottle and two glasses on it. "Have you been...um, sleeping here?"

"Well..." He smoothed his hair with both hands, then adjusted his shirt. "Sleep was not my intention when coming here. But Your Highness has been absent from your rooms for so long, I'm afraid, I've dozed off."

I remained standing by the door. "It's late. You should get some sleep. Please, allow me to walk you back to your rooms."

He pursed his lips stubbornly. His bottom lip slid out a little, making him look like a petulant child.

"Once you walk me to my bedroom, will you stay there with me?" he asked. "Will you spend the night?"

I inhaled deeply, leaning with my back against the door. Tonight was not a good time. But neither had been any other night prior. I couldn't keep avoiding him forever.

He quickly filled a glass from the bottle.

"Have a drink with me." He came closer, offering the glass to me. "Please forgive my intrusion. But Your Highness is a very busy woman. I have a hard time finding even a minute in your schedule for me."

Guilt ballooned in my chest. I had asked him to marry me. I had made him my husband. He was just trying to spend some time with his wife. The least I could do was to meet him half-way.

"Thank you." I accepted the glass with what smelled like an almond liqueur—a little stronger than what I usually drank, but I took a sip anyway as a peace offering.

"Do you like it?" Leafar beamed, hovering over me. "Almond liqueur is very popular at my mother's court."

"It's...um, sweet." I licked my lips, wishing he'd move away a little and give me some space.

Instead, he moved even closer, leaning over me with a hand propped on the door above my head. He was taller than me, likely significantly stronger, too, but I'd never felt unsafe in his presence before.

Not until now.

The way his smile slipped from his face as he ran his eyes over my face then down my chest unnerved me.

"Leafar..." I tried to sound calm, even as my heart leaped to my throat in alarm.

"Kiss me," he croaked, hooking his arm around my waist.

His almond scented breath hit my face as he yanked me to him. The cloying taste invaded my mouth as his tongue slipped between my lips.

Panic jolted through me so violently, my mind blanked for a moment. Darkness rushed in. Pressed against the door, I had no way to escape. I jerked my head sideways, breaking the kiss with a smacking sound of his lips disconnecting from mine.

"Don't." I said firmly, my pulse echoing in my ears with the power of a cannon.

"Well, since you're not coming to me—" he started, but I didn't let him say whatever twisted reasoning he'd conjured up as an excuse.

Bending my leg, I kicked up, hitting him in the crotch as hard as I could manage in this position.

He coughed a breath and doubled over, his hands cupping his cock.

Using the moment, I jumped aside and scurried behind the couch for safety.

"Why did you do it?" he groaned, staggering to the couch, then falling backwards on it with a tortured moan.

"I could ask you the same question." I panted hard, my heart beating high in my throat somewhere. "Only I think I already know the answer. Did your aunt put you up to this?"

"No." He rolled his head on the couch, tousling his golden curls. "But she is getting very impatient too."

I took another step to the side, making sure to keep the back of the couch solidly between us.

"I thought we had an understanding, Leafar. I thought you agreed with me when I asked you to wait."

"But how long can we wait?" he moaned. "If nothing happens, my aunt has already arranged for a public consummation next week." He looked up at me from the couch, his handsome features crumbling in misery. "As a woman, you may not care about it as much as I do. But men have an inherent modesty, and it's just..." he whimpered. "If I'm forced to go through it publicly, the shame would consume me."

Desperation brought him into my room tonight. But it didn't need to be that way.

"Leafar, it doesn't have to come to that. Your aunt is not in this room with us. You can sleep in my bed. I'll take the couch. In the morning, no one will have to know what happened or didn't happen between us at night."

He blinked at me in bewilderment.

"You want me to lie to my family and to the rest of the world?"

I released a breath, feeling deflated.

"No... Of course not. I don't want you to lie..."

There were way too many candles in the room. The air felt hot and stifling, but I didn't trust to turn my back to him even for the few seconds I needed to open the patio doors.

Leafar let go of his crotch and sat up sideways on the couch.

I took a step back, keeping a safe distance from him.

He ran a hand over his hair, then tugged at the collar of his shirt.

"You know that my father..." he said. "I mean my real father, not the current King Consort of Olakrez... My father was executed for treason. That was the official verdict. But the true reason for his execution has always been the royal court's worst kept secret. I knew the truth, even as a child." His fingers found the button of his shirt next, twisting it right and left. "The queen met her current husband years after being married to my father. Divorce doesn't exist in Olakrez. The servant who testified against my father came into a large amount of money right after, then died under mysterious circumstances. And the queen... the queen married her lover a week after my father's death." He turned to face me, resting his hand with the wedding ring on the back of the couch. "My father died because my mother, the queen, didn't desire him anymore."

I could only imagine what it felt like for him to be thrust into all those intrigues at such a young age. Fear must've been with him ever since.

"It will never happen to you," I said with conviction and tipped my chin at his hand. "With that ring, I promised you my protection. No one will ever hurt you here, Leafar."

"Yet you don't want me." His lips quivered. The corners of his mouth turned down in a tragic expression. "By the time my father was my age, he'd already given the queen two children, but even that didn't save him. What chance do I have if your attention wanders elsewhere? If even my youth and good looks aren't enough to ignite your desires?"

"Listen, frankly...I hardly even have any special desires to ignite..." I shook my head. "Leafar, you're not your father. And I'm certainly not your mother. I married you for life, with every intention of our marriage to be successful. But one thing for sure won't help. Cornering me here the way you did, forcing a kiss on me was a very wrong way to go about it."

What he did tonight felt like a huge step back in the development of any kind of intimacy between us. His presence in my room made my skin crawl with unease now.

He looked at me with confusion. "They said that powerful women like being dominated in private sometimes. That if I made the first step, it might excite you enough to...well, to go ahead with the consummation."

"Who said that?"

He scratched his head. "Some of my gentlemen-in-waiting."

"Oh, Leafar." I ran a hand down my face. "Why don't you just ask me instead? Why would you rather solicit random advice from anyone else? Especially about a private matter like this?"

"But you're always busy."

True, I hadn't made it easy for him to find the time to ask. It'd be extremely difficult to catch me between all my events and meetings, even if he'd tried. While I was running around all day, trying to get double of my usual amount of work done, Leafar had nothing to do in the palace. He spent his days fretting about sex or about the lack of it, with the added pressure from all his family and friends who urged him to do something about it.

"I'm sorry," I admitted. "Trust me, I fear the public consummation just as much as you do. I should've found the time to talk to you. I've been incredibly busy, but I should've made the time, anyway. You see..." I owed him at least the courtesy of an explanation. "The advice you got may very well work for some women. With me, however, aggression is a very wrong approach. It terrifies me."

"*I* terrify *you?*" His mouth fell open in shock.

"When you acted the way you did tonight, yes. You scared me."

"But... No." His breath hitched. His face paled. He clung with both hands to the back of the couch. "Your Highness, please... This wasn't an assault. I didn't mean to..."

And now, he clearly feared I'd have him executed for assaulting me.

"Please, calm down." I sighed. "You have nothing to fear. I

promised I wouldn't hurt you. I certainly will never hold your inexperience against you." If there was any chance left for us to rebuild the trust and grow closer, I felt I should start by being honest with him, too, like he'd been with me. "You know I came to Rorrim when I was sixteen. But I didn't just appear out of nowhere. I was born and raised in another world, in a very different one than this one. In my old world, men are usually the ones in power."

His eyes grew bigger as he took my words in.

"Men are in power?" He tilted his head, looking intrigued by such a concept. "But how can it be? Men are not the creators of life like the Great Goddess. Women are."

"Well, the ideology behind it can be twisted either way, even to the point of justifying all sorts of abuse." I clasped my hands in front of me, holding his gaze. "Leafar, I want you to know that I'm not a stranger to fear and pain. I know what it feels like to fear for your life. When I was still a child, before coming here, I was forced to do things against my will... including sexual things. My sense of safety has been compromised, and it often feels like it's been broken irreparably. I don't know if my apprehension regarding sex results from that now, but it's difficult for me to get close to a man or to have sex simply for the sake of sex. I will need a little patience and understanding from you. Please?"

He sat in silence for a moment.

"What is this world that you came from?"

"Does it really matter?" I asked, a little confused by his reaction.

He blinked, smoothing down his hair.

"No. I suppose it does not." He got up from the couch.

"Would you like to spend the day together tomorrow?" I offered.

"A whole day?"

"Well, I have some meetings scheduled, but we can have breakfast and lunch together. I may even find some time for a brief walk in the gardens. Just you and me."

"If you sleep with me tonight, we can have breakfast in bed tomorrow," he pushed.

I refused to leave my safe place behind the couch. Now that my mind had placed Leafar as an aggressor, I couldn't relax in his presence again. Even my offer for him to sleep in my bed while I took the couch no longer seemed viable. My skin prickled with impatience as I waited for him to get out of my personal space.

It was a setback. But I clung to the hope that we could still fix it and move past it together.

"I'd rather have breakfast served on the patio downstairs," I suggested. "It offers such a lovely view of the gardens."

"I'll think about it." He headed for the door, his bottom lip pushed out in that petulant, childish expression of his.

"Or we could go to the games together." I wouldn't give up on trying to save the situation. "Father wishes to see the games if he's feeling better. You can come with us. Would you like to see the games?"

"Maybe." He pushed the door open. "Don't bother escorting me to my rooms, Your Highness. My perfect reputation is beginning to feel more like a burden, anyway."

He left, slamming the door a little harder than was necessary.

Struggling to breathe, I rushed to the patio doors and swung them wide open. The cool night air rushed in, blowing out the candle flames.

I felt many things at once—frustrated with Leafar, angry at the people in his party who kept adding pressure to our already complicated relationship.

But most of all, I felt disappointed and even disgusted with myself, because as my upset husband had just stormed out of my room, instead of rushing after him to try smoothing the things out between us, I stared at the hedge deep in the palace gardens. It hid the stables from view that once served as slaves' barracks.

Eighteen

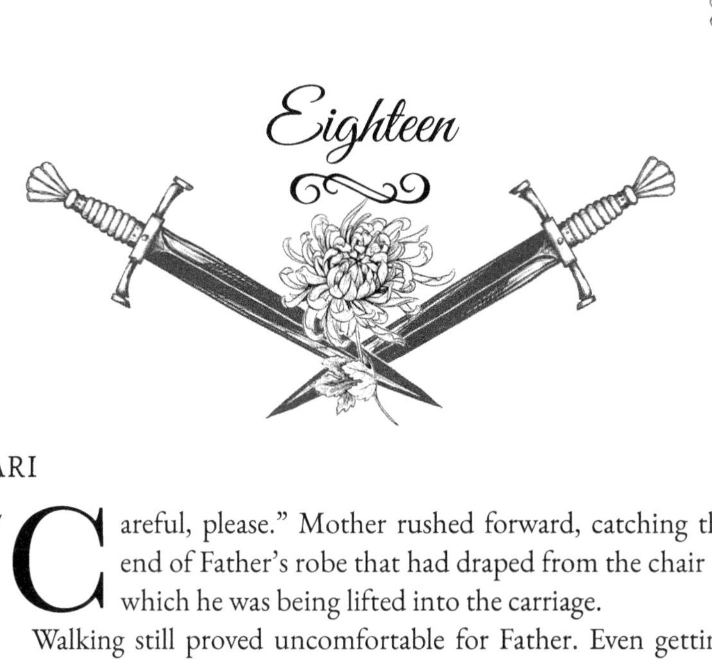

ARI

"Careful, please." Mother rushed forward, catching the end of Father's robe that had draped from the chair in which he was being lifted into the carriage.

Walking still proved uncomfortable for Father. Even getting up from bed left him exhausted and panting for breath. But he insisted on coming to the games today.

"It was almost worth getting hurt," he chuckled, "to have Your Majesty fuss over me all this time."

Mother shook her head. "You should thank Ari for taking over most of my responsibilities. I wouldn't have been able to spend this much time with you otherwise."

Father grinned at me through the open door of the carriage where one of the seats had been removed to accommodate his chair.

"Thank you, sweetie. I'm immensely enjoying the queen's undivided attention every day."

"Just try not to get hurt again, please," I retorted. "If you want to spend more time with Mother, just ask me to free some of her time for you in the future. There is no need to throw yourself under a horse again. Deal?"

He laughed, making a smile tug on my lips in response.

As Mother climbed into the carriage after Father, I walked over to the one I was to share with my husband.

Leafar was already there.

"Morning," I said, taking the seat opposite from him.

"Good morning, Your Highness." He fluffed a cuff of his frilled shirt. The sunlight sparkled in the diamonds and rubies of his new cufflinks.

On Mother's suggestion, I bought the cufflinks and had them delivered to the prince's rooms with a note of apology. I had a hard time finding the words to explain what exactly I was apologizing for. Kicking him out of my bedroom? Delaying the consummation? Marrying him while having feelings I shouldn't have for another man?

As determined as I was to be honest with Leafar, I couldn't tell him about Salas. With his secret past, Salas's situation remained vulnerable, and his secrets were not mine to tell.

Writing the note and giving the cufflinks to Leafar did little to assuage my guilt, but Leafar seemed to enjoy his new jewelry. Stroking the precious stones fondly, he turned his wrist to make the sun play in the brilliant facets.

"Do you like the cufflinks?" I asked as the carriage moved.

He pouted, but far less sulkily than before.

"Yes. They're lovely," he said, demurely folding his hands in his lap. "Your apology was a move in the right direction. The next right step would've been visiting my bedroom last night."

I hated the almost-forgotten feeling of hopelessness that spread inside me at his words. But even more, I hated that it was my own husband who made me feel this way. Though, I managed to stop short of hating him.

Leafar had done everything that was expected from him all his life. Understandably, he expected certain things to happen in return.

"The prized mare of Prince Elbon of Tresed Queendom had a male foal last week," he said unexpectedly.

"Um... Congratulations?" I offered, unsure of how to react to that news.

"With the foul's lineage, he's expected to grow into the champion stallion of the world."

"I suppose he is," I humored him.

What did the mare and her baby have to do with anything right now?

"There is a line of buyers forming already, with the auction starting soon. Since I was forced to leave most of my horses back in Olakrez, I was wondering if Your Highness would be so kind as to put a bid in for me." He tilted his head with a sweet smile on his lips. "It'd be a great way to start a new collection for me."

I'd never bought a horse before. Acquiring them fell under Father's responsibilities. Revlis had been my first and only horse, and even she came to the royal stables long before I started taking horseback riding lessons.

"I'll see what I can do," I replied uncertainly.

The smile slipped from the prince's face, and I feared no amount of diamond cufflinks would put it back there anytime soon.

"My aunt is leaving two days after Queen Anna's ball," he said gravely. "The...um, consummation is arranged for the day after the ball."

With a deep sigh, I ran a hand down my face. The grand duchess insisted on having her nephew fucked by his wife before she left. Publicly, if it had to be.

"I'll talk to her," I promised.

"Don't..." Leafar leaned to me, grabbing my hand. "Please don't aggravate her even more."

"Well, I find it extremely aggravating that she keeps meddling in our marriage."

"She... she cares about me. She wants our marriage to succeed, which I fear is not what you want, Your Highness." He glared at me with an added emphasis in his voice.

"Why would you say that? Of course I care."

"Do you? Really?" His voice rose even higher. "Ever since our wedding, you've been avoiding me and my bedroom."

"That's not true. I have invited you to spend time with me on many occasions." I kept my voice and my temper down, mindful of the coachwoman in the front and the footwomen at the back of the carriage. They couldn't see us, but they would hear the argument if we spoke loudly enough. The whispers about our marital troubles would spread through the palace before we'd even return to the palace.

"None of those occasions included an invitation to your bed," Leafar snapped.

"Is sex the only thing that matters?"

He leaned even closer, staring me down.

"At this moment," he hissed through his teeth with force, "for this marriage to be valid, yes, sex is the most important thing that needs to happen."

I kept my back straight, refusing to cower, but my composure wavered in the face of his aggression. Alarm stirred my anxiety, urging me to flee, but I forced myself not to move.

Anger seemed like a perfect weapon to combat fear. I could let it loose and lash out, but I reined it in. Taking a deep breath in, I clasped my hands and counted my heartbeats until their pounding in my head subsided.

"You married me out of fear of your mother, Leafar, and to please your aunt," I said calmly. "Both are very wrong reasons to tie your life to a stranger."

He huffed in my face.

"What were your reasons for marrying me, Your Highness?"

A white-hot whip of anger slashed through me, but his question was valid.

Morally, I held no higher ground over Leafar. My reasons for marrying gave me no right to look down at him. I married to gain a political advantage for Rorrim and to grow my power in council.

"Why did you even propose to me if you refuse to have me now?" His bottom lip slipped out in that spoiled kid expression that I found rather irritating.

But Leafar was right, I had proposed to him. I'd chosen him over every other man in this world to be my husband. And within days, our marriage was already unraveling.

Guilt twisted painfully in my chest. I had to put more effort into making this work.

Swallowing my anger and irritation, I attempted a peace offering. "I... I can find a few minutes this afternoon. Would you like to have tea with me? I'll have it served on the main patio downstairs. It's a lovely day. You can finally meet my dog. Ria. She's the cutest."

I smiled. If only he would smile back at me to complete this thin, shaky bridge of a connection I tried to construct between us.

Sadly, his sulky expression deepened.

"The place where you should meet me is in my bedroom." He turned away from me and opened the window of the carriage, which effectively ended our conversation, since with the window open, everyone outside the carriage could hear us.

The smile slowly died on my lips.

Leafar felt scared, and he blamed me for it. By rejecting my every attempt at reconciliation, he thought he was punishing me for not letting him have his way. It was childish from him. But Leafar hadn't been an adult for that long yet. In this relationship, I was the mature one.

My frustration with Leafar bubbled into anger against his family. They had molded him into a shape that suited them, and they never stopped pressuring and intimidating him even now when he was a married man.

The urge to turn this carriage around and march into the grand duchess's room right now to demand she stop intimidating her nephew burned through me. The only thing that stopped me was Leafar's plea not to antagonize his aunt. He knew her better than I did and had a better idea about how far her vindictiveness could go. I couldn't risk her delaying her departure for Olalrez. No one would win from that.

I had to think of a diplomatic approach to deal with the duchess, one that wouldn't inadvertently hurt Leafar or deteriorate our relationship with Olakrez to the point of war.

A part of me wished I could just go to his bedroom tonight, take his clothes off, and do what everyone wanted me to do, even if all of them watched if they so wished.

But even if I were capable of such an action, any intimacy between Leafar and me felt unthinkable now. The pressure had grown into coercion and manipulation, killing whatever feelings I could've had for him as a man and a partner. If I attempted sex with him now, I feared I'd break down again, like I did that night with Salas. Except that this time, there wouldn't be the circle of Salas's supportive arms to help me become whole again. There'd be no safety of his understanding, either.

Fear crushed me at the thought of being vulnerable in front of people who might mock me for my weakness. I had no trust in Leafar and didn't count on his support. With him, I had to be the strong one. His respect for me depended on my showing no weaknesses. And without his respect, I feared that our marriage would not survive.

In the days since our wedding, I'd hoped Leafar and I would grow closer. I never expected us to drift even further apart. We were no longer strangers. But the more I got to know him, the less I felt connected to him in any way.

THE ROAD TO THE GLADIATORS' Games Arena was decorated with banners hanging from every streetlight along the way. And on every one of those banners was a picture of Salas.

In all the pictures, he was wearing his costume of the fur cape and the crudely constructed helmet with animal horns and thick rivets. The visor of the helmet concealed most of his face, leaving only a feral scowl of white teeth framed by his wild beard. His eyes in the slits of the visor were replaced by a red glow, further making him appear like a wild beast or some manic demon on the loose.

Through the open window of the carriage, the clamor of the people on the road to the arena reached Leafar and me.

Children jumped around one of the streetlight poles, pointing at the picture of the Mountain Bear on the banner.

"I want to be just like Bear when I grow up." A boy hopped on one foot around the pole.

His father took his hand, stirring him to follow the rest of their family. "You'd better eat all your dinner every day then, to grow as big as he is. Did you see how big Bear is?"

"And strong," another boy said from a group of people walking along. "He fought against a hundred men last week and won!"

"He's stronger than any man," a girl chimed in from the road up ahead. "He fights bears and tigers. He wrestled a sword-toothed alligator last week, and I heard he's going to fight a dragon today."

A dragon?

The games master claimed to have the three-winged dragons in her possession, but I haven't heard of her using them in any of the shows yet.

Also, gladiators usually performed the same act for a few weeks, slowly rotating a few over a year to keep things entertaining. The games master clearly used a different approach with Salas, throwing everything from men to beasts into his acts.

It had only been about a month since I'd last been to the games, but Salas's fame had soared.

The pictures of him were everywhere around the arena too, as well as inside it. Many in the crowd wore animal furs and replicas of his helmet, chanting his name so loud, the music drowned in the noise.

As Father's chair was placed on the royal platform and Mother took her seat next to him, Leafar and I sat to the right side of the royal couple.

"Now I wish we came here last week too," Leafar said, leaning to me. "If this gladiator really is so good, we've been missing out."

I came here for my father and to spend some quality time with my husband. However, apprehension pulsed through me. The last time I'd come here, I watched Salas getting hurt. I didn't want to see that again.

From the rows behind us, a court lady all but moaned. "Goddess, I've been trying to see him in private for weeks now. The games master said he hardly makes himself available to anyone and is already fully booked for months to come. Is there any way to get into the master's good graces and speed things up? I've already made a generous donation for the upkeep of the boys, but she wouldn't budge."

"Do you really want to be alone with that beast?" another woman gasped. "Have you seen him crushing rocks with his bare hands last week? He'd tear you to pieces before you even make it to his bed."

"Does he even have a bed?" someone wondered out loud. "Or does the games master keep him in a cage day and night?"

"Actually, I've heard he's fairly tame outside of the arena," another woman said. "Countess Ciryl claims she's been domesticating him through music."

"Oh, no, I don't want him domesticated," the first lady protested. "I want him to ravage me in all his wild, untamed glory. I'd take him covered in blood and rolled in the arena sand." She sighed wistfully. "If only the games master let me have him for a night or two."

I was glad when the music surged higher and the chatting behind us finally stopped.

Acrobats bounced into the arena. Jumping and flipping in the air while holding long strips of sheer, colorful material, they created a weave of movement and color in ever-changing fantastic patterns.

The crowd's enthusiasm swelled as the gladiators entered the arena. They marched around it, and I counted forty-eight muscular bodies. Salas was not among them.

The weave of multi-colored scarves parted in the middle, and his cage rose from the sand. The man-beast character that Salas portrayed so well raged behind the thick bars. His growls overpowered both the music and the noise of the crowd.

As warmly as the crowd had welcomed their queen and king earlier, they seemed to have lost all restraint when greeting their favorite.

People screamed, clapped, and cheered. They stomped their feet and tossed their helmets into the air. Bouquets of flowers flew to the arena, with precious gems attached to them glistening in the sun. All of it happened before Salas had even left his cage.

For a moment, he stilled completely, staring in my direction, and my heart stilled too. I lifted a hand from the armrest of my chair in a small wave. He lowered his head with a deep rumble through his chest, playing the part of the beast.

A pair of swords criss-crossed his back, and I wondered if those were the ones he'd created himself. Drawing them out, he lifted them above his head, and the crowd quieted in anticipation.

Salas dragged his swords across the bars of his cage, eliciting a powerful melody that mimicked the music played by the horns and drums of the orchestra. I smiled. Countess Ciryl had finally taught him to play an instrument, only the instrument was the cage.

The crowd's enthusiasm exploded with excitement. The chants of Salas's arena name rose high into the sky.

Leafar covered his ears with his hands.

"They're exceptionally loud today," he complained.

They were. And I reveled in their adoration of the man who deserved every drop of it. He played the crowd well, conducting their delight as if it were a powerful orchestra of clapping and cheers instead of instruments.

Even after the cage and the man-beast inside it slid back into the floor of the arena, the chanting of his name didn't quiet down. It rolled and undulated over the crowd that demanded to see their hero again. The pull in my chest resonated with the crowd's demands. I missed him too, the moment he was gone.

"Why did they put him away?" Leafar wondered as the gladiators exited the arena and a set of props appeared for the first act of the show.

I leaned back in my chair, summoning patience. "The games master must be saving the best for last."

Nineteen

SALAS

Deep in the bowels of the elaborate web of tunnels under the arena, I sat on the floor of the cage with my back pressed against the bars.

An energetic staccato of heels clicking against the stone floor came from one of the tunnels. Then Lerrel emerged, carrying a metal mug.

"They liked your swordplay." She grinned, crouching by the cage to hand me the mug through the bars.

"It looks like they did." I'd finally finished my swords, and they turned out functional and quite musical.

"We're sold out for the rest of the year. Can you believe it? Every single ticket is gone. I'm trying to figure out how to add a few more rows of seating. Maybe at the top?"

"As long as it's still safe. Not too high." I took a sip of water from the mug. All that roaring and growling I did in the arena dried my throat.

"Right. We may have to rethink your dragon act if we put seats that high. But isn't it exciting?" She jerked her head, tousling her curls. "So many people want to see you! The royal couple is here too today. Two royal couples, actually. The princess and her new husband came along as well."

Her husband.

The word scraped at my hearing. I struggled to accept the fact that Ari was a married woman now.

The last time I saw her, it felt like no time had passed and nothing between us changed when so many changes had happened lately. Every moment we were together, both in my room and later in the carriage, I had to remind myself she wasn't mine. I had no right to hold her hand, to wish to kiss her, or to remember how it felt to hold her naked body in my arms. Yet those were the memories I'd cherish to my grave.

"Well..." Lerrel got up to her feet. "Are you sure you want to stay here until it's your turn?"

"Yes. I may as well." I took another sip of water.

Metal chains rattled through the tunnels, pulling props up or down for the next act in the arena above.

"Suit yourself. I should go check how it's going up there. Do you need me to send someone down here to bring you anything?"

"No. Thanks. I'm good."

My act was the last one in the games, and I liked having this time of peace and quiet to calm my nerves and collect my thoughts before the performance. Because that was what all of it was—a performance. Even when gladiators got injured, even if they died, ultimately, it was all about how it all looked for the audience.

And tonight, Ari was in the audience too.

Lerrel didn't need to tell me that. I knew the princess was here. Every time the cage rose from the ground, the royal sitting platform was the first thing I looked at. For the past four weeks, it remained empty. But today, she was there, dressed in a shimmering, pale-blue gown, like a fairy princess surrounded by the colorful royal court which now also included her husband.

When I saw them together the last time, the day we brought Rotcod to the palace, the prince came out, but Ari didn't kiss him in greeting. She didn't take his hand. She didn't look at him the way she looked at me, like I was the only person in the world and no one else mattered.

It was no wonder that when she felt scared and vulnerable, she didn't come to him to cry on his chest. She came to me.

"I don't deserve you," the princess had said to a fallen man.

My sense of self-worth had changed over the years. One couldn't live in a society and be completely unaffected by its judgment. When I was younger, the slurs and curses people tossed my way hurt more. As I grew older, my skin grew thicker, better protecting me from the darts of scorn and hate.

However, I never thought of myself as worthless, not even when I was told I didn't deserve to be alive. Even in my darkest days, I always believed that everyone's life was worth living, even the life like mine.

Until that day, however, no woman had ever told me she didn't deserve me. Ari's words kept echoing in my head, resonating through my chest with feelings I knew I shouldn't allow myself to have.

In the orchestrated rumbling and clanking of metal that filled the tunnels, I recognized the hissing of receding lava that came at the end of Falo's act.

Mine was next.

Doing a new act was always nerve-racking. But we'd practiced it enough times for it to go well. I just needed to focus and stick with the script.

I set the mug on the floor outside of the cage. Fixed the helmet on my head and got up.

The floor of my cage shook. The trap door above my head opened, momentarily blinding me with sunlight. The noise of the crowd embraced me as the cage rose to the surface.

I played my part, growling and lunging at the bars until they were lowered, setting me free.

Lerrel took the idea for my newest act from the extensive lore about the Great Goddess's children who defeated the legions of monstrous demons that plagued our world at the beginning of times.

According to the legend, the demons captured Nus's daughter, the Goddess of Governance, and chained her to the top of a mountain for dragons to tear her apart. However, her sisters killed the dragons and rescued her.

Lerrel decided to give the story an unexpected twist by having a wild mountain man rescue the goddess. The games master hoped that the audience would find the unique premise of a man rescuing a woman fresh, entertaining, and fun.

My cage delivered me to the north end of the oval arena. In the south end, the mob of the terrifying monster-demons were already dragging Nave, the actress hired to portray the Goddess of Governance, up a prop mountain.

Nave was wearing a costume designed as ancient armor and looked like she was fresh out of a battle. Her breast plate was dented and scratched, her arm splattered with blood-red paint, and her helmet and sword were missing.

I was supposed to ignore her struggle for now. The savage man I played had to hunt for his dinner first.

Paying no attention to the demon-monsters and the goddess, I went about the prop forest, looking for Daisy, the unicorn goat, that I had to catch for the amusement of the crowd.

Like she was trained to do, Daisy peacefully grazed on a patch of grass behind a brook with a waterfall. I approached her in a crouch from behind and launched for her, but tripped on my bear cape and fell.

Instead of jumping up right away, I stretched on my belly and grabbed her by her hind legs.

The goat bleated, jerking her legs. She turned her head, trying to reach me with the long horn that grew in the middle of her forehead.

I kicked my feet, pretending the struggle was harder than it actually was.

The crowd laughed and cheered. People shouted advice about how best to tackle the goat.

My fall had been accidental, but the rest of it was not. The sound of laughter felt just as rewarding to me as the screams of adoration. It meant people had fun.

The gladiators often took what we did too seriously. They aimed for the image of a perfect, infallible hero without a single fault, which was hard to attain and even more difficult to maintain.

Lerrel often said that there was nothing more lethal for entertainment than boredom, and I discovered that the crowd responded well to an occasional mistake, as long as the mistake was entertaining.

I made it look like Daisy was winning by letting her go, then recapturing her to the utter delight of the crowd. Finally, I hauled her on my shoulders and stomped into the nearest cave.

Inside the cave, a pile of goat bones waited for me with a collar and a leash attached to a ring in the floor, and a carrot.

I put the collar on Daisy. She bleated one more time before I gave her the carrot and knocked on the floor. A trapdoor opened to below, and the goat safely descended to her handlers under the arena floor. I tossed the goat bones out of the cage, as the proof to the crowd that Daisy had met her untimely end as my dinner.

Some in the audience gasped. Others shouted and cheered. But overall, everyone seemed to have a good time, which was all that mattered.

Now came the hard part.

A vibration through the ground signaled the gears were turning, opening the tunnels for the giant fire-breathing worms.

Each worm was about as thick as me and about twice as long. Their proportions made them look more like huge maggots than worms. Pale and blind, they spent most of their long lives underground in the marsh along the shore of the Western Islands, causing no harm unless forced out into the open. If disturbed, however, they spewed fire.

Lerrel had mechanisms to pull the chains through the tunnels below to irritate the worms by bringing them to the surface at certain intervals. She had also marked the openings to the tunnels for me and the others to see where the danger might come from.

The first opening was right in front of the cave. I had to get out or I'd get fried.

I rushed out, and the fire blasted behind me, spurring me forward. Another burst of hot air and flames exploded to my right.

Short blue posts marked the openings in the sand. They weren't easy to spot unless one was looking for them, but the sand over the opening formed a shallow funnel. I noted both the posts and the funnels, then headed toward the mountain with Nave chained at the top.

For the audience, it looked like the wild man was escaping the fire explosions bursting from the sand and came to the mountain for a refuge, then spotted the goddess.

Most of the monster-demons had left already. The few that remained tried to fight me, but I threw them off the mountain quickly enough, unstoppable on my way to the goddess.

Of course, the goddess was supposed to be appalled by my unkempt appearance, and Nave acted that part perfectly.

At the opposite end of the arena, gates opened, releasing the three-winged dragon.

He was a magnificent creature with shimmering royal-blue scales that shone with silver in the sunlight. Massive, the size of about six horses, he soared over the arena, his powerful wings whipping the fire of the worms into an inferno.

"Holy mother of gods." Nave paled.

"It's fine. Lerrel is in control," I assured her quietly, climbing up to her.

The games master stood at the foot of the mountain, hidden from the audience by a prop boulder. She held onto a transparent cord. It was thin but strong, infused by magic, unseen to anyone who didn't know about its existence. One end of the cord was tied to a massive ring in the arena's floor. The other end was secured to the dragon's foot. He lurched higher, but Lerrel jerked on the cord, stopping him from getting away.

Staying in character, I growled and bit with my teeth at the knot of the rope that tied Nave's hands to the mountain. I had two swords on my back, but Lerrel thought untying the rope with my teeth would be more entertaining. She was right, as the noise of the crowd surged when Mountain Bear snarled, bit, and gnawed on the rope—wild and unhinged.

The dragon roared and spewed a burst of fire up into the sky, to the screams of awe from the crowd.

Unlike the orange-red flames of the fire worms, the dragon's fire was bluish white, casting a moon-like glow down onto the arena.

"Open the mirror," I urged Nave, who seemed to freeze in shock, her eyes fixed on the magnificent creature soaring above.

The small mirror on her shoulder was obscured by the remnants of her cape on purpose. She was supposed to reveal it after the dragon's dramatic entrance to make him fly to us. The reflection of sunlight in Nave's mirror would attract the dragon, mimicking the glistening of the mirror trout in the streams of the dragon's native Ekans Isles. The trout was the preferred food of the three-winged dragons, and they hunted it from the air by spotting the sun reflecting on the fish scales in the water.

Once the dragon would come closer, I was supposed to catch its tail. Lerrel then would tug onto the cord again, sending the dragon into a tailspin. He'd roll in the arena, and I'd tackle its third wing, preventing him from rising back into the air. That was the plan.

The dragon beat its wings over the arena, fanning the fire of the worms and raising clouds of sand. His third wing bellowed like an iridescent sail above his back. It helped the creature navigate in the air, allowing the massive animal to make sharp, tight turns during the flight.

Lerrel pulled on the cord. The dragon lurched to the side. He roared, blowing fire and frantically beating his wings.

The games master suddenly dropped her arms. Alarm replaced the calm concentration on her face. She tugged at the barely visible cord, gathering it into a coil with no resistance.

Unrestrained, the dragon soared higher.

"It got loose," Nave gasped. The rope had long slipped from her wrists, only her legs remained tied to the mountain.

"Open the mirror, Nave!" I growled through my teeth, tugging at the knot next to her ankles.

She reached for the shredded remnants of the cape over the mirror on her shoulder.

"Why?" She hesitated, a wave of reflection running through her skin and clothes. "I don't want him here now. He'll kill us."

I couldn't blame her for refusing to be the bait for the unchained beast. The dragon flew in jerky uncoordinated loops over the arena before spiraling downward.

The audience screamed. Those who still believed this was all a part of the show shouted in excitement. The few who'd realized that something was wrong screamed in horror, ducking in the wind raised by the dragon's massive wings.

A blast of white-blue fire set aflame the queen's banners over the top row of seating. Horror spread through the crowd.

Nave grabbed one of my swords from my back.

"Mirror, Nave!" I yelled as the dragon dipped lower over the seats. "Just bring him over here. I'll deal with him."

With trembling fingers, she fumbled with the rags over her shoulder as people screamed for help. The dragon zoomed over the rows of seating.

Then, I saw what the dragon must've spotted too—the royal platform glistened with the sea of gems, diamonds, and shiny fabrics with golden embroidery. The long train of Ari's gown draped down the stairs like a waterfall of precious stones. As she turned, the sun reflected in the lenses of her eyeglasses, just as it would've in Nave's mirror.

"Ari! Run!" I yelled at the top of my lungs.

Over the hissing fire of the worms, the screams of the crowd, and the dragon's roar, she didn't hear me.

Frantically tearing the rags away, Nave finally exposed the mirror to the sunlight.

"He isn't looking here!" she shouted in panic.

The dragon had already turned his back to us, taking the course to the royal platform.

I drew my remaining sword out and slashed through the ropes around Nave's legs.

"Come. Now."

I scrambled down the mountain as Nave followed. Normally, she wouldn't have come down until the very end of the show. There hadn't been the need for her to learn how to move safely across the arena with the worm fires bursting out.

"Fuck!" she squeaked, shrinking from a blast to our left.

"Stay close." I maneuvered between the shallow craters in the sand, running but wishing I could fly faster than a dragon.

The three-winged beast headed for the royal platform. The guards rushed to help the queen and the king, who remained in his chair. They lifted him with the chair and carried him down the stairs. The prince ran after them. Ari followed, but her focus was on the arena.

Through the patches of smoke and fire, our eyes met.

"Run!" I begged. "Run, Ari!"

Even if she could hear me, she had nowhere to run. People rushed to the exit ahead of her. The guards carrying the king were in the way, blocking the stairs.

Several gladiators, led by Noil, headed to us from the fringes of the arena.

"That way." I gave Nave a little shove toward the path between the two short blue posts in the ground that would lead her to Noil. "Stay between the posts."

"But where are you going?" she shrieked.

I had no time to answer.

The princess was trapped.

And the dragon was already there.

Ari ducked, shielding her face with her arm. He sank his claws into her shoulders, plucking her off the stairs.

"Ari!" I sprinted toward the stairs as if my life depended on it, because it did. I could no longer imagine life in the world without Ari.

Leaping over the barrier, I jumped up the rows of seats already vacated by the panicked public.

Wind churned under the mighty wings of the dragon. He flew over me, rising higher and higher, with my princess in his claws.

"Ari! No!"

"Salas!" she cried out in terror.

The long trail of her dress swept above me, like a shimmering sail billowing in the wind. I jumped and grabbed onto it.

The dragon roared, lurching to the side. A mirror trout was a big fish, but not nearly as big as a person. The three-winged dragons were known to carry away a sheep or even a small child occasionally. But the combined weight of the princess and me was likely close to that of a real mountain bear.

It proved too much for the dragon. With a roar, it tried to adjust its grip on Ari but ended up letting her go.

I hit the ground and rolled all the way to the waterfall. As I scrambled to my feet to catch her, she fell into the pond with a splash.

"Ari?" I dragged her out of the water and leaned over her. "Are you hurt?"

It was a stupid question. Her gown was ripped on her shoulders. The dragon's claws left deep gauges in her flesh. Water sluiced down her skin, mixing with blood and soaking the shredded fabric.

"Salas..." Her eyes opened wide behind her glasses. "What happened? What did you do?"

I held her face in my hands. "I made you fall."

Terror melted away from her expression as she ran her gaze over my face.

"That you did," she breathed out. "I have fallen. Hopelessly."

I didn't dare to believe the true meaning of her words.

The sand shifted around her head, and I realized with horror that we lay right in the middle of the opening to the worm tunnels.

"Move!" I rolled to my side, taking Ari with me and shielding her from the worm's round toothless mouth poking from the sand.

Fire blasted from the worm's mouth, scorching the bear hide on my back. Pungent smoke enveloped us.

The dragon had made a tight loop in the air and was now coming back for us.

"Come." I sat up, helping Ari up as well. "We need to get out of here."

"Your cape is burning." She tore at the bear hide frantically. "Take it off."

I opened the buckle on my left shoulder. Coughing from the stench of the burning fur, Ari opened the right buckle for me. We tossed the hide into the pond, where it spattered and hissed in the water on its way down.

The dragon lowered his head on the approach. A worm spewed a spray of flames in his path, and the dragon lurched away. As a fire breathing creature himself, he clearly disliked the flames of others.

I grabbed Ari's arm.

"Come."

She pulled the train of her dress out of the pond, and I helped her gather it all. We only made a couple of steps before the dragon straightened his course, aimed his head at us, and closed his eyes.

"He's going to—" I tried to warn Ari. But there was no escaping the bright blue flame that rushed out of the dragon's mouth toward us.

"Down!" Ari shoved an elbow into my side. I dropped to my

knees, and she tossed the water-soaked train of her dress over us both.

The fabric steamed in the fire. Hot air scorched my lungs. Ari coughed, tossing the train back. The dragon had passed, and we were still alive.

"Smart." I tipped my chin at the scorched fabric of her train that had saved us.

"Thanks." She beamed, climbing to her feet.

The dragon appeared to be momentarily distracted by the screaming crowd rushing to the exits. He blew fire, setting aflame the empty top seats. But he might turn back any minute. I had to get Ari to safety.

I'd lost the advantage of the high ground of the mountain where I was supposed to catch the dragon's tail. Even when the dragon had attacked us, he remained too high for me to reach.

"We have to go," I said.

Ari made a move toward the exit from the arena, but I stopped her.

"The worms." Fire blasted from the ground where she was about to step. "Watch for the blue markers." I tapped a post with my boot.

She nodded, following me between the markers along the safe path. "I was wondering how you do it."

"You watched me?" Thousands of spectators who came to the show watched me every week. But the fact that Ari was one of them was the most important.

"When you're in the arena, I don't watch anyone else," she confessed, running a hand over the scars on my arm. "Though it costs me years of my life when I see you get hurt."

"This time, it was you who got hurt."

The deep scratches bled on her shoulders. It was my fault. I failed to keep her safe. Guilt and worry burned through my chest and tied my stomach into knots. No one had assigned to me the task of protecting the princess, but her safety and her happiness had become my mission. And I failed.

"Careful." I hugged her to me, yanking her away from the path of yet another fire blast.

Led by Lerrel, the gladiators were running toward us from the opposite end of the arena. The royal guards tried to make their way to us from the left. They were closer to us than the gladiators, but the fire breathing worms kept them at bay.

Why were the worms still here? Why didn't Lerrel order to close the tunnels? I feared something must've gone terribly wrong, not only allowing the dragon to get loose but also blocking the mechanisms inside the arena.

Cutting off the gladiators on their way to our rescue, the dragon soared toward us again. The guards raised their crossbows, but their arrows bounced off the dragon's scales, leaving the creature unharmed.

Nothing could stop him.

Ari gathered her train again, but scorched and tattered, it was no longer wet enough to hold back the dragon's fire.

I stepped in front of her, shielding her with my body.

"Salas. No." She gripped my arm, but I didn't know how else to protect her.

We were trapped on a small patch of sand, surrounded by the geysers of fire shooting from the ground, with the dragon heading straight at us.

I lifted my sword, but the weapon was too short to reach the dragon before his fire would annihilate us. I knew it. I knew we stood no chance. The only choice we had was either to die from the fire of the worms or from the flames of the dragon.

"I'm with you." Ari stepped forward, taking a place at my side.

She gazed at me, and I realized she knew it too. She knew this might be our last moment.

"We'll stay together," she said.

Together.

She and I. As it should be. As it always should've been.

Regret, anger, and fear raged inside me. I couldn't let her die. I had more to lose than ever. She gave me everything in my life that was worth fighting for.

My hands flexed on the sword's handle. My fingers suddenly turned transparent, mirroring the arena. I stared at the reflection in disbelief. It hadn't happened to me in so long, I'd almost forgotten why it existed.

Unconquerable fear filled me. But it didn't make me want to hide. It urged me to protect. My fear was not for myself, but for Ari, and it burned through me stronger than fire.

The flame of the worms reflected in my hands. Ari leaned into my side. And instead of trying to contain my fear, for the first time ever, I let it take over me completely.

I let the terror rage through me, filling me with rage too. Inferno stormed all around me, and I blended with it.

I became the storm.

I ruled the flames, sending them toward the dragon.

Twenty

ARI

Fire shot from underground. It leaped onto Salas's hands, engulfing them in flames.

"You're burning!" I screamed and tossed the train of my dress over his hands, trying to beat the fire off his body. But the flames didn't die. They grew even stronger, bursting through the fabric and spiraling around his sword.

"Don't be afraid, Princess," he said in a strangled but eerily calm voice. "Let me fear for you."

Heat radiated from his hands, blowing back my hair. Terror shook me from head to toe. I couldn't let him burn alive, but he wouldn't let me fight it.

"Stand back," he ordered, then dropped his sword and thrust his hands forward.

Transparent spirals of reflection ran up his arms. Fire surged through them like blood coursed through vessels or water filled a dry riverbed after a storm.

Flames surged up from his hands in a continuous stream that grew wider, flowing upwards like a powerful fountain of light and heat.

The dragon stumbled in the air, as if hitting a wall. His blast of blue flame hit sideways, scorching the rocks and setting the prop shrubs aflame. His third wing tilted sharply. His tail whipped through the air, hitting a rock. He lurched toward the ground, losing the lift. Salas leaped up and grabbed the beast's tail, yanking it down. The dragon's wings faltered, and he hit the ground.

Clouds of sand, fire, and smoke rose in the air as the creature rolled on the arena. Salas jumped on top of him, crumbling his third wing under him.

Lerrel and the gladiators rushed to his aid. Two of the men trapped the remaining two wings. They folded them to the body of the dragon. Then, the games master helped them tie the dragon with a barely visible shimmering cord.

The gladiators tried to catch the dragon's head next with the games master holding out a muzzle, but Salas ran back to me.

"Ari. Are you all right?"

I hugged him, pressing my cheek to his bare chest. He wrapped his arms around me, and I kissed his bicep. His skin was slick with sweat and smeared with soot.

His muscles tensed, hard like rock. Reflection ran through his body under my touch. Only instead of the usual undulating wave or a ripple, it crackled like lightning in rugged, broken lines.

"Calm, my darling," I whispered, stroking his back. "Whatever it is you did, however you did it, Salas, you won. It's over. You saved us."

A shudder rocked his body. He tightened his arms around me, holding me closer.

"You're safe," he echoed.

"I am," I assured him.

The dragon's claws left deep scratches around my shoulders, both in the front and on the back. They burned, dripping with blood. But I was alive. I was in his arms, and it felt good.

"I'm fine."

His shoulders dropped with a breath of relief. I slid my palms up his arm. It was warm, but not hot and not burned.

"How did you do it, Salas? You shot fire from your arms. I saw it with my own eyes."

He kissed my hair.

"No fire. Just an illusion, Princess. 'Smoke and mirrors,' like they say."

The threat from the sky was gone. The ground, however, was still aflame with fire bursting all around us. The royal guards gathered on the edge of the arena, but they couldn't get to us.

"Stop the fire!" They yelled to the games master.

"Why are the worms still active?" Salas asked the games master who ran to us.

She looked confused. "I-I don't know."

I'd never seen the games master so unsure about anything. Usually, she had an answer for everything. Real or evasive, but she always had a reply.

"I'll figure it out," she added, much more confidently.

Noil, her husband, rushed to me. "Let me take you to the guards, Your Highness. I know the safe path."

"I'll take her." Not releasing me from his arms, Salas led me through the fire to the edge of the arena where the guards grabbed me.

"Wait." I turned to him as they tried to lead me away. "Thank you..."

It felt so inadequate, but what else could I say with all of them watching us? I couldn't even say his real name out loud here, where they could hear us.

"It was my pleasure, Princess." He gave me a small, polite bow. "She's hurt," he told the guard. "She needs help, quickly."

"Will you be alright?" I asked.

He shrugged a shoulder. "I'll manage. I always do."

"I'll send the royal healing witch to check on you."

He shook his head.

"You need her more than I do. Just..." He hesitated.

"You can ask for anything from me," I assured him.

"Find a way to let me know how you're doing. Please. Let me know how you're healing, Princess."

I held on to his hand for as long as I could. But he let go. He always let me go. And I had no way to hold on to him, either.

"Ari!" Mother rushed to me from the entrance to the arena. "Oh, Goddess, you're bleeding. Get the healing witch here at once," she ordered to the closest guard. "Let's get you back to the palace, my child."

With the dragon recaptured and the fire now contained only to the arena, many people lingered in the vicinity. Some of those who'd run away were now returning in hopes of more entertainment.

"How is Father? Where is Leafar?" I asked as the guards and my mother led me to the carriage waiting for us just outside of the arena.

"I sent the prince to the palace with the king. Both are safe."

"Good. Thank you."

Someone threw a shawl over my bleeding shoulders. A guard helped me into the carriage, along with Mother.

"Oh gods, what a mess," she lamented.

The arena burned behind us. A thick cloud of smoke rose over the poles with burning banners, the pictures of Salas on them smoking and scorched.

With the shock and terror receding, the wounds on my shoulders hurt badly now.

What would've happened to me if it weren't for Salas? How did he conjure the fire that saved us?

"Just an illusion, Princess," he'd said.

But I'd felt the blast of heat on my face as the fire shot up his arms. Yet there was not a single burn on his skin afterwards.

Was it a miracle? It must be.

Twenty-One

ARI

Three days later, the judge reached the verdict in the case that terrorized the city for weeks. The man who brutally murdered women was sentenced to death by decapitation the very next day. He didn't appeal the verdict. There'd be no use if he did. His crimes were too grave to deserve any leniency. He earned the death penalty many times over.

As the crown princess, I was required to attend his execution, but I would've come here either way. Like so many people who had gathered around the execution site that morning, I wished to see the end of the terror with my own eyes.

Mother and I got our seats close to the platform. A few long benches circled the execution site, providing some seating for the spectators. However, the crowd swelled to a size far larger than the benches could accommodate.

There was a sense of relief among the people that morning. The execution meant to put an end to fear that had reigned over the minds of many.

As the guards led the prisoner toward the block with the

executioner standing nearby, I braced to face the devil incarnate in the man who'd killed so brutally.

The blubbering, whimpering man they brought in, however, was nothing like I'd imagined. Tall and thin, he stumbled under the weight of the heavy chains that wound around his torso several times to bind his arms to his body. A heavy metal ball was attached to his right leg to prevent him from escaping. He dragged it behind him, barely able to move forward.

The crowd booed and shouted, but all I could do was stare.

"Monsters..." he muttered, wildly roaming his eyes over the crowd. "Demons are coming. Hide your sons... No man is safe..."

What was he talking about?

Saliva foamed in the corners of his mouth, dripping down his unkempt beard. His dark, overgrown hair fell over his forehead, covering most of his face.

The guards positioned him behind the solid wooden block. One of the guards kept her crossbow trained at his head.

As they pushed on his shoulders, forcing him down to his knees, he stared straight ahead at Mother and me, but he didn't appear to see us. His eyes rotated wildly in their sockets, his chapped lips moving incessantly.

"They won't stop until we are their property..." he chanted. "...until we all are dead. They'll cut our flesh off our bones. Burning... They'll burn us in eternal fire... All of us..."

A guard grabbed his hair, forcing him to tilt his head backward. The sweat-soaked strands fell away from his face, revealing what I first thought was a mask made from clay plastered on his face and never smoothed out.

The guards made him bend over, positioning his head on the block. The executioner raised her axe. The muscles in her tanned arms bulged out. With so few executions taking place in Rorrim, she didn't get to practice her craft often, but she proved her skill by chopping through the man's neck in one swift, clean blow.

The mumbling stopped as the head separated from the body and dropped toward the basket positioned in front of the block to catch it. It missed the basket, however. Bouncing off the edge, the severed head hit the platform, then rolled off it and to my feet.

Mother gasped, jumping from her seat. I got up, too, lifting the heavy skirts of my formal attire away from the rolling head and the bloody trail it was leaving behind.

Blood sprayed my slippers. The head stopped in front of me, the glassy eyes staring up into the sky.

What I'd mistaken for a mask turned out to be a thick layer of scars. Elaborate cuts and badly healed burns covered the man's entire face and neck all the way to the bloodied line at the end of the stub of his neck. His beard grew in uneven patches with bald spots where the skin was too damaged to grow hair.

"Ari." Mother gripped my arm, but I refused to move, staring into the dead eyes of the killer.

"What happened to him?" I asked. "Why does he look like that?"

Mother shook her head. "He was a dangerous man, daughter."

I remembered the incoherent mumbling. The look in his eyes as he had stared at me from behind the chopping block didn't hold much more awareness than the glassy stare of the severed head did.

"He wasn't well," I said softly.

Had the man even realized he was about to die? Had he known why?

"My apologies, Your Highness." The executioner bowed to me, collecting the head.

Watching her toss the dead head into the basket, I remembered the killer's description that Madam Trela reported to us, "Tall. Dark hair. With a beard."

She had never mentioned the scars.

THE SCENE of the execution stayed with me long after I returned to the palace.

I hurried up the stairs to my rooms, eager to get out of my ceremonial clothing. The stiff formal gown compressed my chest, and the heavy mantle weighted down on my healing shoulders so much they ached.

After I stumbled back into my rooms, it took three maids to relieve me from the heavy robes of my formal outfit. They helped me into a much lighter and far more comfortable cotton dress with a high waist and cup sleeves.

I wished it was evening already, so I could take a cup of Salas's tea and go to bed. Whether or not the tea worked, it helped me relax before going to bed. It filled my belly with warmth and my heart with memories of him. Tonight, however, I feared even his magical tea wouldn't erase the dead stare of the severed head imprinted in my mind.

A short while later, a maid arrived with Mother's request for me to join her for tea.

Pressure inside my head threatened to grow into a headache. I needed a few more moments of peace and quiet.

"I'm afraid I'll have to decline," I said to the maid.

"But Her Majesty insists, Your Highness."

That was Mother's way to let me know that her request was actually an order. The matter must be important.

"All right. I'll be right there."

As I approached the drawing room where Mother was taking her tea that afternoon, the guards at the door bowed to me.

"Lady Etah and Lady Gem are with the queen already, Your Highness," one of them informed me. "Madam Trela and the games master have been sent for too."

It looked like Mother was holding an informal meeting disguised as a tea party.

The three women stood by one of the tall open windows into the gardens as I entered. A low table in the sitting area was set with tea, but no one seemed to have any.

"We can put strings with paper lanterns over the pond." Gem gestured across the window at the lily pond out in the gardens. "This way, we'll have plenty of light before and after the fireworks."

Mother nodded.

"Oh, that will look so lovely, Gem." She turned to me with a bright smile. "Ari, dearest, thank you so much for joining us."

"What are you discussing?" I asked, after greeting the ladies.

"The event tomorrow," mother replied. She was giving a ball in honor of the delegation from the Olakrez, whose visit to Rorrim was coming to an end. "I decided to expand the ball. We'll have a garden party and a ceremony before dinner—"

"What kind of ceremony?" I glanced at Gem.

Mother answered for her, "You see, darling, there has been so much...um, upsetting events lately. But the king is doing well. You survived that horrible ordeal in the gladiators' arena. The safety regulations of the games are being overhauled with the help of the council appointed committee." She gestured at Lady Etah, the Head of the Council, who nodded in confirmation. "Now, I decided it was time to bring some positivity into our lives."

"By having a party?"

"Yes." She smiled. "Instead of dwelling on the bad, I wish to highlight the good that has happened by honoring the heroes who keep us safe. Madam Trela and her guards will be invited as the guests of honor, as well as the gladiators."

"The gladiators? All of them?"

My heart beat faster at the mere possibility of catching a glance of Salas tomorrow. Guilt came rushing in right after. Salas was not the man I should be thinking about when I had a husband who had been sulking at me over the lack of attention he was getting from me.

"Madam Trela reported last week," Mother continued, "that one of my gladiators helped capture the murderer who was executed this morning. I thought it'd be appropriate to celebrate the man who helped us keep this city safe. And since one of the gladiators also assisted you to get to safety in the arena—"

"*Assisted* me? Mother, he literally saved my life," I corrected her weak choice of words. "If it wasn't for him, I'd be dead."

Gem rubbed her chin in thought. "Has he ever explained how he ended up defeating the dragon? They say he created a fire?"

Gem left the arena shortly after the dragon had gotten loose and way before Salas used his fantastic abilities to save us.

"That's what I've heard too," Lady Etah said. "Witnesses claim he created fire, which is incredible if it's true. Is he a warlock, by any chance?"

"Why not?" Gem snorted. "He's been many things. It wouldn't surprise me if he also practiced some forbidden magic on the side." She then turned to the window, mattering under her breath, "Is there a line that man wouldn't cross?"

"He's not a warlock," I said firmly.

"How do you know?" Mother tilted her head.

"I just do. But feel free to ask the games master when she gets here."

"All right," Mother conceded. "The point is, two of my gladiators have distinguished themselves in the past few weeks. One helped to apprehend the murderer, and the other one rescued you in the arena. King Trebor suggested a ceremony to bestow the queen's medal on one of them, and I agreed. It will be good for the healing of our people to honor a deserving man after the execution of a terrible one."

"We'll just have to decide which of the two gladiators is more deserving of such an honor," Lady Etah added.

Mother sighed. "It will be a tough choice to make. Saving the city from terror or s the crown princes from the clutches of a dragon? How does one weigh these two great deeds against each other?"

"Why not give them both a medal?" I suggested.

Mother chuckled. "I'm not against honoring a man once in a while when his behavior sets a good example for the rest of the male population. But receiving the queen's medal is the highest honor in the country. We can't give it just to anyone."

"Just last year, you gave two medals on the same day," I reminded her.

"Yes, but that was to honor two very distinguished women. We can't do the same for men. We risk making the award look frivolous."

"But if both deserve it—"

A knock on the door interrupted me.

"Your Majesty," a guard entered, "Madam Trela and the games master have arrived."

The door opened wider, and the two esteemed women entered, followed by a man who had not been announced.

He stayed behind the women, but because of his height that allowed him to tower over them, I could see his face perfectly.

Salas.

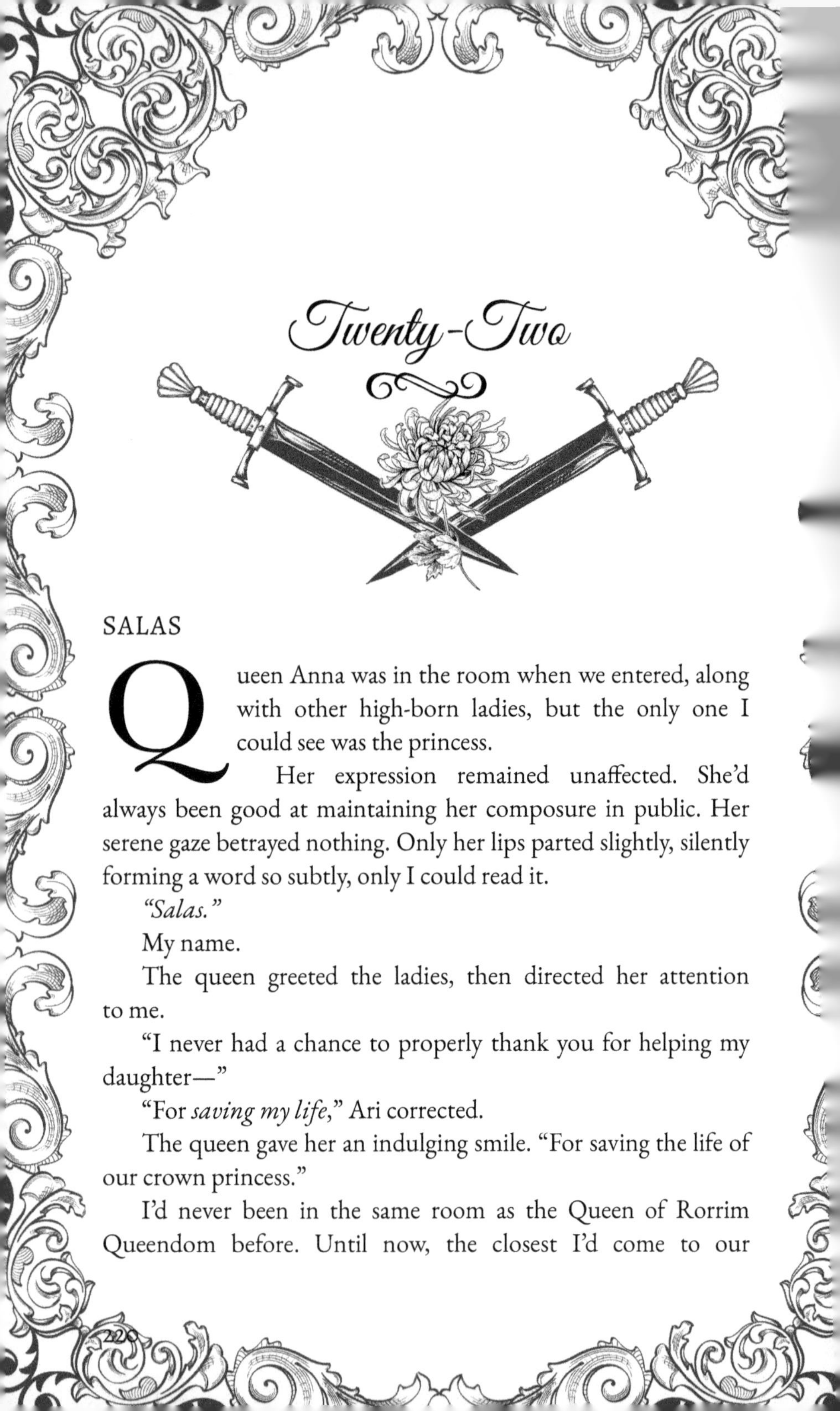

Twenty-Two

SALAS

Queen Anna was in the room when we entered, along with other high-born ladies, but the only one I could see was the princess.

Her expression remained unaffected. She'd always been good at maintaining her composure in public. Her serene gaze betrayed nothing. Only her lips parted slightly, silently forming a word so subtly, only I could read it.

"Salas."

My name.

The queen greeted the ladies, then directed her attention to me.

"I never had a chance to properly thank you for helping my daughter—"

"For *saving my life*," Ari corrected.

The queen gave her an indulging smile. "For saving the life of our crown princess."

I'd never been in the same room as the Queen of Rorrim Queendom before. Until now, the closest I'd come to our monarch was a glimpse of her in the arena. Before I came to Egami, I'd only seen her in pictures.

In a casual lavender dress, with only a modest diadem for a crown, she looked more approachable than ever. Possibly, I'd be more intimidated had I not been so distracted by Ari's presence.

I bowed to the queen, stealing another glance at the princess.

"Thank you." Ari smiled softly.

She looked tired. Her bright summer dress embroidered with lilies-of-the-valley with a green sash tied under her breasts couldn't hide the shadows of exhaustion on her face.

"It is my duty to protect you, Your Highness." I bowed. "I trust you're feeling well?"

It was killing me to act detached and formal, when I wanted to gather her in my arms, put her in my lap, and kiss her scars, both visible and not.

"I'm well," she replied. "Did you receive my thank-you note?"

As promised, Ari had sent me an update on her recovery from the ordeal in the arena. She also included a large bouquet of white roses and a dozen of priceless silk satin shirts. The note said the shirts were to replace the one she'd ruined during her last visit to the gladiators' quarters.

"Yes, I greatly appreciate the note and the presents. I'll never run out of shirts now." I grinned.

Her polite smile grew into a wide grin, too. "You'll never have to wear any other shirts at all."

I tilted my head, peering at her closely. Was my princess jealous?

"Well," Lerrel stepped forward. "Our Mountain Bear is double the hero, Your Majesty."

Upbeat, proud, and as boastful as ever, Lerrel's attitude didn't let anyone in on how much stress she'd been through in the past four days.

The mortal danger that thousands of spectators, including the royal family, had been subjected to at the last games threatened to close our entire establishment for good, and the games master had been working day and night, trying to get to the bottom of what had happened in the arena that day.

The initial investigation conducted by Madam Trela's people in collaboration with the royal palace uncovered that our performance had been deliberately sabotaged. The show animals had been agitated on purpose as traces of unknown substances were discovered in their food. Some of the safety mechanisms had been compromised or disabled. And there were reasons to believe that someone familiar with the show and the arena had done all of that.

Lerrel had been trapped between the necessity to uncover the truth and the need to bury it for good in order to save the games.

Her attire might be as bright as ever, her attitude upbeat, and her smile brilliant and wide. But I knew that she'd used the gladiators' stage makeup this morning to conceal the dark circles under her eyes left by the many sleepless hours she'd endured lately.

"Not only did this man save the princess, but he also helped to apprehend the murderer who was justly executed this morning," Lerrel announced.

"It was also you?" Ari gasped softly, her carefully created neutral expression slipping off for a moment.

"Oh." The queen's eyebrows rose in surprise. "You truly are an exceptional man, aren't you?"

"Thank you, Your Majesty." I bowed my head.

"And the crowd's favorite," Lerrel inserted quickly. "Raeb is our star of the show. Rightfully so. He's strong, kind, and of stellar character and reputation. He was recommended by the most honorable lady chamberlain, and she had never been wrong about any of our boys."

With the mention of her title, the lady chamberlain pressed her lips into a tight smile, avoiding eye contact with me.

"And as we have recently discovered," Lerrel continued to sing praises in the same voice she used when making dramatic announcements in the arena, "he's touched by the divine magic that allowed him to defeat the dragon and rescue our crown princess."

"Oh, about that…" The queen leaned closer to Lerrel. "How did he do that? How did he conjure the fire?"

Lerrel gave her a sly smile. "You know, Your Majesty, we have to keep our secrets in order for the show magic to continue to amaze our audience."

She spoke as if she'd had the full control of what my reflection did that day, when in reality, Lerrel knew even less than I did how it all happened. She'd questioned me in detail, but I could only tell her the same thing I'd said to Ari. It all had been only an illusion. I didn't actually conjure the fire. I reflected and amplified the flames of the worms.

"Just tell me, please, that he isn't practicing any kind of forbidden magic," the queen insisted. "It wouldn't do for us to publicly honor a warlock like that."

"Oh, absolutely not. I give you my word, Your Majesty, Raeb's abilities are strictly of the divine nature. Our magic is of the purest kind."

The other lady present in the room, the one I'd never met before and who hadn't been introduced to me, seemed relieved.

"Well, that's fortunate," she said, adjusting the reading glasses perched on her head over her forehead. "It'll save us the debate about choosing a medal recipient."

"A medal?" Lerrel's face lit up.

"Lady Etah is referring to the conversation we had earlier," the queen explained. "We decided to bestow the queen's medal on one deserving man during a ceremony tomorrow before the ball."

Lady Etah drew tighter her colorful shawl around her shoulders that she wore over her flowing pastel-pink dress.

"Since both heroic actions happened to be conducted by the same man, there is no need to choose." She patted my arm. "Congratulations, sweetie, well done."

The queen turned to Lerrel. "I would like to officially invite you to the festivities tomorrow. Sorry, it is a bit of a late notice, but our planning has been a little chaotic lately, with everything going on. I hope all your boys can come. And maybe you could put on a little performance for us, if it's not too much trouble."

Lerrel's expression brightened even more. Her chest puffed up with excitement. I was happy for her. After all that stress and worry, she needed a little recognition too.

"Absolutely, Your Majesty. It'll be our honor. We're always prepared to give the best performance ever."

"Thank you. We're going to have a lovely celebration tomorrow. Madam Trela," the queen addressed the Head of the City Guards next. "You and your women are also invited, in recognition of your hard work when identifying and capturing the killer."

Madam Trela pressed her hands in orange lace gloves to her chest, looking lost for words. Her cheeks glowed brighter as she curtsied to the queen.

"It's a tremendous honor, Your Majesty."

The queen smiled kindly. "The honor is mine, madam. Today's execution wouldn't have happened if it wasn't for you and your women. It's only fitting to express our gratitude publicly, so the entire court can join me in thanking you." She swept the room with her gaze. "I am looking forward to seeing you all at the palace tomorrow."

It sounded like a dismissal. The meeting was over. Everyone bowed, expressing their gratitude for the invitations and looking ready to leave.

But I didn't come here for a medal.

"If I may ask for a favor, Your Majesty," I said with a bow.

The queen blinked, her eyebrows rising again. She clearly didn't expect me to speak.

"A favor?" she asked. "Is there something you wish for? Well, as the hero of the hour, I suppose you can ask. What is it you want, young man?"

"Not for myself. I would like to request an investigation into the fun houses where Das worked in the past five years."

I might be the only person left who knew Das before he became a murderous monster. I owed it to him and to others who might still be suffering to find out what horrors he'd gone through before he started inflicting the same horrors onto others.

"Who is Das?" Confused, the queen glanced at Lerrel and Madam Trela for explanation.

Madam Trela cleared her throat. "The killer we executed this morning, Your Majesty. His name was Das."

"The killer? But what is there left to investigate? He was found guilty beyond all doubt. You caught him in the act, didn't you?"

The queen stared at me, as did the princess. Ari clearly didn't know until today about my part in apprehending Das.

"I did." I said. "I stopped his attack on Madam Einna, the merchant from the Tresed Queendom. I wish I was there to stop him from murdering his previous victims too. But Das was not born a murderer. His past must've driven him to it."

"You want us to look deeper into his past?" Madam Trela asked.

Ari shifted uneasily. "Are you sure it's a good idea?"

She must be worried about how much of *my* past such an investigation might uncover. But I had to risk it.

I looked into Ari's eyes, now speaking directly to her. "I saw Das's face up close. The scars like his can't be a result of a single accident. Someone inflicted injuries to his body regularly, with various weapons or instruments. The people who did it are still out there, possibly hurting someone else."

Ari nodded with understanding.

"Madam Trela." She turned to the Head of the City Guards. "Why did you never include the killer's scars in the description that you gave us?"

"I didn't?" The woman looked flustered. "I'm so sorry. It must've been an accidental omission."

"How could you 'accidentally' forget about the suspect's most unique feature?" the queen wondered.

"It's rather of a disturbing nature, isn't it?" Madam Trela cleared her throat nervously. "I didn't want to upset Your Majesty or Her Highness with such a grizzly detail."

"Details like that could mean life or death, Madam Trela," Ari reprimanded gravely. "Please don't omit them in the future. Do you know how he got his scars?"

Lady Etah spoke before Madam Trela had a chance to answer. "Could it be that a man like him thrived on violence way before he chose murder as an outlet for it? I'm sure he got into fights more than once during his turbulent, misguided life."

"If that's the case," Ari said, "it'd be easy enough to prove, wouldn't it? We'll just need to talk to the fun house where he worked before his last place of employment."

She glanced at me, and I nodded, letting her know it wouldn't put me in danger. I hadn't worked with Das for many years.

"Well," the queen intervened. "The purpose of our celebration tomorrow is to honor the good, positive things happening in our queendom. If there is a need to investigate the past of an executed murderer, I trust my guards will identify it." She extended me her hand in parting. "Thank you for expressing your concern. I'm looking forward to seeing you tomorrow."

Lerrel tugged at my sleeve firmly, signaling it was time to leave.

Ari slipped her arm into the crook of Madam Trela's elbow. "I'll walk with you, if you don't mind, madam."

"Of course, Your Highness." The Head of the City Guards looked a bit stunned by the princess's attention, but she allowed Ari to lead her out of the room, following Lerrel and me.

"Well, that went well," Lerrel chatted excitedly in a half-whisper, dragging me along the corridor toward the main hall. "You'll get a metal, and the games will live another day. We'll need to figure out what the fuck we're going to perform tomorrow. There's really no time to prepare anything new."

Tuning her out, I focused on what Ari was saying to Madam Trela behind us.

"...I request you'll look into it immediately."

"You want me to go ahead with this investigation, Your Highness? Without the queen's direct order?"

"Yes. Please go ahead with it on my order alone for now. You'll report the results directly to me too."

She did it. Das's past was going to be investigated. Ari believed it was important.

"Raeb?" Lerrel tugged on my arm. "We need to hurry. I have a show to pull off in less than twenty-four hours, remember? And I still need to stop by at the palace stables to see if we can use their horses tomorrow instead of bringing ours all the way out here."

"You don't need me at the stables, do you? I'll wait for you in the carriage."

"Are you going straight to the carriage right now?"

"Right after I'll say a quick thank you to Madam Trela for talking to the queen about me. I didn't get a chance to do it during the meeting." Lerrel seemed to hesitate, so I added quickly, "It can't hurt to stay in good graces with the city guards. We shouldn't take for granted good relationships with anyone in our current situation, should we?"

"Goddess knows you're right." Lerrel heaved a sigh. "You may be my best bet to salvage this shitty situation right now. Without you, we'd be done the moment the princess was taken. If she didn't survive—"

Not wishing to contemplate the scenario of Ari not surviving that day in the arena, I placed a supporting hand on Lerrel's shoulder. "It'll be all right, master. We're getting a medal tomorrow. You saved the games."

"May Goddess hear you and help us." She patted my hand on her shoulder. "Go, be nice to the Head of the City Guards, then go straight to our carriage. The last thing I need right now is someone catching you loitering in the queen's palace unsupervised. I'll see you in a few minutes. It won't take me long."

I had no plan. All I wanted was to see Ari one more time before leaving the palace. The most I hoped for was to say hi to her without people policing every word or gesture passed between us.

The voices from the corridor behind me had quieted by now. Then I heard a door opening and closing and several sets of footsteps spreading in different directions.

Did I miss my chance? Had Ari departed along a different corridor?

As one set of footsteps approached, I stepped from the main hall into the one crossing it to get out of sight of the person approaching. If it was anyone else but Ari, they didn't need to see me "loitering" around.

The new corridor appeared to be guarded by warriors in old-fashioned, all-body armor on both sides. Then I realized these were just empty armor suits displayed from the days long gone, with Rorrim banners and historical tapestries hanging between them along the walls.

The footprints came closer, then the princess passed me by.

"Ari."

She turned and saw me.

"Salas?"

No one ever looked at me the way Ari did, like she finally spotted sunshine at the end of a long, devastating storm. Her shoulders relaxed, her eyes lit up, her lips curved into a gentle smile.

"You..." She stepped closer, and my hands ended up on her waist as if that was where they belonged.

"Is it not enough for you to wrestle bears and dragons in the arena that you have to fight the serial killers in the streets too?" she scolded softly, cupping my face.

"Thank you. For the investigation."

"It has to be done," she said resolutely.

Yet no one of the important women in the meeting this morning understood that. Whatever happened to Das could be happening to others right now, but they were likely employed in fun houses, and saving lives of whores clearly held no value for the state.

Ari's past had damaged her, but it had also opened her eyes to the things that even her mother couldn't see. I sensed it in her the day I met her. She'd been my light after the storm, a breath of fresh air in the suffocating smoke of hatred, scorn, and judgment.

"Thank you," I repeated. "And thank you for the shirts again."

She smiled, not releasing my face from her hands.

"Do you know what it means, darling?" she said tenderly. "You saved my life. No one can question my taking care of you now. I set up a fund in the crown's name for you. The queen made a huge donation too. You will never want for anything. For as long as you live."

"Except that the only thing I want, I still can't have."

"What is it?"

"You."

Keeping in my feelings for her proved impossible. Gods knew I'd tried.

She reached up to me at the same moment as I leaned down to her, and our lips met. I had no time to think or plan for it. The kiss just happened, and now I didn't want it to be any other way.

Somewhere out there, like in another world, doors opened, people walked, their footfalls echoed through the grand halls and corridors of the palace. I didn't want them to see us. I didn't want this kiss to end.

Keeping my mouth on hers, I lifted her in my arms and walked her backwards into the hallway with the silent armored suits standing guard by the wall tapestries. The fervent desire to keep her all to myself for just a second longer guided me behind a long banner and out of sight of anyone who might pass by.

She broke our kiss as I leaned her with her back against the wall, but she wouldn't take her hands off me, stroking my cheekbones with her thumbs.

"I want you, too, Salas. Never stopped. If it's so wrong for me to want you, then why is it the only thing in life that feels so undoubtedly right?"

I couldn't answer it for her. As for myself, I knew why.

Thinking about her had become as natural as breathing. I needed her touch and her kisses to sustain my soul, just as I needed food to sustain my body. Next to her was the only place I wished to be.

Because I loved her.

I loved her so much that I could never tell her that. My love was of no use to a princess. I could give her nothing when she deserved everything.

A stronger man would let her be. I crushed rocks between my hands in the arena, but I wasn't strong enough to break the invisible thread that tied me to her.

She opened the buttons of her dress, and I helped her slide the fabric off her right shoulder. The red healing scars from the dragon's claws marred her skin. I kissed along one jagged line. Breath rushed out of her. She sank her hands into my hair, keeping me close. Slipping my hand inside her neckline, I cupped her breast.

She stilled, pressing her lips to my temple.

It was wrong of me to kiss her, to stroke her breast, to trap her nipple between my fingers... It was wrong for me to crave the sensation of her skin under my palms. Yet it felt right, and I didn't stop. I knew she wouldn't stop me either, as I hiked up her skirt and slid my hand up her thigh.

"You know..." she whispered against the side of my neck. "It's only *your* hands I think about now..." she lifted her head, meeting my eyes, "when I touch myself."

Oh, gods.

"Fuck, sweetheart, you're killing me," I groaned, growing harder than a rock.

Ever since I left her bedroom, she had become my one and only fantasy. It was the most exquisite thrill to discover I was hers too.

I yanked her underwear aside to find her soaking wet already.

. . .

"You think about me as you come on your dainty little fingers, Princess?" I slipped my thick digit inside her, and her inner muscles gripped me.

"Yes…" she whimpered, rocking her hips against me. "I do."

"Do you wish to have my big, rough hands on you?" I found her most sensitive spot and teased it with my thumb. She arched her back, her breath catching in her throat.

"Your hands are big…" She hooked her leg around my hip, opening wider for me. "But they're never rough."

She slid a hand down my stomach and past the belt of my pants, but I shifted away from her touch before she could reach my cock. If she touched me there, I feared I'd lose control. I'd fuck her until she screamed my name and I roared hers, until all of Egami heard us and the entire palace ran here.

Instead, I played her body with my fingers, delighting in her little whimpers and soft gasps of pleasure. This was the best music, the most glorious symphony I'd ever heard.

"Have you seen a man pass by here?" Lerrel's voice suddenly invaded our space.

The games master was looking for me out there, but I had unfinished business. I had to see this intense, beautiful symphony play out all the way to its magnificent completion.

Ari's eyelids fluttered close. She fisted my shirt on my chest, her whimpers growing into moans as she came undone.

Lerrel's footsteps came closer, and I placed a hand over Ari's mouth, working her with my other hand.

"Hush, sweetheart. Shh," I exhaled into her hair as she came on my hand over and over, holding on to my shirt like to a lifeline in a stormy sea.

Slowly, she unclasped her hands, releasing my shirt. I leaned back, dropping my hand away from her mouth, and she opened her eyes.

Lerrel kept searching for me, explaining to someone out there, "…a big, bearded man in a nice shirt with horn buttons. You wouldn't miss him if you saw him."

"You need to go," Ari mouthed.

A veil of regret fell over her gaze. I hated to think she regretted what had just happened between us, but I understood if she did.

She was a married woman now. From my experience, not every woman viewed marriage as a binding commitment or a reason for monogamy, but if Ari did, she'd be feeling guilty about us now.

Her marriage meant nothing to me. It was a political arrangement that forced two strangers to share a lifetime, potentially depriving them both of a chance to find a true connection with anyone else. But if her marriage meant something to Ari, then it mattered to me too.

"I don't want you to regret anything we've had, Princess," I whispered. "No matter how many pure, noble men you'll end up having in your life."

"Should I call the palace guards, master?" a female voice sounded just outside of our hallway.

I couldn't care less about being discovered. But Ari had a lot to lose to be seen with me like this.

"I need to go before they find me and you in here." I tore myself from her and lifted the banner to go out there.

"Salas."

With her dress undone, exposing her right breast, the hard bud of the nipple teased me relentlessly above her neckline. With her lips swollen from my kisses and her skin rubbed to a glow by my beard, she was the vision I'd keep with me forever.

"Salas," she breathed out. "You're still the only one. There has been no one else."

Her words, quiet like a whisper of a breeze, slammed into me like a hammer.

"Why?" was all I could say.

"Raeb!" Lerrel shrieked, turning into the hallway. "By Goddess, there you are."

I let the banner drop between Ari and me, concealing her from Lorrel and the rest of the world.

Ari's secrets were safe with me. All of them.

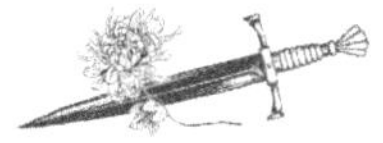

ARI

"Why?"

The word echoed in my head over and over as I listened to Salas's heavy footsteps move away and die in the distance.

Why?

Sliding with my back down the wall, I sat on the marble floor of the hallway behind the banner and hugged my knees to my chest.

I'd never asked myself this question.

Why, despite my getting married, Salas was still the only man I'd ever been with?

I could've at least tried to sleep in Leafar's bed on our wedding night. Maybe it would've made the matters worse between us sooner, but maybe some intimacy could've grown from that. I would never know that now because I'd never given it a chance.

Leafar accused me of avoiding him, and he was partially right. I felt more comfortable away from him than in his company. There was no natural pull that would bring me to him. Every minute I'd spent with him so far had been because of guilt or obligation.

Only now I understood the true source of all that massive amount of guilt that had been plaguing me. My struggle was not about keeping my loyalty to Leafar.

I'd been avoiding sex with him and fighting the expectations of two queendoms because the intimacy with my husband felt like a betrayal of my feelings for the former slave.

I never gave Salas a vow of loyalty. Yet in my heart, I stayed true to him and only him.

Twenty-Three

ARI

Maids fussed over me, putting the final touches on my outfit of the lacy white gown adorned with drops of aquamarine and a long, heavy train embroidered with gold and blue.

I sent a maid to Leafar's rooms. "Please let His Highness know I'll come to take him downstairs in a few minutes."

The prince was supposed to meet me at the top of the grand staircase, but I wanted to greet him in private first, to gauge his mood.

Today was the last ball before the Olakrez delegation's departure. Aside from his personal valet and a few loyal gentlemen-in-waiting, Leafar's escort was leaving the day after tomorrow. I worried he might feel sad or lonely. He was probably fearful about the duchess's threats too.

The enormous train of my dress dragged behind me as I walked along the corridor to Leafar's rooms. It was hard to move in these clothes. Thankfully, today's ceremony required more poise than agility on my part, and after all the outdoor ceremonies, I was supposed to change into a more practical gown suitable for dancing at the ball.

I found Leafar in his dressing room with a whole army of valets and groomers getting him ready.

"Your Highness." He lowered his head as I entered.

The men in the room bowed too.

Dressed in white to match my outfit, Leafar already had a wide-sleeved shirt on with lacy cuffs and turquoise cufflinks. A waistcoat corset in blue-and-gold brocade tightly laced his torso with a gold cord at the back. A cameo pin of a horse carved from lapis lazuli in a gold frame sat deep in the ruffles of his voluminous cravat.

With his hair meticulously coiffed into waves and his chin smoothly shaven, Leafar looked like a prince from a fairy tale. But it didn't escape me how pale his cheeks were or how nervously his eyes roamed the room, unable to settle on anything.

I searched for something to say to cheer him up and put him at ease. "I arranged to put a bid in for that baby horse you wanted."

"The prized foal from Tresed?" He perked up.

"Right. That one." I mentally congratulated myself for remembering to make the arrangements despite everything that had been happening lately. "The stable master said we have a great chance of winning it. My father will personally supervise the bidding process when it starts, and he'll adjust our bid with every correspondence from Tresed."

"Thank you." He beamed, and I would've gotten him three baby horses, despite the ridiculously high price, if only that smile stayed.

Sadly, it slipped away quickly. Worry creased his smooth forehead.

"It's time for us to go, isn't it?" He snapped his fingers at his valet. "My coat."

The man grabbed the white coat with gold buttons and shimmering embroidery along the cuffs and lapels, but I waved him away.

"You won't need it," I said to Leafar. "The day is warm."

Leafar stared at me as if I'd just told him to go out in public naked.

"I can't possibly show up at the ceremony in nothing but shirtsleeves," he muttered, confused.

"You have enough layers on." I gestured at his outfit—the shirt, waistcoat, long pants, and dress shoes with gold buckles. It left nothing but his hands and face exposed. "Any more, and you risk spending the day uncomfortably hot. But come, see for yourself."

I opened the tall glass doors and walked out onto the balcony, inviting him to follow. With my train in the way, I couldn't close the doors behind us, but out here Leafar and I had a little more privacy than in his dressing room filled with people.

"So, what do you think?" I lifted my face up to the morning sunshine. "Today is one of the last scorching-hot days of summer. It will start cooling off soon. But the weather will remain fairly warm well into the fall. Rorrim is north of Olakrez, as you know. The climate here is significantly warmer than what you're used to. It's fine to lose a layer or two of clothing, even for men. I know for a fact that King Trebor is dressing down to a waistcoat, too, and so are his gentlemen-in-waiting. You won't be the only one, if that's your worry."

He chewed on his bottom lip, staring out into the gardens. The ceremony site was on the other side of the palace. But even here, the servants had put the extra strings of lights in the gardens. At night, the lanterns will illuminate the entire grounds with a golden light.

"My aunt wouldn't approve of my showing up in public in any state of undress," Leafar said quietly.

Irritation at the grand duchess' incessant meddling spiked in me once again.

"Your aunt no longer has any power over you, not unless you

let her have it. You're a married man now. You no longer depend on your family for anything."

He glanced at me before quickly averting his eyes again. "Unless the consummation happens tomorrow in her presence, our marriage will be declared invalid. And then..." he drew in a shaky breath, "she'll take me back to Olakrez."

Would she really go through with that? There was no political advantage for Olakrez to reclaim their prince.

"I'll talk to the grand duchess first thing tomorrow morning," I promised.

He paled, turning almost as white as his cravat. "Don't... Please."

"I'll have to," I explained softly. "I can't let her intimidate you like this."

Having sex with Leafar was even less possible than before. Not after I saw Salas yesterday. But I had to carefully consider all implications of my refusal to fuck my husband for his aunt's viewing pleasure. Our marriage might be a sham, already falling apart at the poorly constructed seams, but it couldn't be annulled. I would not subject Leafar to shame and punishment from his family.

The Queen of Olakrez might feel upset about the lack of proof of our physical relationship. She might even use it as a leverage against me in our future negotiations, but I wouldn't let her take her displeasure out on her son.

"You don't have to worry about it, my prince. I will take care of it."

His manicured fingernails scraped against the stone of the parapet as he turned to me with anguish etched on his perfect face.

"How can I not worry, Your Highness? I'll have to go back to Olakrez and..." he swallowed hard, jerking his gaze back to the gardens, "face my mother."

"Leafar." I touched his arm, bringing his attention to me. "Why do you not believe me when I say that no one will take you back to Olakrez against your will? We vowed to trust each other. Why don't you trust me to keep you safe?"

He looked torn, with a haunted expression in his cerulean eyes.

"How much can a husband trust his wife when he doesn't have her love?" he asked.

I couldn't lie to him, not even when I desperately wished to comfort him.

"It has never been about love between us, my prince. But I gave you a vow to protect you in front of this entire court, in front of your family and mine, and I will keep it."

"Until your love for another will step between us," he muttered, gripping the parapet.

"What are you talking about?"

"A vacant heart can always be filled sooner or later, and if it's not with love for me, then with love for another."

The words didn't sound like his. I'd bet my crown, they came from someone else—his aunt, his family, or someone from his entourage—whoever had been feeding him all these insecurities.

But wasn't there some truth to that too?

My entire being was filled to the brim with a strong, passionate feeling that never belonged to my husband.

Was it love?

My heart slammed against my ribs. The day suddenly felt even hotter and its sounds more acute.

That head-spinning sensation of falling that I always experienced when next to Salas, was it from my plummeting to my destruction?

Or was it the soaring thrill of flight?

Had it been love all along that filled me whole and lifted me without wings?

Was that how love felt?

Stunned by the realization, I blinked, turning away from Leafar's questioning stare.

I had nothing to tell him, nothing at all.

Life seemed both more beautiful than ever and dreadfully tangled at once.

"We should go," I said, licking my dry lips. "The ceremony is about to start."

As we passed through the dressing room, Leafar waved away the servant with the coat. I could only hope he did so because he found the day too hot to wear it, not because I told him so.

GEM and her people had outdone themselves, making the ceremony one of the most spectacular affairs that had ever taken place at the queen's palace, especially considering how little time they had to pull it off.

After the procession through the gardens to admire the chocolate fountains framed by the islands of exotic fruit, the waterfalls of expensive wine, and the giant ice sculptures steaming with multi-colored glow from the magical substances added to the ice, we took our seats around a rink over a lawn, and the gladiators' performance began.

Without the magic of the arena, the show relied solely on the men's skills and agility. Other than the palace horses for the opening procession, no animals were involved in the performance, either. Instead, the gladiators demonstrated their skills with weapons in fighting each other.

Salas used his swords against Regit and Raob. Both the light, agile Regit and the stout, heavy-hitting Raob made worthy opponents. The victory over them didn't come easily to Salas. His heavy breathing and the sweat-soaked brow were not an act as he finally raised his swords in the air after defeating them both.

The games master declared Salas the winner, and the Queen of Rorrim announced the great honor of awarding him the queen's medal.

Mother placed on his shoulder the silver sash with the ribbon rosette that held the golden medal paved with precious mirror stones.

"For the incomparable service to the Crown and the Queendom of Rorrim," she declared. "To the special man touched by magic."

Music surged, but it drowned in the applause. The entire royal court and the guests of the palace stood to their feet, cheering and clapping.

Salas held his head high. Rolling back his shoulders, he swept his gaze over the rows of finely dressed nobles applauding him.

For a moment, our eyes met, and a shiver ran down my spine.

I loved him.

It was that simple.

Now that the warm, tender, but all-consuming feeling inside me had a name, I wished I could revel in it.

But all I could do, with so many people around us, was to smile and lift my fingers off my armrest in a tiny wave to show I was happy for him.

He deserved the honor, the admiration, and the applause. His tragic beginnings meant he had a much longer way to climb. But he made it. And he deserved it all.

"Did you petition the queen to award him the medal?" Leafar asked from his seat on my right.

"Me? No." I shook my head, forcing my eyes away from Salas. "Why would you think so?"

"Well, he saved your life in the arena that day, even risking his own life to defy the dragon."

"The queen saw it with her own eyes," I replied. "She also got a report that he apprehended a violent criminal in the city. She decided his heroic deeds deserve the medal. Do you not think so?"

He dropped his gaze to his lap. "I dare not question the queen's decisions."

"But you can think on your own. You have the right for an opinion..." I let my voice trail off, distracted by the gladiators around Salas.

As he basked in the well-deserved glory, I caught a look Falo cast at Salas. It was brief but intense, like a furtive stab of a poisonous dagger.

The next moment, Falo's expression shifted to sweet and flirty as he blew a kiss to Gem sitting next to Leafar and me.

If I caught anyone at the royal court throwing a toxic glance like that at me, I'd watch them carefully from then on. I had to warn Salas to watch his back. He might have enemies among the gladiators that he wasn't aware of. As much as his rise to fame attracted the admiration of many, I imagined, it would also bring forth envy in some.

After the ceremony, the gladiators went to the rooms allocated for them in the palace to change for dinner. Salas was here not as a slave but as a guest of honor. As such, he got a room to spend the night at the palace.

At dinner, Salas sat at the same table as me, just a few seats down on the same side. He'd changed into a dove-gray shirt and a waistcoat in charcoal jacquard. A silver pin depicting two crossed swords on a round shield nested in his simple cravat.

Compared to the ruffles and jewelry of the men at the royal court, Salas's outfit was modest, but it was elegant and suited for the occasion. He wore it well, too, with grace and not a hint of awkwardness about his surroundings.

From this position, I couldn't talk to him. I couldn't even see him unless I leaned over the table, but I felt his presence with my whole being, like always. The awareness of him was visceral. He was in my soul. Every cell in my body came to life when he was near.

Was it love that made me so acutely aware of him?

I never was in love before. I never thought it would feel like this, like a hurricane of thrill and longing, of passion and ache.

How could one hide something like this? I wished to scream to the entire world that he was mine. I wanted to go to him and to hold him like I would never let go.

Instead, I had to remain sitting and chat with the courtiers on topics of no importance like how hot the weather had been lately or how beautiful the gardens looked today.

Once the dinner ended, the party moved into the ballroom. The doors between several grand rooms were open, as well as all doors to the patios outside, expanding the space where thousands of people could dance to the music played by several orchestras positioned in different rooms.

As required, I opened the dancing by taking Leafar into the middle of the main ballroom. We were the first couple on the dance floor under the high cathedral ceiling.

My pale pink evening gown had a far more appropriate skirt for dancing than the white one I'd had on earlier today. The several layers of the light, gossamer material floated around my legs as I led Leafar in the cotillion. He followed me perfectly with the grace of a well-trained dancer.

"We only have one night, Your Highness," he whispered so that other couples on the dance floor with us wouldn't hear him. His sweet smile made it look like he was paying me a compliment, disguising the nervous urgency in his voice.

"I'll wait—" he started, but I shook my head, stopping him.

"Don't wait for me."

I was married to one man while being in love with another. Nothing about this situation was fair. I had no one by myself to blame for marrying without love, then for falling in love so carelessly.

I never acted spontaneously. Every action I'd made, I had thought through. Every step I'd taken, I had valid reasons to take. And yet, there I was in a mess I'd created and pulled two men into it with me. Because I didn't believe before that love existed. That was my biggest mistake. I didn't foresee the things that could hardly be predicted.

No one could untangle it all now but me.

One thing was clear, however, I would never visit Leafar's bedroom again. Making him believe otherwise would be a cruel lie.

"Don't wait for me, Leafar. Get a good night's sleep tonight. I'll talk to you tomorrow, after my audience with your aunt."

At my mentioning the grand duchess, he swallowed hard and bit his lip. The influence of that woman over her nephew was strong. Maybe with her leaving the country, he'd learn to relax and find more joy in life. Right now, the poor thing looked anything but joyful.

"You know what? Why don't you come to my living room after breakfast tomorrow?" I offered. "You can spend the morning there while I'm meeting with the grand duchess. Bring a friend or two to keep your company. Stay the whole day, if you wish. No one will dare bother you there, not even your aunt."

"It's very kind of you, Your Highness."

"You don't have to face her at all other than to say goodbye just before she leaves."

The music ended. The prince bowed to me, allowing me to lead him off the floor and to the sitting area between two sets of open patio doors. My mother and father sat in armchairs, surrounded by a group of courtiers, including the grand duchess and a few of Leafar's gentlemen-in-waiting.

"Oh, I can't wait to dance again," Father stirred in his chair.

"Patience, Your Majesty." Mother patted his hand on the armrest. "You've just started to walk again. One step at a time, please."

A valet handed Leafar the coat he'd abandoned in his dressing room.

"Put it on," the grand duchess replied to his questioning glance. "Dress as a decent young man, Leafar. You're not one of them." She tipped her chin at the group of gladiators at the other end of the room. All of them were in shirtsleeves like many of the court gentlemen, including my father.

Indignity flared in me, scorching my chest. But Leafar obediently turned around, allowing the valet to put the coat on him.

"You look lovely tonight, my prince," I said calmly, before turning to the grand duchess. "There is nothing indecent about my husband, Your Grace. His upbringing instilled the unshakable sense of propriety in him that nothing could corrupt."

Sadly, that was as much as I could rebuke her in public without causing a scene and potentially a political fallout with Olakrez. Mother looked tense already, watching me with concern.

I didn't insist on Leafar taking off his dress coat. Doing so would put him on the spot and undoubtedly result in an argument with the duchess when it wasn't about her, or me, but about Leafar and his ability to stand up for himself.

There was strength in him. Though, his ways of getting what he wanted tended to be sulking and manipulation, but I hoped that with time, he'd learn to speak his mind and defend his point of view in a more straightforward manner.

Giving his aunt what she wanted, Leafar quietly moved away from us with the group of his gentlemen-in-waiting

One of the Olakrez ladies chuckled, pointing at the gladiators.

"Those boys are natural. Just look at them mingling with the nobles as if they weren't of a low birth themselves."

"They act like they belong here," a gentleman scoffed.

Mother lifted her head. "Tonight, they're our guests of honor."

I smiled at the courtiers politely. "Some of those 'boys' did more for the queendom in the past few days than many people of the court have done in their entire lives."

"One of them saved our daughter's life," Father reminded everyone. "Wouldn't it be lovely, Your Majesty, if you asked our hero to dance? I'm afraid no one had asked him. One would think his card would be filled by now, but I haven't seen him dancing yet."

The dance floor had filled quickly. Gem danced with Falo. The games master and her husband were also there, swirling in the quadrille.

"I'd rather stay with you, dearest," Mother cooed, not letting go of Father's hand. "But I'm sure Princess Aniri would welcome the chance to express her gratitude to him for saving her from the dragon. What do you think, my dear?" She looked at me.

"If you insist, Your Majesty," I replied quickly and headed across the room before anyone could object and stop me.

Was it reckless of me to accept Mother's suggestion so eagerly? Was it careless of me to approach in public the man I loved in secret?

The music stopped as the quadrille ended. Now, all eyes were on me as I crossed the dance floor toward Salas.

He bowed to me, as did the men who flanked him on both sides.

"May I have this dance?" I offered him my hand as the orchestra played the first notes of polka. "That is if your card still has any space for me." I tipped my chin at the sage-colored card pinned to his belt on the left. All single men at the ball had a card like that for the women to write their names in to claim them as partners for each dance.

"It's full, Your Highness," he rumbled quietly. "But only because I can't dance any of that..." He gestured at the floor where the couples were gaining speed in a whirlwind of polka. "Despite my dance teacher's best efforts, I've only mastered the waltz. They're going to play it twice tonight. Both times, Lerrel already auctioned to the highest bidders this morning."

Despite his words, he took my hand, as if accepting the invitation, anyway.

"The waltz is such a lovely dance, isn't it?" I smiled, squeezing his hand. "There is no reason it can't be played three times instead of two tonight."

I lifted my free hand and snapped my fingers at the orchestra. The snap couldn't be heard over the noise in the room, but the conductor caught my gesture over her shoulder and immediately halted the music.

"Waltz, please," I ordered in the relative silence that followed.

She nodded and raised her arms. A new rhythm filled the ballroom.

Salas smiled as I led him onto the dance floor where the couples have regrouped to adjust to the change in music.

"The power of the crown princess," he said.

"Sadly, that's all there is to my power." I sighed.

I was powerless to even tell the man I loved how I felt about him.

What would he do if he knew? Would he feel elated like me? Or would my love just add another complication to his life?

Doubts and hesitation entered my mind.

How did he feel about me?

Salas had been my rock in a stormy sea from the moment we met. He'd been my steady, unshakable support to lean on both in my thoughts and in real life. I knew he cared about me. But love was such a new feeling to me. I barely recognized it in myself. How could I tell it in others?

Meanwhile, our time together ticked away with every note of the waltz. It'd end soon, and I hadn't said anything to him yet. We twirled around the dance room, Salas following my lead with unexpected lightness and grace.

"You're a pretty good dancer," I blurted out.

"For a man my size, you mean?" he teased.

"I didn't say that."

"But you thought it, didn't you?" He chuckled as I dropped my gaze. "You'd be right, though. With my size, I need to be exceptionally good at this. Imagine if I stepped on a woman's foot. She'd probably be left with a limp for the rest of her life."

Why was it so easy to talk to him about anything or nothing? I wished this dance would never end, and I feared it would end too soon. It was ending already.

"Salas, I..."

What could I say here, in the middle of the dance floor, surrounded by the court that was always hungry for gossip? What could I do if my obligations tied me more effectively than chains?

The last notes of the waltz died, leaving us in a momentary

silence. Couples bowed to each other, parting. Yet Salas still held my hand.

"What bothers you, Princess?" he asked, acutely attuned to my moods, like always.

I couldn't give him an honest answer. With only the two of us left on the dance floor now, all attention was on us.

"I never realized before how short the waltz was," I said with a neutral smile.

He bowed, leaning forward and bringing my hand to his lips in an elegant gesture.

"Meet me at the old barracks when the ball is over," he said so quietly; I stared at him to make sure I hadn't imagined hearing it.

He gave me one of his warm, comforting smiles and walked away without waiting for me to lead him back to the gladiator group.

Meet me at the old barracks...

My heart leaped with a thrill at the chance to see him without the entire palace watching us.

But how could I do it?

An even more important question was—should I?

Not even the strongest emotions could change the course of our lives. In our case, love could only bring pain and heartache, and in Salas's case, a threat to his freedom and possibly his life.

It was reckless of me to fall in love with him. It'd be heartless to drag him into it with me.

My love was mine to bear. Alone. And in silence.

Twenty-Four

SALAS

I told her to meet me here because I wanted to see her, and I had a feeling she wanted to see me, too, without the attention of the court. The dance had been way too short. It took everything I had to let go of her when the music ended.

But would she show up?

I couldn't answer that question with certainty.

Ari knew what she wanted to be, and she built her life accordingly. I loved that about her, her unwavering sense of direction and her faith in her purpose.

She made decisions based on reason and consideration. But there was nothing reasonable about meeting a former whore in a former slave barrack, was there? She'd chosen a life partner already, and it wasn't me.

But here I was, like a love-sick puppy, waiting against all odds for my princess to appear in the door.

It was dark in here, save for the sole candle I'd brought. The slaves had been long gone. The horses had been moved, too, since the princes of Tresed and the Western Islands had departed. But the faint smell of horses still lingered in the air. Personally, I found the scent warm and comforting. I liked horses, even if I would never ride one.

The wide door creaked open.

"Salas?" Ari walked in, and for a moment, I forgot how to breathe.

She wore a dark cloak over a simple flowery dress. Yet to me, she looked more regal than ever. My princess, who could never be mine.

"You came," I exhaled.

"I did. When I shouldn't have." She adjusted her glasses, clutching the side of her cloak with her other hand.

She was nervous. She probably hadn't slept well the night before, and today had been exhausting for everyone. I wished I could wrap her in a soft blanket and bring her to bed, then hold her while she slept peacefully.

Only I doubted she'd find peace any time soon. Something gnawed at her, more than the usual business and concerns of her occupation.

I took a step toward her. "You know one of the many things I love about you?"

She peered at me closely. "Tell me."

"That you know what you want, and you go for it."

"I do?"

I nodded firmly. "You wanted justice for me, and you worked on it. You knew you wanted me in your bed, and you got me. You want to make this world a better place for everyone, not just for the select few, and you're doing everything to get into the position to make it happen. And right now, you want to come to me for a hug. Only for some reason, you're hesitating." I paused, giving her a chance to argue, but she didn't say a word to contradict me. "Would a glass of wine help you relax?"

She blinked, taking a look around.

"You have wine here?" She finally noticed the silver tray on the upturned barrel next to one of the stalls.

"It's a good one." I filled two glasses with a splash of wine each, then put the bottle back on the tray next to the candle and the wide lily pad I'd filled with raspberries on my way to the barracks. "I stole it from the queen's palace."

"You stole it?" She laughed.

It was a short, nervous burst of laughter that died quickly. But I loved hearing it, anyway.

"Well, it was served to the guests at the party. I figured that since I was an officially invited guest this time, it was for me too." I handed a glass to her, then clinked it with mine. "To you, Princess."

She barely touched her wine, glancing back at the tray with the candle and the berries.

"It almost looks like a date," she muttered softly.

A date?

That wasn't my intention. I'd found a quiet place for us to talk, since she'd looked at the ball like she desperately needed to talk to someone. And also, because I had something to tell her too.

While I watched Ari dance with the prince tonight, I realized I couldn't stay in Egami for much longer.

I stayed because she needed me. I wanted to be here for her as someone she could trust, because just like big hugs and genuine kisses, trust was a rare commodity in the palace. After what happened yesterday, however, I realized I couldn't trust myself around Ari. I couldn't watch her going through life as a wife of another man, dancing with him, bearing his children, and growing old at his side.

If she came to me for help again, I couldn't trust my well-intentioned hugs not to turn into something more. If she looked at me the way she did back in the hallway yesterday, I couldn't guarantee she wouldn't end up coming on my hand again, or worse.

The problem was that in my mind, Ari belonged to me and only me. When in reality, she never was mine. I didn't lure her here to convince her otherwise or to change anything. This wasn't a date.

Yet as I set the glass back onto the tray, I heard myself asking, "What if it was our date? Like the one we planned, remember?"

She had to stop me right then and there. But she didn't.

"There are no horses here." She smiled with a glance down the aisle between the stalls. "Wasn't I supposed to teach you how to ride a horse on our date?"

Oh, I could turn this into a real date so quickly, our heads would spin. The consequences would be dire for both of us, but I found it hard to care about the consequences right now.

"I planned to take you swimming," I reminded her. "But I'm afraid that can't happen, unless you don't mind scandalizing the court by swimming naked in the lily pond with me."

"Would you really go swimming naked?" She gave me a teasing smile. I loved it when she smiled carefree like that. "Where is your male modesty, sir?"

"If you wanted modesty, my sweet princess, you shouldn't have looked for a date in the gladiators' quarters. Or slaves' barracks. Or a fun house."

"All proved to be the right places for me to find my perfect date. If only I knew how to keep him." The smile left her. "We can't date, Salas, with or without swimming. I can't court you, remember? I'm a married woman."

As if that was the only reason why she and I could never date. Even imagining it seemed like a sin. Yet I came closer to her, anyway.

"Then, I will court you. In your old world, a man can court a woman, can't he?"

I watched her carefully when speaking about her old world. She didn't flinch. The dark memories she harbored wouldn't ever go away, but she had brought the demons of her past under her control. My strong, beautiful princess.

"Yes, Salas. In that world, men court women. And in another life, I'd be so...so happy to be courted by you."

Tears glistened behind her eyeglasses. Her tears undid me. Always.

"Please, let me hold you, Ari."

Her wine glass fell onto the hay strewn floor, spilling the priceless wine.

She stepped into my arms like coming home. It was more than a hug. More than a date. Because Ari and I were more than all of it. Larger than life itself.

It didn't matter who reached first and who followed, whose lips touched another's mouth, or whose cloak fell off first. When we kissed, nothing else mattered.

I wanted to make her feel better. Whatever weight pressed down on her, I wished to lift it. I wanted to be the one who put a smile on her face. But when she pulled away, tears still glistened in her eyes. And the most devastating thing was that they were there because of me.

"I made you cry."

"No." She shook her head quickly. "You..." She drew in a long breath, then exhaled quickly. "You are my happy place, Salas. I go to you in my thoughts when I can't come to you in person. You are with me, despite the guilt and the heartache. And I'm keeping you in my heart, despite it all."

The guilt and the heartache...

That was what I caused for her. I wished to give her the world, but all I gave her were tears. My decision to leave grew even more solid with that realization. Not for me, but for her.

Ari's life could never include me. Yet I'd been sticking around for one and only reason—it was so fucking hard to leave her.

I'd taken every chance to stay in Egami, but for what?

To hunt the seating area from the arena for the rare glimpses of her on the royal platform? For even rarer conversations, filled with dread of imminent parting? Because no matter how strong our bond was, no matter how passionate our encounters turned, they were always going to end with us parting.

"Sweetheart..." I brushed the tears off her cheeks with my

thumbs, wishing I could erase all her sorrows just as easily. "It will be better soon, I promise." With me gone, she wouldn't have to go through all these emotions in the same maddening cycle over and over again. "I'm leaving Egami, Princess. It will be simpler that way."

"You're *what?*" She gripped my arms as if I were walking away already. "But why?"

But she knew the reasons. And in her mind, I believed she agreed with them too. She had a smart, practical mind, my sweet princess.

"No..." she exhaled, pressing her forehead to my chest. "I know I can't hold you. But how am I supposed to let you go?"

My heart was breaking, but at the end, it'd be easier for her without me standing between her and her duties.

Her body shuddered with her next breath. "When I'm with you, I never feel guilty. It only feels like a betrayal when you leave. I can't keep watching you leave, Salas."

The utter devastation on her face gutted me.

"Come with me," I said. "Let's leave together."

I must've lost my mind. Where would I take her? What could I offer her? But as her eyes opened wider, I saw our future in them because I could give her something no one else could.

"I can make you happy, Ari. No other man can."

Because no one knew her the way I did. No one loved her the way I loved. And no man could love her more than I did.

"Where would we go, Salas?" Her voice was soft. Her eyes lit with a dreamy expression.

"North, where it's warm, even in winter." Cold felt especially bitter when one was on the road, I knew it firsthand. "I'll find a job easily this time. Thanks to you, my shameful past is more distant now. No one would hesitate to employ a former gladiator of Her Majesty."

"We'll live in a small house on a beach somewhere?" she joined in the fantasy with me. "You'll make swords, and I'll cook us potatoes for dinner in every way I know how."

"I love potatoes." I smiled. "Almost as much as a rabbit pie."

She smiled, too, despite the tears that glistened on her eyelashes like dew drops.

"It'll be a beautiful life," she said with a wistful note in her voice so sorrowful that I instantly knew our future together was only a dream, just like that date we would never have. "I will kiss you whenever I want."

I held on to the dream with everything I had. "And I will make love to you whenever and wherever we wish."

She rose on her tiptoes, and I met her lips with mine. It was a desperate kiss, deep and hungry.

"I can't come with you, Salas," she whispered fervently, clutching the shirt on my chest. "I wish I could, because you are the only one who makes me truly happy. But many people would suffer if I left. I can't... I'm... I'm not free."

She would never go anywhere with me. Not because she'd hesitate to leave behind the luxurious life of a princess and not because of my past, but because Ari had a purpose and obligations, and no one could steer her away from them. Not even me.

She slid her palms up my chest.

"Let's have this date, Salas," she said softly. "Let me love you one more time, please. Just this once."

Just this once.

The words sliced through me like a blade.

"This once," I echoed, unbuttoning her dress so fast, I nearly ripped the buttons off.

I tugged her dress off her shoulders and freed her breasts. Cupping one, I rolled the nipple under my thumb, and she moaned, arching into my touch.

The sweet, sexy sounds she made sent a rush of desire through my body. My cock swelled with heat, straining to leap out of my pants. Sucking a breath through my teeth, I rocked my erection against her belly, my mind growing blank from lust.

Before Ari, being with a woman had always been methodical for me. Over the years, I'd worked out a system and used it, adjusting it slightly, depending on what worked best for each client.

But Ari wasn't a client. She never had been. With her, I lost the ability of any logical thinking. There were no thoughts in my head, just feelings in my chest and sensations all over my body.

Tugging her dress lower, I kissed every sliver of her exposed skin. I placed a string of kisses along her collarbone, then between her breasts. I caressed each nipple on my way down, eliciting sweet, whimpering moans from her lips.

I trailed my kisses down her stomach as her muscles contracted and her skin pebbled with shivers of pleasure.

Worshiping every part of her body, I fell to my knees and tugged her skirts down her hips, taking her undergarments with them. I kissed the patch of dark hair between her thighs, drinking in her scent and committing to memory every sensation of loving her.

She raked her hands through my hair, gently stroking my skull with her fingers. I freed her leg from her dress and placed her thigh on my shoulder. She moaned, rocking her hips against my tongue as I dipped it inside her.

She was already wet, so wet for me, my princess. I reached as deep as I could with my tongue first, then replaced it with my finger, while licking and sucking on her swollen clit. She moaned louder, her breathing turning erratic. Her fingers flexed in my hair.

Ari was lost to pleasure now, completely consumed by the need to orgasm, and I held the key to her climax quite literally in my hand.

"Salas." She yanked my head away from her. "You..." she panted. "I want you with me... Inside me. Please?"

I rose to my feet, and she leaned against me, her body melting into mine.

"The clothes..." She tugged impatiently at my shirt, ripping it off over my head. "And these..." She unbuttoned my pants and shoved them down my hips.

Her frantic need for me rolled with a swell of heightened desire through my body. She wanted me, no one else. I didn't help her with removing my clothes. There was something especially arousing in having her do it for me.

She let out a long breath, raking her fingers through my chest hair.

"I missed you, Salas. Every moment when you aren't with me, I miss you."

My heart ached as if a thick rusty chain tightened around it. I missed her too. Even now, when she was still in my arms, I already dreaded the years I had to spend away from her.

She deserved a royal bed, but all I could offer her right now was a half of a haystack in the corner. I spread my cloak over it and laid her on top of it.

"It's not a royal bed, my princess."

"I don't care." She wrapped her arms around me, pulling me closer. "I've spent many lonely, sleepless nights in a royal bed. I'd much rather be here with you."

I watched her face as I entered her, slowly sliding into her slick heat until her hips cradled mine.

Her eyelids dropped half way. Her chest rose and fell with her deep breathing. She gripped my shoulders so tightly, her fingernails dug into my skin. The slight sting of pain made every nerve in my body stand on end. Heat rushed to my cock, urging me to move.

I pulled back, slowly dragging out her pleasure and mine. She inhaled, her body following mine, unwilling to separate. Shifting my hips forward, I angled them so that the top ridge on my cock pressed to her clit with my next thrust.

She gasped, and her expression melted into one of pure pleasure. A sweet, tender smile played on her lips.

"It's so good, Salas... You feel so, so good..."

I tried to stretch it out for as long as I could. But she felt fantastic, so perfect, I knew I wouldn't last long. When it came to her, I lost all control.

"I can't, Ari, I—"

"Yes..." she whispered.

Pressing harder, I pumped faster. Her eyes opened wide as her thighs trembled. I waited just a little longer, just until she couldn't speak and could no longer breathe. When her body stilled before her pleasure erupted, I let it go too.

Our bodies rocked together in a fantastic dance of bliss, perfectly in tune. And when we came down from the crest, we came down together.

I didn't want to move away, but I shifted my weight off her.

"Stay." She clung to me. "Please. Just a little longer."

"I'm here." I cradled her in my arms. "I'm not going anywhere. Not yet."

She ran her hands up and down my back, my arms, and my sides, letting her fingers explore every dip and ridge of my body.

"I want to remember this moment, Salas. For as long as I live."

Twenty-Five

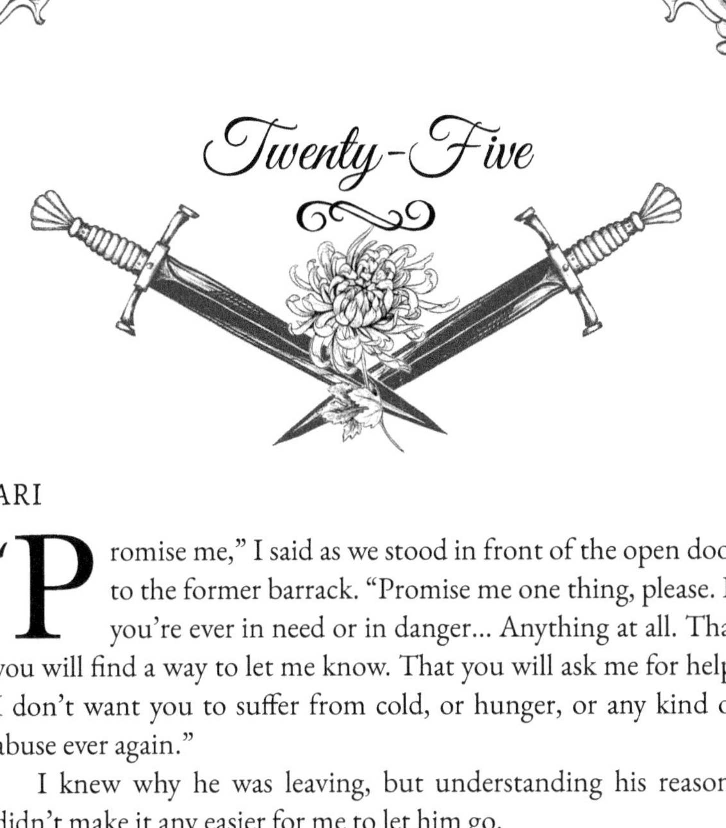

ARI

"Promise me," I said as we stood in front of the open door to the former barrack. "Promise me one thing, please. If you're ever in need or in danger... Anything at all. That you will find a way to let me know. That you will ask me for help. I don't want you to suffer from cold, or hunger, or any kind of abuse ever again."

I knew why he was leaving, but understanding his reasons didn't make it any easier for me to let him go.

"I'm not a child anymore, Princess. I'm in a much better position to take care of myself now. You don't need to worry about me."

But I would. I knew I'd spend many sleepless nights thinking and praying for him. Salas was the strongest man I knew, but he was also a kind man, and kindness could be exploited by unscrupulous people.

"Beware of those who might pretend to be nice but are only waiting to backstab you. Like that gladiator, Falo. I wouldn't trust him."

"I don't trust Falo, either, princess." He smiled, brushing away a strand of my hair. "He doesn't even pretend to be nice."

"Promise me you'll ask me for help if you need it, please," I begged.

"If it'll ease your worry, then yes, I promise." He gently ran a thumb over my chin before cupping my face. "But I want you to promise me something in return."

"What is it?"

He peered at me intently. "You do what you have to do, Princess. Be the best queen that you can be. Accomplish everything you have to accomplish, make the lives of our people better, and get your name in the history books like you were destined to do. But once it's all done and you finally believe you deserve some happiness, I don't care how late in life it may come or how old we both may be by then, you come to me, and I will spend the rest of my life making you happy."

He was right. He could make me truly happy. But I couldn't do the same for him. I couldn't give him the easy, simple happiness he craved. He wouldn't get it with me because nothing about my position was simple or easy. My coming into his life had been making it increasingly more complicated. To the point that he had to leave it all behind now.

Tears choked me, and I couldn't say a single word in reply.

He didn't force me to speak. Wrapping his arms around me, he just held me close until I found my breath again.

"I'll go first," I said around a painful lump lodged in my throat. "Wait for a minute before leaving too."

It was impossibly hard to leave his arms. But I'd seen him walk away from me too many times already. I simply had no strength to watch him leave me again.

Walking briskly, I stared straight ahead. The world turned blurry from tears, but none spilled anymore. I'd cried enough. Tears never helped.

I had a destiny to fulfill and a country to rule. I gave up my happiness for Rorrim. Now I faced a lifetime without Salas, and I had to find the strength to go on.

At the end of the gardens, I stopped to collect myself and rein in my sorrow because I didn't trust anyone to know how I felt. I couldn't tell a single person in that grand palace that my heart broke tonight.

A golden string of a spider web stretched across the end of the path between the hedges. It shimmered in the dying lights of the lanterns left after the ceremony. The summer was coming to an end, and I'd hardly even noticed it go by.

I'd spend the summer mostly in the palace. I'd never found the time to go swimming. Salas had been my one and only breath of fresh air all these weeks. With him, I finally learned what happiness meant. And I had to let him go.

Many busy, lonely summers lay ahead of me now, spent in council meetings, or in the throne room, or at dinners with many important women from all over the world who might not mean much to me but meant a lot to the queendom.

Such were the duties of a princess.

Sweeping with my hand ahead of me, I tore the golden string of the spider web and left the gardens on the way to my rooms.

There was but an hour or two left of the night. I held no hope of sleep. All I wanted to do was to bury my face in a pillow and let it choke the screams of my broken heart.

"You have company, Your Highness," the guard at the door to my sitting room warned me.

"Company?" I groaned and ventured a guess, "Prince Leafar?"

Who else would visit me at this hour?

She nodded, opening the door. "And his escort."

His escort?

I entered the room, coming face to face with the Grand Duchess of Olakrez, the Leafar's very persistent aunt.

"I believe our audience is scheduled for later in the morning, Your Grace," I said, with a voice colder than the ice sculptures at the ceremony today.

"The matter can no longer wait, Your Highness," she replied in an equally icy tone.

Several ladies from the prince's escort were here as well, including the duchess's personal adviser. They lingered around my sitting room, fanning themselves with embroidered fans and drinking cherry wine and ice water. Leafar wasn't with them.

The duchess snapped her fan closed. "The Queendom of Olakrez demands you fulfill your agreement with us and make Prince Leafar your husband in every sense of that word."

I'd requested the meeting with the duchess, intending to fight her on it, but I had no fight left in me. I felt too broken inside, too tired, and too numb to argue.

"Where is Leafar?" I asked wearily.

"The prince is in your bedroom," the duchess informed me. "He's waiting for you to perform your marital duty."

She headed for my bedroom door. Her entourage of highborn ladies stirred, ready to follow her in.

I quickly stepped forward, positioning myself in her path.

"The prince expressed his desire for privacy," I said. "I wish to honor his request."

"I'm afraid his wish can no longer be honored, Your Highness. You can't be trusted to fulfill your marital duties in a timely manner anymore. Goddess knows you've had plenty of time to do it since your wedding."

I'd been trying to postpone the inevitable. Subconsciously, I'd dreaded to betray my feelings for Salas. But that was over now. Salas was gone. All I had was a life of duty ahead of me and an unfulfilled responsibility right in front of me.

The duchess came face to face with me.

"I will not ask where you spent the last hour, Your Highness." She wrinkled her nose. "I can only assume by the smell from your clothes that it was somewhere awfully close to the horse stables." She shrugged, spreading her arms aside. "Women have needs that their husbands can't always fulfill. I certainly won't question your affairs outside of your bedroom as long as you fulfill your duties inside it right now."

"Of course, how can you question my 'affairs' if the Queen of Olakrez is known for keeping a harem of handsome boys for her pleasure?" I retorted, holding her stare.

"The queen is well within her rights to do as she pleases," the duchess huffed. "She has ensured an heiress of the royal blood for her throne, and everyone knows it takes more than one man to satisfy a woman. I don't question your desire for other men, Your Highness. It's your lack of desire for your own husband that presents a problem. I am not leaving your chambers until I am fully satisfied your duties to our countries have been fulfilled. Otherwise, I am taking Prince Leafar back to Olakrez tomorrow."

Going back home was Leafar's worst nightmare. I couldn't allow her to take him. But I also suspected the duchess' threats didn't have as much weight as she wanted me to believe.

"We both know the prince is of little value to the queen at this point," I called her bluff. "If the marriage is annulled, his status as a former husband won't possibly be the same as that of a pure, virginal groom. The queen won't be able to find another match for him as advantageous as his current match with Rorrim."

The duchess glared at me.

"His reputation is now forever stained. Thanks to you."

"It's a good thing then that I don't care about his reputation. Prince Leafar's value to me isn't tied to his purity, and his wishes are important to me. He is a citizen of Rorrim now, and in Rorrim he shall remain."

The duchess's mouth fell open, but she didn't rush with a reply. A calculation was behind her narrowed eyes.

I had to drive my point home, in front of all these witnesses.

"I want you to acknowledge the fact, Your Grace, that my husband is to stay in Rorrim when you leave tomorrow."

"Only if he is your husband in every sense of that word," she insisted. "To spare his modesty, however, I am willing to give you a chance to rectify the situation right now, with only me and my escort in attendance, as opposed to a far greater number of witnesses at the public consummation tomorrow."

"If I 'rectify the situation' tonight," I said with a calm confidence I did not feel, "There will be only the prince and I in that room. No one else."

"How can we be sure it happened if we don't witness it with our own eyes?" the duchess asked suspiciously.

"You'll have to take my word on it."

"Like I said, Your Highness. My faith in your word on this particular matter has been severely shaken."

"How about Leafar's word then? I know he confides in you. He wouldn't lie."

The duchess blew out a derisive laugh. "I'd be a terrible stateswoman if I believed the words of men."

I leaned with my back against the closed bedroom door.

"What would it take for you to accept it once it has happened, Your Grace? Because I swear on everything that has any value in this world, you are not watching me fuck your nephew."

The duchess didn't flinch at my choice of words. The lack of decorum didn't faze the seasoned politician like herself.

"If you're implying I'll derive any kind of pleasure from watching you defile the prince, you're very mistaken. I'm simply looking after his interests."

"Good. Then our goals align. I wish nothing but the best for your nephew too. He begged me to 'defile' him in private, and I shall oblige. You're not setting foot in my bedroom."

"I am not leaving—"

"Suit yourself. Feel free to stay in this room for as long as you like. Now if you excuse me, I have a husband to bed."

I placed a hand on the handle of my bedroom door and paused just enough to make sure they wouldn't rush me in their eagerness to get in.

The duchess squared her shoulders, angling her head down like a bull, ready to charge.

"I'll give you thirty minutes, Your Highness, before I enter this room. If you're not done by then—"

"I need longer than that," I interrupted her hurriedly, my fake composure slipping. "I need to take a bath first."

"Well, then you'd better hurry." She remained relentless. "At least on his first night with a woman, my nephew deserves better than a wife who reeks of horses and other men."

I swallowed that insult as a punishment for all my lies and silently entered my bedroom.

Not finding Leafar in the sitting area, I peeked behind the silk screen to find him in my bed. Wrapped in my blankets, he slept on his side with his mouth open and a string of drool glistening in its corner.

I quickly slipped into the bathroom and had a shower. I made the water as hot as my skin could stand without blistering. Lathering the sponge with the rose soap, I scrubbed every part of my body, washing off every trace of Salas's touch.

Despite my best efforts to hold them in, tears ran down my cheeks. I'd broken promises and lied just for a chance to experience a sliver of stolen happiness with the forbidden man. As a result, I made everyone around me miserable and drove the man I loved out of the city.

Now, I had to lie to myself that I didn't need Salas in my life, that I could do just fine without him. I had to deny any chance of happiness to myself to keep everyone else happy.

And so it had to be.

I dried my skin with a towel, put on my robe, and walked over to my bed to finally have sex with my husband.

Leafar blinked at me, sitting in bed with the blanket pressed to his chest.

"Did I wake you up?" I asked. "I tried to be quiet."

"I wasn't sleeping," he lied, but I didn't hold it against him. I'd told far worse lies myself. "Um... my aunt?" He looked around as if expecting the grand duchess to jump out from behind the screen.

"She's in the sitting room. It's just you and me here tonight."

He looked confused. "But she should be here."

"She gave me thirty minutes to... consummate in private."

He perked up.

"Really? I guess we better hurry then."

He tossed off the covers, revealing his completely nude body and his already partially erect penis. His shyness seemed to have melted under the heat of his eagerness to get it over with.

"Wait." I stopped him by raising a hand. "I have a few conditions first."

"What kind of conditions?" he asked warily.

"You'll lay down on your back and will remain in that position during the whole thing. Please."

"All right." He readily agreed, plopping back into the pillows. "Isn't that how it's always done? The wife is always on top."

I closed my eyes for a moment, forcing the cherished memories of Salas's large body moving over me out of my mind. I didn't want to remember it right now, not when I was about to get in bed with someone else.

"Can you also not grab me while we are...together?" I asked Leafar.

He squinted at me from the pillow. "You don't want me to touch you?"

"Can I trust you not to restrain me or hold me down while you're touching me?" I fisted my hands, already dreading an impending panic attack.

He was so young, so inexperienced, and I was so fucking jumpy. Not knowing what to expect from him, I couldn't trust him, and I feared the worst.

"It'd be kind of hard to hold you down if you're on top," he pondered.

It was not impossible for him to roll me over. He was stronger than me. But I wasn't going to give him any ideas about that now.

"Just try not to overpower me. Let me do all the work, at least tonight. Please?"

"As you wish." He threw his arms to his sides. "I'm all yours."

All mine.

Whether I wanted it or not.

I lifted my robe out of the way as I climbed onto the bed. He bit his lip, watching me straddle his legs.

Was he hard enough for us to proceed? He didn't look like he was. Goddess knew, I wasn't ready at all.

How was I supposed to fix it?

I never had to think about things like that with Salas.

Salas…

With him, it'd just happened. In the most amazing way.

My chest squeezed so hard, I nearly bent over in pain.

I couldn't think about him right now.

I couldn't remember…

"Your Highness?" Leafar's worried voice reached me as if through a fog.

In this relationship, I was the one who had to make it happen. I had to be strong. I tugged at the belt of my robe, untying it.

"It's all good," I said, trying to sound comforting, then shrugged the robe off and tossed it aside.

He ran a curious gaze up and down my naked body as I tried my best not to blush. It wasn't shyness that crippled me, but the uncomfortable feeling from how wrong this whole thing felt.

Unease creeped up my spine, threatening to paralyze me. I had to get it done and over with. Quick. Like yanking out a tooth.

"Sex is supposed to be enjoyable." Salas's words came to me.

And then, *"Some things take time."*

I didn't have time. I fought for it and lost. But I had to at least try to make it enjoyable for Leafar.

I plastered a smile on my face and leaned over him.

"Just relax, my prince." I slid my hands up his perfectly smooth chest.

His muscles strained under my touch.

Relax.

Relax and enjoy.

The words jolted me with alarm. I stiffened, dreading where my mind was about to go. Coercion led Leafar and me into my bed tonight. I'd been forced, and my mind reacted, threatening to veer off into the darkness once again.

Unlike my panic attack with Salas, however, there were no gentle arms cradling me, no soothing words to support me. I couldn't count on anyone but myself to get me through this.

"Ahh, it feels good." Leafar let go of the sheets he was clutching and gripped my hips. Sliding me forward over his cock, he bucked his hips up.

"Wait..." I pushed against his chest.

"How much longer do you want me to wait?" he snapped, his fingers digging into my flesh. "Have I not been patient enough?"

It wasn't his fault. He didn't know me. Maybe I didn't give him enough chances to get to know me, but he had rejected every opportunity I gave, and the more I'd learned about him, the further away it drove me.

Fighting against his grip, I scooted back.

He glared at me.

"It's because of *him*, isn't it?"

I froze, startled. "What are you talking about?"

He pulled himself up into a sitting position. With his fingers locked on my hips, I straddled his thighs.

"I'm talking about that slave turned gladiator you've been fornicating with."

Blood stopped in my veins.

I licked my dry lips. "Who told you about him?"

"Did I even need to be told?" he scoffed. "Everyone saw how you looked at him in the arena during the games and at the ball tonight."

I could deny it, but I'd lied enough. Leafar was my only future, and what kind of future would that be if we built it on lies?

"I'm sorry, Leafar." I took a deep breath. "I'm sorry I met him before I met you. I'm sorry my feelings for him grew out of my control. I'm sorry I can never regret meeting him. But if I hurt you in any way, I hope we can find a way for you to forgive me, because hurting you was never my intention. Your safety and your position in Rorrim were never threatened. And now..." I swallowed hard. "He's gone, Leafar. I'll never see him again."

"Oh, he is gone," he lashed out. "Absolutely. I made sure of it."

My muscles tightened in apprehension. "What do you mean?"

"Powerful women take lovers. It's a fact of life." He spread his arms to the sides in acceptance of that fact. "Women will be women. My feelings aren't hurt," he scoffed. "I knew my place long before I came to Rorrim. As your husband, I'm supposed to celebrate whatever makes you happy. And if it takes several random men to satisfy you, so be it. But if it's just one man, there is always a threat of him eventually taking my place. Especially a former whore, whom you went through the huge trouble of elevating to a royal gladiator."

"How do you know all of that?" I scrambled from his lap, almost falling off the bed in the process.

"Another gladiator kindly informed me, so I knew where the danger lies." He followed me into the sitting area behind the screen.

"Who else knows?" I didn't bother putting my robe on, grabbing my discarded dress instead. It might smell like horses, but I had no time to look for anything else.

Butt naked, Leafar watched me, his eyes flicking nervously between my face and my clothes. "Where are you going?"

"Who else knows, Leafar? Whom did you tell about Salas?"

"Salas?"

"The man whose secret you just so righteously threw in my face."

His handsome features scrunched with disgust.

"He's a whore, Your Highness. Why would you even want to associate yourself—"

"You put his life in danger." My shaking fingers got trapped in the dress as I tried to straighten it to put it on. "Do you not realize that?"

"Well, according to the Rorrim's laws, he should've been long executed," he replied casually.

Burning with both anger and terror, I tossed the dress aside.

"What do you know about our laws?" Then it dawned on me. Leafar wasn't foolish, but he had a weakness that allowed him to be manipulated. His weakness was fear. "Who put you up to this? Your aunt?"

He paled.

"No. My aunt can't know about a whore in your bed. Think about the scandal it'd cause in Olakrez."

"Who, then? The gladiator who told you? Was it Falo?" I knew it was. "Who else knows?" I gripped his arms and shook him so hard his teeth clunked. "Whom else did you tell?"

"Your mother, the queen."

"What?" I dropped my hands from his arms.

Mother would be furious. She must be, since she didn't even call for me to speak with me about it. I had to talk to her at once. I'd get her out of bed if I had to. Maybe I could still salvage the situation somehow.

"And the head councilor, Lady Etah," he added.

My heart dropped.

Salas' secret was no longer a secret. The council knew.

I blew out a breath, scrambling for what to do now.

Leafar spread his arms aside again.

"I had to, Your Highness. Who else has power over you? Who else could possibly put an end to it and make you behave?"

"Me." I pressed a hand to my chest. "Me, Leafar. You should've talked to me. That's how trust builds between people. We should've been able to discuss things between us, instead of talking to others behind each other's backs."

And now what? Was I too late to do anything about it?

Cold sweat chilled my spine.

"Oh, Leafar." I shook my head. "You let your fear rule you. And now, an innocent man may die."

"He isn't innocent!" he shrieked. "He's a whore who has no place in the palace, in the arena, or in your heart. Your association with a man like that is disgusting. Mother would've never accepted your marriage proposal if she knew. You're a princess, for gods' sake. Why did you need to fall this low? Did you not have enough handsome men at the court to fornicate with? Did you have to fuck a dirty whore?"

I raised my hand to slap him for the insult. No one would fault me if I did. According to the laws of Rorrim, it was perfectly legal for me to hit him. But the same laws would have him executed if he slapped me back.

How wrong all these laws turned out to be, and I had worshiped them for so long.

I dropped my hand without touching him. Grabbing my dress from the floor, I tossed it over my arm, then did the same with my cloak.

Wearing nothing but my shoes and my glasses, I shoved the door into the sitting room open and marched out.

"Guards!" I yelled.

"Your Highness?" Leafar ran out after me.

His aunt and her entourage rose from the armchairs, staring at us in shock. The door to the hallway opened, and two guards rushed in.

Leafar faltered. Realizing he was still completely naked, he cupped his crotch with his hands and promptly retreated behind the bedroom door.

I placed my clothes over the back of the couch, then took the dress from the pile and shook it out.

"My highly esteemed ladies," I announced, putting the dress on over my head. "The prince's reputation is fully and irreparably tarnished. I hope he's now sufficiently defiled for your liking, Your Grace." I bowed my head to the Great Duchess while closing the front buttons of my dress.

I didn't explicitly confirm the consummation, but I knew how my words would be taken in conjunction with both of us emerging naked from the dark bedroom. I owed this much to Leafar. No matter what, he was my responsibility. His aunt had to deliver the report of our marriage being valid to his mother, and they both had to leave him alone.

"Well..." The grand duchess moved her startled gaze from me to her nephew, who was peeking at us from behind the door.

The duchess clearly hesitated on how to proceed in this situation. Plenty of witnesses saw us naked, including the palace guards. It'd be foolish of her to insist Leafar remained untouched and pursue an annulment. It also would be impossible for his mother to bank on his pure reputation again and find another high-standing wife for the prince. Their best bet was to leave him in Rorrim, just like he wished.

The prince didn't even need to lie. All he had to do to get what he wanted now was simply to keep quiet. And he did, not saying a word.

One of the guards stepped forward, tentatively gripping her crossbow.

"Your Highness? Do you need help?"

"Yes. Please send for Prince Leafar's valet to help him get dressed and escort him to his bedroom. My prince needs his rest. He had a very, *very* busy night."

With the emphasis on that word, I glanced at Leafar, wondering if the trust we'd pledged to each other and broke could ever be restored.

Tossing the cloak over my shoulders, I left the room. With the hood low over my face, I headed to the east wing of the palace, where gladiators were staying for the night, including the guest of honor who'd been lauded as the one touched by magic still that morning, only to become a hunted fugitive now.

Twenty-Six

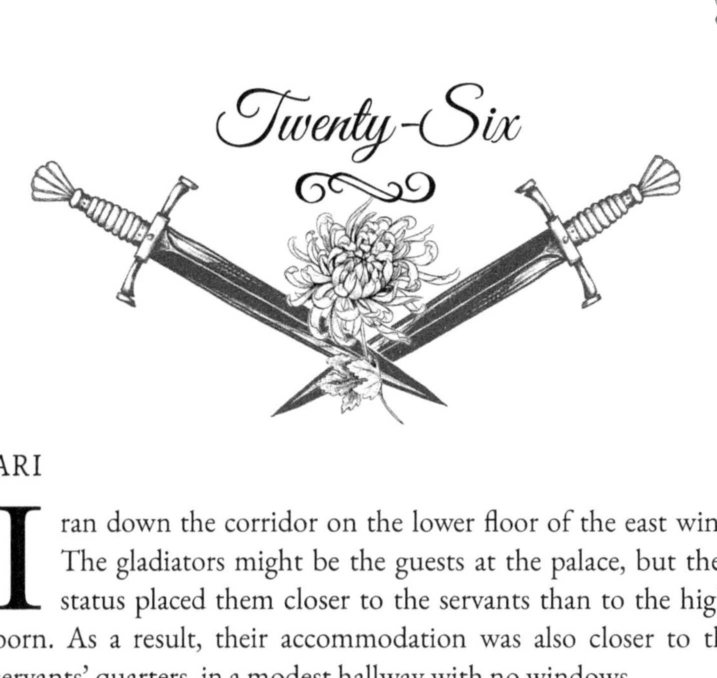

ARI

I ran down the corridor on the lower floor of the east wing. The gladiators might be the guests at the palace, but their status placed them closer to the servants than to the high-born. As a result, their accommodation was also closer to the servants' quarters, in a modest hallway with no windows.

The door down the corridor behind me opened, and I slowed my pace, trying to step as quietly as possible on the wooden floors.

"Your Highness?" the games master called.

Cursing under my breath, I turned to face her. "How did you know it was me?"

"I recognize your shoes." She tipped her chin at my flat-sole slippers as she approached me. Her attention to detail proved even more acute than I thought. "You wore them when you came to our neck of the woods to look for Raeb the other day. Dare I assume you're looking for the same gladiator again?"

"What if I were?" I asked carefully.

I could use her help to find Salas. My only other option was to knock on every door in the hallway in search of him.

"Then I would ask you what for?" she replied just as cautiously, drawing a long, colorful shawl around her shoulders.

The games master was an ambitious woman. Driven to succeed, she'd cut corners and stepped over heads when needed. But I hoped she cared about her gladiators more than just the means to her success.

I took a chance. "I'm afraid his life is in danger."

She didn't seem surprised to hear it. A hard expression set behind her dark eyes that peered at me intently.

"He deceived us all, didn't he?"

There was more sadness than anger in her statement, which prompted me to ask, "Do you believe he deserves to be punished?"

She gave me a guarded look. "That's the law, isn't it?"

"Did the consideration of the law prompt you to betray him?" I prodded.

"I wasn't the one who did it."

"But it was one of your gladiators who informed the prince, wasn't it?"

She shifted uncomfortably, huddling deeper into her shawl.

"If Your Highness will forgive me, I prefer not to give any names at this point. Will it suffice to say that our investigation into um... certain recent malfunctions in the arena uncovered a few concerns with one particular individual?"

"Falo," I said with certainty. "Was he the one who sabotaged the act with the dragon too?"

She arched an eyebrow. "How do you know that?"

"Just a lucky guess." I waved her off, not willing to get into lengthy explanations, but it seemed the world of the gladiators didn't differ much from the royal court where people competed and jostled each other out of the way in their strife for favors and fame. "Falo has been upstaged in the arena recently, hasn't he? Did he feel bitter about it?"

The games master heaved a breath.

"Fame is addictive, and losing it can be excruciatingly painful for some. Falo will be punished severely, according to his crimes, but on a personal level, I don't judge him harshly."

"Is that how you found out about Salas's secret?"

"You know his real name too? I bet you knew his secret all alone. Isn't that why you sent Lady Gem to persuade me to accept him on my team?"

"How do you know it was me who sent her?"

"I didn't know for sure." She smiled slyly. "But now I do."

Blush heated my cheeks. How easily I'd walked into her trap. I was too frazzled, too worried, too in a rush to pay attention.

"Please, tell me where he is?" I begged.

She tilted her head, studying my face. "Are you angry at Salas or worried about him? Because that would make a huge difference in how I'll answer your question."

We weren't in the court of law. At this point, the games master didn't have to speak with me at all.

"I worry about him," I confessed. "Always have. I need to warn him. The queen and the council know his secret, and the royal guards may be coming for him soon."

She sighed heavily.

"They already have. I sent them to the gladiators' quarters."

"Is that where he is?"

"No. Reab... I mean, Salas left Egami before it all happened. He gave up the job that he was so good at, that so many boys in his position would kill for, and I can't shake the feeling it has something to do with you."

She pinned me in place with her accusatory stare. But the weight I carried already crushed me harder than anything she could do or say to me.

"I only ever wished the best for him," I said, crestfallen.

"You know what I always tell my boys about the favor of powerful women? 'Use the fire of status and money to keep you warm but don't come too close or it will burn you.' It seems Salas didn't listen, and now he lost it all."

"All except for his life, which he may lose too if I don't help him. Do you know which way he left? I have to warn him. He needs to know he's in danger."

"If you ride horseback, you can probably catch up with him on the road out of Egami. He went on foot. He said he'd take the North Gates out of the city."

"Thank you." I made a move towards the stairs up to the main floor, but the games master caught my arm.

"Salas is the strongest man I know, Your Highness, and I've seen my share of strong men. But he has a big weakness. His instinct to protect is far greater than his sense of self-preservation. He struggles to hurt anyone weaker than him, even to defend himself. I had to design his acts in the arena with that in mind. If the guards attack him, he'll hesitate to hit a woman, which may cost him his life because the guards will not hesitate to hurt him."

Twenty-Seven

SALAS

Leaving the city, I didn't look back. This place had given me the only woman I'd ever loved. But it took it away from me way too soon. Happiness teased like a flash of sunshine before it disappeared, leaving nothing but cold solitude.

Once again, I walked alone on a deserted road, heading into the unknown. Only this time, the future didn't look as bleak.

I had a letter of reference from the games master of the royal gladiators tucked in my pocket. The letter would open many doors for me, anywhere in the country. My shameful past seemed that much further behind me, hopefully no longer able to catch up with me.

The work at the forge I'd done for the gladiators had improved my skills. There were blacksmiths who needed helpers in every part of the country. With Lerrel's reference, I didn't doubt I'd get a job wherever I chose to settle down. My plan was to head north, toward the coast on the border with Olakrez. I hadn't seen the ocean before, and the north seemed as good a direction as any.

I'd made it past the city gates, heading toward the forest that surrounded Egami.

Thumping of hooves came from behind me. There were very few travelers on the road at this early hour.

"Salas!" the familiar beloved voice cut through the stillness of the morning.

My princess rushed to me. She was a vision on her white horse, with her dark cloak trailing in the wind behind her and her unbound hair flying around her lovely face.

For one thrilling moment, I believed she'd chosen to leave it all behind and was coming with me after all. Then I saw her pensive expression.

She stopped her horse, and I caught her in my arms as she jumped from her saddle.

"Ari? What happened?"

"They're after you," she panted, struggling to catch her breath. "...the royal guards. Mother knows..."

"What does she know?"

"About your past. The queen knows your secret, Salas. The council too. The royal guards are on their way to arrest you. You need to hurry."

She looked terrified, but I wasn't scared. For years, I'd been leaving with the expectation of my past catching up with me sooner or later. It looked like it had finally happened. The timing could've been better. But then again, it also could've been worse.

"Here." Ari shoved the horse's reins into my hand. "Take her. She doesn't like going fast, but she will if you need her to. She can also ride at a steady pace for days with little rest."

"I don't ride horseback." At least she didn't bring a riding crop with her.

"I know. But now, you must." She took my face in her hands. "You need to get away, Salas. Nothing good awaits you if they catch you, believe me." I held her tight, and she kissed my face, whispering against my skin, "Remember our dream, my love? The one where I teach you how to ride a horse?" She brushed away a tear from her cheek. "Well, at least that part of our fantasy came true, didn't it?" She smiled at me through tears. Then yanked at the reins to bring the horse a little closer. "Salas, this is Revlis. She'll be a good horse for you."

"Hi, Revlis," I said, not looking at the horse. I saw nothing else when Ari was in front of me. I wondered if she even realized that she'd just called me her love.

"Revlis, this is Salas." She petted the animal's cheek. "Keep him safe for me. Will you, girl?" She looked back at me. "She's a perfect horse for an inexperienced rider. Trust me, you don't have to be afraid."

"I'm not afraid."

"Good. Do you see those two birches at the edge of the woods?" She gestured at the forest to the left of the main road. "That's where the hidden path starts. Not many people know about it. I've taken Revlis there many times. She knows the way and will take you all the way through the forest, past the waterfall, and to the other side of the river. The guards are looking for you, but they will turn back by nightfall. You'll just have to stay safe for a day. One way or another, I will convince Mother not to send them after you again. I swear, I'll do everything to stop the hunt for you. I just need some time to make it happen."

"I'll be fine."

"Please, please stay safe. You are my happy place. Whenever I'm cold, hurt, or lonely, I think about you to help me cope. I need to know you're safe and well, so I can go on too."

Wherever I was, no matter how far fate would take me away from her, I'd never be truly alone anymore because she was in my thoughts, and I was in hers.

I couldn't tell her how I felt, but I put all my love for her into our last kiss. Gripping the back of her head in my hand, I kissed her like my next breath depended on it.

"I'll live," I promised her. "For you."

I climbed into the saddle while Ari held the horse for me. The mare shifted uneasily under the weight of an unfamiliar rider but calmed down as Ari petted her.

"You know what to do, girl," Ari said to her horse gently. "Take him to safety. And I'll see you both again one day."

One day.

I held on to these words of hope as Revlis quietly moved toward the path between the birch trees. I didn't look back, no matter how much I wished to do it. It took all my focus simply to stay in the saddle.

One day, the pain of losing her might ease. One day, I might look up at the stars and not compare them to her freckles. One day, the peals of her laughter stop dancing through my memories.

Or maybe a miracle could happen, and one day, I might be able to say to her, "I love you."

ARI

As an inexperienced rider, Salas looked unsure in the saddle but steady enough for me not to worry about him making it across the river safely. As Revlis turned toward the forest, I headed back to Egami.

I didn't look back. I'd watched him leave too many times already. Today, it was enough for me to know that he was safe. And he would stay safe. Until I'll see him again. Because I would see him again.

As I walked back to the city along the deserted road, I knew with certainty that sooner or later, I would come searching for him, and I would find him, no matter how far life would take him from me. My love would help me find my way back to him. Knowing it helped me walk away from him now, instead of running after him.

A large group of riders on horseback exited the city. I recognized the palace uniforms they wore.

Were they after Salas?

If so, they were too late.

With a furtive glance over my shoulder, I made sure he'd made it to the secret path and was out of sight already. As the guards would head further down the road, searching for him, they would actually increase the distance between them and the man they were after.

Pulling the hood of my cloak over my head, I stepped to the side of the road to let them pass me. But as the riders approached, my gaze crossed with the woman who led them—Gem.

Her eyes narrowed, and I ducked my head down quickly. But it was too late. She knew me too well to be fooled by my cloak. And there was only one reason for me to be here at this hour.

"This way!" she screamed, steering the guards off the road.

Our path through the forest wasn't a secret to Gem. She knew it better than I did.

"Gem!" I rushed off the road after the guards.

She slowed her horse, only to shake her head at me with her lips pursed in disappointment.

"Don't, Gem. Please," I begged. "Let him be."

But she spurred her horse, catching up with the guards. Taking her place ahead of them, she led them right to the spot where the path began.

"Don't!" I ran after them in vain.

Safety proved to be just an illusion, like happiness was only a dream.

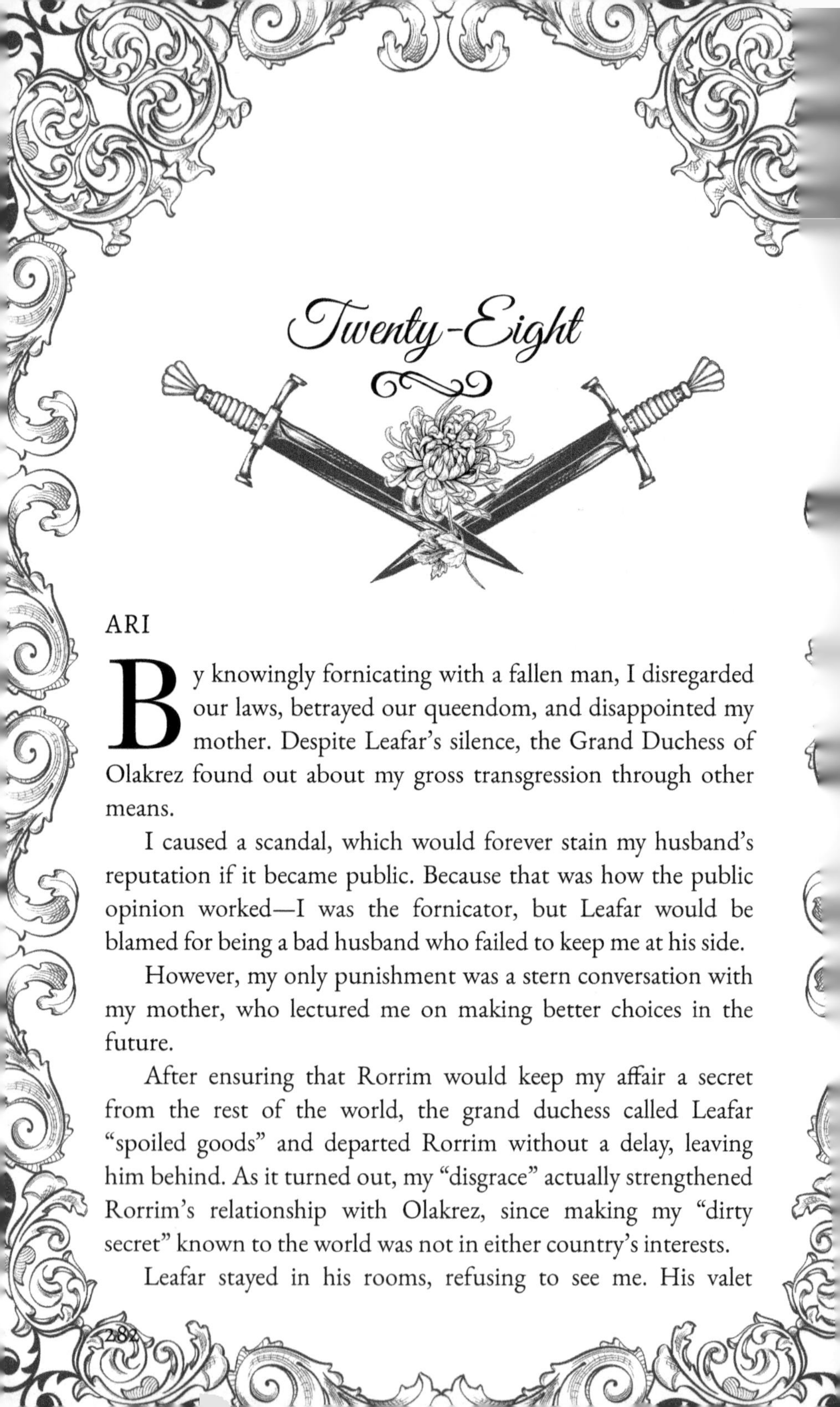

Twenty-Eight

ARI

By knowingly fornicating with a fallen man, I disregarded our laws, betrayed our queendom, and disappointed my mother. Despite Leafar's silence, the Grand Duchess of Olakrez found out about my gross transgression through other means.

I caused a scandal, which would forever stain my husband's reputation if it became public. Because that was how the public opinion worked—I was the fornicator, but Leafar would be blamed for being a bad husband who failed to keep me at his side.

However, my only punishment was a stern conversation with my mother, who lectured me on making better choices in the future.

After ensuring that Rorrim would keep my affair a secret from the rest of the world, the grand duchess called Leafar "spoiled goods" and departed Rorrim without a delay, leaving him behind. As it turned out, my "disgrace" actually strengthened Rorrim's relationship with Olakrez, since making my "dirty secret" known to the world was not in either country's interests.

Leafar stayed in his rooms, refusing to see me. His valet

informed me that my presence in his bedroom was no longer desired and that from then on, the prince would charge the Crown of Rorrim for any public appearances with me at the price negotiated through the royal council.

The games master announced that Falo retired from the gladiators and decided to spend the rest of his life in peace of the countryside in an undisclosed location. After the damage his sabotage had caused to the games from the very first act of Salas, Lerrel could've pursued a life of imprisonment or even the death penalty for Falo, but she chose to just banish him instead.

The scandal of the crown princess's affair with a former man for hire was hushed up with minimal consequences for the crown before any rumors even got a chance to form.

The one person who stood to pay dearly for all of it was Salas.

Because of his connection to me, his case never went to a judge. To keep it private, he was tried by the royal council, with only the council members and a few trusted guards present. The investigation was rushed, with the trial taking place only two days after his arrest. They couldn't wait to deal with the undesirable as fast as possible, to erase him from existence, like a shameful stain on the history of the royal family.

The two days leading up to the trial I spent in the royal library, poring over every legal document I could find that might help me defend him.

Yet on the morning of the trial, I approached the throne room empty-handed. There simply was not a single law in Rorrim that was on Salas's side. In the entire history of the queendom, not a single case had been successfully argued in favor of a fallen man.

Instead of books, notes, or scrolls in my arms, I had a dagger hidden under my purple council robe. I didn't condone violence, but I couldn't give up on Salas. I intended to pass the dagger on to him, and if diplomacy failed, I was determined to try anything and everything to free him, including breaking him out of jail.

The guards opened the doors into the throne room for me, and I entered the place I always held sacred in my heart. To me, this was the heart of Rorrim. Everything that was pure and noble about the queendom resided here. Now, I feared cruelty and injustice reigned here too.

The queen wasn't in the room yet, but all twenty-four councilors were present. They bowed to me in greeting—a differential treatment that was nothing but decorum. My opinion mattered here only as long as it aligned with the established norms. When I went against the norms, I never won.

Lady Etah, the Head of the Council, peered at me above her reading glasses. "Greetings, Your Highness."

"Greetings." I walked across the open space in the middle with the white marble rose inlaid on the floor and took my seat to the right of the queen's throne.

Mother arrived shortly after. Her long purple mantle swept over the white rose of peace on the floor on her way to the throne.

She'd said she wasn't angry with me, just disappointed with my choices. Her disappointment cut deeper than her anger would. But in this case, I couldn't regret my choices. In fact, if I had to make them again, I would. I'd choose Salas every time.

Four trusted guards, armed with swords and crossbows, entered the room. Behind them, two more led Salas in. His hands weren't bound, and I realized why when he tripped over his feet, then ran his unfocused gaze across the room. They had drugged him into submission. The guards weren't here to subdue him. They helped him walk because he was so heavily sedated, he might fall without them holding his arms.

My heart ached seeing him like that. I bit my lip and clasped my hands in my lap so tightly, my fingernails dug into the skin of my palms. The sting of physical pain helped me focus enough to speak.

"The accused is inebriated, Your Majesty," I said firmly. "He doesn't have the clear presence of mind to defend himself. We should postpone the trial until he's mentally competent."

At the sound of my voice, Salas jerked his head up. His chest expanded with a long breath as the guards seated him in a carved armchair facing the queen, with the white rose of peace between Mother and him.

"The accused is not the one in charge of his defense," Lady Etah argued. "Lady Wal is. And she is in full control of her mind. Are you not, Lady Wal?"

"I am, Head Councilor," Lady Wal replied with a soft smile.

They wouldn't let me defend Salas, citing conflict of interests. They'd tried to ban me even from attending his trial, but I was a full member of the council, and as such, I had the right to be here today.

Lady Wal, a soft-spoken, tall woman in her fifties, rose from her seat and cleared her throat, checking her notes.

Since the law was not on his side, Lady Wal spoke primarily about Salas's character. She praised his record as an obedient, hard-working slave. She outlined his rise to fame in the gladiators' arena, portraying him as a man well-loved by the public. She brought up his role in apprehending the violent serial killer. Finally, she highlighted his heroic actions when saving me from the three-winged dragon in the arena. She mentioned his magical ability to wield fire, but Lady Etah promptly dismissed that part.

"The accused's peculiar command of magic is irrelevant to this case," she said. "Depending on the verdict reached today, however, we can conduct another investigation at a later date. It might be in the interests of the crown to determine exactly what kind of forbidden warlock magic this man might be practicing."

She tapped with her quill at the scroll in her lap, peering at Salas, as if trying to decide whether she preferred him beheaded as a former whore or burned at the stake as a warlock practicing black magic.

"Considering the accused's exemplary behavior," Lady Wal concluded, "I believe that an execution would be too harsh a punishment for this man. I therefore petition Her Majesty and the highly esteemed royal council to replace the execution with an imprisonment for life. Let's give him a chance to think about the choices he's made and regret the harm that he's done."

My heart sank into my stomach with dread. A dungeon cell for the rest of his life—that was the highest leniency Salas could hope for, even in the eyes of his own defender.

Lady Etah unfurled her scroll. "The council understands the defender's position. However, the law in this case is clear. Death penalty is the only appropriate punishment for this man."

The queen nodded, and so did the rest of the council members.

My insides froze in horror.

"The gravity of his crime," Lady Etah continued, reading from the scroll, "is further exacerbated by the long period of time during which his deceit took place. He's had years to repent and confess in his crimes to the law enforcement authorities, yet he never did that. Any leniency for such a hardened, unrepented criminal would be a grave mistake on our part."

Her every word fell heavily on my chest. Fear threatened to spike into panic, but I refused to give up hope.

I jumped to my feet. "Why don't you prosecute me? I was the one who ordered Salas to my rooms. I lied for him. Making him a gladiator was my idea. I was the mastermind of his deceit. Prosecute me."

Lifting her reading glasses up to her forehead, Lady Etah gave me a chilling look.

"I beg your pardon, Your Highness, but we didn't gather here this morning to pass judgement on *your* behavior."

"But why not?" I argued. "After all, it takes two to have an affair, doesn't it? Shouldn't I be sitting there, next to him?"

"Aniri," Mother intervened in the firm voice of a parent imploring her child to behave.

But I hadn't been a child for a long time now, and this wasn't a child's play. Salas's life was at stake.

"Once again, Your Highness," Lady Etah insisted, "the council is not judging your personal involvement in this case. We all make mistakes occasionally. Clearly, this vile man saw a young woman of high standing with a bright future ahead of her and took advantage—"

"And there it is." I raised a finger in the air. "The only reason you spared me from a trial is because I am a woman and of high standing. Anyone else would've been right there, judged with him. You're concerned about my bright future. But what about his future? His life? If men and women are equal—"

Lady Etah shook her head.

"But they're not, Your Highness. Men and women are not the same and never were. Goddess put a man below a woman to serve, protect, and obey her, and she did it for a reason. Only when men know their place can our queendom prosper."

Salas's crime wasn't his relationship with me. It wasn't even the deceit that he was charged with. He dared defy the norms. Now, his mere existence threatened the established order, and as such, he lost his right to exist.

Lady Etah ran a hand over her silver hair pulled into a high up-do. "We gathered here today to reach a verdict on the matter at hand. Only the accused himself or his defender can speak on his behalf. And since Your Highness is not his defender, I suggest—"

Salas cleared his throat unexpectedly. Pushing with his hands into the arms of his chair, he rose heavily.

"I'll speak," he said.

His voice was rough. He winced when he tried to swallow. His throat must be dry. His gaze still seemed slightly unfocused and his stance unsteady, but he squared his shoulders with determination.

Lady Etah waved at him to sit down. "Your defender has already presented your case. I fear you lack the education and credentials to add anything of substance to your case."

"You said I could speak. That's the law, is it not?" he glanced my way for confirmation.

I nodded quickly.

"Everyone has the right to defend themselves in the court of law," I said firmly, then turned to the guards. "Can Salas have some water, please?"

I'd defend him until I ran out of breath, until my voice broke, and my brain fogged from exhaustion. I would use my dagger to draw blood without hesitation too. But Salas had a voice of his own. All his life, he'd been silenced. Now was his chance to be heard.

"The deeply esteemed ladies of the royal council," Salas moved his gaze from one face to another along the semi-circle of seats, "Your Highness..." His rough voice warmed a little when his eyes paused on me. "Your Majesty." He bowed his head to Mother. "If you wanted me to think about my life choices, you didn't need to bother imprisoning me. Goddess knows that most of my life, I've been doing exactly that. I've been thinking about the choices I've made when I had any choice at all."

A young male clerk in a tight purple uniform with crisp white collar and cuffs trotted in with a glass of water and handed it to Salas, then waited until Salas hungrily emptied the glass before taking it from him and leaving the room.

"May I take you through those choices with me, ladies?" Salas asked.

A murmur rolled through the council.

Lady Etah furrowed her forehead. "I don't see how it's..."

Salas explained before she could stop him, "You are all wise, highly educated women. So maybe you could tell me where I went wrong?" He paused, but no one interrupted him this time. "You see, my mother died when I was twelve. It devastated our family and left my father and me homeless. I believe her death marked the beginning of my misfortunes. However, you must agree, I have no control over the matters of life and death. The blame for her illness and death lies only with the gods."

The councilors shifted in their seats while Salas continued.

"Many would say I was fortunate that a highborn lady took me in. And at the beginning, I thought myself lucky too. But the lady was the one who took my innocence—"

"Now..." Lady Wal waved a hand nervously. "We really don't need to know the details."

"You don't want to." Salas nodded. "Speaking of sex makes people uncomfortable, doesn't it? I know what it's like. No one speaks of what happens between a man and a woman. No one taught me about sex, either. I was too young to know about such things they would say, even when I was already doing all those things with the lady. Maybe if I had any prior knowledge on the subject, I would've been better prepared to deal with her advances. I was told to stay away from girls. But no one taught me that the real danger could come from an older, powerful woman of high standing. No one taught me how to say no to someone lauded as my benefactor, someone I was supposed to be grateful to and obey her every word."

I drew in a shaky breath, clutching my hands tighter. Salas had been open with me about his past, but I could only imagine what it must be costing him to speak about it this frankly to a room full of strangers. It took a different kind of strength, one that I didn't think I possessed.

"Was that where you think I might've taken a wrong turn?" he asked. "That I somehow should've known what obeying her would lead to? That I should've fought her? Would it appease you if I pushed her away, got charged with an assault on a woman, and was executed? None of what has followed would've happened then. I would've still died a criminal, but not a whore."

He paused, waiting for a reply from the council, but none came. Lady Wal's cheeks bloomed with crimson. Lady Etah stared straight ahead over Salas's shoulder. Others listened, avoiding eye contact with him too.

"I started working in a fun house because my only other option was to freeze to death on the side of a road. Was that the wrong choice to make?" He tilted his head. "Should I have died instead? It looks like this has been my life's biggest mistake—I chose to live." He paused, his throat bobbed with a swallow. "It all went only worse from then on. You see, once a man tripped on the moral path laid out for us by society, the only thing he can do is fall. There is no recourse, no atonement, no turning back. No way up."

He ran a hand through his hair. The gesture appeared to cost him his balance. He swayed sideways. I jerked, ready to help, but the guards steadied him.

"I never blamed anyone for my misfortunes but myself and the cruel fate. But maybe I should have?" There was an accusation in his question. "If the odds are stacked up so high against you, how far can you really make it on your own? Men have so few options in this world—"

"There are good reasons for that," Lady Etah pointed out.

"I know." He exhaled a humorless laugh. "Trust me, I was a diligent student as a child and studied the scriptures well. I know all about the ideals every man should aspire to. Only the scriptures stay silent about what happens to those who fail to meet those ideals. You see, a man can only play one role in life. He's to be a husband and father. There is no occupation for him otherwise." He ran his gaze over the row of councilors, finding me. "By the grace of Princess Aniri, I got to experience what it's like to have an honorable occupation that brings people's admiration instead of their scorn." He turned to the queen next, speaking to her directly. "The man you're condemning to death today is the same man you celebrated as a hero who saved the princess. Just a few days ago, you called me 'special' and 'touched by magic.'" A bitter half-smile crossed his lips. "I am still me. But oh, how your opinion about me has changed."

Mother inhaled deeply, stoically holding his gaze.

"You wanted me to think about my life choices," Salas addressed the entire room. "I have, and I will continue to think about them for as long or as short as my life may be. But I want to ask you all to think about the choices you give to men and boys in Rorrim. How many of us could've had a better life if given a chance? How many boys out there have the potential to be the princess-saving heroes but will end up in fun houses or frozen on the side of a road instead? I'm not asking for leniency for myself," he concluded. "But I implore you to think of the lives you could still save. What happened to me is happening to others out there, and our laws allow for that to happen."

When Salas went quiet, I held my breath, waiting for the reaction from the council. A few of the ladies shifted their feet. One or two sniffled softly. Mother seemed contemplative.

Lady Etah pointed her quill at the councilor, who was taking notes of the proceedings.

"This is the kind of rhetoric that can never leave this room." She gave the councilor a pointed look. The woman nodded and promptly ripped to pieces the last two pages of her notes.

Everything that Salas had said was erased, just like they wanted to erase him from existence too.

Mother lifted a hand in a call to attention.

"I'm willing to consider a life imprisonment instead of the death penalty for this man," she said. "He might've turned out better had the state collected him as an orphan after his mother's death, or maybe if the church intervened in time."

"Your Majesty," Salas sighed. "If you think the lives of state wards are any better, you're sorely mistaken. Mine is just one case of many. A fundamental change is needed to stop and prevent the sufferings of many."

But his plea fell on deaf ears. Even if they spared his life, he'd be rotting in the dungeon for nothing.

"Your position is noted, Your Majesty." Lady Etah folded her hands in her lap. "Is the council ready to take a vote?"

Lose his life or lose his freedom. Such were his options. Neither was good enough. Salas deserved better.

"Where are you going, Your Highness?" Lady Etah called after me as I rose from my chair and headed to Salas.

Diplomacy didn't work.

I reached inside my robe and drew the dagger.

Twenty-Nine

SALAS

"**B**ack off!" Ari pointed a long dagger at the guards.

The queen paled. "Ari? What are you doing?"

"Stay in your seat, Mother," Ari snapped. "Everyone, stay where you are and listen—"

The Head of the Council rose from her seat.

"Take the prisoner away," she ordered the guards. "Now."

A guard shoved against me, sending me back into my chair.

The fucking sleeping potion. It'd been two days since they shot me in the back with the crossbow bolt laced with the potion during my arrest on the forest path. But once it'd entered my bloodstream, the aftereffects had been taking forever to wear off.

Another guard pointed a crossbow at my head.

"I said stay back." Ari lunged forward and slashed at the woman's arm, drawing blood.

My mouth fell open in shock.

Was it the same princess who had so adamantly claimed she had no aptitude for weapons?

The guard groaned. Her injured arm jerked to the side. Her weakened fingers released the bolt. It missed my head and embedded into the shoulder of another guard. Both guards then stomped on their feet unsteadily before crashing down to the floor.

"Is there a sleeping potion on your dagger too, Princess?" I staggered to my feet.

She shrugged a shoulder, looking focused and tense. "Beat them at their own game."

Sleeping potion was a nasty thing. They tried to give me some with tea that morning. Once I'd realized what it was, I poured it out when no one was looking. I was glad I didn't drink it, finally finding my footing now.

When two other guards trained their weapons on Ari, a hot bolt of anger shot through me. They could do whatever they wished to me, but how dared they put her in danger?

"Not the princess!" the queen shouted.

The councilors gasped.

I grabbed the arm of a guard so hard, she spun, sending her crossbow bolt up into the ceiling. Wrapping my other arm around the second guard, I pressed her hands to her torso and bent her over, her bolt hitting one of the marble petals of the rose on the floor.

"Guards!" The Head Councilor yelled at the top of her lungs.

The doors to the throne room swung open, and an entire army of guards poured in. Most women had crossbows, but seemed confused where to shoot.

"Ari!" the queen screamed in panic, running across the floor to her daughter, but the guards separated her from us. "Don't shoot the princess!" she yelled at the guards.

"Get away from him!" Ari held out the dagger, protecting me. "This is not a trial. It's a joke. You just can't wait to be rid of him. But he's not an inconvenience to be swept away and forgotten. He's a person. You can't erase him. I won't let you."

Her hand trembled slightly. Her eyes brimmed with tears, but her voice came loud and firm.

The guards formed a semicircle in front of us, their potion-laced weapons aimed to kill.

Lady Wal craned her neck, peeking over the shoulders of the guards.

"Your Highness, it's such a foolish notion on your part. He isn't worth all this aggravation."

"He's worth everything," Ari replied adamantly.

I gently moved her behind me. The two of us retreated to the left, toward the frame shrouded in black velvet on the wall. There was nowhere to retreat any further.

Hugging my waist with one arm, Ari held the dagger in her other hand. She was ready to fight for me. She'd already attacked a guard. But if she actually killed someone, I feared, even the queen could not protect her from the consequences.

"I'll take it, sweetheart." I freed the blade from her trembling fingers.

I'd fight my own battle. Ari had already given me more than anyone could. She made my life worth fighting for.

"Salas..." She wrapped her arms around me. Her body was shaking. Her eyes were open wide in horror. Tears streamed down her face.

"You'll be alright," I promised.

She'd be safe, even if that was the last thing I did in this world. My crimes were mine to answer for. She was innocent.

"Do you trust me?" she asked unexpectedly.

"You know I do."

"Then fall with me, Salas."

I stared at her, unsure what she wanted me to do, but willing to do whatever it took to erase the terror from her face and from her heart.

"Kill the man," Lady Etah ordered.

The guards rushed us, their crossbows aimed at my head.

"Fall with me!" Ari screamed, shoving me backwards. "Now!"

And I did.

I pushed away from the floor with my feet, letting my body

fall backwards against the wall with the giant frame behind the black velvet.

The fabric fell. The frame held a mirror that reflected my face when I glanced at it over my shoulder. Then a ripple distorted it as my elbow hit the surface.

Instead of shattering into pieces, the glass in the mirror turned into a pool of liquid darkness. Ripples of light and shadows enclosed us.

And we fell through it. Ari and I. We fell together.

ARI

Horror seized me. The play of light and shadows disoriented me. Memories rushed me.

Once again, I was scared. Only my terror wasn't for me this time. I felt helpless to save the man I loved, and terrified at the thought that I'd be forced to watch him die.

It wasn't the mother's arms that held me this time as I crashed through the mirror, but his. Salas held me tight. Somehow, he managed to keep his bearings in the chaos because he turned, hitting the floor first and keeping me on top of him unharmed.

We landed in the darkness. I glanced back at the large mirror on the wall behind me. Mother's pale face stared back at me, her features distorted in the expression of horror. The guards' crossbows remained aimed at the mirror.

"Don't shoot!" Mother yelled. "Don't break the mirror!"

Scrambling to my feet, I leaped aside, out of the line of view of anyone in the throne room. A swell of darkness flooded the mirror, washing away the view of the throne room.

"What the fuck was that?" a dry, unfamiliar voice croaked nearby.

Loud music with a hard beat boomed from a distance. Multi-colored lights from the floor below pulsed to the music, casting their glow onto the concrete stairs.

A flash of a lighter in the corner illuminated a group of young men sitting on the floor and heating something in a metal spoon held over the flame.

One of them got up from a crouch, whipping under his nose with his sleeve.

"Bitch, where did you come from?" he sniffled.

I tossed a glance around as my eyes had gotten used to the dark. It was the same mirror I'd come through to Rorrim ten years ago. The same stair landing in the orphanage. The white painted doors to the girls' bedroom were now boarded up, the white glossy paint scratched and chipped. The wooden parkette floor was broken and filthy. But the mirror was still there—probably too plain, too old, and too heavy to move it anywhere else.

I raised both hands, taking a step away from the junkies.

"I want no trouble, guys." The familiar fear zapped through me, as if it had never left. As if the past ten years had never happened. "I'm leaving."

"The fuck you are." Another one got up, his eyes glistening wild in the darkness.

"Not until we have some fun first," the first one chuckled, shuffling closer.

Two or three more shapes lurked in the shadows, unsteadily swaying on their feet.

"Come on, baby. Get over here, warm my dick—" The last word got stuck in the guy's throat, choked by his own shirt, as Salas lifted him by the scruff from behind.

"That is not a way to talk to a woman," Salas gritted through his teeth.

The guy kicked his feet, dangling in the air and gasping for breath.

"Hey!" His buddy stepped forward.

A switchblade opened with a click.

"He has a knife," I warned.

"Not anymore." Salas knocked the knife out of his hand with a casual gesture, as if swatting a fly away. "Ari, where is the way out from here?"

"Um... This way." I waved a hand down the stairs.

"Perfect." He tossed the guy down the full flight of stairs. "Go work on your manners, boy. Next?"

The one who had lost his knife ducked after his weapon, but Salas caught him by the back of his pants.

"Let me go!" the man squeaked. "Hey, we didn't know she was with you."

"And what difference does it make? How is disrespecting a woman when she's alone any better than when she is with a man?"

He tossed this one down the stairs, too, then grabbed another one.

"Women are our birth givers," he lectured the thug, lifting him over the staircase. "They are the foundation of our society. The gods made them physically weaker than men, to give men a purpose too. What is our purpose as men?" He asked the guy.

"I... I don't know, dude. Really—"

"Wrong answer." Salas tossed him down the stairs like a trash bag.

The remaining two tried to sneak past him, but he caught them both, grabbing them around their torsos and lifting them both off their feet.

"Our purpose in this world is to protect our women, gentlemen," he said firmly. "Will you remember that? Protect. Not attack."

"Yes! Sure!" they yelled as he sent them both rolling down the stairs too.

"Do you think they got it?" he asked me, after they all scrambled away at the bottom of the stairs.

"Let's hope they did." I shrugged, feeling positive they got nothing.

I took a look down the stairs to make sure they were gone, then picked up the switchblade from the floor.

"I'm sure there is more of that down there. Be ready." I hiked up my long purple robe of the Rorrim's Council and took the first step down. "Well, for what it's worth, welcome to my world, Salas."

"Wait." He placed a hand on my shoulder. "Can you return to the palace the same way we came?"

He gestured at the mirror on the wall. It remained dark, reflecting nothing but the dirty opposite wall of the landing. Maybe I could still see my mother and the throne room if I stood in front of it. But I wasn't going to try.

It felt like an enormous weight fell off my chest. Salas was safe. His secret no longer threatened his life. And for once, I didn't have to say goodbye to him.

Our future remained murky. But in this world, we could have a future. Together.

"No." I shook my head. "The one thing I want to do in life I can't do in Rorrim. I can't be with you there."

"Ari." Placing both his hands on my shoulders, he turned me to him. "You had terrible things happen to you in this world. I know how much you despise it. I can never give you what you're giving up."

I took his face between my hands.

"But you give me what no one else can, Salas. You make me happy. They will kill you back in Rorrim. Here, we can be together. It's a very simple decision for me, really. I'm no longer alone in this world. I have you. You will protect me. When society fails to look after one of us, we'll look after each other."

He stared at me intently. His eyes flicked between mine as if trying to read the truth. I held his stare, having nothing to hide. I'd go anywhere, as long as he came with me.

"Then let me say to you something I never could say before." He brought his face closer to mine. "I love you, princess. Maybe not from the first day we met, but definitely from the first time we kissed."

Air rushed into my lungs, making me feel lightheaded with happiness.

"I love you, too, Salas. And it feels so fucking good to say it out loud at last," I breathed out before his lips touched mine, taking my breath away.

Thirty

ARI

6 MONTHS LATER

Sharp whistling cut through the hot summer air as I approached the bus stop. Three young men lingered in the shade of the bus shelter, playing cards and passing a booze bottle between them.

"Hey, babe, want a drink?" One of them shoved the bottle with a cloudy liquid my way.

I shook my head and stepped closer to the only other person at the bus stop—a middle-aged woman in a long-sleeved dress.

"Bitch! I'm being nice to you!" the man shouted.

I kept my gaze down, doing my best to ignore him. I knew from experience that any kind of acknowledgement would make it worse. By being nice, I'd provoke further advances. By being rude, I'd risk a physical assault. By ignoring them, I could only hope that they'd forget about me soon and return to their game.

Another man pulled on the arm of the first one, taking the bottle from him.

"Leave her. An ugly cow. There are much prettier chicks out there."

"But that's disrespect!" the first man raged. "My booze is not good enough for her? Who does she think she is?"

I prayed the bus would come soon, but it was nowhere in sight yet.

The woman gave me a critical look.

"Walking around half naked in public like that," she hissed under her breath. "What else do you expect?"

It was a hot summer day. I wore a spaghetti-straps tank top, but my maxi skirt was even longer than the woman's dress. Two of the three men were topless, the third one had a soiled tank top on. Yet according to the woman, *my* clothes were the problem here.

I shrugged, ignoring them all, and reached in my book bag for my phone.

The technological advances during the past decade had been fantastic and on the verge of magical. Even after four months of owning a mobile phone, I still couldn't believe how easy it was for me to talk to Salas from anywhere in the city.

I flipped the phone open and pretended to dial the number. Salas would be in his workshop this afternoon. There was no need to bother him with an actual phone call.

"Hi, baby," I pretended to speak to him. "I'm at the bus stop now. Should be home in thirty minutes." I made a pause, as if listening to his reply. "I love you too."

The three guys cringed, returning to their game. The fake phone call didn't always work, but more often than not, men would back off when they realized I had a boyfriend. Uncanny, how much more respect men had for the boyfriend they never met than for the woman standing right in front of them.

Thankfully, the bus arrived just a few minutes later. I climbed in, then watched the cityscape passing by in the window.

Not everyone was as awful as the three men at the bus stop. I'd met many decent people in this world in the past few months. I deeply admired my professors at the university. I'd made good friends with quite a few students in my classes. Salas and I had a kind old man for a neighbor.

Sadly, kindness still wasn't a quality admired in men. Instead, it was often viewed as a weakness. The kind, decent men I'd met often felt out of place in their own world.

That said, a lot of changes had happened in the ten years that I was gone.

The corruption and abuse at the orphanage had eventually come to light, and the establishment was closed. A nightclub opened in that building instead.

The night Salas and I arrived from Rorrim, the club security picked up the junkies at the bottom of the stairs. They tried to detain Salas and me as well, but didn't get far with that. The club owner watched Salas toss his man all over the dance floor, then offered him a job as a bouncer that very night.

We rented a small room in the city and stayed in it for a couple of months. Salas worked nights. And I became Ira again. I restored my identity to join other girls from the orphanage in testifying in court against its management and benefactors. It proved healing to see justice happen for once.

The city had changed in many ways. Neon signs popped up along the major streets. Private cafes and restaurants had opened. In my old school, we only had one classroom equipped with a handful of clunky, gray computers to learn basic programming skills. Now, the internet cafes were everywhere.

Through the internet, Salas had connected with a museum that was looking for a master blacksmith to restore and create a few replicas of swords and daggers for their re-enactment exhibits.

Despite the many positive changes in the country, finding a job was still difficult. For the first two months, I'd spent every day filling in applications for jobs in shops, restaurants, and factories. But even a decade later, it was still all about whom you knew, not what you knew.

Since day one, Salas had been our only provider, which was

new to him. He relished being able to support us, but I knew he disliked his job at the nightclub. When the chance came for him to work at the forge again, I sold the jewelry I was wearing when we came from Rorrim. He quit his job, and we rented a small, one-bedroom log house with a workshop on the outskirts of the city.

The project for the museum had opened more doors for Salas. He started getting regular orders from other museums, hobby stores, weapon enthusiasts, and cosplayers from all over the country and beyond.

Things were going so well that instead of wasting my time looking for a job that I couldn't find, I started taking classes at the university.

The bus dropped me off at the end of our street. My steps grew faster the closer to home I got. Instead of going to the front door, I went straight to the workshop connected to the main house by a short walkway.

Salas had put the fire out already and taken his thick gloves off, but he still had his leather apron on over his navy-blue tank top.

"And there is my princess." He beamed as I entered. "How was the class?" He opened his arms wide for me, and I ran into them.

His hugs were a true home to me. With his arms around me, it didn't matter what world we lived in. Salas was my home.

"It was good." I exhaled, dropping my heavy book bag to the floor and twining my arms around his neck. "But being here with you is so much better."

I rose on my tiptoes, reaching for a kiss, and he quickly found my lips with his.

The door to the walkway connecting the workshop to the house was open. A delicious smell wafted through it.

"What's for dinner?"

"Meat pie."

My mouth watered. "Are you making your famous rabbit pie?"

"No rabbit. Again." he sighed. "Just chicken. The store didn't have rabbit meat. It looks like I'll have to go to the forest to trap some if I ever want to make a rabbit pie in his world."

I chuckled. "I'm sure chicken is just as good."

Sliding my hands behind him, I hooked my fingers into the belt of his jeans. I still hadn't gotten used to the fact that Salas wore jeans now. But he made any clothes look good, including these.

"When is the chicken pie ready?" I asked as he kissed the side of my neck.

"In about ten-fifteen minutes," he murmured against my skin, cupping my breast through my top. "I have enough time to make you come at least once before dinner."

"Mmm, best appetizer ever." I tugged at his apron. "Are you keeping this on?"

He leaned back with a smile.

"Sure." A spark of humor glistened in his honey-brown eyes. "Just the apron, nothing else. What do you think?"

The sound of someone clearing their throat behind me made me pause.

"Mother?" I turned around to a small stand-up mirror on Salas's workbench.

I'd brought it here the last time I'd spoken to her and forgot to take it back to the house.

The Queen of Rorrim Queendom stood on the other side of the mirror, dressed in a purple-and-gold evening gown.

"Good evening, daughter," she said in a formal voice with a quick glance at Salas, who still held me in his arms. "I have a few minutes before the dinner in honor of the delegation from the Western Islands, and I wished to talk to you."

"Is everything okay?" I stepped out of Salas' hug reluctantly.

Mother was a busy woman, even more so since I wasn't there

to help her now. She had little time to spare but made an effort to find a few minutes to speak with me almost every day.

"Greetings, Your Majesty." Salas inclined his head.

The queen gave him a brief nod, without a word of reply. But it was better than before when she refused to acknowledge his presence at all.

"How is Father doing?" I asked the queen.

"The king is well," she replied in the same formal tone.

Salas took off his apron and hung it on the hook by the door.

"I'll go check on that pie," he said, heading for the walkway to the house.

Mother followed his departure with her gaze. A wrinkle of displeasure formed between her eyebrows.

"Is that how you allow him to walk around, Ari? Does he not have enough clothes to put on?"

It took me a moment to remember that Salas's sleeveless tank top would be highly inappropriate for a man to wear back in Rorrim. Salas still refused to wear anything sleeveless out in public, even on a hot day.

"It's summer here, Mother," I reminded the queen since it was currently the middle of winter in Rorrim. "Salas works at the forge. It's hot." I shrugged. "What's so scandalous about it, anyway? It's just arms. We all have them, don't we?"

Mother shook her head.

"That world is not good for you, dearest. It's such a twisted place."

"No world is perfect, but I'm safer here now than before. I have Salas. He supports and protects me. Without him, I'd have no roof over my head. He pays for everything. Amazing, isn't it?" I teased. "Apparently, a man is perfectly capable of running a successful business if given the freedom to do it."

She waved that off. "I'm sure you're helping him, dearest, even if just with your guidance and advice. And you don't need his support or his protection." Mother still blamed Salas for taking me away from Rorrim and from her. "You would be perfectly safe here, home in the palace."

"I would. But Salas wouldn't be. He'd be dead or rotting in jail. I couldn't let that happen, Mother. I love him." I paused, considering whether to share with her the secret I hadn't even shared with Salas yet. "I want to ask him to marry me."

Her chest heaved in the tight bodice of her dress.

"Oh Ari, sweetie." Her voice turned pleading. "Is it necessary? That man is such a wrong match for you."

I didn't expect her to meet the news with enthusiasm. But she took it better than I'd anticipated.

"I've had the perfect match before, haven't I?" I argued. "It didn't turn out that great, did it? How is Leafar doing?"

A divorce law existed in Rorrim, though it was rarely used, not because marriages were so perfect there, but because with so few options for men to support themselves, they held on to their wives even at the expense of their own interests, happiness, or identities.

"The prince is recovering in your summer estate," Mother said. "Gem has been keeping him company whenever she has time to spare from her duties at the palace."

"Gem? Really?" That came unexpected, until I remembered that she'd always favored handsome, golden-haired men. "Does the prince welcome her visits?"

"He seems to enjoy them, from what I heard. Why? Would you rather I put a stop to that?"

"No." I shook my head quickly. "Not if they like each other. Leafar can spend his time however he wants. He's no longer married and doesn't have to worry about his reputation. I can only protect him from any unwanted contacts, but I can't tell him whose company to enjoy. As long as he's safe and happy."

Mother pursed her lips. "With the full access to your allowance, he certainly has the means to keep himself happy. The number of horses he's ordered so far probably exceeds the number of servants at the estate by now."

I knew for a fact that happiness was not in money. After searching for it all my life, I'd finally found it in Salas's arms. But if Leafar needed money to feel happy, I was glad I could give it to him.

We'd promised no love to each other, because love was never meant to be the foundation of our marriage. But trust was, and we both betrayed each other's trust.

Because of Leafar, the man I loved had nearly gotten killed. But because of me, Leafar was now living as an abandoned ex-husband, bearing the stigma of the divorce that had never happened in Rorrim's royal family before.

I'd never trust Leafar again, but I promised to protect him, and I tried to keep him safe, even from a distance. I also hoped that he'd find true happiness that fear had prevented him from searching for before.

"I miss you, daughter," Mother exhaled.

Her shoulders under the high collar of golden lace dropped. She looked tired.

"Mother..." I shoved a stool closer to the workbench, then sat on it and pressed a hand to the mirror.

I could see Mother and speak with her, using any mirror in this world. However, she could only see me in the ancient one in the throne room. A twister of emotions swirled through me, yet the mirror's surface remained as hard and smooth as ever.

After crossing through the mirror twice already, I still didn't understand exactly how it worked and didn't know how to control it.

Not every emotion seemed to open the portal. Both times, I had been terrified to the point of passing out. The first time, I feared for my life. The second time, for Salas's. Both times, I also felt helpless, with no way out but leaving the world I was in.

In the throne room that day, I remembered hugging Salas when he staggered back and my elbow pushed the velvet shroud into the surface of the mirror. That was how I knew the portal was open. That was when I told him to fall through it with me.

And he did. He put all his trust in me and did what I asked. He fell with me and let me save his life.

Mother placed a hand against the glass from the other side of the mirror.

"Do you think you can come back soon, darling?"

I heaved a sigh. I missed her. And Father. And my silly puppy. I missed the purpose I had in Rorrim, the hope of making it a better place for everyone.

I was currently taking Political Science courses at the university. A credential in that area of study wouldn't help me with getting a job in this world, but the knowledge it gave me and the deeper perspective on governance, diplomacy, and politics could be helpful back in Rorrim.

"I can't come back, Mother. Not until Salas is my equal there, the way he is here."

She petted the glass before dropping her hand away.

"Well, I'm willing to file a petition with the council to spare his life."

That wasn't enough.

I shook my head. "He doesn't deserve jail, either."

"But Ari, he broke the law."

"Then the law is unfair and needs to be revised."

Every time we'd had this conversation, we'd come to the same standstill. The fundamental laws of Rorrim had been in place for so long, they'd become sacred. No one would change them for the sake of one man—a slave and a former whore. But I saw it as more than just saving Salas. Some time ago, I promised him to make changes to benefit the most disadvantaged groups of the Rorrim's society, and I held on to the hope of fulfilling that promise one day.

"Maybe..." Mother bit her lip. "Maybe we could make a special allowance in his case. I've spoken to several councilors already, and most seem amenable to the idea of granting him a reward for the service he performed for the crown. They admit that by saving your life and apprehending the murderer, he deserves an exceptional leniency. Instead of the dungeon, we can house him in your father's old hunting cabin. He'd be guarded and supervised, of course. But you will be able to visit him as often as your duties permit."

"You want him to become my kept man? My pet? How would that be any different from being locked in a dungeon?"

"The king's hunting cabin is much more luxurious than a dungeon cell," she pointed out haughtily.

"A gilded cage is still a cage, Mother."

"Ari, this is a very reasonable compromise. He keeps his life. You keep him as a lover. Moreover, any daughters resulting from this...um, arrangement will be recognized as your legitimate heirs. They will be put in the direct succession line. Is that not the greatest honor a man of his standing could ever hope for? If he gives you a daughter, she'll rule the queendom—"

"There is no talk about children yet," I stopped her. "Salas had the surgery, like all men in fun houses are required to have."

"The surgery is easily reversible." She waved me off. "The healing witch can undo it in no time, or we can hire the warlock Rotcod again. He performed a true miracle for your father. As a part of his reward, I granted him special permission to attend classes at the medical school. So, his skills are certainly improving. Your lover will be in good hands."

"Salas is not just my lover. He's so much more, Mother. I love him. I want to marry him. Here, he's free and my equal. If we ever return to Rorrim, that is exactly what he has to be there too." That said, this was the nicest idea she'd come up with for him to date. The progress was slow, but it'd been at least moving in the right direction. "But thank you. I do appreciate your thinking about it. I'll keep thinking too."

SALAS

I got the pie out of the oven and put it on the small table in our tiny kitchen. Everything in this house was small, but it was ours, and that was all that mattered.

Ari entered the room quietly, having finished her conversation with the queen.

"How are things back in Rorrim?" I turned to her.

"Good. Everyone is well."

She looked tense, like she often did after those conversations.

"How is the pie?" She managed a smile.

My Ari was great at pretending. She'd mastered a range of neutral expressions and had a stellar control of her voice. But I knew her. Over the months we'd spent together, I'd learned to read through it all.

"The pie can wait. Come here." Sitting down, I pulled her to me. "Do you miss Rorrim?"

"No," she said quickly, then added, "Well, some things... I mean people and pets, mostly."

Unlike me, Ari had left a family behind, parents who loved her, pets that she adored, and the crown that she'd been proud to wear.

"They're all well." She smiled again, effortlessly this time. "It's all good, my love."

I loved it when she called me that. Warmth rushed me. I tightened my arms around her, drawing her closer between my knees.

I had little back in Rorrim, but even I missed a few things from there. With the constant noise in this world, I missed the quiet when the air was so still that one could hear birds chirping from anywhere and at any time of the day. I missed the water that tasted like fresh wind and glacial ice instead of a cleaning agent and rust like it did here. As little magic as I'd had in my life before, I missed it here too. This world had not a speck of magic.

But I'd gained so much more. Here, I could be myself. No one would even think about tossing the word "whore" into my face.

In this twisted place, even the truly promiscuous men weren't shamed. They were celebrated instead, with women they'd slept with being called their "conquests." It was women who were called whores instead, even if they didn't sell sex for money, even if they had no sex, even for no reason at all.

During my two months working as a bouncer in the nightclub, I'd heard men call women all possible derogatory terms for simply rejecting their advances. The treatment of women was appalling here, and it almost always went unpunished.

The drastic change of cultural norms had a whiplash effect on me. I often wished to get Ari away from here, even if it'd cost my life to return to Rorrim. She gave up everything to bring me here. Her birthright, her ambition, the very purpose of her life, she left it all behind to be here with me.

I found her lips with mine. She slid her hands down my neck and over my shoulders. I kissed her face, following with my kisses the familiar map of her freckles. With a soft moan, she pressed her body to mine, and I trailed my kisses down her neck then along her collarbone.

The pie was waiting, but she breathed out, "Don't stop, Salas. I need to feel you."

I needed her too. Always.

Clothes were simpler in this world—no laces, not too many buttons. I slid down her shoulder straps, then unhooked her bra, releasing her breasts. Each was more than a handful, but I had large hands. When I cupped a breast, it hid in my palm completely. The bud of the nipple poked between my fingers, and I squeezed it gently, making her gasp in pleasure.

"Salas..." she murmured my name as I kissed the tip of her other breast.

For both Ari and me, sexuality had been warped from a young age. The two of us were still learning how to enjoy intimacy without guilt or shame, how to have sex with no other purpose but to enjoy each other.

But our love was built on trust, giving us a safe place to learn it all.

I pulled Ari onto my lap. Straddling my thighs, she reached for the closure on my pants while I hiked up her long cotton skirt.

Desire zapped through my groin as she wrapped her warm, little fingers around my cock.

"There it is." She smiled with satisfaction, freeing my erection while I took off her underwear for her.

She ran her fingers along the row of elevations on the underside of my shaft. I was so hard, my cock pressed to my belly. She didn't pry it away, rubbing herself against it instead, up and down the hard bumps. I gripped her hips, pressing her closer.

The slick, tantalizing sensation of her heat grinding against the head of my cock made my mind reel with need. I strained my muscles, holding back.

As her moans grew louder, her mouth slacked open, and her eyelids dropped half-way, I grabbed her and got up from my chair, then flipped her onto the table, next to the chicken pie.

She gasped, wrapping her legs around my hips.

"Together, Salas…" she moaned, rolling her head on the table.

"Yes, sweetheart. Always together." I slid inside her with a thrust that pressed my ridge to her clit.

She gripped my shirt as I thrust harder, making the table shake and shift. Tossing her head back, her thighs trapping me in a vise, she came around my cock so hard, her moans probably could be heard all the way at the bus stop, and I finally let it go too.

Pleasure burst through my veins as my release filled her. Sex with her was incomparable to anything I'd ever experienced. I could stay like this forever, with our bodies merged and our souls connected.

With her hair spread over the table, her top down to her waist and her cheeks blushing, she was the most beautiful thing I'd ever seen.

I flicked her nose with mine. "I could eat you, instead of the pie. All night long."

She remained serious, however, gazing at me intently.

"Marry me, Salas," she said, breathlessly.

Marry me.

Just a few months ago, I didn't dare dream of ever hearing these words from her. Ari always treated me like an equal. I knew we belonged together, but there was a world where I would never be accepted as her husband.

She stirred under me uneasily, probably concerned by my silence.

"I know you deserve a better proposal," she said. "I was going to do it properly, in a nice place somewhere..."

"Ari," I shifted off her, "I don't care for grand gestures. But if you ever return to Rorrim... Your marriage with me would never be accepted there."

"I'm not going back." She sat up. "Even if there was a way, I'm not going back to the place where you can lose your life or your freedom. You proved to me that happiness is real. I refuse to live without it now. I refuse to live without you." Taking my face between her hands, she ran her thumbs over my cheekbones. "Will you be my husband, Salas?"

A ripple of vulnerability ran through her expression as she waited for my reply. As if I would ever refuse her.

"I feared you'd never ask." I smiled.

"Is that a yes?" Her eyes lit up with hope. "Please say yes."

"Of course it's a yes, sweetheart. How can it be anything else?"

She hugged my neck with a puff of relieved breath against my skin.

I reached over to the wooden jewelry box inlaid with mosaic from ironed straw. The beauty of having a small kitchen was that everything in it was within arm's reach.

"I made something for us." I took out a matching pair of rings from the box. "By this world's tradition, both a man and a woman wear a wedding ring, right?"

"In this *country*, yes, they both wear one, on their right ring fingers."

I opened my hand, displaying the silver bands I'd made in my workshop between working on orders.

She gasped in delight. "You made them?"

"I did. For both of us."

I was a blacksmith, not a jeweler, but I was proud of how the bands turned out. I even managed to etch a design in the silver. I kept it simple, borrowing the cross-stitch pattern from the shirt that Ari gave me as a gift back in Rorrim.

"It's gorgeous." She took the smaller ring and lifted it to her eyes, inspecting the design. "That's the embroidery on your shirt, isn't it?"

I nodded. "It seems like all life-altering events happened to me lately while I wore that shirt. And you've been with me for all of them. I figured it was fitting."

"There is an engraving inside too." She looked closely and read, *"You are my happy place."*

"You said it to me, remember?" Of course she did. It was clear from her expression that she never forgot those words. "You have become my happy place, too, Ari."

Her eyes glistened with tears behind her glasses. She sniffled softly and quickly buried her nose in the side of my neck.

My Ari was the strongest woman I knew. Her emotions were just as strong, too, powerful enough to transcend worlds.

I cradled her in my arms, kissing her hair.

"I can't wait to marry you, sweetheart."

"You are my happy place, Salas," she murmured against my skin.

"And you are mine."

Patreon

For more illustrations to this and other books by Marina Simcoe, including NSFW art, please visit the author's Patreon:

A Look in the Mirror

TRILOGY

Downfall of a Princess
Rise of a Fallen Man
War of Smoke and Mirrors

Seven Horny Sins

Let Me Claim You
Let Me Win You
Let Me Feed You

The World of the River of Mists

Joyless Kingdom Trilogy

Somber Prince

Joy Guardian

Pleasure Trader

Wingless Crow Duet

Wingless Crow

Crownless King

Fire in Stone Duet

Fire in Stone

Hearts of Fire

Serpent's Touch Duet

Serpent's Touch

Serpent's Claim

Madame Tan's Freakshow Trilogy

Call of Water

Madness of the Moon

Power of Rage

About the Author

Marina Simcoe likes to write love stories with human heroines and non-human heroes who just can't live without them. She firmly believes that our contemporary world could always use a little bit of the extraordinary.

She has lots of fun exploring how her out-of-this-world characters with their own beliefs, values, and aspirations fit into our every-day life.

She lives in Canada with her very own extraordinary hero, their three little offspring, and a cat who is definitely out of this world.

facebook.com/MarinaSimcoeAuthor

instagram.com/marinasimcoeauthor

amazon.com/author/marinasimcoe

bookbub.com/profile/marina-simcoe

goodreads.com/MarinaSimcoe